# HARDCASTLE

## JOHN YOUNT

RICHARD MAREK PUBLISHERS,
NEW YORK

Library of Congress Cataloging in Publication Data

Yount, John, date.
  Hardcastle.

  I.  Title.
PZ4.Y85Har [PS3575.O89]      813'.5'4      79-21977
ISBN 0-399-90061-6
PRINTED IN THE UNITED STATES OF AMERICA

The author would like to thank the John Simon Guggenheim Foundation and the National Endowment for the Arts for their support while this book was being written.

*This book is for my father*
*John Luther Yount*
*who lived part of it and inspired it all.*

# SWITCH COUNTY, KENTUCKY, SUMMER 1979

HIS VISITING GRANDSONS, lounging on the living room rug like young animals resting in the heat of the day, asked him to tell about a shooting he was mixed up in, but he would not accommodate them. It didn't seem quite possible to say anything about a time so long before they were born, about a time when, indeed, he could not have imagined them. They asked about the shooting in a spirit of fun, but he could not answer in the same spirit. Yet just at that moment, and certainly not by accident, his wife came in from the kitchen drying her hands on her apron and sent the boys off to dig worms for fishing and sent him and his small granddaughter off to the store.

And so it is that he finds himself walking down the highway toward Elkin feeling strangely contentious, out of kilter with himself, and even a little mislaid in time. He is sixty-seven and on some level or other he is perfectly aware of that, but he is also bemused at the fact. Oh, he knows well enough he could account for his age as a man might account for an extraordinary amount of money he finds has slipped through his fingers. Sure, he could think back and satisfy himself that nothing was lost, but merely spent. Yet the odd notion persists that, if he knew just how to do it, he might shake himself awake and discover that he is young after all and had only dreamt otherwise.

"Pappaw," the little girl says. "Pappaw?" And she tugs on his forefinger until he comes back to the present moment and realizes she is

9

shying away from a bright yellow automobile pulling up to stop beside them.

"Mr. Music, can I give you a ride into town?" the driver asks and leans over the steering wheel to peer out at them from his sanctum of vinyl and chrome and Nashville songs. He looks freshly scrubbed and is wearing a clean, fancy shirt, but there is yet a little coal dust in the hollows of his ears. Still, to William Music he seems somehow as damnably innocent and ignorant as the two small boys he'd left digging worms behind the barn.

"I thank you, no," Music says. "We'd as lief walk it."

The driver nods, flips a hand up from the wheel in acknowledgement, and the dazzling yellow car rumbles off. It doesn't go fast but its wide rear tires, throbbing engine, and raised hind end threaten terrific speed at any moment.

In his peculiar mood William Music looks after it a moment before he gives a little snort of laughter. Well sure now, he thinks, buying such as that is one way for a man to keep himself and his family poor until he goes on strike, gets himself hurt, or until the hard times come again. Yes, and how many are there in Switch County any wiser, he wonders. Yes, and who could say the hard times won't come again? He does not wish to be hard on the man, or on himself, but he can find no other terms for his regard than to think that nothing lasts save man's unteachable nature.

# 1

## MORNING, WICHITA, KANSAS
## OCTOBER, 1931

DAYLIGHT WAS LITTLE more than mist and blurred edges when William Music sprang up from the weeds and ran beside the Missouri Pacific freight train rumbling out of the switchyard. Other men appeared—ragged, dirty, ghostly in the grey half-light—running too. Music ran beside a boxcar, slid the door half open, threw in his paper parcel, and heaved himself in behind it. Before he even raised himself from his belly, he saw that the boxcar was already occupied by a huge man wearing bib overalls and no shirt or shoes. The big man was propped against the far wall, his hands draped over his knees and his head hung between his shoulders as though he were weary or asleep. Music righted himself, collected the paper parcel he'd thrown in before him, and said, "Howdy," but the man's hooded, groggy eyes drowsed only a moment upon him before they lost focus and his head lolled again toward his chest.

You ain't used to being rousted, are you, Music thought. Despite the hard reputation of the Wichita railroad police, he could see why they'd left the man alone. He appeared to weigh two hundred and thirty-five or forty pounds and was nearly as hairy as a dog.

For a long time he kept the weary figure located, at least in the tail of his eye, and plotted a countermove or two in case he should be rushed. There was nothing in the paper sack he carried but his suit coat, an old newspaper, and a tin pot for cooking, no money in his pockets except

11

eleven cents; but the giant of a man wouldn't know that. Still, all through the morning and early afternoon, while Kansas at track side fell behind and Kansas in the distance seemed to keep pace, the man didn't stir. The freight blew its whistle from time to time, slowed here and there to clatter past a shabby depot, but never stopped; and only those boes and stiffs who had run it down and swung aboard when it left the switchyard that morning were going to catch it, for it was hell-bent for St. Louis, and there hadn't been a single grade steep enough to faze it.

To occupy himself, Music sat in the half-open doorway of the boxcar inventing the scene of his homecoming. It would be early evening. The sun wouldn't have set behind Howard's Knob, but the shadows would be long and cool when he turned off the county road just out of Shulls Mills and mounted the washed-out wagon road up toward the house and barn. His father would be out by the barn. His posture, the set of his shoulders, unmistakable. He'd be riving out shingles someone had ordered, say; and the wooden mallet would be striking the froe and bouncing once after each lick, which was his father's style. The sound would go *whop-pop*, *whop-pop*, *whop-pop* until the bolt split evenly. His father would not notice him, dreaming as he was in the rhythm of his labor. There would be no one else about, his two brothers, Earl and Luther, being back on the Knob with the mules and the sledge, say, bringing out one last load of oak before supper. He would walk up within a dozen feet before his father sensed him and let the mallet bounce twice on the backside of the froe to make a little flourish by way of acknowledging and greeting whoever had come. The sound would go *whop-pop-pop*, and his father would look up from under the brim of his old straw hat, see him, recognize him, and tuck away every sign of surprise and joy almost in the same instant they flashed across his face. "Well," he'd say in the calmest, easiest sort of voice and extend his hand. "We got that fine diploma from away off in Chicago," he'd say, as though in answer to a question, as though the diploma from Coin Electric had just arrived, although no question had been asked and the diploma would have arrived a year before. "Come on in," his father would say, and the two of them would start toward the house, but they wouldn't get there before his mother appeared on the porch, the cessation of the blows of his father's mallet together with some sure, sudden instinct having brought her to the door, eyes already brimming with the knowledge that it was he. "Will," she would say, "Lordy mercy, Will!"

She would surely say something like that. She would throw her hands up with joy. She would weep. For that reason, somehow, he could take the vision of his homecoming no further. His father, a quiet and private man himself, respected privacy. He would ask no questions, make no show. Seeing him come home after nearly two years—ragged, broke, hungry—would be enough to make him keep his peace. Not so his mother. It was not in her nature to leave a thing be.

Music got up to stretch his legs. He was light-headed, and his joints felt unstrung. At last, after so many days of nothing to eat, his innards had quit growling and rumbling, passing along the volume of emptiness inside him. The machinery of his digestion had grown quiet, sullen, painfully tight; and in his mouth there was the constant and unhealthy taste of brass. He remembered a greasy spoon on Maxwell Street in Chicago where a man could get a good-sized hamburger, potatoes, and coffee for a dime, the hamburger and potatoes served, not on a plate, but on a piece of newspaper. There were no seats and no flatware save spoons. So deep in his own thoughts, he was, he turned to describe to the big man propped against the far wall the dimensions of the hamburger, his hands already measuring it out in the air. But he caught himself before he spoke, and blew a little snort of laughter through his nose. The big man still slept, trembling all over with the motion of the boxcar. You're run to ground, ain't you, Music thought and pondered him for a moment, the bald spot on the crown of his head, the hair bristling even on his shoulders. There was a wound on one of the man's bare feet about the size of a fifty-cent piece. It was beginning to scab over, but around the edges the flesh was a bright and unlikely shade of red. Maybe, you goddam bear, Music thought, *I* ought to jump *you*. Kill you. Eat you. There'd be enough to last me all the way back to Shulls Mills, Virginia. He couldn't help the laughter that escaped him; and the massive head rose, but the eyes were hooded and only a rim of iris showed beneath the upper lid.

Music turned and leaned his shoulder into the doorjamb and looked out. The boxcar rocked, the wheels clicked, the air roared by; but in the distance Kansas kept pace. It seemed to go on forever. Closer, the infrequent houses and barns that slipped behind, the roads, the few trees, seemed interchangeable; and it required a leap of faith to believe there might be anything else. Rivers. Oceans. Mountains, say.

Somehow the man's foot caused Music's old wounds to itch, and he rubbed first one calf and then the other, remembering how he had regained consciousness in the line truck on the way to the hospital, the

13

foreman driving, a working buddy calling again and again: "Hey, Music! Music! Goddammit!" He returned to the living with all his joints aching as though they had been pushed inches toward the center of his body; his lungs raw; and the calves of his legs, where the rivets had been, cooked as done as pot roast. He woke with the immediate knowledge that his working buddy had pulled the wrong fuse jacks and allowed him to get into twenty-three hundred volts. His life hadn't exactly flashed before his eyes, but something nearly as peculiar had happened. He had seen his grandfather sitting in the kitchen, his warped hands lying one atop the other upon the head of his cane, saying to him as though it were a matter of great importance: "Hear that rooster a-crowin. He says, *'Kikere kikere kie!'* " That's what his grandfather had told him, his rheumy eyes bright with the only German word he knew, besides *Musik*, the name that, two generations before his time, had been brought from the old country to the new. When the electricity hit him, he'd had a vision of that, and oddly of Roanoke when he had gone there to the tobacco auction with his father for the first time, their wagon coming around a turn in the road behind the sleepy mules and the house lights, street lights, and the colored lights of businesses spread suddenly below him in the valley.

He'd been done with his schooling and had been working as a lineman for almost three months when his working buddy made that mistake and allowed him to learn things that Coin Electric did not teach. He had learned that twenty-three hundred volts did not, under all circumstances, kill a man, if he happened to have his safety belt on and his spurs dug in and therefore didn't fall and kill himself that way, if the juice didn't hold him fast but slapped him back, and if the pole in question happened to be a very dry chestnut pole and therefore not the best ground. He had learned that, in one split second, electricity could enter where you touched it, leave through rivets in the leather shin straps of your spurs, and in no longer time than that, find and violate all of you, down to your deepest, most secret core. Still, if his job had been there when he mended, he would have gone back to it.

In four days, maybe five, he'd be home. He wondered how it would be and what he could tell them. He took a deep breath and rubbed the stubble on his face. Well, he could bring them news. The boom had never quite found the way to Shulls Mills; he doubted that the bust had either. He could tell them about the depression. He could tell them about the jobs he'd had: unloading boxcars at the freight yards in Chicago from three to five in the morning and working as a dishwasher to send himself

14

through Coin Electric's ninety-day course. He could tell them how once when he'd had his lineman's job and had been flush, he'd been robbed by two men armed with socks. That's right, he'd tell them. The socks were mates; pretty; each blue silk; each, it turned out, with a stone about the size of a hen's egg in the toe. He'd tell them how, when the men with the socks had told him to empty out his pockets, he'd laughed and knocked the closest one flat on his ass; and how that one had later pleasured himself by kicking him in the ribs before taking his money, his pocket watch, his cigarettes, and, finally, even his shoes; and discovering the twenty-dollar bill he kept in one shoe against just such a possibility, had somehow taken great offense, called him a low son of a bitch, and folding the twenty carefully away into his shirt, had jumped with both feet on the center of his chest. He had been just on the fringe of consciousness, not quite able to roll away, and he had heard his breastbone crack and—he'd swear to it—felt some of his pride leak out and something like humility enter in to take its place.

He could tell them how hard it had been to find any sort of work at all, even for a day or a few hours. It would be a difficult thing for them to understand since on their ragtag mountain farm there was never a shortage of work to be done. He would tell them how he had knocked about here and there. How at last he'd heard they were trying to hire linemen out in Salt Lake City, Utah, and were offering a good wage but weren't having much luck finding trained men; how he'd ridden the rails all the way out there only to learn it was nothing more than a rumor. And he could tell them that's when he'd decided to come on back home.

He didn't know what he'd tell them, but no such things as those. If he told them any of that, he'd be telling them how he'd been beaten, turned tail, and run.

His hunger was gnawing at him, and he was thinking he ought to stretch out and try to get some sleep when some stiff in a car up the line shouted, "Sooey, pig! Soooeeey!" The voice, made faint by the noise and speed of the train, seemed to hang beside the track like a signpost before it was snatched behind. Music saw a swale sheltering a house, barn, and a few trees, and then a field of corn stubble before he glimpsed the sow and the litter of piglets. "Hot damn!" he said, and on a sudden impulse snatched up his paper parcel and leaned out of the boxcar, holding on until it should rock again toward the cornfield. "Whoa!" the big man said behind him, roused at last. "Catch yourself, fool!" But he had already leapt into a violent rush of air, and in the next second, into a helter-skelter

15

and even more violent conflict with the earth. He rolled and bounced and kicked up the dirt beside the railroad bed, it seemed to him, for hundreds of yards. He was surprised more than scared. The dizzy contortions of body and limb registered, oddly, without pain, and after a while it seemed to him that he had been able to withdraw somehow toward the center of himself, where he was relatively inviolate and bemused, like the stationary dead center of a rolling wheel. He was even able to hear hooting and jeering from the boes on the freight.

Later, after the train had blown past and gone and he had picked himself up, he discovered that his tin cooking pot was bent nearly flat, that he had lost a shoe, that the side of his face was skinned a little, and his right forearm and left hip were skinned a lot. He limped a little way down the track looking for his shoe before he felt suddenly so dizzy and weak he had to sit down on a tie. Although the freight was out of sight, he could still feel the diminishing vibrations of it, still hear its almost inaudible song along the rails. He blinked and rubbed grit from his eyes and spat it from his mouth. "Didn't kill me," he said, as though offering a final argument to a side of himself that took a strange, grim pleasure in pointing out his stupidity. He ran his tongue around the inside of his mouth, collecting grit, and spat a viscous string of dirt and blood. Slowly his strength seemed to return, and he got up and limped down the railroad track, his shoeless foot feeling vulnerable, almost somehow amputated. When he saw the shoe, it was forty feet out in the cornfield, pointing away from him as though striking out on its own. He climbed down the short embankment, crossed the fence, and took it up. It was scuffed, but less than the one that had stayed on his foot, less than the rest of him. He sat down and put it on and felt whole again. He could not afford to let himself consider exactly where he was or how far he might have to walk before he could catch another freight.

The sow and the litter of pigs were a hundred and fifty yards away. Nearly a half mile beyond them, the roofs of the house and barn rose just above the swale—the owners of the pigs no doubt lived there—but there was no one in sight. He got up again and started out, but after he had closed considerable ground, the sow took note of him and began to lead her piglets away; and he had to trot, and then run, to get any closer. His side hurt but there was no help for it. The piglets began to squeal as he gained on them, and the sow, realizing at last that her litter could not keep up with her, stopped abruptly and turned to face him. Her flat nose handled the air, speculating on his motives as her piglets overtook her and swarmed behind her flanks. He came on, and as if with sudden insight, she seemed to start, as though she would turn and bolt away, but she did not. Some of her litter held their ground in the shadow of her protection as he bore down on them; others broke and ran. For a second time she started—a sudden spasm that seemed to force a grunt out of her and lift her off the ground in its violent agitation—and more of her litter deserted her. A great staple in her nose he hadn't seen before, pig eyes bleared with what seemed an ancient hatred, a funny downward bow in her neck which kept her snout high, at last she charged, two confused piglets charging with her.

"Hot damn!" Music shouted, his voice rising so far above its usual register it cracked and broke; and just as he and the sow were about to collide, he jumped her. He overtook and scooped up a piglet, and his ribs pained him sharply, but there was no time to rest for he heard her already behind him, clattering through the corn stubble. He made for the fence with the piglet screaming and squealing under his arm, and the sow, he could tell, closing on him. He slowed a little, glanced over his shoulder, and chose exactly the right moment to jump up and to the side; and for a second time, she rushed almost directly beneath him. He could feel the terrific weight and momentum of her in the near miss. She slewed halfway around before she hit the four strands of barbwire and had a violent, momentary fit, extricating herself. It was nearly time enough. He had angled a little to one side but never ceased to run for the fence. He had his right hand on the fence post, his left leg over the top, and his right foot on the second strand when her snout slammed into the shank of his right leg with almost, but not quite, enough force to topple him back into the cornfield. But he fell the other way. Still, somehow she caught the cuff of his trousers and shook it with twice the strength of a dog before she lost her grip and left him lying on his shoulders on the other side, the piglet still clamped under his arm and one foot cocked up over the top strand, where his pants cuff was hooked on a barb.

She seemed to stand back a moment to grunt and think, which allowed him to get one leg under him and the other loose from the top strand before she tried to get at him through the fence. He kicked at her face. "Shitass! Git away!" he shouted and scrambled up the slight embankment to the railroad bed. "Jesus," he said and tried to catch his breath. Sweat rolled down his ribs, and his legs shook. He gave a quick look toward the house and barn in the swale. No one was in sight.

The sow grunted to her litter, but the scattered piglets were hesitant,

17

nervous. Still she grunted to them, and skittish as they were, they gathered. She dropped her snout close to the ground and seemed to be counting them out of the top of her head as they straggled in. She knew, Music thought, that her tally would be one short—the one kicking and squealing under his arm—but she had to confirm it. When she had, she kept pace with him inside the fence while he limped back down the line to collect his paper parcel. He crossed the tracks and went down the far embankment to walk out of sight of the sow and to keep from being quite so visible from the farm. The piglet he clutched ceased its squealing and struggling only long enough to baste his side with a string of wet, clinging turds.

Half a mile down the track, with apologies, he took out his pocketknife and cut the piglet's throat. Three miles after that he came to a trestle over a creek, and under the trestle he dressed out his supper, washed his shirt, and sponged off his pants, finding one moist, soft pig turd in his pocket and another pressed between the waistband of his trousers and his side.

He built a fire and cooked the carcass whole. The flesh, where it wasn't charred, was white as milk and sweet, and although he wished for pepper, and most of all for salt, the piglet was delicious. He ate his fill, then wrapped the rest in newspaper and tucked it away inside the paper sack. He spread his shirt to dry by the fire, put his suit coat on over his undershirt, and permitted himself the luxury of rolling a cigarette from the small store of tobacco he had left. Lying back with his arms behind his head, he watched sparks from his fire rise up toward the trestle and wink out. "Fool, yourself," he said.

The next day, twenty miles or so down the track, sore in every muscle, he came to a town and caught himself a milk-run freight going east.

# 2

## EVENING, SWITCH COUNTY KENTUCKY

A DAY OF pork and two days of nothing, and William Music was hungry again. He held on to the side of the coal car with his right hand, to the paper sack with his left, and leaned out over the railroad bed. The train was not going fast, but there was no good place to jump. The edge of the railroad bed gave way to a rocky bank down to a river. He looked up the line, searching for a wider spot, and saw an ellipse of gravel and cinders perhaps a dozen feet across with a stand of poplar and water maple guarding the abrupt slope to the river. He tossed the paper sack away first, so that he would be committed to follow it, and jumped. He thought he was going to be able to keep his feet, but he couldn't even though the train was going no more than ten or twelve miles an hour. The fall hurt his ribs again, and he collected some cinders in the heel of his hand. Slowly, as though he were an old man rising after a nap, he propped himself up into a sitting position; and while the train clicked and clattered on past, he picked cinders from his palm. It was a shallow, bright pain that caused his mouth to water.

When he had cleaned some of the grit from the hot abrasion, he groaned, rose, picked up his sack, and started back down the line toward the little mining community the train had just come through. It hadn't looked like much the first time, but as he approached, it looked far worse. The coal tipple looming beside the tracks seemed empty, derelict, as though no coal had rattled through it in a long time. There was no smoke

19

coming from the power plant, and the corrugated sheet iron of its roof and sides seemed to house yet another volume of deep and long-undisturbed quiet. At last he saw the padlock on the powerhouse door and blew a snort of disgusted laughter through his nose. He had a knack, he decided, for jumping off trains into places that weren't quite places at all, but a kind of no-man's-land between places. He leaned back and looked at the wooden sign high up on the tipple. It was scummed over with coal dust and bled through with rust from the bolts that held it. In bold letters it said: BEAR PAW COAL. He wondered how long it had been out of business, cursed himself under his breath, and went on. He crossed the railroad track and a tilted wooden bridge over the river, making for the road he had been glimpsing for an hour or so, winding along the western side of the valley. Just across the bridge there was a long, low building on his side of the road, and on the far side, a row of shacks strung out to the south with smoke rising from two or three of the chimneys. "Ain't a ghost town anyhow," he told himself, but he wasn't much encouraged. It looked like a place where an empty belly would be hard to fill.

He decided he would turn north on the road, since if Shulls Mills didn't lie directly east, it didn't lie south; that would be Tennessee; southeast would likely be North Carolina.

He calculated he had close to an hour and a half to find something to eat before dark. He'd seen a fair number of homesteads scattered along the valley, and now and again a coal camp too, though probably, he thought, no better off than the Bear Paw; still there had to be some sort of food around. Chicken, he decided, was what he wanted. That's what he'd keep an eye out for. If he couldn't find a chicken, then surely, he thought, he'd come across a garden with maybe some turnips or carrots still in the ground, or maybe a potato mound covered over for the winter, or cabbages, say; but he wanted a chicken, a hen with eggs in her.

Just as he came abreast of a large, ramshackle building on his left, a man leaning against its gallery, whom he had not seen, straightened and stepped toward him. "Evenin," the man said.

He was slight, with a frayed work shirt buttoned primly around his neck, looking, like the rest of his clothes, as though it had belonged to a larger man. One empty sleeve of his jumper was pinned to his shoulder. "Evenin," Music said.

Underneath the broad-brimmed felt hat, which sat absolutely level on the man's head and which Music would have taken for black but for a lighter band of grey where the hatband was missing, the face studied him

20

so calmly that there was something just short of insolence in it. The man's face, grey with stubble and streaked with snuff or tobacco at the corners of his mouth, was impassive; his eyes, speckled and hard as pebbles at the bottom of a stream, did not leave Music's. Some slight movement behind the man caught Music's attention, and he saw another man and a half-grown boy sitting on the gallery of the building, their backs propped against the wall. "Got some white here that'll keep the cold out if ye've a mind," the man said, his face expressionless, his lips scarcely moving.

For a moment Music did not understand. It was as though he'd thought the one-armed man, planted so woodenly before him, had had another purpose altogether in stopping him, as though he'd somehow read the larceny in his heart and was going to tell Music what happened to chicken thieves in that part of Kentucky. Corn liquor, the man was offering him. Moonshine. And in the light of that, the man's gnawed, impassive face seemed almost benign. "I've had no corn liquor in a long time," Music said, his tension leaving him so suddenly he gave a little bark of laughter.

"Twon't find better in Switch County," the one-armed man said. "Hit's doubled and twisted." The man cleared his throat and spat. "If ye've a mind," he said, "hit's twenty cent a pint. Twenty-five if ye aim to trade with clacker."

"There's not but eleven cents in my pocket, mister," Music said, "and I guess I've got no clacker, for I don't know what it is."

The man nodded almost imperceptibly. His eyes the nondescript color of pebbles never left Music's face. "Yes," he said, "I taken ye fer a stranger."

"I'm headed up Virginia way," Music said. "Bound home, if I can get there." He heard in his voice the queer, slightly formal manner that spoke to him of home.

Again the man nodded almost imperceptibly, his jaws flexed thoughtfully. "You'll want to take care hereabouts, for Switch County tain't so comfortable for passing through as it might be."

"I'm obliged," Music said. He wanted some of the man's whiskey but didn't quite know how to deal with him. There was no one like mountain people, he thought, for making a simple business awkward. It was embarrassing for them to buy and sell, and so they approached the matter too bluntly or else circled it endlessly, either way stymied and shamed by their own awkwardness. Give the city man his due, Music thought; he can trade with you in the blink of an eye. He could feel that he and the

21

one-armed man were going to stand where they were for a long, long time unless he could somehow clear the air. He shifted his package from one arm to the other and stroked his chin. "I don't guess," he said, "you'd care to do eleven cents' worth of business?"

The one-armed man remained impassive. He looked off at the horizon, he chewed, spat. He looked at the ground before his shoes and the ragged and begrimed cuffs of his trousers. His hat brim waggled slightly. He turned his head and spat again. "Dwight," he said, without turning toward the two figures lounging on the gallery, "see can ye find airey sort of bottle thereabouts."

Music saw the boy rise and step through what had once been a window into the bowels of the building. Presently he emerged, dropped down from the porch, and came up carrying a pop bottle caked with dust. The boy's hands and bare feet were black as a raccoon's, and at the crown of his head, his hair rose in an unruly swirl, like the topknot of some strange bird; yet there was dignity in him somehow, in his eyes, the set of his chin. "Will this'un do?" he asked. "Hit's all I could find."

"Hit'll serve," the one-armed man said. He took it, turned it upside down, and gave it a shake. Nothing fell out. He rubbed it against his thigh as though shining an apple until it was possible to see through it. He blew into the neck of it and handed it back to the boy. "Hold hit still," he said and drew a pint mason jar out of one of the baggy pockets of his jumper. He clamped the lid of the mason jar under the stump of his arm and with no trouble opened it without spilling a drop. But skillful and steady as he was, he could not pour a stream as small as the neck of the pop bottle, and Music could hardly stand to watch.

When the pop bottle was three-quarters full, and the mason jar two-thirds empty, the man ceased pouring. He managed to set the lid back on the mason jar as much with his armpit as with the stump of his arm. He spun the lid down with one flick of his thumb. He dropped the mason jar in his pocket, took the bottle from the boy, and, without a word, extended it to Music.

"I thank you," Music said and took the bottle and paid him. "I surely do." He swallowed in anticipation, whisked his palm over the mouth of the bottle, leaned back his head, and drank. Before he swallowed twice, the moonshine peeled his gullet all the way to his stomach and filled him with fire. A mist of tears washed his eyes and dampened his eyelashes.

"Hit's stout fer hit's doubled and twisted," the one-armed man said, "but tain't any cheap busthead."

Music had no voice, could not speak. His eyes swam in tears. He offered the blur of the one-armed man the pop bottle. "No manners," he managed to say, his voice no more than breath and whispers despite the volume of air which left his throat.

The one-armed man shook his head. "Stomach ain't stout no more. Little buttermilk and biscuit, and maybe a dab of navy beans, is all I can handle without aggravation."

Music bobbed his head again and again, since it didn't yet seem quite possible to speak above a whisper. He raised the pop bottle in a gesture of salute and parting, and swung his head toward the north up the road. He cleared his throat, although it seemed already as clear as a whistle, and in a voice that was stronger, if not his own, said, "This'll ease my travels." He nodded almost formally to the man and the boy standing before him and even to the man sitting on the gallery of the building. "I'm obliged," he said and turned to go.

"Ye'll come to Elkin a little ways up the creek," the one-armed man said behind him, "but I wouldn't fetch up. There's them in Elkin that's mean-spirited. I'd keep on to Valle Crucis, son. Tain't but seven mile."

Music raised the pop bottle in acknowledgement and went on, surprised to feel a certain warmth in his joints already, a looseness, as though they had been lightly oiled. His ribs didn't hurt so much either. Nor did he walk far until all the spots where he was stiff sore seemed to attract warmth and easement from the corn liquor. Even his hunger dulled and warmed and grew almost sweet, as though it weren't, after all, serious or important. About a mile up the road he stopped and took another drink. It didn't seem so wickedly strong as the first. His eyes scarcely teared. Still, he could feel the machinery of his body change gears again and settle into a slower rhythm, even as he breathed out the warm, sweet fumes of it, even as he watched the fog of his breath hover before his face until it disappeared.

How cool and serene the evening was, how still. As though cotton plugs had been drawn from his ears, sounds he hadn't noticed before seemed to reach him from great distances up and down the valley. Someone's dog was barking back toward the Bear Paw, his voice as short and precise as hammer blows; somewhere away, a cow was bawling, long and soft and consonant at first but raucous as the bleating of a sheep before it was done; and north toward Elkin, in perfect miniature, he could hear the slamming of doors and the voices of children. It is fall, he thought with wonder, as though he had known the month of the year but not the season. There was a field yet green on his right with long beige grasses at its edge, swirled and cow-licked by the wind. Some of the trees still held color, some were bare; already the unrelinquished leaves of the oaks were brown. Up the mountains toward the tops of hogbacks and ridges, there were laurel thickets and pines, the green of them deep and lusterless against the pale blue sky. He stood still for a long moment as though pondering what he saw: the mountains, the valley, and across it, the long, smooth arc of the railroad girdling the abrupt slope down to the river. The rails shone like quicksilver in the remaining light, and here and there snatches of the river he could see shone too, but softer, duller, like melted lead or pewter. And as if some strange wisdom lay in noticing such small things, he realized that he was indeed almost home, that after covering an unthinkable distance, he was nearly there. All the valley had to do was broaden out a little, the mountains rise a little higher with slopes a little less abrupt, and he would be there. It wasn't more than two hundred miles or so farther. He wiped his mouth on the back of his hand, refusing to think into words or acknowledge the feeling that the distance didn't matter, that he could come no closer—the sharp, sudden certainty that home existed in time and not at all in space. He wondered what the proof of "doubled and twisted" corn liquor might be. There was a warm spot the size of a silver dollar in the center of his head, and his balance was no longer quite sure. He climbed down into the right-hand ditch, cut a limb from some scrub maple, whittled out a stopper, and plugged his whiskey. Back up on the road, he dropped the bottle in his sack and went on.

The chicken he wished to find was nowhere to be seen. In a mile and a half he hadn't passed a single homestead until he rounded a curve and saw a dirt road leading up into a narrow hollow on his left, but as he drew abreast of it, he saw no house and barn, but instead, another row of shacks, their front door stoops clinging to the bottom edge of the road and stilts holding their backsides above the steep bank behind them. Still, there were people there, for smoke rose almost straight up from every chimney, and here and there the mellow, rosy bloom of a kerosene lamp lit a window. And there were children playing in the road before the shacks, Negro children, girls with heads full of pigtails, boys of all sizes, most of them in motion and almost all indistinguishable from the color of the earth but for the rags and tatters of the clothing they wore; and there were men lounging on the high side of the road, one or two standing, one or two sitting against the bank, all of them black, head to foot, clothing and all—dull, lusterless, coal-dust black, save for the metal shine of a dinner bucket or a carbide lamp. The high, musical litany of the children playing and the occasional bass or baritone remarks of the men pleased him and stopped him on the road. He saw himself mounting the wide path into the hollow, sharing his whiskey with the men, talking trivially, laughing; they might just tell him where he could find that hen he was looking for. "Evenin," he called out to them and raised his hand. The voices of the men ceased at once, and all eyes turned toward him. The shouts and laughter of the children, the running to and fro, subsided more slowly; and their eyes turned toward him as well, with only a little cautious movement among them to get a better view. "Evenin," one of the men said at last.

But for the just audible goings-on inside the shacks, no one spoke or moved, except one figure who crept among the children and past an isolated woman or two toward the washed-out wagon road. It was an old man, or a broken one. He stopped at the edge of the road and leaned on a walking stick. "You a Hardcastle man, white folks?" he asked.

"Don't know what a Hardcastle man might be," Music said and laughed. "What does one look like?"

The old man leaning on his stick was not amused. He appeared to think the matter over and turned his head toward the men lounging across the rutted-out road as though to see what their opinion might be. They were quiet, looked uneasy, offered nothing. The man with the walking stick swung his head toward Music again. "You be some kinda law?" he asked.

"No, uncle," Music said, "I'm just passing by."

The man labored slowly across the road to the others, and they spoke together in indistinguishable voices for a moment.

The children began to stir, as though a spell cast over them were beginning to fail. The few women gathered together to whisper.

At last a large man with a dented carbide lamp clipped to his cap took a step in Music's direction. "We ain lookin fo trouble, white man," he said in a deep, strong bass. "You got no truck in Mink Slide."

Music did not know what to say. Suddenly he couldn't even remember what had already been said. He suspected he had made some blunder; was somehow drunker than he knew. A moment before it had seemed an easy thing to mount the rutted byway up into the hollow, to pass his whiskey among them, to warm himself before their conviviality as before

25

a fire. "We ain lookin fo trouble," the man said again, and Music nodded and raised his hand that he understood, although he did not.

A quarter of a mile further down the road he was still puzzling over it when, around a curve, the narrow valley opened out for another coal camp. Elkin, he thought.

It was bigger than the Bear Paw and lay under a blue haze of smoke. North and on his left there were two rows of company houses perched along the foot of a mountain and three or four buildings across the road from them. At the base of the mountain to the northeast, across the river and the railroad tracks, there were electric lights burning at the power plant and tipple, and along the conveyor to the mouth of a coal mine which was a third of the way up the mountain. Although it was not yet dark, many electric lights were burning in the houses and in one or two of the buildings across the road from them; and shabby as the community was, because of the lights it looked somehow festive as well. Just to his right was a schoolhouse, and upon a field of hard-packed mud and scrappy grass, white children were playing ball, the failing light notwithstanding. The team at bat slouched against a backstop of sagging supports and broken chicken wire, talking among themselves and haranguing the pitcher. But the pitcher, twelve or so, wearing a man's old suit coat for a jacket, the sleeves rolled back, the hem striking him at midthigh, paid them no mind. He took his windup and fired the ball down the center of the strike zone, the suit coat he wore seeming to start its delivery a full second behind the boy inside it, and to stop its follow-through a full second after the boy had ceased to move. The batter ignored the pitch, took one and then a second practice swing.

"Ezel, you out!" the pitcher said.

"At ain't nuthin but a lie," the batter said; "that ball were a real groundhog."

"Outta there," the catcher said.

The batter hunched his shoulders, turned. "Nobody ast you nuthin," he said. "I'll stomp a mudhole in yore ass."

The infielders came in to argue. The ragged group leaning against the backstop snapped upright and advanced toward home plate. A base runner on first broke for second, hesitated, and then beat it for third. In grave and noncommittal silence a group of smaller children and girls looked on beside the road. All, anyway, but one small, blond girl who stood, birdlike, on one bare foot; the other, toes curled, propped against her shin. She watched Music instead.

26

"What do you think, missy?" Music asked her as he passed them by. "I think he was out."

The girl sucked her thumb, rubbed the sole of her foot slowly up and down against her shin, and made no answer. Despite the fact that her joints seemed swollen and nearly purple with the cold and she was none too clean, there was about her a kind of fair-skinned, fine-boned beauty that made him shiver, since he knew all at once, without knowing quite how, that she was feebleminded. He rolled his shoulders uncomfortably and picked up his pace. On the ball field, argument gave way to shoving.

At the north end of the playground, as he passed the small, one-story schoolhouse, the sound of scuffling and the hubbub of grunts and cries followed him. Except that the windows were so dirty they resembled the scales of a snake and the building was altogether scummed over with coal dust, the schoolhouse might have been in Shulls Mills, what with its single wooden step up to the worn doorsill and each of its four corners supported by stones.

Beyond the schoolhouse there was a lot, cluttered with timbers and rife with weeds. Then a small grimy depot, once painted mustard yellow. The railroad crossed the river upon a wooden trestle, ran beside the depot's empty platform, and then crossed back again. Above the depot there was a boarded-up movie house; something nèither Shulls Mills nor any of the other farming communities around it ever had. Between the double doors and the ticket window there was a faded poster which advertised *Rio Rita* in "Marvelous Photourama."

Across the highway the small company houses were made of rough, unpainted lumber; and perched on short wooden posts above the hardscrabble earth, they looked as much alike as blackbirds on a fence. As he passed them by, he could smell the odor of side meat frying in skillets; the sulfurous odor of burning coal; and from outhouses over pits too shallow or too seldom limed, the rank odor of human dung. The stink of it made his stomach roll, but it seemed to bother no one else. Here and there he could see shadowy figures at ease upon the porches; and as though nothing at all tainted the air she breathed, an old woman came toward him down the opposite side of the road, a peck bucket full of water hanging from each gnarled hand. She made slow, shuffling progress, listed heavily with every step she took, but not a drop of water licked over the brims. On his right two miners leaned back in split-bottom chairs upon the gallery of the commissary and, with eyes ghostly white in their black faces, watched him pass. The peace of evening seemed to be upon them too, what with the sky yet a light, mother-of-pearl grey, and, all about, the earth dark-toned and slipping toward dusk. Music nodded to them, said, "Howdee," and they nodded and spoke in return.

He kept his pace up the road. Across the river and the railroad tracks, there were two coal cars painted the color of rust parked on the siding, a mountain of two or three hundred tons of nut and slack coal just behind them. A sign on the huge, blackened tipple said: HARDCASTLE COAL CO. Smoke rose from the burning gob pile, smoke and steam from the power plant; but with every step he took away from Elkin, the stink of the coal camp diminished and the subtler odors of the earth returned: the faint mustiness of dying leaves and grasses, the glass-clear odor of the river, and, from high up on the hogbacks and ridges, the faraway breath of pines. All at once he could tell from the sweet, sharp kiss of the air upon his face and hands that it would likely frost and be achingly cold before morning. He saw no reason to try to make Valle Crucis if he could find something to eat, some reasonable shelter before he got there. He was either going to have to find shelter or sit by a fire and tend it all night. The second possibility made him remember the whiskey inside his sack; and although he knew he should have no more just then, he stopped and got it out. He took only one swallow, but it warmed him at once. He held the bottle against the sky and saw that it was still half full. Hellkatoot, he thought, if I need to, I can sip on this and walk till morning.

# 3

## REGUS PATOFF BONE

THE SHACK SAGGING into the mountain had a tin roof and an open dogtrot down the center, with what looked like two rooms opening off either side. A small barn and a corncrib rose behind it, and down in front and to the north there was a low structure not much bigger than six feet square that appeared to be a springhouse. But what interested him most was a saddle of land southwest of the barn, where he was certain he could see the ghost of a kitchen garden, the standing up of cabbage stalks, the withered vines of pole beans clinging to stakes. Behind that, where the land was steeper, three widely spaced haystacks loomed darkly against the side of the mountain. Even if the garden ain't got nothing in it, he thought, I can dig me out a place in that far haystack and sleep like a babe.

He stepped off the road in the near darkness, watched awhile, and listened. There was no movement anywhere around the homestead, and he heard nothing. There was no light in the rooms off the north side of the breezeway and none in the front room off the south side, but the air and earth around the left rear corner of the house were polished a faint yellow. Music suspected the kitchen occupied that corner. Those who lived there might have settled themselves down to eat; still, he thought, someone might yet be in the barn, milking, say, or doing some other chore.

Although the springhouse was no more than twenty-five yards from

29

the front porch, he decided to take a look at it first, if a springhouse it was; and as quietly as he could, he covered about half the distance from the highway to the house, walking, not upon the wagon road, but to one side of it for fear of stirring gravel or stones. He stopped again to listen, cocking his head, scarcely breathing; and below the surface quiet, he did hear sounds, very faint but there: the squeak of an oven door, the rattle of a pan, then the squeak of the oven door shutting. At last the receptacle of his ear grew so crowded with the underpinnings of silence, he was unable to sort them out. He heard water trickling somewhere and another sound he took to be from the barn—the rhythmic whisper of milk spewing into a pail, he thought, but he discovered it was only the stirring of his own clothing as he breathed. He went on toward the small, low structure until he found that it was, indeed, a springhouse; but just as he was lifting the latch of its door, a dog barked. He nearly bolted, but on a sudden impulse let himself inside. The dog seemed to pause and listen before he bayed with more authority. "Hush up," he heard someone tell it, a woman's voice, he thought. The dog made one or two more croupy, grumbling barks and ceased.

Inside, the springhouse was totally dark and full of the liquid comment of water running through it. "Hellkatoot," Music whispered to himself, and all of a sudden reeling drunk, he sank down on his haunches and did not move for minutes, waiting for his dizziness to pass. Excitement seemed to have pumped him so full of alcohol that, even when he did begin to inch about on hands and knees, his dizziness came back and he nearly fell sideways. It's only that I can't see nothing, he thought, and allowed himself to rest again. At last, feeling about in the dark, he discovered the edge of the cooling trough and what seemed a large crock covered with a rag, and beside that, a gallon mason jar. Carefully he lifted the mason jar from the trough and unscrewed the lid. It was heavy and therefore full of something, but it was more faith than the nearly nonexistent sweet, chalky odor that told him it was milk. He drank until his stomach stretched and the mason jar grew lighter. "I thank you," he whispered. He felt around for the lid, put it on again, and set the jar back in the trough. He rested again. "That's better," he said. He felt for his paper parcel and, as quietly as he could, opened the door.

Although he expected it, the dog made no comment. Outside in the lesser dark, he closed the door carefully. It made no sound he could hear, for it was hung from leather hinges, and he realized only his carelessness with the latch had caused his trouble getting in. He began to sneak back

30

down the hill, thinking it best to go down to the highway and make a big loop around from the south, rather than risk crossing directly in front of the shack. Even so, the dog began to bark before he'd gone two steps; but it was, he realized all at once, inside the shack, and he went on.

In the moony darkness he searched the garden end to end, finding only two turnips, one of them no larger than a crab apple, and a handful of beans with hulls as tough as leather. He took his coat out of the paper bag and put what he had gathered inside with the hope that tomorrow, on the way to Valle Crucis, he might be able to add enough to it to make himself a stew.

He was cold and almost put on his coat, but thought better of it. It would be best to save its warmth until he settled down for the night; digging out a place for himself in the haystack, like walking, would warm him. In any case, he was only cold on the surface—his skin merely a size or so too small—not bone-cold.

On the south side of the haystack most distant from the house he began to dig. About a foot above the ground, he burrowed into the faint warmth of it, into the slow, sweet fire of its rot and fermentation. When at last he was done, he turned around, eased himself in feetfirst, and covered his lower body with hay. He spread his coat over him and heaped as much hay as he could upon it, and at last drew the paper sack under his head and rested the base of his skull on the bottom of the cooking pot inside it. "Ahh," he said and wished only, and belatedly, for another taste of the moonshine tucked away inside the sack and for a smoke, but he made no move to get them. He looked straight up at the stars and the pale moon, which, as it rode in the cold night sky, seemed to smoke faintly around its rim. Wrapped in the warm, musty sweetness of hay, he was drifting toward sleep when some rattletrap of a car or truck passed on the highway below him. He listened as it went on toward Valle Crucis. No, it had paused to idle where the wagon road from the shack emptied into the highway. No, he heard a grench of gears and the slower growling of the motor. The goddamned thing was climbing the wagon road toward the shack. He could hear the gravel crunch, the jolting as it negotiated the ruts. The motor idled, shuddered, stopped. He heard the thump of a clutch pedal released from the pressure of a foot, a metal door squawk open and slam shut. Why didn't that knothead of a dog bark? he wondered, and knew at once it was because the dog recognized who had arrived. Hellkatoot, he thought, and looked wildly about, taking stock of the pasture, the uneven line of woods a few hundred yards above him, the

31

ghostly remains of the garden below. None of it seemed to offer any real cover. He felt ridiculously trapped, as though someone had dropped a haystack on him and pinned him on his back, but then the steps and breezeway of the house grumbled woodenly underfoot, and at last a door opened and closed. He sighed, realized he had been holding his breath. "Shitass," he said and squeezed his crotch. If it hadn't been for the icy air upon his face, he would have gotten up and scouted out the shack, but he was warm and his eyes were grainy with fatigue. All right, he thought, what the hell, so someone came in behind me.

His nose was cold and drained a thin, watery liquid upon his upper lip. He sniffed. What's the man gonna do, he asked himself reasonably, come out and check his haystacks? Why, hell no, he thought, and carefully, moving one part of his body at a time, he turned on his side without loosing his covering of hay. Still, in some corner of his mind, he was bothered that the place was not so settled in for the night as he had thought, although it did not keep the warmth from soothing him or the whiskey and milk from working on him like a potion.

Nevertheless, he did not know he'd been asleep when, some time later, he became aware of two things simultaneously: a cold wet spot on his forehead and an intense pain in his ear where the weight of his head seemed to mash his ear against the tin pot as cruelly as between the jaws of pliers. The moon, too, seemed excessively bright even through the slits of his eyes. Slowly, more asleep than awake, he began to turn to his other side, realizing as he did that something had touched his forehead moments before, that it was standing now at his back, that indeed there were two figures behind him where there had been none.

He leapt broad awake and bolt upright, flinging off both coat and hay in a sudden eruption. The dog sprang back. The man said, "Easy, cousin," and pointed a pistol exactly where the dog's nose had touched his forehead. Music could see very little of the man's face because of the carbide lamp on his head, but he could see that the man carried not only a pistol, but a sack and a rifle in his other hand.

"What in hell you think you're doin?" Music asked him.

"Ye got that on the wrong foot, ain'tcha?" the man said. "You the one holed up in my haystack like a rat in a corncrib." He let the hammer down on his pistol and slipped it into a shoulder holster underneath his jumper, apparently satisfied that Music was not dangerous, sitting as he was with his hands flat against the ground behind him; at least not so dangerous that the little falling-block, single-shot, .22 rifle couldn't deal with him, for he changed it to his right hand, thumb on the hammer. The man turned his head slightly to nod at the dog, and Music glimpsed a bit of the man's nose, cheekbone, and chin until the light struck him again full in the face. "I reckon ole Fetlock was tryin to tell me ye bin in my springhouse too. Ain't much coon dog," he said; "don't never know what he's gonna tree."

"I owe you a bellyful of milk," Music said.

The light bobbed slowly in acknowledgement. "And the better part of a haystack," the man said. "Git up."

Music got up and bent to retrieve his coat and his sack.

"Nope," the man said. "Stand about five feet yonder way if ye will." He waved Music back with the rifle barrel, knelt and patted Music's coat around the pockets, picked it up, and seemed to weigh it in his hand. He picked up the paper sack too, felt it, weighed it. "What's in here?" he asked.

"A soda bottle with a little liquor in it and a cooking pot."

The light bobbed. "Step on out toward the house," the man said.

"Can I have my coat?" Music said. "It's chilly if you ain't under a haystack." The coat came flying at him, and he caught it and put it on.

"Step on out," the man said, and Music started for the house. The dog, nose to the ground, quartered ahead of him, and the man walked a few paces behind.

The window at the rear corner of the house was still lit, and as they drew closer, Music could see a woman moving about inside. They ducked under a clothesline with a ragged shirt and a flour-sack towel hanging from it, passed a black iron washpot, and stepped up on the breezeway of the house. There was stovewood stacked along one wall of the breezeway and a galvanized washtub, a lantern, and various tools hanging from spikes along the other. Music turned to look at the man, who waved with the barrel of the rifle and said, "Right in there, cousin." Music lifted the latch, and the hound slinked past him as he stepped into a kitchen, mellow with lamplight and smotheringly warm from the cookstove.

The woman he had seen through the window might have been fifty or so, but it was difficult to tell. Although her hair was a rich red-brown without any grey, her face was a net of wrinkles; and though she looked ruddy and strong, she carried her head at a peculiar angle, as if she were slightly deaf or bent with rheumatism. "Howdy," she said to Music.

"Ma'am," Music said, but the woman's attention seemed to bend

33

around him toward the rifle pointed at his spine. The man had shut off his carbide lamp and taken off the cap it was clipped to. He was taller than Music by a head and had hair the color of a lion's mane.

"What's this here?" the woman asked.

"Jumped this feller outten a haystack, Momma," the man said. He took one of the two chairs from under the kitchen table and set it by the door to the breezeway. "Sit ye down," he said to Music, and Music sat, anger slowly beginning to bristle along his scalp. He had been caught in the wrong, and the man had the privilege, maybe even the obligation, to curse him and run him off, but not to draw the thing out like this.

The man ambled to the other end of the room, put the gunnysack, Music's paper parcel, and the little rifle down on the sideboard. He dragged the other chair from beneath the table for his mother. She sat too, her head cocked to one side as though she were listening to something beneath the floorboards of the house. Settling himself into a curl under the table, the hound tasted the inside of his mouth and sighed, his lips fluttering softly. The man leaned back against the sideboard, crossed his arms over his chest, and looked at Music.

What the hell, buddyroe, Music thought and speculated on the man's strength and the distance between them. He was rawboned, lean, and Music guessed he'd be awkward but tough as hickory. He wished they weren't so far apart. It would take two, perhaps three, steps to reach him, and although he no longer had a weapon in his hands, there was the butt of the pistol showing just inside his open jumper. Finally there was the woman, who might get knocked about and hurt. He thought about trying to get away, but the odds of that seemed longer yet. His chair was propped against the door to the breezeway, and there would not be enough time to get up, turn around, snatch the chair aside, and get out. No, he thought, it would be better to take the man's gun away. As though he were shifting for comfort, Music leaned his weight a little forward, taking some of it upon the balls of his feet; but somehow, though he was tuned to make a sudden leap, he made no further move. Whatever there was of forbearance and good sense sitting in the central chamber of his brain did not abdicate as it often did. Perhaps it was the woman with her head tilted humbly to one side, her large, chapped hands folded in her lap, her eyes looking somewhere in the vicinity of his shoe tops; perhaps it was his sense of wrongdoing; or the complicated but somehow benign atmosphere of that place; but for some reason the possibility of action drained away. Music scratched the back of his head, wiped his mouth,

34

sniffed. "Well," he said at last, "I got in your springhouse for a fact and drank me some milk." He made a gesture toward the cement sack with his forefinger. "If you look in my poke yonder, you'll find two turnips and a handful of pole beans I grubbed outta your garden." He inclined his head toward the far-off field. "I expect that haystack I bedded down in needs fixin if it ain't to molder." He took a deep breath and raised his eyebrows quizzically. "I think them's the damages," he said. "I trust they ain't none of em shootin offenses."

As though Music had not spoken, the man said, "What business ye got in Switch County?"

"No business," Music said. "Didn't know that's where I was."

The man wrinkled his brow, tilted his chin to the side. "That don't seem hardly likely," he said.

"I been through lotsa places I couldn't name," Music said. "I'm headed to Virginia, and this here place is in my way. If I didn't come through here, I'd have to come through somewhere else."

"That makes a right smart of sense to me," the woman said.

"You ain't heard of the National Miners Union, I reckon," the man asked.

"Lots of poor stiffs are trying to organize these days," Music said.

The woman rocked herself ever so slightly back and forth in the chair.

"That yer answer, is it?" the man asked.

Music frowned, confused, wondering if he was beginning to catch the drift of things. "I've heard of the United Mine Workers and the West Virginia Mine Workers, I guess," he said, "but I don't know that other outfit." He thought of the one-armed man, the way the niggers had acted in that Mink Slide place, the trouble and killings he'd read about in the newspapers at one mine or another, in one state or another. Hellkatoot, he thought.

"Well," the man said, "they're makin a ruckus in Harlan County and down in Pike and Perry and Bell." He studied Music, seeming to grow more embarrassed all the time, his neck flushing red even to his ears, like some overgrown schoolboy who had been made to recite when he didn't know his lesson. "I won't monkey with ye," he said at last. "Are you a unionizer or no?"

Music felt his own ears warming with embarrassment, as though being a unionizer was so far from the truth there was no good way to argue the matter. It was as if someone had accused him of being a fence post or a

35

pinto pony just to hear what he would offer to the contrary. "I been knockin around out west," Music said, "knockin around most everywhere, it seems to me. But for every fellow that's got a job"—he made a vague motion with his hand—"there's three more lookin. No, mister," Music said, "I ain't no organizer for your union, nor much of anything else. I'm just tryin to get back home to Shulls Mills, Virginia."

For some moments no one spoke, until the woman, sitting woodenly in her chair and looking at no one, said in a soft, almost dreamy voice, "I expect yer a-thinkin we're right cross." She sighed. "Leastwise that's the appearance I'd put on us. My folks come from Virginia," she said, "just over to Big Stone Gap."

The man rubbed his chin uncomfortably. "If yer what ye claim, I'm right sorry to be a-diggin in yer business," he said. He shifted his feet. "Still yet, I probly ort to carry you to the sheriff and let ye tell yer story to him."

"You some kinda law?" Music asked.

"More's the pity," the woman said. "Mine guard is what he be, and a deputy sheriff into the bargain. Ye hungry, I reckon?"

The warm, sweet smell of biscuits and gravy and the complicated odors of other foods had been with him since he entered the kitchen, although he'd had no chance to acknowledge them and what they were doing to his stomach. "I don't want to trouble you," Music said.

"Shaw," the woman said and rose. She went to the woodstove, removed one of the lids and poked the fire up, added a stick or two of wood from the box beside the stove, and went to the cupboard over the sideboard. "Twon't be fancy," she said. "I wasn't studyin company."

"I thank you, missus," Music said.

The woman made him no reply. The man dragged up the chair she had vacated and sat heavily down. He propped his elbows on the table, massaged his face, and, with a sudden wry expression, laughed. "I ort to believe ye, I reckon," he said. "Don't seem any man's luck would run so poor, and him an organizer, as to land smack in a mine guard's lap."

"Set up to the table," the woman commanded Music. "They's coffee still hot, and the rest's a-comin." Music did as he was told, and she placed a chipped, enameled tin cup before him which bathed his face in steam and another before her son.

"How long ye been on the road?" the man asked.

"I don't know how to answer," Music said. "I ain't been home in better than two years, but I've been most of that time in Chicago." While the man listened patiently and the woman labored over the stove, he told what he could about Chicago; about learning the electrician's trade, and about hard times catching him there. He did not know how to tell why he'd stayed, or how rough and lean it had been. With some embarrassment, he told the story of traveling all the way to Salt Lake City, Utah, because he'd heard there was an electrification program going on there and linemen were being hired for big money; and how, finally, when he learned that no such thing was true and caught himself one morning sifting through the garbage cans behind a hotel, looking for something to eat, he had thought, at last, of going home. He did not tell them it was hard to remember he had a home, that even as he sat before them, he was not certain he had the right to return. When he had left home in the beginning to seek whatever he sought, hadn't he renounced it? Struggling to get by day after day and month after month, hadn't he lost even a proper memory of it? He did not tell them that, for he didn't understand it himself; and, like taking hold of twenty-three hundred volts or being robbed, it was, in any case, too personal a thing to tell.

"Regus," the woman said from the stove, "you ain't goan carry him to the sheriff, aire ye?" She was rounding off a plate with navy beans and some sort of meat in a white gravy.

The man called Regus frowned and ran his forefinger back and forth under his nose. He looked at Music. "I'd hate to think you wuz guying me," he said, "and me swallowin it. Hit ain't no folks anywhere that's believed as many lies as them in Kentucky. I reckon we don't ken the difference." He shifted his feet under the table and sighed, inclining his head toward the woman at the stove. "Nawh," he said at last, "I reckon I ain't."

The woman took a pan of biscuits from the oven, propped three of them precariously atop the food on the plate, and set it before him. The odor was so delicious Music felt dizzy. "You get to it now," she said, "fore hit cools."

The woman went off into the front room, Regus sipped his coffee, and Music began to eat. The food was even better than it smelled. He was sure, in all his life, he had never eaten anything so good. The meat—he thought it was rabbit to judge by a wide, flat thigh and skinny shank he could see—was cooked in a white gravy, mildly sweet, very peppery and fine; and the biscuits and beans, too, were delicious. Presently the woman reappeared carrying a large, black, leather-bound Bible pressed against her breast as though it were an infant. "Mister," she said, not quite

37

looking at him, her head tilted to one side after her fashion, "can you read writin? I mean ye no offense if ye can't," she added.

"Yes'um," Music said through a mouthful of food. He was confused—he had been since the man and dog had startled him awake—but he felt blessed, as well, with great good fortune.

"Now, I thought you could," the woman said. "I'd not have ast if I'd had airey notion ye couldn't." She put the Bible down gently on the table and folded her large, rough hands into her apron. "I'd take it as an awful favor if you'd read me a mite of the Gospel after ye've had yer supper. I ain't a-chargin ye to eat by it. Hit's just so long since I been to a church meetin," she said.

Music bobbed his head and swallowed. "It would be my pleasure, missus," he said.

Across the table from him, Regus rubbed the palms of his hands together thoughtfully. "I'll be back directly," he said and rose. Beneath the table, the hound scrabbled up and brushed past Music's shins to follow the man out upon the breezeway.

Music gulped down coffee and stuffed his mouth with food. The woman took the coffeepot from the stove and filled his cup again. "I'bleve you wuz near perished, son," she told him; and as if he were one of her own, and without asking his preference in the matter, she replenished his nearly empty plate with what remained in her pots and pans. Music took a scalding sip of coffee and determined to slow himself down, but he could not. The woman began to heat some water on the stove. "I'll not have ye think," she said, keeping her back to him, "that I've been a-beggin your pardon for my son. I ain't," she said, her voice calm, but full of such quiet conviction that he paused over his plate, his jaws packed, part of a biscuit arrested halfway to his mouth. She turned toward him, her head to one side, her eyes focused on a point no higher than his shoe tops but with the power, somehow, to make him go still inside, as though she looked him dead in the eye. "Regus Bone's as good a man as ere ye'll chance to meet," she said. "Hit's the times that makes us ill and sets us all agin one another."

His mouth, stuffed as it was, went as dry as if he had been chidden. He swallowed three or four times to make room for speech, seeming to swallow each time whatever he was going to say before he quite knew what it was. The woman continued to look in the neighborhood of his shoes. He had no notion how he could feel penetrated by such indirection. "Eat your victuals, son," she said at last and turned back to her labors

38

just as a sudden pounding came from the other side of the house. There were three heavy blows and the pounding ceased. "Now what do ye reckon he's a-doin?" she remarked, scraping the remaining scraps of food from her pans into a slop bucket.

As hungry as he had been, as good as the food was, he had eaten past his appetite. Still, slowly, grimly, as though he could make up for past hunger, he put the food inside himself and braced to keep it there over his stomach's objection. The pounding took up once more, and after three blows, abruptly stopped again. Music pushed part of a biscuit around his plate, gathering every last morsel, feeling sick from the richness of the gravy, the salt and pepper, which he was not used to. Outside on the breezeway the man's footsteps rumbled woodenly, the dog's claws clicked, and something heavy was dropped roughly down. Regus came in, crossed the room, and sat down again at the table. The hound slinked beneath it, circled and collapsed, his elbows rapping against the floor like sticks.

"What was all the fuss and a-poundin?" the woman asked.

Regus did not answer. He took his cup of coffee between his large chapped hands. "You'll bed down in the front room acrost the dogtrot," he said to Music.

"Hit ain't fittin," the woman said.

"Hit'll do," Regus said.

The woman turned from cleaning skillets and pans as though to argue, but she did not; instead she folded her hands into her apron for a moment and then, seeing somehow that Music's plate was empty, she took it from the table. "Yore coffee's ice-cold," she said to Regus.

"Hit's all right," Regus said, but he was looking at Music, his eyes grey as dawn. "I expect you'll read to Ella outten her Bible now," he said.

Music took the Bible up. "What part would you like to hear, missus?"

The woman stood at the stove with her hands folded into her apron. "I'd like hit if ye'd begin at the start," she said.

Regus got up, stepped into the front room, and reappeared at once with a rocking chair, which he placed just inside the door by the woodbox. "Set yourself down, Momma," he said.

Music half turned from the table so as to catch the light from a kerosene lamp in the windowsill, and slowly and with great care, he began. " 'In the beginning,' " he read, " 'God created the heaven and the earth.' "

"Amen," the woman whispered and rocked herself, her eyes closed in concentration.

" 'And the earth was without form, and void; and darkness was upon the face of the deep.' "

"Amen," she said.

He read to the end of the second chapter of Genesis and stumbled only over the names of the rivers flowing out of Eden and one or two other words. At the beginning of the third chapter of Genesis, she stopped him. "That'll do," she said, "that'll do handsomely. You read s'purty and s'fine; but if ye'd just as soon, I'll not hear of the serpent this evenin."

Music closed the Bible and gave it to her, and she held it against her breast. "I never had a finer supper, missus," he told her. "I'm obliged to you."

"I wasn't studyin company," she said, but her voice was far away.

"Well," Regus said, "if I ain't to go coon huntin like I'd started, I reckon hit's time to bed down."

"That room ain't fittin," the woman said, letting the Bible sink to her lap, her voice once again strong.

"They's a tick in there," Regus said, "a tight roof. Hit'll serve as well as airey haystack."

The woman did not speak further. She looked reproachfully in the direction of Regus's shoe tops, got up, and went into the front room. She returned at once with a heavy quilt and gave it to Music, who had gotten up with Regus. "I'm grateful," Music said.

Outside on the dogtrot, Regus took the lantern hanging on a peg by the kitchen door, lit it, and handed it to Music. "Ye'll be shet in," Regus said. He wiped his forefinger back and forth under his nose. "I ain't so quick to ken a fellow as Momma," he said. "I'll need to think ye over." He looked embarrassed. Even in the lamplight Music could see the flush creeping up his neck toward his ears. "I nailed the winders shet, and I'm goan wedge a prop agin yer door." He spat off the end of the dogtrot, his ears red. "I'll let ye out come mornin and carry ye acrost the county line." For a moment neither of them spoke. "Hold on," Regus said. He went into the back room across the dogtrot and came out with a chamber pot, which he handed to Music. He picked up what appeared to be a rail lifted from a fence. "Twon't be airey way out but one," he said, "and that's over me."

Music lifted the latch and went in the room. Regus shut the door behind him. The rail thumped against it and squawked tight. Music

40

raised the lantern and looked at the strings of leather britches beans, apple snits, and rings of dried pumpkin hung from the low rafters. Against the front wall there were small, straw-filled bins of potatoes, onions, turnips, and carrots. There was no furniture in the room, but on the floor in the northwest corner there was a tick discolored with ancient stains. He dropped his quilt upon it, set his lantern and chamber pot on the floor, and stood for a moment considering the quality of his luck. "Jesus," he said, puzzling over being captured, questioned, fed, asked to read from the Bible, and, finally, penned. He didn't know if he should be grateful or mad. "Jesus," he muttered, and sat down on the tick, noisy with dry cornshucks. He gazed stupidly at his feet and tried to puzzle it all out, but his mind refused to work. After a moment, more asleep than awake, he took off his shoes, rolled his coat for a pillow, turned the wick down on the lantern, and blew out the weak rim of flame. He lay back against the rustle and crackle of cornshucks and covered himself with the quilt. "Hellkatoot," he whispered.

# 4

# A JOB

HE WOKE THINKING he was watching a red-tailed hawk, harried by crows, barrel-rolling over the ridge behind his father's house. The crows dived at it in odd, dead silence while the long, piercing whistle of the hawk drew him out of sleep; yet the moment he opened his eyes he knew where he was, even before the sound faded. It wasn't a train. A steam whistle from the coal camp back in Elkin, he guessed. He shifted on the cornshuck tick, surprised to feel none of the stiffness that plagued him when he'd slept on the ground or in a boxcar. He felt good, well fed, rested, as though all he needed to restore him was a single meal and one night in a house.

As if he had gone to sleep only a moment before, the question of his luck still haunted his thoughts, but it seemed suddenly clear to him that, in the small but important matters which kept a man from day to day, he did have luck, good luck. He merely did not have it on a grand scale. He would not go home driving a car and wearing a fine suit of clothes, but afoot, ragged, and possessing only the simple luck that had kept him. Still, if a man could learn to be content with that, where was the blame?

Across the dogtrot he heard sounds. The household was awake. He sat up, eyed the chamber pot distastefully, and decided to knock on the door to be let out. He put on his shoes, got up to try the latch, and found the door opened easily onto the breezeway. The dog was curled outside and, by way of greeting, raised his head and gave Music a huge, whining yawn, stretching his jaws, vapor rising from the ridged roof of his mouth and long curling tongue in the morning air. "Fetlock, is it?" Music asked him, and the dog sneezed and thumped his tail against the floor. "You son of a bitch," Music told him and stepped off the end of the breezeway, making for the outhouse, but just at that moment the kitchen door opened and Ella Bone appeared. "I thought I heard ye," she said. She waved him away. "Go on about yer business. I'll set ye out some wash water." She disappeared back into the kitchen before he could thank her.

There had been a frost, as he'd expected, and the metallic smell of it was still in the air, although the grass and earth were rimed with white only in the lee of the house and corncrib where the sun had not yet reached. His breath steamed before him, and the sun warmed his shoulders.

The rank outhouse had a catalogue in it and a rusted bucket half full of corncobs. The smell and look of it were as familiar to him as his childhood, and he considered it for a moment in the light of the distances he had traveled, the cities he had seen and dwelt in, and almost without rancor he began to laugh.

When he approached the house again, he saw that a flour-sack towel, a cake of homemade lye soap, and a smoking pan of hot water had been laid out for him on the simple shelf beneath the kitchen window. He rolled his sleeves and washed his hands and face and the back of his neck, scrubbing so vigorously and with such great pleasure he did not hear Regus come up behind him.

"Would ye like the use of a razor then?" Regus said, and Music turned, but his eyes were bleared and burning with lye soap and he could scarcely see.

"If it wouldn't trouble you," he said. "I left mine in a pawnshop out in Dodge City."

Regus bobbed his head and went up on the dogtrot carrying a bucket of milk.

In order not to waste the use of soap and hot water, Music thought better of merely washing his face and hands and stripped off his shirt and undershirt and bathed his chest and arms, which smoked too in the cold air. Regus brought out a razor, cup, and brush and hung a leather strop for him from a hook at the end of the rough shelf. He left the things without a word and went back into the kitchen. There was a shard of mirror propped in the window frame, and Music squinted into it as he

43

lathered, scarcely recognizing the wild-looking face covered with better than a quarter inch of stubble which stared back at him. No goddamned wonder they shut you up, he told himself. His shirt and undershirt were rancid and offensive when he put them on again, but there was no help for it. He cleaned the razor, stropped it, and dashed out his water.

"I'm obliged to you," he told the woman when he carried the basin and shaving things back inside.

"Well," Ella said, "you look a sight better. Lay em yonder," she said, motioning toward the sideboard. "Just got the milk strained, and Regus stepped down to the springhouse with it. Set ye down to breakfast. Regus'll be on back ere you get yer chair pulled up."

He put the shaving things on the sideboard. "Missus," he said, "you've got no call to feed me again. I could run a week on that supper last night."

She caught up the hem of the ragged apron tied about her waist and used it to open the oven door and take out a pan of biscuits. "Set up to the table. I'll not have ye hungry in this house, nor hear the contrary."

Music did as she bid him, and in a moment she put a plate before him with biscuits, eggs, and a slab of bacon on it. "Eat them victuals, son," she said, and he found it easy to accommodate her, for his appetite was fierce, as though it had taken no more than supper the night before to reestablish the habit of eating. She set a cracked, lidless tureen of gravy and a second plate of food on the table just as Regus's heavy footsteps sounded upon the dogtrot. He came in and, all in one motion it seemed, set his bucket on the sideboard, pulled his chair up to the table, and covered his biscuits and eggs with gravy until his plate was swimming in it. "If it won't fer gravy," Regus said apologetically, "a lot of little babies would have died."

"I've heard that," Music said and laughed and took some gravy himself.

But it was as if the two of them could think of nothing further to say, for they gave over at once to silence and eating. Nor did Ella speak. Yet somehow an awkward prelude to speaking seemed to grow in the room. Music could sense it so strongly that by the time the two of them had finished and Ella had replenished the coffee in their chipped enameled cups, his ears had grown warm with it.

At last Regus cleared his throat, and after a moment said, "Momma's got the gift of prophecy in her dreams." His neck was rosy, but his voice was calm and even and his eyes were perfectly serious, as though he were

44

delivering a speech he had practiced. "She's stronger with the Lord than most folks," he said and ran his finger back and forth under his nose. "She says you are to stay with us."

Music looked at the woman by the stove, her hands rolled into her apron, her head tilted to one side after her fashion. Her face was without expression and she offered no word. Hellkatoot, he thought, what sort of hocus-pocus is this?

"Momma ain't often wrong with it," Regus went on, "only once in a great while."

"Hit ain't never the dream ner prophecy that's wrong," Ella said. "Hit's just that I don't, ever time, ken the proper meaning."

"I think I'd best get on to Virginia," Music said after a moment, "but I thank you."

"Tain't no thanks due us," she said. "Hit's only that the dream said otherwise."

"Well," Regus said and raised his brows, "well, I said I'd carry ye outten the county, and so I will; but if you want to pull some time as a mine guard, I can get ye in. I'll not try to fool with you that it's airey sort of proper job, for hit's not." He propped his elbows on the table and held the enameled coffee cup between his large, chapped hands. His expression was serious for a moment before his eyes seemed to flash with a sudden humor. "Still yet," he said, "the pay's all right, three dollars a day, and you can draw it in money or clacker as ye choose." He sucked his teeth and turned to look at the woman, although he continued to speak to Music. "But if you'd just as lief go to Virginy, I'll carry ye acrost the county line, and Momma will have to read another feller into her dream."

Ella Bone gave no sign, but merely took their plates from the table and set them in the dishpan.

"What's this clacker?" Music asked, as if it were the only question he was capable of, as if his decision rested on the answer.

"Why hit's scrip," Regus said and laughed. "I beg yer pardon," he said, "you done already said you wuz just passin through." He scratched the back of his tawny head. "Hit's minted off in Cincinnati, I think it is. You can't trade on it except at the commissary. Hit don't sound right a-jinglin in yer pocket, don't ye know, not like proper money."

"I guess I'll hire on," Music said.

Ella Bone raised her hands as though to deliver a blessing and said, "Praise His name."

# 5

## HIRING ON AND
## SWEARING IN

AS THE MODEL T truck pecked along the highway into Valle Crucis, Music rode with his elbow out the window and a skinny cigarette, more spit and paper than tobacco, hanging from his lips. He felt both wildly happy and a little peculiar. He would have taken any sort of job for three dollars a day and asked no questions; it was only that the woman's dream bothered him, as though, once again, he had done something half-cocked such as jumping off a highballing freight into the middle of Kansas. Still, he reasoned, he was riding and not walking, fed and not hungry. Clean-shaven, his hair wetted, tamed, and combed, he was even on his way to a high-paying job; and as the Model T pecked and growled through Valle Crucis, past the depot and stores, the hotel and courthouse, he felt almost important, at least until the truck began to growl up a long hill with fine, big, white houses fronting either side of the street. At one, grander even than the others but for worn and faded awnings shading the windows and the huge front porch, and a little peeling paint here and there, Regus pulled up and stopped.

The two of them got out and walked around to the back, where there was a pavilion, a pool with a fountain in the center and many marble benches parked comfortably in the shade of trees and shrubs. Wealth, Music realized, made him nervous; but it didn't seem to bother Regus, who banged loudly on the door and turned his head to spit when a thin, grouchy-looking colored woman appeared. They had business with Mr. Kenton Hardcastle and she should fetch him, he told her.

46

Without speaking to them or inviting them in, she scuffed away into the bowels of the house, from which, presently, they saw an old man in a starched white shirt waving a Panama hat to signal he meant to meet them in front. They rounded the house again and mounted the wide veranda, waiting until the colored woman opened the door and held it and the old man came through.

He was the sort of old man whose chest had receded while his belly grew proud, so that the front of him seemed to be all britches with a set of shoulders riding on top. "Sit. Sit," he said, waving his hat toward two white, wingback, wicker chairs. They sat, but he did not. Still, he seemed absolutely at rest, as though, splayfooted, his chest collapsed over his belly, he had achieved a perfect balance of stresses. He shook his hat thoughtfully at Regus for a moment. "Regus Bone," he said.

"That's right," Regus said and spat over the railing into the yard.

Kenton Hardcastle plopped the hat on his head. "Well, state your business then, Mr. Bone."

"I've brought the extra man to pull my shift with me, if ye'll hold still for him," Regus said.

Hardcastle turned to Music and gave him a look of cold, insulting appraisal. "What's your name and where you from?"

"Bill Music," he answered. "I come from Shulls Mills, Virginia."

"I pay damned good wages," Hardcastle said, "and I generally like a big bastard for my money." He studied Music a moment more, as if sizing him up for a fight. "But if a feller is downright mean and don't scare a whit, he might do."

Somehow Music got the notion that Kenton Hardcastle used himself as the absolute measuring stick by which to judge a man's mettle. Hardcastle's age and shape being what they were, it was almost, but not quite, laughable. "Hell," Music said, smiling in spite of himself, "I'm fearless."

"That's what I need," Hardcastle said. "I won't have a guard on my payroll that a miner can run over. If you don't have iron, you don't draw wages from me. Have you got what I'm lookin for?"

"If I don't, I'll leave," Music said.

"I'll see to it," Hardcastle said. "I expect to get a hard case for my money and I expect something else: when I ask you to do a thing, no matter what it is, I want it done right then, no excuses and no questions. Do you understand me?"

"Yessir," Music said, although he was beginning to wonder if he did.

47

"These are bad times, and I'm in a fight," Hardcastle said. "There's unionizing scum all over this state, and many a smart coal man will lose his operation and his holdings if he can't be tough. But, by God," he said, "that won't happen here! You'll keep a keen eye out or answer to me. And you'll not let a single one of those seditious sons a bitches get anywhere near Hardcastle Coal Company. You understand me?"

Since he didn't know what else to do, Music nodded and said that he understood.

"All right," Kenton Hardcastle said. "I'll call the sheriff and the mine foreman." Perhaps in lieu of a handshake, he fetched a cigar from his shirt pocket and made poking motions toward Music with it until Music understood and took it. "Mr. Bone will tell you what you need to know," he said and waved them away.

When they were back in the Model T, Regus chuckled softly. "That old sucker never give me no cigar when I hired on, but then again I never thought to tell him I was fearless."

Music turned to look at Regus and saw in his face an expression so completely without spite or malice that he laughed himself, as much with relief as anything. "Christ," Music said, "I guess I thought I was making a joke."

"Ha," Regus said, "if you want Kenton Hardcastle to know yer jokin, ye'll have to tell him, for he'll never guess otherwise." He turned the Model T out of Hardcastle's driveway and back toward the center of Valle Crucis. "Well, now we've got another prince of a feller to see," he said and spat out the window.

The prince of a fellow turned out to be as surly a man as Music had ever met. After the first ten minutes in Sheriff Hub Farthing's office Music began to wonder just how much three dollars a day was worth to him; he had been arrested and thrown in jail by friendlier men. Still the sheriff swore him in and, stiff with anger, slapped a badge down on the edge of his desk for Music to pick up. He was still trying to get his mind around being a deputy sheriff when Farthing—a wide, if not quite fat, man who seemed to be all over, uniform and all, the color of ripe wheat—pointed a finger at him and told him he was a deputy sheriff only as a favor to Kenton Hardcastle and only for the purpose of keeping unionizers, foreigners, and goddamned miners in line; and if he shot up anybody, he'd better make damned sure it was one of those and that he did the shooting on company property, or anyway close enough to drag the goddamned carcass back on company property.

"You get any other ideas about what that badge can fetch you in Switch County and I'll yank it quicker than a cat can lick its ass," the sheriff said.

Hellkatoot, Music told himself when they were again in the Model T and on the way to Elkin, it's a depression and a man would be a fool to turn down three dollars a day. But the affairs of the morning had left him dizzy and confused. He took out his pocketknife, divided the cigar Hardcastle had given him, and gave Regus half, wondering just what he had gotten himself into and shaking his head in disbelief.

"Hub Farthing's got all kinds of kinfolks scattered around this county he'd like to see have yore job," Regus said and laughed. "Hell, mine too. So don't expect him to take a shine to ye. But old Kenton Hardcastle believes in hiring mine guards that ain't known in the county. The miners won't be bluffed so easy by a feller they've known all their lives. No," Regus said, "they'll run over them and face them down if they's a row." Regus chuckled and shook his head. Kenton Hardcastle was a clever old scalawag, he explained. Clever enough to make three fortunes, even if he had lost two of them and grown both mean and nearly crazy trying to keep from losing it all. "But he will," Regus said. "Ain't any money in coal no longer, not even fer the hotshot operator like him."

The times were gone, Regus said, when a man could make a killing in the coal business. Hell, it wasn't 1920 anymore. In the spring of that year coal had brought as much as fourteen dollars a ton right at the tipple, he said; and he himself had often made close to fifty dollars a day, working, as he was, nearly a six-foot seam of Pocahontas coal. He laughed and said he'd had to take thought and study how to get rid of his money in those days, but he'd done it. When he could take a number-three coal shovel and load thirty ton a shift—if he didn't mind threatening to whip the motorman a dozen times a day in order to get empty coal cars, and didn't mind working so hard he'd spit black cotton—he'd seen no virtue in not buying anything that pleased his eye. Oh, he'd gotten rid of his money, he said. He'd never known anyone dumb enough to dig coal who was smart enough to save his money, and that included operators. He looked over at Music and grinned. "The depression around here started in the fall of 1920," he said. "We got nearly a ten-year lead on the rest of you folks. Oh," he said, "hit picked up for a bit in '26 when the miners overseas struck, but that didn't last. Only just long enough fer a lot of fools to throw down their plows and take up a pick and shovel and then git caught and commence to starve like the rest of us."

49

"How'd you wind up in Switch County at a job like this, if you don't mind me askin?" Music said.

"Accident and bad luck, ye'd have to call it." Regus switched the cigar from one corner of his mouth to the other, squinting and grimacing from the heat so close to his lips. Finally he plucked the butt from between his teeth, inspected it, pinched away the coal, and folded it into his mouth like a chew of tobacco. After a moment he raised his eyebrows in surprise and pleasure, spat out the window, and told about a slate fall in a Harlan County mine where he had once worked. He had been eating lunch in the main drift with his working buddy, two other miners, the motorman, and the brakeman when the top let go without a sigh from the slate or one creak from a timber. A hunk of slate about the size of a coal car had come down on his buddy, a fellow named Lon Harmon. The brakeman had been pinned too, and broken up, and lost a leg as a consequence. But he himself had only gotten bruised and had his scalp laid open; for when the top let go, he had scrambled and thrashed about trying to get out of the way, and somehow everything had come down just right, so most of the weight was resting on what had already fallen and very little on him, although he was buried to the waist. He hadn't even gone out, for there was never a moment when he couldn't hear the motorman crying, "Great God A'mighty, great God A'mighty!" over and over again, even after the roof quit coming down around their ears, so that finally Regus had shouted, "Shut up, you damned fool, and dig us out!" spewing pieces of the raw turnip he had been eating from his mouth. Straight away the motorman began to weep and dig, telling later how he'd thought it was teeth and jawbone that Regus had been spitting, what with his scalp torn and his face covered with blood.

It had taken them a long and awful time to get the slate off Lon Harmon, Regus said, but it never mattered for he was mashed flat as a toad on the highway. Those had been pretty good days when the pay was all right, so he had bought the little shirttail farm in Switch County from Harmon's widow, who had no money to speak of and wanted to go back to her folks over in West Virginia. It had been Harmon's old place before he quit it and went to digging coal.

Regus mused a moment and snorted. "Hit was more disrespect for the dollar than charity that notioned me to buy it," he said. "I never wanted it, ner thought about it until a year or so ago." The chewed cigar appeared on Music's side, tucked in Regus's cheek like a walnut. Regus turned his head and spat out the window. "I was in a mine over in

50

Letcher County that was strikebound and fast going to hell," he said. "Hit was owned by Hardcastle's brother-in-law, a feller name of Royce Perry. Little operation it was, with about enough contracts to keep it going just a little in the hole all the time. I was running a short-wall machine for him. But when they struck him, and he lost what few buyers he had fer his coal, and the drift commenced to fill up with water here and there, and the top to come down, hell, I knew he was gonna go under.

"When I started to get hungry, I let out to him that I was about to head over this way and try my hand at farmin." Regus turned his head and spat out the window again and raised his eyebrows. "Turned out a mine guard had just been killed down to Elkin, and Royce got me the promise of his job. Royce was a-workin himself as a mine foreman for Consolidated Coal Company in Jenkins, last I heard. Lost all his holdings. You see how it is then," he said, tucking the lump of the cigar into his cheek and looking at Music; "I'm about as new to Switch County as you be. Hell, what with me and Momma," he said and laughed, "you may have more friends here than I do."

Just at that moment they passed Regus's homestead. Clothes fluttered from the clothesline which ran from the corner of the house to an old, blasted walnut tree, and Ella Bone straightened from a galvanized tub beneath the line to shake out a dress. When Regus saw her, he beeped the horn and he and Music waved. She turned and shaded her eyes with her hand to look after them, but didn't wave back. "Momma did take to you," Regus said, "but there's one thing that tends to worry me about all this here, and that's how we figure to arm ye." He looked at Music and raised his brows and grinned. "I don't reckon you got a pistol on ye I don't know about?" he said.

"Never carried one," Music said, and blushing, he added, "I never even fired one."

"Hmm," Regus said and rolled the lump of the cigar from one cheek to the other and back again, "well, we'll have to sort something out."

"I always hunted a lot," Music said, "but it was with my daddy's old hog rifle, a muzzleloader, don't you know?" Suddenly he wondered what he was doing hiring on as a mine guard, a deputy sheriff, for Christ's sake? He knew nothing about Switch County and coal mining, about guarding property against unionizers and Reds. How the hell was he supposed to recognize a unionizer if he saw one? What did he want with a job that would make everybody his enemy? He was suddenly homesick.

51

He felt a longing simply to be on his way home, or anywhere, to have only the problems of finding shelter, a little something to eat, a freight to jump.

"You ever bark a squirrel with it?"

"No," Music said, "never did." Hell, Music thought, hold on a minute and let me think.

"Ever shoot any deer with it?" Regus asked.

"Four," Music said.

"Any wild turkey?"

"A few," Music said.

"Ain't much game around here no more," Regus said. "Most of it's been killed off and put in the pot."

The valley opened out a little to Elkin: the strings of shacks on the right; the commissary, movie house, depot, and school on the left; and across the river, the tipple, powerhouse, gobpile, the empty coal cars parked on the siding.

"We'll see can we catch Bert Maloney without us having to get in that damned rathole mine," Regus said. "Yonder's his coupe down to the powerhouse."

Regus turned left just before the commissary and crossed the plank bridge over the river. Under the Model T the planks clattered against the strippers like a volley of pistol shots. Music could get no space to think, and there was a giddy feeling in his stomach, as though he were on a swing in the middle of its downward arc.

Just as they pulled up beside the green Chevrolet coupe, the mine foreman stepped out of the powerhouse door. He was about Music's height, but heavier-set. He wore broad green suspenders over a relatively clean khaki shirt, and upon his head was a miner's cap with a carbide lamp clipped to it. Regus got out and walked around the front of the truck. "Bert, I'd like ye to meet the new mine guard," he said. "This here's Mr. Bill Music."

Music stepped down from the cab of the truck and stuck out his hand.

"Hydee," the mine foreman said and gripped it briefly. "I'll hafta let Regus show you about and fill you in," he said in a high, almost feminine voice. "We're fixin to catch a visit from the state mine inspector; just got a call from Elsie Coal Company over the ridge."

"Didn't know the state inspector ever got any closer to the mine than the commissary," Regus said.

"Yeah," Bert said and grinned, "but you can't count on that sucker. He don't like those low drifts, that's a fact; but if he was to ride into the mountain, it would cost twice as much to buy him off. Hell, they's so much water back in there, the sucker might drown." He turned his back on them, looked at the mountain, and spoke without turning his head. "Got to get a couple of one-arm johnnies in yonder and pump a little out, maybe brattice about half the son of a bitch off," he said and began to move away across the railroad tracks toward the tipple.

"Talks a little funny, don't he?" Music said.

"Hmmm, don't let him fool ye. He's the second-hardest man around here. The first is comin yonder," Regus said and pointed to two men coming across the plank bridge toward them, one wearing a black, broad-brimmed hat, and the other a straw skimmer such as a city drummer or a college boy might wear.

"Which one?" Music asked.

"The one a-wearin his gun straight down over his pecker," Regus said. "That's Grady Burnside. The one in the fancy hat, that's Cawood, his nephew—ain't nuthin but a mean, fool kid." Regus gave a little snort of laughter. "He won't last. Some miner, or one of them niggers down at Mink Slide, will likely kill his ass fore he ever sees twenty-one."

The two of them came on across the plank bridge toward where Music and Regus were standing. They were pretty big men, half a head taller even than Regus.

"Ay, Regus," the younger one shouted, "you gettin any gravel fer yer goose?"

Regus turned his head and spat, and when the two of them drew up, he said, "I'd like ye boys to meet Bill Music, the new mine guard."

"Music," Cawood said and laughed with great good cheer, "Music? What kind of a name is that?"

Music shrugged. He wasn't even looking at Cawood, but at Grady, whose great, long face had two beardless, waxy scars, one on each cheek. "The one I was born with," he said, and he and Grady exchanged a nod.

"Zat right," Cawood said. "You gettin any frogjaw fer yerself? Nawh," he said, "hangin around with Regus I don't guess you would be, but I can put ye on to some. I don't mind ye eatin my fuckin pussy, but don't want ye fuckin my eatin pussy."

At last Music was able to look from Grady to Cawood and nod to him as well.

53

"I guess I'd best show Bill on around the place, so he'll know what to guard," Regus said. "See you boys in the mornin."

"Yes," Grady said.

"We'll hold this shit heap till you get here," Cawood said.

After Music and Regus had drawn off a few paces, Regus said, "That Cawood's a charmer, ain't he? Jesus, hit's a wonder to me that someone ain't cored him like an apple before this. Grady, though"—Regus jerked his head to one side as though in awe—"Grady's done already been killed once or twice and won't stay dead. Sid Hatfield, for one, shot him to pieces nearly ten year ago."

As the two of them went on toward the commissary Regus explained how Grady Burnside had once been a Baldwin-Felts detective, Baldwin-Felts being a kind of private police hired by the coal operators to shoot up or otherwise run off any unionizers they could find; to ferret out miners who were union members; get them fired and blackballed; and finally to see to it that the miners and their families were evicted from company housing, taken off company property and dumped somewhere beside the road with neither job, nor shelter, nor sometimes—if they happened to owe the company any sizeable bill at the commissary—even any personal belongings. "That was Grady's kind of work," Regus said. "He taken to it, like a bee to honey. But he run into a hard case in ole Sid Hatfield."

"Any relation to that Hatfield and McCoy bunch?" Music asked.

"The very same," Regus said. "Sid Hatfield was the grandson of ole Devil Anse Hatfield and was the high sheriff of Matewan, West Virginia, when Grady and him run snout to snout. Hatfield was always on the side of the miner around there, which made him an odd case and got him crosswise of the Baldwin-Felts," Regus said. "Don't know exactly how the Baldwin-Felts came by it or what the charges were, but thirteen Baldwin-Felts showed up in Matewan one day with a warrant for Hatfield's arrest." Regus turned his head and spat out the chewed lump of the cigar. "Hatfield and Mayor Cavell Testerman met the Felts men there at the depot down by the river and commenced to argue over the warrant. Al Felts himself was with em, and I guess they had their minds set on taking Hatfield one way or another, but when the shootin started and Hatfield yanked them two forty-fours of his'n, I expect maybe even Grady Burnside would have as lief been somewhere else. Testerman got shot down and killed and Al Felts too, and six other detectives, and three more a-lyin wounded, and three—Grady with em—jumped into the Tug River and swum back to Kentucky."

54

Regus laughed. "The miners around here say if Grady hadn't been yellin for his momma, that forty-four slug Hatfield put through his cheeks would have blowed his face off."

"Hellkatoot," Music said.

"Yeah," Regus said, "I reckon so." He ran his finger back and forth under his nose thoughtfully. "He must have been yellin somethin though, for if that forty-four had caught teeth, gum, or jawbone, I reckon it would have took his face off, sure nough."

"Shitass," Music said. "Hellkatoot."

"Yeah," Regus said, "I guess Grady was shot in the bacon too and in the foot, although the tale I hear is that he shot hisself in the foot, being so busy duckin and dodgin an all."

"Well, did they get that Hatfield feller?" Music asked.

Regus shook his head and let out a little bark of laughter. "Not right then. There wasn't nobody in shape to git him, I reckon. I heard that Sid Hatfield came out of that scrape without a mark on him. It's a fact, though, they cored him about a year later. He was being brought to trial for the murder of the Felts men, and when he was a-walkin up to the courthouse fer trial with his wife on his arm, a Baldwin-Felts man shot and killed him there on the courthouse steps." Regus shook his head. "That was in the Pikeville paper. His wife and friends had someway talked him out of wearin his pistols into the courtroom."

The two of them mounted the steps to the commissary. "Some say that Grady was the one what shot him," Regus said, "but hit's others swear he showed up here at Hardcastle to commence bein a mine guard before his face even healed up."

Music stopped on the gallery, a sudden empty feeling in his stomach. It was as if the machinery of his body simply balked without asking any sort of permission. Regus stopped too and raised his eyebrows in question. "You ever shoot anybody?" Music asked, the question unanticipated, automatic, embarrassing.

There were three miners lounging in split-bottom chairs at the other end of the gallery in front of the open window to a tiny post office. They were talking among themselves. Two filthy black and one relatively clean, all three with carbide lamps on their heads.

Regus stepped toward Music and said quietly, "Never did, but don't let on."

For all the humor in Regus's eyes, Music didn't feel much better as they entered the pungent, cool gloom of the commissary and passed a rack of men's suits and another of women's dresses, faded by the sun and mantled with fine black dust. The store was huge and seemed to contain everything imaginable. There were shoes, stockings, underwear, hats, and bonnets; there were picks, shovels, drill bits, carbide lanterns; there were kegs of powder, cans of carbide; there were tins and cans of food, bins of produce, sacks of flour and beans, of sugar and salt. Toward the far end there was a long counter with a paymaster's window on the left and a cold-drink cooler and a glassed-in candy case on the right. It was a cavernous space, which, never mind that the stores of articles seemed as dusty and settled in as the furniture of an ancient, unused room, nevertheless filled Music's nostrils with seductive odors: the raw, warm smell of leather, the similar but sharper odor of freshly ground coffee, the unaccountably sweet odor of clothing and yard goods. Behind the counter a clerk with a goiter on his neck the size of a baseball watched them approach.

"Cecil," Regus said in greeting.

"Hydeedo," Cecil said.

"This here's Bill Music," Regus said. "He's hired on as a mine guard."

"Hydeedo," Cecil said and nodded to Music. "We fixin to have more mine guards than miners, ain't we?" He went off into a peal of high, girlish laughter and then shook hands with himself and answered, "I reckon yer right," and laughed again.

"That's right," Regus said in an absolutely serious voice, "Mr. Hardcastle's thinkin about gettin shut of the miners altogether, windin this whole shebang down and settin us to guard it so nobody don't run off with the slag heap. I reckon ye'll be on the county directly."

For a moment Cecil's jaw dropped, but then he recovered and laughed, although the sound was without its original high-pitched joy. He shook hands with himself once again. "You like to guy a feller, don't ye?" he said to Regus. "You got some tradin to do today?"

"Not me," Regus said, "but Bill might fancy one thing or another."

"A sack of cigarette tobacco," Music said, "and a shirt."

Cecil scooped up a bag of cigarette tobacco and a book of papers from beside the candy case and set them before him. "The shirts are yonder," he said, nodding his head toward a dusty counter.

Music picked out a work shirt of heavy, strong material but was surprised at its price. A fancy dress shirt in Chicago cost no more than forty-seven cents, and the work shirt he had chosen was forty. "Christ, you're kinda stiff on yer prices, ain'tcha?" he said and dropped the shirt on the counter.

56

"You betcha," Regus said and sucked his teeth. "Nobody ain't never been known to git him a bargain at the company store. That ain't what it's for, is it, Cecil?"

"Now don't start," said Cecil, "I'm a carryin ever soul in Elkin, near about, and these prices ain't outta line considerin."

"Sure," Regus said. He stroked the end of his nose tentatively, squinting over Cecil's shoulder. "You got a paper poke?" he asked.

"Sure," Cecil said and drew one from beneath the counter and shook it open with a single snap of his wrist. "What'll ye have?"

"Fetch me down one of them kegs of powder," Regus said.

"What fer?" Cecil said and laughed. "You ain't goin back in no drift and blow you a coal face, aire ye?"

"Hand her down," Regus said, and Cecil pulled his head back, frowned, and then reached down a twenty-pound keg of powder.

Regus pulled the bung and poured a double handful into the paper bag.

"What ye doin?" Cecil said. "That there's a four-dollar keg. Some dumb miner'll try to wind my clock over that."

"Charge him three-ninety-nine," Regus said.

"I kain't do hit!" Cecil said. "That's a four-dollar, twenty-pound keg."

Regus ignored him. "How's this compare with what you use to shoot in yer daddy's hog rifle?" he asked Music.

"Looks about the same," Music said; "little coarser."

Regus replaced the bung and rapped it tight with the heel of his hand. "Pass down another," he said.

"Lookie here now," Cecil said, but Regus silenced him with a raised finger.

"This here's company business, not private," Regus said; and grumbling and muttering to himself, Cecil passed down a second barrel of powder from which Regus withdrew roughly the same amount. "Now," Regus said, "what does ole Bill owe ye, minus the powder fer which we ain't a-payin?"

"Forty-two cent," Cecil said, his chin drawn sulkily in toward the goiter on his neck.

"Well, then, mark him down," Regus said.

"I kain't do hit," Cecil said, his voice growing high and shrill. "I ain't got no pay slip on him."

"Hit'll get to ye by and by," Regus said and folded down the top of the paper bag and slipped it in his jumper pocket. He nodded to Music to pick up the tobacco and shirt.

57

"I kain't do hit!" Cecil said.

"Then draw yer pistol," Regus said, winking at Music and already turning away, "but you better shoot Bill first, cause he ain't like me; he'll kill you quicker'n a snake."

Music followed Regus down the dusty, pungent aisle of the commissary, the hair bristling on the back of his neck and a weak, giddy feeling in his stomach until he heard Cecil muttering behind them, "Ain't nobody ever tells me nuthin." Music's knees felt weak. "Come in here and walk off with all kinds of tucker," Cecil muttered; and then louder: "You better not be guyin me, Regus, or I'll debit you forty-two cent!"

Outside on the gallery of the commissary, Regus nodded to the three miners still lounging by the post office window, but only one of them made anything like a nod in return; and as though regretting it or disowning it, he turned his head immediately and spat across the railing onto the crumbling pavement of the road.

After Regus had showed him around the powerhouse and tipple, pointed out a boundary of timber the company owned up on the mountain behind the strings of shacks, showed him property lines, and driven him down to Mink Slide, the two of them returned at last to Regus's small homestead, where, from a trunk in Ella's room, Regus withdrew an ancient .44 pistol wrapped in an oilskin. He placed it carefully on the floor and rummaged in the trunk until he found a cavalry holster and, finally, a small musette bag which turned out to contain a leather pouch of balls, a tin of corroded percussion caps, a flask of powder, a bullet mold, and a cleaning rod. The two of them carried it all into the kitchen and set it on the table, where Regus unwrapped the pistol and, with his eyebrows up and humor dancing in his eyes, said, "Well, hit sholy looks like a pistol; must be a foot and a half long. I reckon you'd get a man's attention if ye pulled it on him."

"Ugly old thang," Ella Bone said. "Hit's an abomination is what hit is."

"Now, Momma," Regus said, "a mine guard has got to provide his own arms. This'un is just somethin fer Bill to carry till he can git him a piece a little more up to date."

"New er old they're an abomination, and I'll not listen more, ner hear about it," she said, and she left the house and went out to the barn.

"That's Momma's strongest word," Regus said. "She don't throw it around." He handed the pistol to Music holding it by the barrel. "But I

58

don't know that this here is such a grand idea as it seemed," Regus said. "Reckon you can make it shoot?"

"Jesus Christ," Music said as he took it, "must weigh five pounds." He turned it over and over in his hands, looking at it. "I don't know," he said. "I think so."

For the next hour or so he and Regus discussed, dismantled, and cleaned it. Music thought the balls should be patched but could find no patching material in the musette bag. Regus had seen his father shoot the pistol when he was a boy, and didn't remember him using any sort of cloth, but his memory of the time was very dim. Still, when Music set one of the .44 balls atop a cylinder, he could see there would be no room for a patch. Finally, after they thought they understood the gun's operation, they took it and all the paraphernalia outside, Fetlock weaving in and out of their legs and dancing in excitement at the mere sight and smell of a gun. Music poured the slightly lumpy black powder from the flask into each cylinder, leaving only enough room for the ball. He placed the first ball atop the cylinder, centered the sprue, and rammed the ball home with the levered plunger beneath the barrel. The ball was enough larger than the chamber that seating it sheared off a thin ring of lead. "You're right," Music said, showing him; "for certain there ain't room for a patch."

When Music had the pistol fully loaded and capped, Regus found an empty sardine tin in the trash heap below the barn. With great flourish and ceremony he set it upright against the mud bank below the outhouse, stepped off twenty-five paces, and said, "Well, see what you can do."

"Go ahead," Music said, offering him the pistol.

Regus didn't even look at it. Instead, his eyes lit with humor, he looked at Music, cut himself a chew of tobacco, and bit it off the blade of his pocketknife. He tucked the quid in his cheek and said, "I think the feller that loaded that goddam horse pistol ort to have to shoot her," and he stepped back and stuck his fingers in his ears. In the loud, flat voice of a deaf man he said, "I ain't so sure she won't blow up," and spat an amber stream of tobacco juice out before him.

Somewhat uneasily Music sat down, cocked the hammer, rested his elbows on his knees, and holding the pistol with both hands, took careful aim. He squeezed the trigger. The hammer fell, but the gun did not fire. "Shit," he said, "no good, damn percussion cap."

"Aire you goan shoot that cannon er not?" Regus shouted behind him.

59

"It didn't shoot," Music said.

"What?" Regus shouted.

"It didn't go off," Music shouted.

He cocked the hammer again, steadied himself, took aim, and pulled the trigger; and this time the pistol bucked and roared, and when the smoke cleared, they saw a very large hole in the mud four inches above and two inches to the right of the sardine can.

"Whooee!" Regus shouted.

Behind the barn, Fetlock began a croupy baying.

Music fired again and there was a second hole two inches from the first.

"Whooee!" Regus shouted.

Fetlock came around the barn, drew up by the corncrib, and looking from one of them to the other, confused but happy, bayed again and again, his front feet bouncing off the ground each time he gave tongue.

Ella Bone even appeared for a moment on the dogtrot, shading her eyes with her hand to look at them, before, shaking her head, she went back into the kitchen.

Music recocked the piece and fired a third time, and the pistol thundered like a cannon. Flame and smoke fanned out before him, and the recoil flung his arms over his head, nearly knocking him over backwards.

"Hot damn!" Regus shouted behind him. "Aire ye hurt, Bill Music?"

Music rocked forward again on his buttocks, and his feet came to rest on the ground. Regus hurried up beside him while Music turned the pistol carefully this way and that in his hands, looking at it as though it might decide to fire again, willy-nilly. Nothing, however, appeared to be wrong with it.

"Did she blow up?" Regus said.

"I don't know," Music said, still inspecting it at arm's length as though it were a deadly serpent; "I don't think so." His ears were ringing so badly he could scarcely hear; and his trigger finger, which he had just discovered was burned black, was beginning to hurt. "I don't know what happened," he said. "Kicked like hell."

"Look," Regus said and pointed through the thinning smoke, and Music saw a third hole in the bank in line with the first two, and yet a fourth hole three feet further to the right.

"Seems to have shot twice, someway," Music said and cautiously looked at the open end of the cylinder. At first it appeared all the chambers were empty. "Great God," he said, "I think the son of a bitch emptied itself." But then he saw that there was one charge remaining. Fetlock came up, low to the ground and trembling, his whining scarcely distinguishable from the ringing in Music's ears. "Christ," Music said, "it's like a cannon full of grapeshot, for God's sake. Here." He handed it to Regus. "There's one chamber still charged; you shoot the son of a bitch!" Delicately, at arm's length, they passed the pistol from hand to hand.

Regus chewed on his quid of tobacco and turned the pistol inquisitively this way and that, inspecting it. "I don't know as I'm curious," he said.

Music shook his left hand as though he were drying it of water and sucked his burned trigger finger for a moment. "Hell," he said, "it can't shoot but once now; there ain't but one load left in it."

"Yawl didn't grease it, didya?" Ella Bone shouted from the dogtrot, and they both turned to look at her where she stood, her hand shading her eyes. They looked at each other.

"Grease it where?" Regus asked. "Didn't know we wuz supposed to grease it."

"I reckon they's lots of things you don't know," Ella Bone said and went back into the kitchen.

"I think we need to have a talk with Momma," Regus said. "It was her daddy used to carry the contrary thing."

Music sucked his burned trigger finger. "Empty the son of a bitch and we will. I'm nearly deaf as it is."

"Well," Regus said uncertainly, "stand back."

Music stood back and stuck his fingers in his ears, and Regus cocked the pistol and brought it slowly down on the sardine can. Music, standing to the side, saw the hammer fall, but nothing happened. He took his fingers out of his ears and said, "Cock her again; it's the next chamber that's loaded."

Regus made his knees wobble. "This here piece could make a man gun-shy," he said, but in the same smooth, mechanical motion he cocked the hammer and brought the pistol to bear on the sardine can, which, when the pistol spouted smoke and flame, went sailing over the top edge of the bank.

"I took a little Kentucky windage on it," Regus said apologetically, "since you seemed to be shooting a mite high and to the right."

61

Still, when they retrieved the can from the field above the bank, they found it virtually unscathed, the ball merely having brushed its bottom edge. They set it again where it had been before and went in to talk to Ella, who, it turned out, knew all sorts of things they didn't know. Her father had put a layer of cornmeal down on the powder before seating the balls and had put a layer of hog lard over the tops of the balls after they had been seated in the chambers, all in order to keep more than one chamber from going off at a time. The lard alone was good enough in cold weather, Ella explained, but when it was hot, the lard would sometimes melt and run out, and therefore wouldn't work. Music sucked his trigger finger and listened closely. The cornmeal, Ella said, worked in any weather. Finally, with an edge of disgust in her voice, she said, "Let me see the abominable thing, for I disremember it."

Regus handed it over obediently.

Ella took it, raised the hammer to half-cock, and rotated the cylinder. "Yep," she said, "I ken the problem now. Wouldn't load but five shots in this here one. They's some that have little notches to rest the nose of the hammer in betwixt the nipples, but this here one ain't so sure. Ye'll want to let the hammer rest on the empty chamber; otherwise a hard knock might jest set her off."

Regus looked at Music and raised his eyebrows. His mother gave him back the pistol.

"I thank you, ma'am," Music told her.

"Hmph," the woman said, "if I thought the two of ye wouldn't shoot up the place, ner yer feet, ner lose an eye, ye'd have no word from me."

Somewhat humbled, the two of them found that, thereafter, the pistol practice went much better. Music discovered that, one out of three shots, he could hit the sardine tin, and that blasting powder, crushed with a spoon against the bottom of a saucer, worked as well as the powder in the flask. Only the green, corroded percussion caps could not be made dependable; and without much hope they set out to Valle Crucis for others.

But at the Farmers' Hardware store off the courthouse square a clerk knelt behind the counter and rummaged far back on a dusty shelf to set tin after tin of percussion caps before them. He passed the tins over his shoulder, blowing the dust from the top of each as he found it. There were caps of many sizes, including two tins of size thirteen, which fit the old Walker Colt perfectly. Even though the tins contained one hundred

62

caps apiece, they bought them both, as well as ten pounds of lead, which, including the new shirt and tobacco, put Music a dollar and twelve cents in debt.

Home again, the pistol cleaned and loaded, they discovered the problem of the cavalry holster, which, no matter how it was worn, would not permit the pistol to be drawn with the right hand. "Hit was the sword they used in the right hand," Ella explained as she watched them struggling with it and puzzling over it.

"Well," Regus said, "hit was yore poppa's."

"I don't care nuthin for hit," Ella said. She looked at his shoe tops and shook her head. "I reckon you want it rigged up on the chest like yourn," she said to Regus.

"Would be best," Regus said.

"God forgive me," Ella said, "give it here." And while they heated the bullet mold atop the stove and melted lead in a small tin pot shoved in the firebox, Ella removed the flap of the holster, reversed the belt loop, and measured Music's chest and shoulders again and again with a little string of rag.

By the time they had sixty or so acceptable, shiny .44 balls cooling on a rag beside the stove, Ella had contrived a shoulder holster of great utility and comfort, even though the sight of it caused Regus to pinch his eyes shut and shake his head with laughter. Since no extra leather or buckles were in the house, Ella had made the necessary straps and hangers from a feed sack patterned with bright blue and pink cornflowers, and to fasten the contrivance together she had used the largest buttons she could find, which happened to be made of yellow glass and were somewhat larger than twenty-five-cent pieces. Even with his coat on, Music looked ridiculous, since a four-inch-wide band of the material circled his middle like an outrageous cummerbund and the huge Walker Colt made a lump beneath his coat as large as if he had strapped a full-grown rabbit to the left side of his chest. Only the butt of the Colt peeking out from beneath his lapel suggested otherwise.

As a consequence, all through supper and even twice during the Bible reading, often without even looking in Music's direction, Regus would suddenly begin shaking with laughter. When, during the fifth chapter of Genesis, he took a third fit of laughing, Ella raised her hand to silence Music and said, "Son, if ye've no respect for the Scriptures, I'd as lief you took yerself off."

"I'm sorry, Momma, I surely am," Regus said, but shaking his head

63

and laughing still, he got up and went out upon the dogtrot, closing the door behind him.

When Music had finished the fifth chapter, Ella said, "Son, I reckon I could listen to ye read till the Lord called me home, but ye shouldn't let me misuse you so."

"It's no trouble," Music said. "My momma used to read the Bible to me and my brothers every night until we got nearly grown."

"Did she then?" Ella said. "That's so fine. It's ever been a sorrow to me that I can't read the Scriptures for myself. Sometimes I used to open the book and just stare at all the writin thinkin to myself that if I just stared long enough, hit'ud come to me what it meant, don't ye know." Ella laughed and sighed. "Did ye ever hear such foolishness?" She threw her hands up as though astounded at her own simplicity. "I do it still yet sometimes. Ain't got no sense," she said.

After a moment Music said, "I'd borrow paper and pencil from you if I could. Bein set up here and all makes me think I ought to send my people some word. I guess you sort of remind me of home."

"Why surely, son," Ella said, "if I can find any such things."

"I hate to bother you, missus," Music said.

"No bother in it," Ella said. "I know they's a stub of a pencil around here sommers." She went off into her room, where Music could hear her rummaging around. "Don't know as I can find you paper fit to write on though." Music could hear drawers opening and closing and things rattling around. "Well now, here," she said, "I don't see why this won't serve."

When she returned, she handed him a chewed red stub of a pencil and a yellowing piece of heavy white paper, which, when he unfolded it, turned out to be something very like a death certificate for someone named Cleveland Edward Bone. After a moment Music saw that it had been issued by a mining company and entitled Ella Cody Bone, as the dead man's spouse, to receive thirty dollars a month compensation until she remarried or until her death.

"I reckon ye can use the back of it well enough," Ella Bone was saying.

"No, missus," Music said, "this is important and you need to keep it."

"Aww, son," Ella Bone said, "I know what hit is, and that company has long since gone broke. Hit ain't worth a thing in this world. You jest mark out the front and write on the back. Hit's right nice paper."

But Music would not use it. He found a paper bag instead and cut a square from it with his pocketknife. He felt called upon to say something to her, to thank her for all her help, for taking him in, to console her for the death of her husband nearly ten years before, but she was already busy over the sink with her pots and pans. "You write yer folks and tell em I'm a-feedin ye and keepin ye out of the weather," she said cheerfully.

Outside, Regus was sitting on the back edge of the dogtrot, Fetlock curled in the soft dust of the backyard before him. He still seemed amused. "I don't know, Bill," he said, "maybe they'll take ye as crazy mean." He shook his head and laughed. "All them damned little flowers," he said, "and them big yeller buttons, and that god-awful hog's leg. Sheeit, I got no notion why, but I think ye'll carry it off someway." His shoulders shook and he made little snorting noises, but then all at once he cleared his throat and spat and seemed to get control of himself. "This ain't no kind of world," he said, "fer a feller of my good sense." He cleared his throat again. "Here," he said, "you better take this," and he extended his hand, in which Music could make out a chrome-plated derringer and some shells.

"No thanks," Music said.

"You better take it," Regus said. "Leastwise you can load this'un in less than half an hour."

"No thanks," Music said. "If I ever get in so much trouble I got to draw that Walker Colt, if I ain't out of trouble by the time it's empty, I don't think that thing will help me."

"You don't never know," Regus said.

For a moment Music stood still and watched the moon where it hung above the barn. It seemed to touch the comb of the barn roof with light, the far edge of the corncrib, the rim of Ella Bone's black iron washpot, so that all of them looked rimed with frost. "Would you care for a drink?" Music asked.

"That would be handsome," Regus said.

Music went into his room to get his corn liquor and was surprised to find a chair, half an upside-down oak barrel with a clean rag over the top of it like a tablecloth, and a tick of nearly twice the thickness of the one he'd slept on the night before. There was a lantern on the barrel top, together with his paper sack, and the room had been swept and tidied. He took the pop bottle from the sack and went back out on the dogtrot. "Your momma really fixed me up," he said, sitting down beside Regus.

65

"Yeah," Regus said, "she's got you sleepin on hay. Already after me to rig up some kind of bedstead."

Music uncorked the moonshine and passed the bottle to Regus, who took a drink, pursed his lips, exhaled silently, and passed it back. They drank until it was gone.

"I've got to work out some room-and-board pay for your momma," Music said after a while.

"Ha," Regus said, "I'd like to see you try to get that past her."

They sat and watched the pale moon where it rode above the barn.

"My people haven't heard from me in a while," Music said at last. "I thought I'd write them. Tell them where I'm at."

"For sure," Regus said and nodded. "I'll bid you good night then."

It took him a long time to start the letter. In a wash of yellow light from the lantern, he smoothed the piece of brown paper again and again with the side of his hand. He had written: "Dearest Poppa and Momma," and nothing more; for when he put that much down, the impulse to write left him. There seemed, at last, nothing to be said in a letter. Strangely, only after he had lost heart and nearly crumpled the paper did he begin to write, drawing each word carefully with the bitten stub of the pencil. "I am in Kentucky and alright," he wrote. "Have hired on as a mine guard and living with good folks who took me in. I will stay here a while then come on back home." He read over what he had written. "Don't look for me as I will write and tell you when I strike out," he added. He thought for a while and then, smiling a wry smile, wrote: "Tell brother Luther and Earl to stay on home as it's hard times, and to say hellow to any pretty girl they see for me." After much thought, after smoothing the paper again and again, he began once more to draw slow, careful letters upon the square of brown paper bag. "I hope and trust you are all well and alright as I am. Your son, Bill." He read the letter over carefully, decided it would do, folded it, and put it aside to mail the next morning.

# 6

## GOON

WHEN HE AND Regus rode into Elkin, clattered across the plank bridge, and stepped down from the Model T truck in the smoky-grey light of morning, Ella Bone's rig and the huge Walker Colt caused him no embarrassment whatever, at least none beyond what he felt already for wearing the stiff new shirt with the badge pinned to it and carrying any sort of gun.

Grady and Cawood Burnside came toward them from the direction of the powerhouse.

What was it about them, Music wondered, that made them seem to own the cinders and gumbo they walked on, the very firmament? Without quite thinking it into words, he knew at once it was the grim, taciturn, penetrating threat that seemed to look out of Grady's eyes as though, if he thought of it, he might spit on you, or your mother, or your father, or your wife and the babe in her arms. And Cawood? That bastard. With him it was a matter of sheer cockiness.

The straw skimmer, more ornament than covering, sitting on the back of his head, Cawood bawled, "Ay Tune, gettin any wampus?" But then, all at once, Cawood noticed the two or three inches of pistol grip sticking out from underneath the lapel of Music's coat, and his eyes seemed to bug taking in the lumpish bulk of a weapon nearly the size of a beagle pup strapped to the left side of Music's chest, and he said no more. The proportions of the pistol seemed to unman him and take him aback. If he noticed Ella's colorful and flowery bellyband or the large yellow buttons, the sight did not amuse him. It was, Music thought, as Regus had predicted, or perhaps, in a more general way, as Kenton Hardcastle had: there was power in being a stranger; power, for the moment at least, in the eccentric and unforeseen rig. He could see the effect of it written across Cawood's unintelligent face and protuberant eyes, as if deep inside him something had just said, "Whoops!"

Not Grady, however. He had seen the pistol grip too, the vague outline of its size and shape; and upon his long, scarred, horse face there was no expression whatever. He merely swapped the stump of his cigar from one corner of his mouth to the other and chewed it solemnly, speculatively. What was he thinking? Music wondered. Whether the weapon was some sort of sawed-off shotgun or an outsized pistol? How quickly Music could get the thing unholstered? How willing he was to use it? You sons a bitches, Music thought.

Grady and Regus had begun to talk about something, but it was as if Music's frustration, the machinery of his own thinking, were making so much noise he couldn't hear them. What in God's name, he asked himself, was he doing here? Cawood had begun to speak too. Music understood only that Cawood was talking about not having let anyone run off with the tipple during the night, and he caught the flavor of Cawood's new tone—a kind of deference toward the five pounds of iron strapped to his chest—but he did not hear enough to be able to answer. It didn't matter. Regus and Grady had finished whatever they were saying to each other, and Regus had started off toward the powerhouse. Music followed, merely nodding to Cawood in passing.

"Hey, Regus," Music said, as the Burnsides were crossing the plank bridge and Regus was about to enter the powerhouse. Regus turned with his eyebrows inquisitively and somehow humorously raised. "I don't like the goddamned job," Music said.

Regus looked at him a moment longer before incredulousness gave way to laughter. "I wish I'd thought to time ye," he said. "What ails ye, man?"

Music knew exactly what ailed him until he tried to phrase it and found that it had no name. There was merely a hollow feeling in his chest touched somehow with the cool breath of shame.

"I reckon so," Regus said, as though he understood. "Come on, now." The two of them entered the powerhouse, where the hum of the steam turbine and the windy whir of wheel and belt seemed to make Music's uncomfortable feeling more complex. It wasn't just the badge and pistol, or even the arrogance of the Burnsides. It had something to do with him, personally, as though, long ago, when he had decided to leave Shulls Mills, Virginia, he had dared just such a situation as this. It was as though the thug in Chicago who had found the twenty-dollar bill hidden in his shoe, called him a low son of a bitch, and jumped into the middle of his chest had somehow guessed him capable of it.

"This here's Big Cigar Green," Regus was saying, introducing Music to the nigger who kept coal shoveled into the boiler.

Beneath the black man's rag of a shirt, sleeves missing at the seams of the shoulders, his chest swelled in perfect proportion like the breastplate of a Roman soldier. His arms were massively sculptured and black as pitch. He and Music nodded to each other. "Cap'n," Big Cigar said.

The thug with the stone in the sock knew something, Music was thinking. Knew that when he had hidden the twenty in his shoe, he had anticipated the robbery and therefore somehow participated in it. There was a kind of collusion between him and the robbers in that act, a brotherhood; but what was more, he had tried to cheat them at their own game.

"This here's Too Sweet," Regus was saying, introducing the nigger who kept the wheels and belts greased.

Music nodded, and Too Sweet—all elbows, knee joints, and angles— nodded back. "Boss," Too Sweet said, his eyes like knobs of porcelain in his black face as he tried not to look at the pistol grip and the lump under Music's coat.

"And yonder's Tom Harmon, chief head-knocker around the power-house," Regus said.

"Hydee," Harmon said.

"Hydee," Music said, and all at once he knew exactly how he felt: he felt like a man who had been falling and was anxious to hit bottom and have it over. When he'd caught himself going through those garbage cans behind the hotel in Salt Lake City, he had known the fabric of his ambitions simply could no longer hold him up, and he was going to land back in Shulls Mills, where his father and brothers scratched out a living on their ragtag farm as though they couldn't conceive of anything better, as though they had never even thought of another way to live. He had made, at last, a kind of peace with that. He would hit bottom and start all over again, new and humble. He didn't like being fetched up in Switch County with the sensation of falling still in his bones. But how could he explain that to Regus or anyone? He wasn't sure it made any proper sense. Perhaps it was only that, being a man who didn't like to leave a thing half done, he wanted to fail completely if failure was what fate had marked him for.

Regus showed him the bunk where they would take turns sleeping on the night shift and handed him a copy of the new contract which Grady had told him they were to take around for the miners to sign. The Burnsides had gotten the niggers in Mink Slide all signed up the evening before, Regus explained. They would have to sign up the rest.

"You ort to read her over if ye can, so's you can tell them that asks what they're signin. Ain't many of em that won't know, but they's some will forever have to hear it."

Music sat down on the bunk to read the document. It was full of legal-sounding words he could only guess at from the context; still, the message was clear enough. The miners agreed to join no union. They agreed that no one but members of their immediate families had the right to "ingress" or "egress" to and from the company houses they occupied. The contract made it clear that all streets, alleys, or lanes about the premises were private property subject to any police regulation Hardcastle Coal Company might make. It warned that a miner's employment could be terminated for breaking any regulation and that on termination of his employment, the employee forfeited all rights to occupy company housing immediately. The company had the right to enter at any time the premises of any "domicile," and the lessee expressly waived any benefit or protection to which he might otherwise be entitled by law.

"Sons of a bitch," Music said, "this thing even claims, if a man owes the company any money when he gets evicted . . . "

"The company can keep all his truck," Regus finished. "Sure," he went on, "I can't handle the fancy words in it myself, but I know what she boils down to. I've signed my share of them things. Hit ain't nuthin but a simple ole yeller-dog contract; and what with cold weather comin on, and the National Miners Union organizing whomsoever they can, I reckon ole Hardcastle wants to remind everybody that he means business." Regus ran his finger back and forth under his nose and laughed. "Hit ain't like they ain't signed nearly the same thing before. Come on," he said, "let's us get started."

They left the insistent heat and noise of the powerhouse, Music with the contracts and Regus with a checklist of names. Outside, Elkin looked like a picture drawn in black, sepia, and shades of grey. The cold, silver sunlight polished the surface of the river, windows scummed over with coal dust, and fingers of frost retreating into the shade. No one gave them much trouble.

Even with most of the children in school, the small, four-room dwellings they entered were often crowded, and Music wondered where so many could lie down to sleep. Even the cleanest of the houses smelled like a fart in a paper sack from the coal being burned for cooking and upon grates for heat. Often the sulfurous odor of coal was complicated by the stink of dirty bodies, clothing, and linen; and almost always, another kind of odor, persistent, somehow ancient, but not quite identifiable, as though, at last, it was the profound odor of poverty, existing as solidly as a mildewed and dusty trunk locked away in an attic to be passed down generation to generation. No one gave them much trouble. Hardcastle had been working shifts for a long time, and only about a third of the men, or fewer, were back in the mountain, so there weren't many houses where they had to leave a contract to be signed later. Matter-of-factly Regus explained to the women of such houses that there would be no scrip paid, no advances on scrip given, and no trading at the commissary until the contracts were signed and turned in to Cecil. More often the man of the house was there; and grimly, his jaw as rigid as a horseshoe, he signed and shoved the paper back to Music, sometimes without one word being spoken on either side. Usually the womenfolk hung back, inside the doorways to other rooms, where often the walls were papered with pages from catalogues or magazines. There were old people in many of the houses. Often there were two or three children too young for school: here a child clinging to its mother's skirts; there another, nose jeweled with snot, sitting upon a sprung and cluttered divan; yet another squatting on its heels, the ragged cloth ends of a sugar tit sticking, like a flower, from between its pursed lips. In almost every house someone was holding an infant; sometimes a babe was being held by a child of no more than three or four, but with such unself-conscious grace and skill, such comfort and naturalness, there seemed in neither small head any clear distinction between what it was to be a parent and what it was to be merely a brother or sister.

One man, scarcely thirty and all but toothless, asked, "In whichwise is this contract different from the ones I done already signed?" Other men wanted to know if they were still going to get their twenty-two and a half cents a ton. Few of the men were able to read the document, or even tried. Perhaps half could sign their names. The others made their marks, and

71

Music copied their names below and witnessed their marks with his own signature.

Now and again there were houses without a wage earner, where a widow woman lived. Kenton Hardcastle charged no rent or utilities for allowing them to remain, but he paid no compensation either. These women, too, had to sign or make their marks on the contracts. In one such house, where the front porch was broken and sagging and they had to go around to the back to get in, a young woman who looked no more than seventeen opened the door. She had her hip cocked a little to one side to accommodate the small child who straddled it. She also looked so angry that, for a moment, Music was struck dumb; but he came to himself, ran his finger down the checklist of names on Regus's clipboard, and said, "We're lookin for Mrs. Merlee Taylor."

"Who's come, Merlee?" someone asked from another room. In the next moment a woman appeared in the doorway; a woman bent nearly double upon herself, who looked up at Music from beneath her widow's hump like a turtle peering out from under the dome of its shell. Her gaze could mount no higher than Music's belt buckle.

The young woman, however, stared him directly in the eye. "Ain't nobody, Aunt Sylvie," she said in a voice so bitter and flat Music felt his heart shrink. She turned and handed off the child to the old woman, who, withered and bent as she was, could not hold the infant to her breast, but merely support it before her under its tiny arms as though she might be teaching it to walk.

"Give it here," the young woman said to Music, and he gave her the contract and pencil. She signed her name, propping the contract against the doorframe and handing it back at once.

Music said, "Thank you, ma'am."

She shut the door in his face.

Behind him Regus fingered the hair growing out of his shirt collar and looked at the ground, his neck and ears red. His eyebrows rose as though he might offer some word, but he merely tucked the quid of tobacco into his cheek and spat, turned on his heel, and went on toward the next coal company shack. Music followed behind.

Two contracts later, when they were done and walking toward the powerhouse, Regus's neck and ears began to redden again, as though a low-watt bulb had been switched on just beneath his skin. "A couple of years back, her husband was down at the commissary," Regus said. There was no question who *her* was. "He picked out some little ole head kerchief for her and stuck it in his pocket, don't ye know." Regus shook his head and sucked his teeth. "The story I heard was that the son-of-a-bitchin mine guard shot him down on the spot."

"Hellfire," Music said, "nobody kills a man over a kerchief."

"Wouldn't want to think so, would you?" Regus said. "But as to that, I saw one miner kill another over a goddamned game of marbles."

"On purpose?" Music said.

Regus snorted, jets of fog billowing from his nostrils in the cold air. "He shot him twice in the head with one of them little snubbed-off thirty-two pistols."

"Yeah, but a goddam kerchief?" Music said.

"That's the story I heard," Regus said. "Some far kin of Hardcastle, the mine guard was. Little crazy. Taken it personal, like the man was stealin outten his own pocket. Thought he owned the place cause his kin did, I reckon. Heard he yelled out, 'I seen ye, I seen ye,' and shot the young feller down without further word ner caution." Regus tugged at the hair at his throat. "Was that mine guard's job that I taken, after somebody shot half his head off one night."

They had stopped walking and were standing on the bridge over the river. "Who shot him?" Music asked.

Regus cocked his head, raised his eyebrows quizzically, and spat off the bridge into the river. "The dumb son of a bitch," he said, "could have been might near anybody. They found him a-layin right yonder," he said, nodding toward an iced-over rock his bright tobacco juice had splattered. "He claimed he never meant to shoot the young feller. Meant to shoot the floor twixt his feet to scare him. Now I've seen all kinds," Regus said, "but I never met the man who was so poor a shot as to take the bottom of a man's heart off when he was aimin betwixt his feet." Remote and preoccupied, Regus looked at the river where the mine guard had been found, then away at the hazy, blue-grey mountains rising against the sky, and finally at Music until whatever sober thing had been in his face was gone. "Such a feller gives us gun thugs a bad name, whichever way you look at it," Regus said at last. "The worse yet, if folks was to believe we couldn't hit within five feet of where we wuz aimin."

The humor behind Regus's eyes seemed all wrong, but it was there—calm, steady, insisting on its right to color whatever it might choose. Regus sighed and steam billowed from his nostrils. "Less us see what kinda grub Momma put in the dinner buckets," he said. "We done already worked more this mornin than we'll generally work in a week.

73

This here job, ole Bill Music, is mostly a matter of standin around lookin mean."

*Why, you low son of a bitch,* the robber had said, looking down on Music where he lay just on the fringe of consciousness, legs helter-skelter upon the sidewalk and curbing of Maxwell Street and one all-but-oblivious hand feeling his head where, already, there were knots the size of goose eggs. The big man had passed Music's shoes to the smaller man, folded the twenty-dollar bill into his shirt pocket, and jumped into the middle of Music's chest. *Maybe,* Music said to the big, shabby man, wherever he might be, *maybe so.*

That evening when Music and Regus had begun to take turns with the watch, Music went to the commissary and had Cecil grind him a pound of coffee. Having received official notification that Music was a mine guard and taking alarmed, sidelong glances at the bulk of the Walker Colt under Music's coat, Cecil was very quick and nervous about filling Music's order, talking nonsense all the while in a frightened, hopeful effort toward comradery.

Music carried the warm, fragrant bag of coffee around to the back door of Merlee Taylor's coal company shack and knocked; but when the door opened, it was the old woman who stood before him. She did not speak; she simply stood absolutely still in the doorway, bent over upon herself like an ancient question mark.

"Here, missus," Music said, trying to give her the bag of coffee. "Please," he said, for she seemed not to understand and made no move to take it.

The young woman appeared then, her dress front unbuttoned nearly to the waist, her sweater pushed off one shoulder so that the child she carried could nurse.

Music was instantly embarrassed.

The young woman glared at him. "Ain't we seen enough goons fer one day?" she said. "What do ye want now?"

"Please," Music said to the old woman, shoving the coffee at her; and when, at last, her long, bony, crooked hand turned palm up and received it, Music backed away and was gone. The smooth white flesh of the girl's breast, the pink ellipse of her nipple a shade lighter than the pink of the baby's lips, stayed behind his eyes, so that it was difficult for him to see how to walk.

# 7

## THE LATE SHIFT

NO MINER HAD said more than two words to Music since he'd hired on. But Gay Dickerson and Worth Enloe were not ordinary miners. They were company men. They ran a Jeffry Short-Wall machine on the night shift, undercutting coal faces in the various rooms so that miners could shoot the coal and work it out the next day. Perhaps because they had steadier and better-paying jobs, they weren't so bitter and close-mouthed. Still, Music was surprised when, a week after he had hired on, the two of them squatted at the entrance to the drift mouth and passed a little time with him. They chewed and spat and spoke of days when mining coal was a proper occupation; and Music, leaning against a coal car, the pistol grip of the huge old Walker Colt sticking out from beneath his coat and over his heart like a pump handle, was happy to listen.

"Hit use to take a right smart of skill to get coal," Worth Enloe said. Tirelessly he sat on his heels. The pucker of forever grimy skin around his ruined eye twitched where once a powder charge had gone off in his face. "These fellers that is now and gets their five ton wouldn't have dug two in them days. Weren't no undercuttin machines and weren't hardly no special crews." Worth Enloe spat and his blind eye twitched. "A man had to lie on his side and undercut the coal face with a pick, and when he went to bore holes fer his shots, why, there weren't no electric drill. He taken an auger and braced hit agin his chest and turned her by hand. He

75

knew jest how much powder to use to get the job done, and he packed his dummies right. Clay dummies and not airey old bug dust like these fools. Why, the proper miner could break down a coal face so hit could be worked to advantage," Worth said. "He done hit all. Laid his track, done his cleanup and dead work, knowed how to set props so the top didn't come down on him . . . "

"Hit's the goddamned farmers and niggers what mostly get killed ever whipstitch, cause they don't know how to mine coal and ortten to be back in no drift noway!" Gay Dickerson said. Music could see that Dickerson had wanted to get a leg in the conversation for a long time, but something about the older man's slow, brooding voice had kept him out, just as Worth's silence kept Dickerson from going on. The silence, the twitch of skin around the ruined eye where coal dust had been blown into the flesh beyond the reach of years of scrubbing, seemed to say there was a different point to be made.

"Back when the labor was all by hand," Worth said at last, "there wasn't no lack of work for a proper miner. The coal brung a good price so a man could make a decent livin. But when the smell of money gets out, you don't know what's gonna come callin from downwind. Hell, operators come from all over and started tryin to mine coal up ever little creek and holler. Hmm," he said and shook his head and spat, "ain't no tellin how many coal seams have been ruint by folks that didn't know nuthin bout minin. Cain't nobody get the coal outten lots of those mines now. Trouble is, fer ever operator that come down here to mine coal and get rich, they was a hundred poor sons a bitches throwed down their plows and started diggin it fer him. Lots of them operators went bust and then went on back where they come from, but most poor miners didn't have nothing and nowhere to go, ner a dime to get there." Worth's bad eye twitched. "They're still right here in the coalfields. They's too many miners, and too many machines a-gettin the coal too fast, so hell, hit ain't worth nuthin."

"They'd be a proper livin yet for what few real miners is left," Gay Dickerson said. "Lord knows they ain't many real miners. No old-timey miner would load the crap these fellers shovel into coal cars. You ort to watch the rock and slate that comes outten this here drift. You ort to watch how many times they got to shut the tipple down cause the slate pickers can't keep up with it."

Music rolled himself a cigarette while Worth and Gay listed the multitude of things that had gone wrong with mining. The machines, which not only got the coal too fast but made the work more dangerous, so that a man was as likely to get electrocuted or mauled by some damned machine as he was to get killed by a slate fall or an explosion. The unions, which were often crooked and took more in dues than the men ever got back in benefit; which made trouble and called strikes, got folks fired and caused scabs to get brought in who stayed on in the coalfields when the strikes were broken because most of them didn't have any place to go back to either. The state mine inspectors, who came around and got bribed, or who didn't get bribed and shut down a mine for one reason or another and threw everybody out of work. The operators, who underbid one another to get contracts and then took the money out of the miner's wages in order to be able to sell the coal for next to nothing. The government, which, whether local, state, or federal, always threw its weight against the miner if there was trouble. The damned housing. The goddamned commissary.

Finally, they came full circle, back to mining itself, which, they conceded, some way or other got in a man's blood and unfit him for anything else, never mind that it would break him, and cripple him, and starve him out besides. Worth Enloe's bad eye twitched many times in succession, and all at once Gay Dickerson stood up and stepped on the heel of his right rubber boot with the toe of his left, and, drawing his naked foot out of the boot, showed it to Music. There were no toes on the foot except for the big one. "I was sixteen when I let that happen," Gay said cheerfully. "Already had me a wife and two youngins. Went to sprag a wheel on a full coal car and didn't get the sprag stick jammed in right, and the damned thang run over my foot. My workin buddy felt the car bump and says to me, says, 'What in tarnation wuz that?' and I says, 'Why, nuthin, just only the coal car run over my foot; didn't hurt.' 'Great God on the mountain, son,' he says, 'yer hurt whether ye know hit or don't.' He come around and commenced to get me out of my boot but seen it was full of blood and left off. He laid me out atop a coal car and called the driver and tole me, when I got outta the drift, to git to the doctor quick. But I never. I walked on back to my house and set down to take a look. I wuz surprised, I tell ye, when I saw they wadn't nuthin but little ole tags a skin holdin four of my toes on. Felt lucky I'd had my foot on the rail in sech a way as to save the big'un. My wife jist nearly fainted when she seen hit, but I sent her off for her sewin shears to cut the damned thangs aloose." Gay Dickerson laughed and turned his pale foot this way and that, looking at it in the electric light at the entrance to the drift

77

mouth. "Now you may think I'm a-guyin ye, but hit never hurt until I commenced to cut them little flaps of skin that was along the bottoms of the toes." With a quick motion of his head he spat a stream of tobacco juice a good ten feet to one side. "My wife couldn't stand hit, don't ye know, and run right outten the house. But boy, I'll tell ye, I'se just as glad she were gone, fer cuttin them toes off hurt like fire. You wouldn't think it, but by the time I got that first toe cut aloose, they wuz beads of sweat the size a buckshot popped out on my forehead." Gay shook his head at the memory and giggled, put his boot on again, and squatted as before. After a moment, as though it were an unimportant afterthought, he mentioned that some years later a slate fall had broken his pelvis.

When Gay stopped talking, Worth Enloe sniffed, twitched his bad eye, and looked straight before him without speaking. Oddly Gay seemed to catch his mood and didn't talk any more either.

Music rolled himself another cigarette in the hopes the two of them would start up again. "I don't mind tellin you it scares the hell out of me to think about crawlin back in a mountain tryin to cut hunks of it out to carry off. Seems like it would always be waitin to come down on your head."

They did not reply, and Music began to realize that, somehow, they had talked each other into a change of mood. They seemed to have slipped into a puzzled and benumbed indignation at how little, after all, the proper knowledge of mining and the price of their wounds and infirmities had bought them. He could see it in their faces, the set of their shoulders, the way they stared before them. The very atmosphere around them seemed to be changing, and in it Music felt a growing resentment toward him he hadn't noticed before. It seemed to harden into shape even as he became aware of it, as though, because he was an ignorant stranger, they had thought to instruct him, only to realize, somehow, in some manner, they had been playing the fool.

At last Worth Enloe rose, primed, and put the spark to the carbide lamp on his cap. "Gay, goddammit," he said, "hit ain't no clacker a-laying around out here."

Gay Dickerson, looking confused and ashamed, got up and lit his lamp as well; and quick as that, the two of them began to duck walk back into the low drift.

"Well, goddam," Music said to himself, looking after them.

The light from their lamps bobbled deeper into the mountain, and the cool breath of the coal mine seemed to wash out of the drift mouth in their

78

wake, the odor of the bowels of the earth tainted with man piss and mule dung. Late season crickets grated slowly, haltingly in the cool night air. And a little at a time it came to him that, though they might have started out treating him with native forbearance and courtesy because he was a stranger, they had somehow realized as they talked that he wasn't a stranger at all, but an old enemy, hired to keep them in line and paid for by their labor. They had not listed him in their litany of complaints, but there he was, wearing a badge and gun; and if they had forgot that for a moment, they had remembered it soon enough. It was only that the other miners, not so well off as Worth and Gay, never forgot, not even for a second.

But hellkatoot, Music thought, if it weren't me rigged out with a damned pistol and a badge, it would only be somebody else. Only a fool would turn down three dollars a day in such times. He had never made so much money. Even when he worked as a lineman out in Chicago, he had made only fifteen cents an hour, and that for working twenty-three hundred volts, hot, and with shitty equipment. At Hardcastle, he worked only every other day and still made an average of ten and a half dollars a week; that was forty-two dollars a month. If he worked only a few months, he wouldn't have to go home like a bum, a whipped dog. He could buy himself an automobile if he desired it. A single month's pay would buy a sound used one.

He could see himself turning off the county road onto the washed-out wagon road up to his house, the motor of a dark blue, four-door Chevrolet chortling pleasantly under the hood. His father, out by the barn, would watch the car approach, quiet, suspicious, his instincts alerted to deal with some stranger, possibly a drummer, possibly the agent of some unknown trouble about to assail him from the larger world. His mother, looking through the kitchen window, as yet only curious and surprised, would utter a scarcely audible "Now who in the world?" His brothers, never even thinking to be curious or mistrustful, would merely be delighted at the sight of an automobile which was about to come to rest, if only for a moment, upon the stones, mud, sawdust, and chicken shit of their own, personal barnyard.

Yes, he thought, that's the way it would be.

And later, after all the greetings and talk, during which his brothers could not help being more interested in the car than in him, he'd take his brothers for a ride, and there would be joking and laughter and high, good spirits. And later still, he would take his father and his mother to church, say, and his father would be silent and grave, perhaps puzzling over whether or not he approved of an automobile in the family, having already acknowledged, without quite knowing it, that there were things in the world, like riding in cars and airplanes and lodging in fine hotels, that were not appropriate to his station in life. So he would sit puzzled and dignified and not altogether happy. His mother, dressed in her finest, would be scarcely less confused, but flustered and giddy as well; for, whatever else the automobile might mean or signify, it would be a sign to her that her son had gone off into the great world and not only survived it and come home, but had somehow wrested from it an expensive marvel he had mastered and tamed to his purpose, which, at the moment, seemed to be nothing more profound than conveying her to church like a grand lady.

Yes, he thought, yes, that's the way it would be.

Far back inside the mountain the Jeffry Short-Wall machine began to eat noisily at the coal face in some room or other, and Music came back to himself as though he had actually, even physically, been somewhere else. He withdrew Regus's pocket watch and checked the time. It was eight-thirty and Regus was no doubt asleep upon the iron cot in the powerhouse, where, at ten, he would enter to wake him, give him back his watch, and take his place upon the cot. In the meantime he was, he realized, supposed to be roaming. Since he had hired on, Kenton Hardcastle wanted two guards on his property at all times and wanted at least one of them on the move.

He started down the mountain beside the conveyor, descending at once through a thin gauze of smoke which hung suspended no more than a hundred and fifty feet above the valley. It was as though he had slipped below the still surface of a lake, and beneath it he became aware of a double sound: what seemed to be the distant cadence of preaching overlaid now and then with sometimes grave, sometimes joyous, cries. Now and again the preacher's voice, if that's what it was, submerged completely beneath the hubbub from the congregation. He paused for a moment and listened, and at first he thought he had fooled himself and what he heard was only the distant belling of hounds somewhere down the valley, but then he heard voices say quite clearly, although in perfect miniature, "Praise Jesus. Hallelujah."

There was a church meeting going on somewhere. Down toward Mink Slide, he suspected.

At the foot of the mountain he passed beneath the black, hulking

80

structure of the tipple and went on down the railroad siding. But curious as he was, he could hear nothing but the noise of his own footsteps, the liquid murmur of the river, and, from the powerhouse, the hum of the steam turbine and the windy whir of wheel and belt. He crossed the bridge and came up by the commissary, where an outside floodlight lit the gallery and a night-light glowed from within. Still, there was nothing but the confabulation from the coal company shacks directly across the street: somewhere among them, bits of talk; somewhere, the grinding pop of a rocking chair; somewhere, the incessant, soft crying of a child. But then, far off to the south, he heard a single voice, high and nasal and without the least vibrato, begin to sing, joined by the end of the first melodic phrase by other voices, which sang over and over again:

I am the man, Thomas, I am the man.
I am the man, Thomas, I am the man
I am the man, Thomas, I am the man
Look at the nail prints in my hand.

He went down the street past the boarded-up movie house where, Cecil told him, everyone in Elkin had once spent part of Saturday night since, each week, tickets for every member of a miner's family were stuck in his pay envelope and the price was automatically deducted from his wages. It was a practice that had ended three years back, when someone tried to burn the movie house down one Friday night while Kenton Hardcastle, his wife, children, and housekeeper were watching *Rio Rita* by themselves. A tattered and faded poster beside the double doors still advertised *Rio Rita,* but only the Hardcastle family and the colored housekeeper had ever gotten to see it, although every miner in Elkin had had the price of admission deducted from his wages. The building still sagged toward the right rear, where the fire had burned through some of the supports. Giving the scorched rear section of it a passing glance, Music fancied he could still smell the sweet, creosoty stench of the long-dead fire.

The singing had stopped by the time he got to the depot, but he had isolated a shack at the end of the second row of company houses where a ragged, hoarse voice was reciting: " 'Who shall separate us from the love of Christ? Shall tribulation, or distress, or persecution, or famine, or nakedness, or peril, or sword?' "

"No, oh no," a woman's voice said, and a jumbled chorus of voices added, "Amen."

Sure, Music thought, seeing in the moony dark the simple rough cross fixed to the porch roof. He had noticed it the week before when he and

81

Regus took the new yellow-dog contracts around to be signed. *Church* was printed upon the arms of the cross and *holiness* down the shaft in such a manner that the first *h* in *church* began the word *holiness*. The small, quiet man who lived in the house—Music even remembered his name: Bydee Flann it was—had read the contract over carefully and appeared to be angry; but he had only covered his face with his hands for a moment before he signed the paper and handed it back. Music remembered it all very clearly because he'd felt a deep need to apologize to the man, although he had not done so. Full of curiosity, he crossed the broken pavement of the road and climbed the bank toward the three rows of company houses.

" 'As it is written,' " the weary voice said, " 'for thy sake are we killed all the day long; we are accounted as sheep for the slaughter.' "

"Yes, brother. Amen," said the congregation.

"Yea, but I tell ye, we cannot be torn-nah from his grasp-pah!" the preacher's voice said with sudden raw volume just as Music came abreast of the lighted window of Bydee's house and looked in upon the crowded room.

"Amen," someone said.

"Hallelujah."

"Lord, we know only a little," Bydee Flann said in a voice so ruined it sounded like a wood rasp. "In our ignorance we don't know what to hope for, ner what to pray for."

"Amen."

"Amen."

He was not, Music saw, somehow quite the man he had seen before. It wasn't just a matter of the rough, ragged work shirt having been changed for one of those old-fashioned white dress shirts with the replaceable celluloid collars—although Bydee's had no collar at all—and his patched work pants having become a pair of black dress pants worn slick and green as the body of an old housefly; it was a matter of strength and dignity and authority. Sweat glistened on his cheeks, and not a member of the congregation so much as coughed or moved while he traced his finger along the page of the open Bible before him and, in his soft, hoarse voice, read: " 'For we know not what we should pray for as we ought; but the Spirit itself maketh intercession for us with groanings which cannot be uttered.' " Bydee Flann, become preacher, nodded his head with profound understanding and stood back a step from the rough, homemade

82

little lectern before him. "Thank God," he whispered, "thank God." He pointed his finger at an old woman who sat with four children on one of the makeshift pews, nothing more than a plank supported between two chairs. "Thank God for yer suffering, sister," he said.

"Thank you, Jesus," the woman said.

"You," the preacher said, pointing to a man who sat looking at the floor, his huge hands hanging between his knees. The man responded, "Thank you, Lord," somehow knowing at once where the preacher was pointing.

"You and you and you," the preacher said pointing to other members of the congregation, and there was a chorus of answers; the women seeming to thank Jesus; the men, to thank the Lord.

The preacher went back to the open Bible upon the lectern and read again in his hoarse, ruined voice: " 'The Spirit itself beareth witness with our spirit, that we are the children of God. And if children, then heirs; heirs of God, and joint-heirs with Christ; if so be that we suffer with him, that we may be also glorified together. For I reckon that the sufferings of this present time are not worthy to be compared with the glory which shall be revealed in us.' "

The preacher stepped back and raised his hands and closed his eyes. Sweat soaked his shirt through under his arms, made a dark streak down his back. "Praise God," he said. "Hallelujah."

"Hallelujah."

"Amen."

"Children of God," the preacher said. "Heirs of God! Do you want more than that? Do you need more than that? You better love your suffering!" he shouted. "You better thank God for it! He keeps strict account! Didn't He allow his only son to be cursed-dah and spat upon and nailed-dah to the cross?" Raising his right hand over his head, his forefinger protruding like the barrel of a gun, the preacher walked among his congregation. "Child of God-dah, ye'll sit on His right hand-dah!" he shouted, pointing his finger at a small blond girl Music had seen standing beside the ball field that first night he had come through town. "Heir of God-dah," the preacher shouted, pointing to a woman whose narrow, wrinkled face looked close to both ecstasy and weeping, "ye'll dwell in Glory!" He paced back and forth, singling out members of his congregation. "For though the body be dead-dah because of sin-nah; the Spirit is life-fah because of righteousness! Rejoice!" he cried. "Rejoice!" He

83

pointed his finger at a rawboned, lantern-jawed man who sat toward the rear of the small, crowded room, a man who was half a head taller than anyone else. "You are called-dah! Justified-dah! Glorified-dah!"

The man loomed up. His eyes, which had been feverishly upon the small, grey-haired preacher, rolled back into his head as though he were going to faint, and he began to tremble and shake, head to foot. Outside the window, Music took an involuntary step backward as the tall man's jaw seemed to unhinge itself and wag, and a rhythmic and unintelligible succession of syllables issued from his mouth while only the whites of his eyes showed and his body continued to shake and jerk. Across the room another man rose. He was bent nearly double, and his mouth, without the superstructure of teeth, collapsed upon itself again and again as he spoke a low and singsongy bass. A woman rose too and added her voice.

"The Spirit is upon them," the small, sweat-soaked preacher said. "Hallelujah."

The preacher took up his Bible and held his free hand out before him, the fingers spread as though he were delivering a benediction. He closed his eyes. Sweat dripped from his nose and the point of his chin. "Is there one among you with the gift of interpretation touching his heart and spirit? Do they speak to God or man? Rise and tell us." The little blond girl got to her feet but her great, luminous, pale blue eyes did not blink, nor did she speak a word. The preacher acknowledged her and let his arm fall to his side. For a moment his chest rose and fell as if he were resting from a great labor; but at last, over the babbling of the others, his spent voice took up, hoarse and ragged and halting: "'For I am persuaded, that neither death nor life, nor angels, nor principalities, nor powers, nor things present, nor things to come, nor height, nor depth, nor any other creature, shall be able to separate us from the love of God, which is in Christ Jesus our Lord.'"

Somehow, much moved and much shaken, Music retreated across the hardscrabble earth. He did not know what he thought, but more like a thief than a watchman he crept between the coal company shacks, scaring himself unduly when, by accident, he kicked an empty food tin, which bounced and tinkled away in the darkness.

At last he climbed down the bank and got across the road to the depot, where he took comfort in the small yellow light glowing over the empty platform. From the church across the road, voices took up the final hymn.

"Holy Rollers," he told himself. "Sure, that's all they are." He laughed a weak, panting laughter and got out the makings and rolled himself a cigarette. "Takes all kinds, I guess," he said, aware, suddenly, that he was talking to himself, and almost in the same moment, aware of why. The old familiar world he thought he knew, understood, and had always dwelt in seemed to be slipping away. The old familiar Bill Music too. As unsatisfactory as they were, he wanted them back again. "Hellkatoot," he said.

A little nervously he started back up the street toward the other end of town. For some reason he wanted to be closer to Merlee Taylor, who had not been in Bydee Flann's congregation shouting "Amen," speaking in tongues; not her, she was a hard case. Twice since he had taken her the coffee, he had returned with other things; once with a peck of potatoes, once with five pounds of side meat. When he'd arrived with the peck of potatoes, she'd given him a long, cold look, turned her back on him, and gone off into another room, leaving him to set the potatoes on the sideboard and take himself away. When he'd arrived with the side meat and put it into her hands almost in the same moment she appeared, she had given him a look just as long and penetrating. "Sure," she'd said, "but if ye think I'm in your debt, you're a fool surenuff," and she'd shut the door in his face.

# 8

## COON HUNT

"THAT BONEHEAD," REGUS said. "Look at him. He's about as smart as a cloud of cow-shit butterflies."

In a big-footed, ear-flopping leap, Fetlock cleared the branch, let out a croupy bark, and began to cover exactly the same part of the cornfield he'd covered before, even sticking his head in the same corn shock to snuffle and snort before he began to clatter through the moony corn stubble, now and again raising his handsome voice to tell them that, by God, he smelled coon. He had already unraveled the maze of scent once and followed it across the branch to spend twenty minutes working the scrub oak and chinquapin thickets up the hill on the far side before the trail seemed to cool and he'd come back to the cornfield to start over.

"He run him backwards, I bet," Regus said.

Music, who had twice in the past week gone to see the one-armed man, passed Regus a pint mason jar. "He's got a pretty good nose. Hell, the track he's on ain't no fresher than last night, for certain," Music said.

Regus tipped his head and drank and passed the jar back, shaking himself all over as though with a violent, sudden chill. "Yeah," he said, "but he ort not to sound on a trail as cold as that. I don't think he's got any sense."

Music drank. Through eyes bleared with water he saw Fetlock quartering back to the same corn shock he had visited twice before. Likely the coon had found himself a stunted ear of corn there and had spent a little time digging it out. Fetlock stuck his head in the corn shock once again before he began to cover the same ground over and over, turning and wheeling and working very low down and fast.

"Dizzy bonehead," Regus muttered. "Lessen we want to bide the night right here, we gonna hafta hep that animal."

"He does seem to be runnin in pretty tight circles," Music said.

"He's about five minutes away from runnin right up his own butt," Regus said and stretched out his hand. Music put the mason jar in it, both of them watching the hound. "I swapped four dollars fer that feather-brain," Regus said in a dreamy voice. "Feller said his daddy was a bluetick and his dam, a redbone." Regus shook his head. "Don't hardly see how they could have whelped such nonsense as that." He took a drink, gave another nasty shiver, and passed the mason jar back again. Regus whistled and Fetlock skidded to stop, but he merely gave Regus a quick look before he swung back to work again, and Regus got up to fetch him.

Music took another drink, spun the lid down on the mason jar, and followed, carrying the little falling-block .22 rifle and a burlap sack. His own notion was that Fetlock was going to make a fine coon dog. "All that hound needs is more huntin," he said when he caught up to Regus. "He just ain't savvy yet."

Regus took off his belt and looped it around Fetlock's neck and crooned to him, "Whoa, whoa now," for the hound was excited by the attention and the hunt, wanted to get back to the puzzle the coon had left him, and was nearly choking himself in his happiness and confusion over how he was supposed to do it on such a short leash.

"Maybe," Regus said, "but I ain't so sure there's enough coon left in Switch County to train the genuine article on; never mind this critter here. Whoa, pup, settle down," he told Fetlock. "I was thinkin we might strike out up the mountain back in behind Mink Slide. They's a sight of fox grapes back yonder and a good-size branch a-coming off the mountain where I've seen more than one coon track."

"Let's do her then," Music said.

Regus tried to lead Fetlock away, but the animal was unable to remember for more than a moment that there was a noose about his neck and seemed bent on choking himself. Regus stooped, picked the hound up, and carried him.

"If that branch is big enough to have crawdads in it, we ought to find coon," Music said. "There ain't nuthin a coon loves more than crawdads."

"I bleve we done fell in with a honest-to-God coon hunter, ole pup," Regus said to the hound bucking and struggling against his chest.

They crossed the split-rail fence and went south by the haystacks and then turned west up the mountain. "I did some coon hunting when I was a youngin," Music said. "Had a good dog too, but I'll bet yourn will be better."

Fetlock heaved against Regus, whined and licked the bottom of Regus's chin, and then struggled some more; but, being held fast, the hound groaned deep in his chest and, looking doleful, as if he had suddenly grown old, at last allowed himself to be carried without further commotion. About two hundred yards up the mountain, Regus set him down and released him from the belt. "Now," he said, "if you strike something goin in a straight line, ye got a fifty-fifty chance a runnin it in the right direction."

Each of them had a drink while Fetlock quartered this way and that.

Regus lit the carbide lamp on his cap. "I grew up in a coal camp and don't know a terrible lot about coon huntin," he said. He got out his plug of tobacco and offered it to Music. Music shook his head, and Regus cut himself a chew and bit it off the blade of his pocketknife. "I only got to go four or five times as a little chap over in Pike County, but I took a deal of pleasure from it. Anyhow," Regus said, rubbing the back of his neck and laughing, "if ever somethin strikes you wrong, Bill Music, I'd as lief know it. Don't think yer a-pokin another man's fire. Speak on out."

"Absolutely," Music said, already feeling the warm effects of the moonshine. "I knew there was bound to be somethin in Switch County I understood even if it's only coon huntin. Lead on. Lead on."

The pale moon, the high icy stars were sowing seeds of a hard frost. Over the spiced mustiness of the woods, Music could smell the frost coming. It was a flat, cold odor like the odor of iron or wet rock. His breath billowed out before him, and his face was stingingly but pleasantly cold. Every so often Fetlock doubled back to check on them and then quartered ahead to range far out of sight. They traversed the mountain to the southwest, weaving through chinquapin and laurel thickets until below them they could see the blue-white lights of Elkin and Hardcastle and, further to the south, a narrow string of soft, yellow lights from the kerosene lanterns in the shacks of Mink Slide, lights glowing in the otherwise pitch-dark valley like souls in perdition.

Music was somehow unreasonably glad to be on the mountain, to be hunting, to be more than a little drunk, to be three times and three ways removed from being a mine guard. "Hey, Regus," he said all at once, "I'm damned if I understand it."

A step or two ahead of him in the moon-dappled woods, Regus drew up and turned his mild face. It was a face that nearly always seemed to have humor lurking just below the surface, as though humor, turned hard as bone, were its foundation. "What's that?" Regus said.

Music fetched the whiskey from his pocket, unscrewed the lid, and passed the mason jar to Regus. "There ain't a miner in Elkin that don't hate the sight of us," Music said.

"That's a fair statement, I reckon," Regus said. He tucked the chew of tobacco into his cheek, spat, and drank.

"Well," Music said, "you were a miner, and your father before you."

"Yes," Regus said and passed the jar back.

"Well, shitfire!" Music said. "I don't understand what would make you cross over to the other side." He took a drink, and then in the whispery voice the whiskey left him, said: "Looks to me like it would go against your grain."

"Is that what's fetched you up then?" Regus said and began to climb again toward the southwest.

"Hellkatoot! One of the things," Music said, keeping about a half-step behind him. "It's against my grain, and I never dug the first shovel of coal."

"Then how come yer a-mine guardin?" Regus asked.

"You're duckin me," Music said.

"Yes," Regus said. "But if you throw a stick in the creek, hit'll float so long as hit don't suck up the water. I aim to float," Regus said. "Does that satisfy you, Bill Music?"

"It don't," Music said, "shitfire, no it don't."

Regus made a soft sound like laughing. "All right," he said, "my poppa was a miner and a union man in the bargain fer all hit fetched him."

The two of them made slow, steady progress up the mountain, more

89

athwart the grade than with it, walking abreast when they could, Music dropping a step behind when they couldn't; and Regus talked in his slow, humorous voice.

"I was a trap boy," Regus said, "bout thirteen when I learned how it is with the miners. We had us a checkweighman at that mine by the name of Lightfoot. A mean sucker who had a hump on his back and whose habit it was to point over his shoulder at it and say, 'See that, fellers? Now that's just how them coal cars better look when they come outten this here drift.' Them coal cars was supposed to carry two ton, and that's what the miner got credit for, but I'd guess he had em loadin maybe five hundred pound extra the way they were rounded off on top. And hell," Regus said and laughed, "if that son of a bitch seen a little slate in what a man had loaded, he would, like as not, dump out the whole shebang, and the miner who loaded it would lose credit for the car." Regus stopped for a moment and caught his breath and then started up the mountain again. "Well," he said, "coal was sellin high and times were good, and Poppa and some others snuck around and organized, there being a U.M.W. man down from Pennsylvania to egg em on." Regus let out a short, soft bark of laughter and gave his head a little sideways jerk. "Well, when the miners stood up on their hind legs and made their demands," he said, "they was prouder of getting rid of Lightfoot and electin their own checkweighman than anything else. Even than gettin a decent wage for yardage."

"Well then," Music said, "the union did some good."

Regus nodded and spat. "Sure," he said, "sure, when times were good, hit was a fine thing. But when the price of coal fell and the company wanted to cut the miners' wages, why, my poppa and them others bowed their necks and struck. The operator brought in scabs. The miners carried their guns down to the picket lines. The operator hired on a dozen mine guards, ole Lightfoot among them; and boy, everybody had a fine time shootin up the place." Regus snorted. "Somebody put the wind through Lightfoot right off, and they was other shootins too, and the national guard came on down, and Poppa and the others had to back off and think her over, which was when they got time enough to notice that the Pennsylvania organizer was nowhere in sight, nor the union funds either, which had been collected in dues."

Regus stopped walking and propped his hand against a tree to rest. "They was about a dozen miners brought up on murder charges for Lightfoot and a couple other guards that got themselves killed. And they was maybe sixty or so got fired and evicted, Poppa with em. We damned

90

near starved out that time," Regus said and shook his head and laughed. "Not that hit taught Poppa a damn thing; he brought the same sort of trouble on himself till the day he died. Got himself blackballed so he couldn't get a job without he made himself up a new name." Regus shook his head. "He got hisself caught and fired more than once before him and the others ever even had a chance to make their first demand."

Fetlock came loping back through the underbrush, and without so much as giving them a look, cut up the mountain above them and doubled back, his nose to the ground as though he were being pulled along by a wire through it and had to run in order to keep from being dragged. Regus took a step or two and set his foot on a blowdown.

"I don't know as I've learned airey thing but this," he said. "One miner by hisself might have a little sense, but two together has got half as much sense as one, and three has got less sense than two, and any more than three in one bunch has got no sense at all. That there is the trouble with unions." He swapped his quid from one cheek to the other and spat. "Hit never seemed to me to cause the operator no trouble to find one poor man who would fight another for the same no-account job." Regus chewed thoughtfully and shook his head. "Hit don't matter, near as I can make out, which side you and me is on," he said.

For a long moment neither of them spoke; then Regus made a short sound like laughing. "Can ye strap that on, Bill Music?" he said. "Aire ye happy now?"

"Nope," Music said.

Regus laughed. "I reckon," he said. "I reckon so."

"I'll have to settle for drunk," Music said and fished the mason jar out of his pocket, but somewhere above and ahead of them, Fetlock struck up.

"Lord," Regus said. "Listen! Listen at him sing!"

"He musta run smack over somethin!" Music said. He spun the lid down on the jar and dropped it in his pocket, and both of them scrambled at once over the blowdown. Unlike Regus, Music had no lamp on his head, so he ran into things and fell many times, but he kept up; and all the while Fetlock's croupy, baying voice rang in the dappled woods, telling them: "He came this way, passed over this ledge, skirted these briars, crossed this log," and they thrashed after it. By the time they had covered three or four hundred yards, Fetlock had gone into full cry, a beautiful chop-mouth yammer which seemed to leave the hound no space for breathing.

91

"Hallelujah!" Regus said in a winded, ragged voice, "listen at him sing."

All at once the hound's belling changed again, no less constant, but somehow easier, satisfied, a sound almost like yodeling.

"By God," Music said, "I bleve he's treed a'ready."

The two of them thrashed through blowdowns and scrub until, fighting out of a net of grapevine, they came in sight of him standing on his hind feet, his forepaws up on a sweet birch, and his big-eared, slender head raised to the sky, talking out of the front of his mouth to what was in the topmost branches.

Regus tried to lean against a spindly white pine no taller than he was and nearly fell when the rubbery trunk bent to one side. "Ain't that," he gasped, "handsome?"

"Mercy," Music wheezed and dropped to his knees and then pitched forward on his hands. After a moment he felt for the mason jar in his pocket and found it whole. "Mercy," he said again and lay down on his back. Regus came over and sat down beside him, and they passed the jar back and forth while Fetlock bayed and bounced on his hind feet as though he thought, if he just got started right, he could climb the tree.

Finally, in a voice still a little breathless, Regus said, "I don't see airey thing up in that tree."

"It's there," Music said. "Fetlock says it is."

"I don't see airey damn thing," Regus insisted.

The two of them struggled to their feet and began to walk around and around the tree; and indeed, its slender, leafless branches, outlined against the sky, seemed to contain nothing at all. Regus's carbide lamp did not help them much, but still, Music thought, they should have been able to see eyes glowing with the reflected light the lamp cast. When he was young and hunted alone or with his brothers or father, they had built fires beneath the trees, and the coon's eyes would glow when it looked at the fire. Still, on bright moonlit nights such as this one, the animal would often look at the moon instead. But at last Music spotted a thickness about one of the topmost branches that had no business being there.

"I see him," Music said.

"Where?" Regus said.

"Yonder," Music said, "on the south side, bout four foot out from the trunk. Ain't a coon, I think. Too small. It's a possum."

"Can you shoot it?" Regus asked.

"Sure," Music said, "but we never did shoot possum. They'd be all

92

right, I guess, but possums ain't too careful about what they eat. We always used to pen em up for a week or so and feed em a little buttermilk and cornbread. They're fine eatin then."

"All right," Regus said.

"Why don't you tie ole Fetlock up so he don't kill it, and I'll climb the tree and shake him out," Music said.

"All right," Regus said.

"Get a stick to hit him with when I shake him out. Don't kill him. Just give him a swat to make him sull, and then catch him by the neck and drop him in the sack."

"All right," Regus said. He took hold of Fetlock and petted him and crooned to him and bragged on him, but Fetlock was for talking to the opossum and didn't want to be led away. Regus had to loop his belt around Fetlock's neck again, but even so, he lunged for the sweet birch on his hind legs, his forefeet pawing the air, and Regus had to let him come back to the tree while he got out his pocketknife and took the belt off and made another hole in it to fit Fetlock's neck so that the belt could be buckled and the hound could be led away without strangling himself. Finally Regus was able to tie him to the little white pine, having bragged on him and petted him until he seemed to get it through his head that Regus was proud of him, and so, settled down a little, although he still danced and bayed.

Regus began to whittle on the limb of a maple at the edge of the clearing until Music stopped him. "That's a club. You'll kill him with that," Music said and cut a limb himself, a little bigger around than his thumb. "Smack him with this," he said.

"All right," Regus said.

Music took three or four deep breaths and began to climb the birch, but halfway up he ran out of strength and had to hang on. The tree had no limbs until very near the crown, and Music, a little dizzy from the whiskey, and his arms and legs trembling with fatigue, began to wonder if he was going to make it.

"How come yer a-stoppin?" Regus said from below.

"Cause I'm bout to fall out on my goddam head," Music said, surprised that even his voice sounded weak and shaky.

"Well," Regus said, "so long as nobody don't tell the possum. He might take a notion to shake the tree."

Instantly Music could imagine, somewhere above him, the opossum gritting its teeth, wrapping its tail around the limb, and getting ready to shake him out. The vision made him slip about six inches down the trunk before he got himself in hand and, with the last of his strength, struggled upward until he could catch a limb big enough to support his weight. "Mercy," he said in a hoarse whisper. He hung on until his strength returned and then climbed far enough into the crown to be able to set his foot on a limb half the size of his wrist. He was soaked with sweat and shaky. "You ready, damn you," he called down.

"Sure," Regus said and laughed, "I'll swat whatever hits the ground, be it man or beast."

Music leaned far out from the trunk, took hold of the opossum's limb, and began to shake it. Almost at once the opossum flopped loose and fell. Regus kicked it over the instant it hit the ground and struck it with the stick too; but Music didn't get to see what happened next, for he realized suddenly that the whole tree had started over. "Shitfire," he said, "look out!" He held on with his hands and swung his feet out, but when the tree had dipped its top halfway to the ground, it broke suddenly at its butt end and came down hard. The top of it brushed Regus, who jumped clear, but it gave Fetlock an awful swat, and he thrashed about in its small, topmost branches. Music himself was soundly jarred and stunned.

Regus spat and ran a finger back and forth under his nose. "Wouldn't think a man would want to ride a tree over like that when the sap's down," he said.

"It wasn't my intention," Music said, sitting spraddle-legged where he had fallen. "Where's the dog?" Music said, looking around. "Did I kill it?"

Fetlock crouched shivering, blinking, and chastened among the small limbs of the crown.

"Nope," Regus said, "don't appear you kilt nor lamed nobody."

Music felt suddenly for the mason jar and found it miraculously whole. "Mercy," he said.

"Prime, fat possum," Regus said, holding it out by the scruff of the neck for Music to see. The opossum's eyes were half closed and its lips were drawn back in a death grin. Its mouth, a little open, exposed its pale, lolling tongue, sickly pink gums, and sharp teeth—an excellent death act but for the rim of iris and pupil, which never quite disappeared above the eyelid and so allowed the opossum to keep keen track of things, dead as it looked. Regus took the opossum over to Fetlock and let him have a smell and told him he was a fine hound dog, but Fetlock seemed as wary as he was pleased, since Music had just dropped a tree on him and he wasn't sure how that fitted in with the rest.

While Regus got the sack and dropped the opossum in it, Music let the fierce impact of his fall drain out of his feet and butt, had himself a drink, and considered the sweet birch. It had been nothing more than a large sucker growing out of a stump rotted off almost even with the ground; there were other suckers there too, eighteen or twenty inches up. Now, why didn't you notice that before? he asked himself. He sat where he was and took another drink while Regus untied Fetlock. Immediately the hound started back the way he had come.

"I wonder if he aims to run that possum back into yesterday," Regus said.

"I don't know," Music said. "Maybe he's goin home. Hell, he found us a possum and we hit him with a tree. Maybe he's thinkin, if that's the way it's done, he ain't so sure he likes it." Groaning, Music rose and brushed at the seat of his pants. "Cain't say I blame him," he said.

But Fetlock came back through the tangle of grapevines and trailed the opossum to the base of the sweet birch, circled to the sack Regus held, and then gave the whole length of the tree such investigation as he dared, approaching it and springing back, or sneaking up on it, tight as a fiddle string, legs bent, muzzle to the ground, watching the birch out of the top of his head as though he thought it just might make a jump and land on him again. Music watched Fetlock circle and work until he came back to the sack Regus held, where, at last, he seemed to get it all sorted out and went off across the ridge to the southwest, hunting something else. "He's a damned fine hound," Music said, "and he's got a forgiving nature too. Now," he said, "we've greased the skillet. Do you still have the itch for coon?"

"I do, Bill Music," Regus said, "if you'd just as lief?"

Music smacked his lips tentatively. The soles of his feet had quit stinging and the numbness had gone out of his spine. He passed the jar to Regus. "Have a drink," he said.

While Regus tucked his quid into his cheek, spat two or three times, and drank, Music rotated his pelvis in a gentle circle, trying to straighten the kinks in his backbone. "The next tree is yours to climb," he said.

Regus shook himself all over like a wet dog, shuddered, and handed the jar back to Music. "Sure," he said.

Music dropped the jar again in his pocket. "Lead on," he said. "Lead on."

"Now, you take them niggers down in Mink Slide, as a fer instance," Regus said, as though what he had been saying before Fetlock struck across the opossum's trail had been in perfect suspension, as though no

95

more than an instant had passed, "they come in on transportation when the folks down to Hardcastle went on strike."

So, Music thought, the alcohol in him making him feel particularly canny and wise; so, Mr. Regus Patoff Bone ain't completely satisfied with himself, now, is he?

Regus swung the sack with the opossum in it across his shoulder and began to walk. "Ole Too Sweet told me once that he'd rather be one-eyed and broke back in Alabama than be in Mink Slide with fifty dollars in his pocket. I'll bet you couldn't find one white miner at Hardcastle that wouldn't like to lick his calf over again either. "Hell," Regus said, "Hardcastle shut the mine down the selfsame hour they struck, and sent him a recruiter off to Alabama to fetch him some strong buck niggers. Sure, that recruiter went down offerin five dollars a man, new overalls, and transportation to Switch County to any darky that wanted to dig coal. Give em a big sell about how much money they'd make, how they'd be their own bosses, how the company would provide houses for them to live in. Sure they come, you bet," Regus said, and turning toward Music, he walked squarely into a dogwood tree and struggled with it for a moment before he fended it off and went on; and Music, as though from a position of lucid sobriety, thought to himself, Hellkatoot, he's drunk as a snake. "Course the recruiter never told them poor niggers they was going to have to work out the five dollars, the damned overhalls, and even the goddamned ride to Switch County," Regus said and giggled. "Never told them they was a-comin as scabs and would likely get kilt, nor that Kenton Hardcastle planned to marry them off the selfsame moment they stepped down from the goddamned cattle cars onto Hardcastle property."

"What?" Music said.

"Sure," Regus said, "you betcha." He turned around, and the soft explosion of his laughter boiled like smoke in the light of the carbide lamp. "That goddamned Hardcastle had recruited black women from the whorehouses in Louisville, and when his bucks pulled onto the siding, he let them women pick whosomever they fancied and married them on the spot."

"Hell," Music said, "is he a justice of the peace too?"

"Nawh," Regus said, "ain't nothin of the sort, but them niggers didn't know that. Ole Kenton Hardcastle was ever a man to profit by another's mistakes," he said, and went on to explain that other coal operators always had trouble with black scabs because they would not stay in a place where there weren't any women for them; and where there were women, the bucks would fight over them and there would be knifings and

96

shootings and trouble, so Hardcastle had figured a way to get around both difficulties at the same time. It even worked to his advantage that the striking miners had heard about the trainload of scabs coming and had ambushed the train a few miles away at Theta Gap, where it was moving slowly up the steep grade. They had shot up the cattle cars with the colored scabs in them, and three or four of the poor niggers had been killed and a half dozen others wounded. And a bunch of the miners had come back into Elkin with their rifles and shotguns to finish what they'd started at Theta Gap, but they were held off by the sheriff and a bunch of deputies and mine guards. Still, the poor black fellows climbing down from riddled cattle cars into such a situation were in no position to make a fuss over a little thing like being married off to women they had never seen before. They had already been shot to pieces coming through the gap, and across thirty yards of cinders and gumbo was a bunch of ragged, angry men who wanted to start in again and do a better job. So it was, in a hell of a tight and scared, they listened to Kenton Hardcastle marry them to strange women. Straightaway after that, they were marched off under guard to the shacks that had been flung up in Mink Slide, where, for nearly a month, guards had to be posted in order to keep the striking miners from killing them and in order to keep them from sneaking off and beating it back to Alabama.

"I heard the guards didn't do a hundred-percent job either way," Regus said, and then all at once he stopped talking and went down on one knee. He seemed to study the ground in front of him for a moment before, with great dignity, he took off his miner's cap, rid his mouth of the quid of tobacco, and vomited. "I believe," he said, sitting on his heels, his hands propped on his knees, "I've had more of that shine than I can keep surrounded." He sat very still for a few moments. "I surely do apologize," he said, "but I'm a little dizzy, not bein a drinkin man."

All at once Music felt dizzy himself, as though Regus's honesty had made him aware of it. The mountain seemed to turn on its base, counterclockwise against the spread of stars, and he had to hold on to a branch of laurel and bend his knees for better balance.

"Ahh," Regus said, "this ain't no kind of world for a thinkin man." He seemed to ponder that a moment and then vomited again before he nodded his head as though in firm agreement with himself. He picked up his cap with the carbide lamp on it and handed it to Music. "You lead, Bill Music, and I'll follow. The light don't do me no good noway if I can't walk where I'm lookin."

For a long time they climbed the mountain behind Mink Slide. Once or twice Fetlock doubled back to check on them and then went on ahead, having slowed down considerably, as they had. Music felt guilty and somewhat chastened for having gotten Regus drunk and for having had so much to drink himself. In spite of the cold, the liquor had put a fine mist of sweat across Music's forehead, as though he were ill and in a fever, although he felt all right. Still, when they crossed a spring branch, Music knelt and drank from his cupped hands, and icy as the water was, washed his face and the back of his neck. Regus drank too, and they sat for a while and rested and talked a little. The talk was easy, quiet, without the least bantering. Music told about a night when he and his brothers were coon hunting along the Mill River in Virginia, and a young dog, about eight months old and brave if not smart, had caught a coon in the middle of the river and been drowned by it and damned near caused the drowning of Music's younger brother and himself. The coon had simply climbed up on the dog's head and held him under. Music told how his younger brother had jumped in trying to save the dog, for it was his and he prized it, there being almost nothing else in the world that belonged to him alone. So Music had had to jump in to get his brother out, although he could not swim a stroke. He had pushed his brother and shoved him and even kicked him into the bank before he swallowed so much water he could do nothing more. He had thought he was dying. He had heard, in the water or in his blood, the deep tolling of a bell going BONG . . . BONG . . . BONG. But then the current had taken him into shore, and his two brothers had dragged him out, more dead than alive. They had worked on him, trying to mash the water out of his lungs while he puked and wheezed. They had never spoken a word about it to their father or mother, for Music hadn't wanted it known how little sense they had exhibited. They had only told about the silly young dog catching the coon in the middle of the river and getting drowned for his trouble.

All the while Music talked, Regus listened intently, his mild face strangely without a trace of its usual humor. It would have been a good thing to have brothers or sisters, he said, but Ella hadn't had any luck with her babes, having lost two of them to thrush before they were a year old and another to the epidemic flu. She had almost lost him as well, which would have been an awful shame for her, he said, as though counting himself for nothing and taking her perspective in the matter entirely. He'd had the dysentery and the camp doctor had given him up, but an old granny woman had begun to doctor him with some sort of medicine, and he pulled out of it. Ella had thought the medicine miraculous and had copied down the name

98

of it so that she could name him after it and, therefore, honor whoever had invented the potion which had saved her son. They had not learned until Regus was in school that Ella had not copied down the name of the medicine at all, but only the abbreviations stamped on the bottle: "Reg. U.S. Pat.Off."

Although something about Regus's face changed a bit in that moment, so that Music felt it would have been all right to laugh if he wanted to, Music did not feel like laughing. Regus brought out his plug of tobacco and offered it to Music, who raised the palm of his hand and shook his head. After Regus had cut himself a chew, he said, "I'd be obliged though, Bill Music, if you didn't let on to Momma ye know how I got my name. Hit's caused her a right smart of embarrassment." Regus swapped his quid from one corner of his mouth to the other, tucked it in his cheek, and spat. "She's right sensitive about it," he said, and his eyes crinkled at the corner, "though I don't see why. It's a good enough name. I think I'd favor it over Castor Oil, say."

They both laughed then, and after a moment Regus fished out his pocket watch and read it in the light of Music's carbide lamp. "Eleven-thirty," he said. "I reckon if we're to get any sleep a'tall, we ort to pack it in."

"Yes," Music said, "but we could let the dog take a cast or two and catch him up when he doubles back." He took the mason jar out of his pocket. There was two inches of whiskey left in the bottom. He set the jar in the spring branch and propped a heavy, flat stone on it to hold it down. "Who knows," he said, "we might come back this way some night, and it would be good to have a taste waiting on us." He dried his hands on his britches and rubbed them together. "What say I build us a fire till Fetlock shows?" he said.

"Sure," Regus said.

But Music had barely gathered a little squaw wood and lit it when Fetlock came loping by to check on them. He was so tired his shoulders and rump were bouncing like a child's rocking horse, and when Regus clucked to him, he came willingly. Music kicked out the fire and gathered up the little falling-block .22 rifle and the burlap sack with the opossum in it. Regus put Fetlock on the leash he'd made of his belt. And the three of them began the long walk home.

Registered United States Patent Office Bone, Music thought; surely that wouldn't make a woman carry her head so humbly or keep her from looking another human being in the eye. Naming Regus in such a manner was a grand gesture, no matter how it had turned out. To think of it, to be

99

hunting, to be mellowed with corn liquor beyond even the reach of fatigue, put him in a wonderful mood. It seemed to him he hadn't been so content since he'd left home, since, indeed, the last time he'd been hunting back in Virginia. He hadn't been out for coon then, but for turkey—his secret weapon a turkey call he'd made from a piece of cow horn with a nail driven into the tip. No call ever imitated the yelp of a hen so faithfully as his did when a small stone was grated against that nail. At the top of Howard's Knob he had hidden himself and made one single yelp; and way off, a gobbler had answered: *"Chobalobalob, chobalobalob."* And he had set the barrel of his father's hog rifle in the crotch of a tree, pointing it toward the sound; for if the gobbler came at all, he would come straight as an arrow. Without calling again, he waited half an hour while daylight climbed the dome of the sky. It was late spring, and redbud and dogwood were in bloom together and the first green-gold of leaves had begun to show. There was mist in all the low places hiding the valley, and mountains rose out of the mist like islands in a sea. Nor did he move until the gobbler appeared, running fifteen or twenty feet, and then stopping to puff himself up and strut with his wing tips dragging the ground, and then running again. With infinite slowness, so that the turkey would not see him move, he inclined his eye to the rifle sights, and the third time the gobbler paused to puff himself up and drag his wing tips, he shot. The gobbler hopped into the air—perhaps startled, perhaps he meant to fly—but he was atumble and askew, and his wing beating was to no purpose. And, at last, when he had come down off the mountain with the tom turkey flouncing, warm and heavy against his back, he had known he was going to leave home. It was not a thing he had gone up there to decide. He had not caught himself making the decision. He had merely been aware that he had made it. Ambition had little to do with it. His fascination with electricity had little to do with it. It was another matter entirely. It seemed to him now, walking athwart the dark mountain with Regus and Fetlock at his back, that he understood it; and far more in earnest than in whimsy, he thought to himself that a man could live in the Garden of Eden only so long as he didn't know where he was.

# 9

## CHANGES

ALL OF THE material was a little faded and dusty on the outside, but if the bolts were flopped over a few times, the colors turned bright and handsome. One piece of cloth seemed very beautiful to him—wine it was, with small grey and blue flowers—and he waited with his hand upon it as though the commissary were bustling with customers and someone might buy it out from under his nose. His stomach felt raw and his head hurt, but the two of them had just drawn wages for a four-day workweek, which, for him, meant nine dollars and thirty-six cents above and beyond what he had charged, and his sudden inspiration to buy her material for a dress gave him comfort. After all, even though twice he had been able to beat Regus out and buy the victuals and supplies that Ella had sent them for, he still had five dollars tucked away back in his room, and there was no reason not to buy the cloth if it pleased him. He had accumulated quite a lot of money for so little work, and he could spend some if he wished to. Never mind that Miss Merlee Taylor had not so much as smiled upon him. Mrs. Merlee Taylor, it was. But never mind that either. He wished he had shaved though, as Regus had done. He rubbed the stubble on his chin and waited for Regus and Cecil to quit trying to top each other with hunting stories so he could ask about the material.

Regus leaned against the counter, talking in his slow, humorous voice and drinking from time to time from an orange soda pop. Cecil had gotten the best of the coon-hunting stories, and Regus appeared to have gone on

101

to bigger game. He looked fresh and pink as a baby, doubtless, Music thought, because he'd had the good fortune to throw up most of the corn liquor he'd drunk; no amount of shaving could account for his clarity of eye and high spirits.

"It was a smallish bear, wouldn't weigh more than a hundred pound," Regus was saying, "but there it was, setting right tip-top of an old black gum snag, when there wadn't nobody, includin me, thought there was a single bear left in Perry County."

"When was this, you say?" Cecil asked, both interest and the shadow of doubt upon his face.

"Bout ten year ago," Regus said, "when I was a young pup full of piss and vinegar." Regus took a pull of his orange soda. "I admit to bein right excited," he said. "Had to pin the rifle barrel agin a tree to take a steady bead, but I cored him. The only thing was, I hope to die if that sucker didn't fall right backards down inside that damned ole snag. I waited and a-waited, hopin he'd climb out, but he never. Didn't know what to do. Thought of trampin on back down the mountain to fetch a bucksaw and some hep, but someway, didn't want to do that. It would sort of spoil it, ye know, to hafta fetch someone to hep out. I thought I'd give a try to climb up there and get him out myself."

"Shoot," Cecil said, "you wouldn't catch me climbin down inside no tree with a bear that moughten be dead."

"Yessiree, that's about what I was thinkin," Regus said, "but the whole time I was scrabblin up the outside of that ole snag, I never heard nuthin out of him; and after I got up on top, I chucked a bunch of bark and crap down in there and didn't hear nuthin either. Couldn't see much though, for toward the bottom of the snag it was pretty dark. Turned out he was dead as a hammer. Wadn't no trouble to get down to him, but I couldn't get that sucker outta there to save my life. I'd grab aholt of his tail and get him up maybe two or three feet and then lose my purchase again the inside of that black gum and go right to the bottom, or I'd lose my grip on his ole knob of a tail and drop him." Regus's head twitched to one side and he sucked his teeth. He ran his finger back and forth under his nose and looked at Music, who couldn't decide if he'd imagined it or if Regus had given him the merest hint of a wink. "They tails is kinda slick, ya know," he said, "like as if ye'd taken and sorta oiled the fur a little. Well, I tell ye, it wadn't long till I had wore myself out. I mean I had just about give up." He took another swallow of his orange soda and shook his head in wonder. "It was right then that I got my real surprise. I was settin on that bear, sweatin and a-thinkin and a-scratchin my head, when, I'll be damned, if somethin didn't darkey the hole."

"Say what?" Cecil asked.

"Yessir," Regus said, "I mean plumb shut out the light. Scared me nearly to death when I figured out it was a second goddamned bear a-backin down on top of me."

"Get outta here," Cecil said and looked away over his shoulder as though to call upon a third party to witness the nonsense he was having to endure. "I ain't so big a fool as that," he said; "get outta here with that stuff."

"Yessir," Regus said, "ole momma bear herself, backin right down to see how her youngin was a-doin, I reckon."

"Sure, sure," Cecil said and shook hands with himself after his fashion. "I reckon you shot her too," he said and laughed.

"Well, I probably would have," Regus said, "if I hadn't a left my rifle out on the ground. I surely don't think hit would have been smart, though. I don't know as I would have cared to be shut up in a hollow snag with a wounded momma bear and a dead cub. Course I might have been able to shoot her enough to kill her, but then she would have fell on me, and there bein no way around her and all, I expect I'da smothered betwixt the two of them. No," he said and straightened up from the counter, "I reckon I done the proper thing, all right." He drained the last of his orange soda, set the bottle down, and fished a nickel out of his pocket which he placed deliberately in Cecil's palm.

"Well?" Cecil said.

"Well?" Regus responded, raising his eyebrows quizzically.

"Well, goddam!" Cecil said, the goiter on his neck swelling, "you feed a feller that bullshit until he acquires a taste for it . . . "—he waved his arms around as though shooing flies and grew red in the face—"you cain't just leave it there."

Regus's eyebrows rose another quarter of an inch, and he turned to look at Music as though for explanation.

"You ain't a-foolin nobody," Cecil said. "Go on ahead and tell me what ye done and put me outta my misery."

"Oh," Regus said, "why sure. I just only stayed right quiet, took a good grip on the small bear, and when the momma got down where I could, why I clamped my teeth in her ass and grabbed a handful of fur. Lordy," Regus said and gave a little bark of laughter and shook his head, "she clawed me and that dead bear both right up outta that tree quicker

103

than you could spit. When we got to the top, I just pushed her off, and she broke her neck."

"Course you did," Cecil said, looking disgusted. "Shitfire, I don't see why I didn't think of that myself."

"Me neither," Regus said; "was near about the only thing to do." He sniffed and ran his finger back and forth under his nose. "Come on, Bill Music," he said, "less us get outta here fore Cecil gets back everything Hardcastle paid us in wages."

In spite of himself, Music flushed. "Not yet," he said; "there's a trifle here I'd like to buy."

"Jesus, what's that?" Cecil said. "I thought I'd listened to that great load of nonsense for the price of a soda."

"I'd like to know what amount . . . " Music cleared his throat; his ears heated up. "That is," he said, "this cloth here, how much of it would it take to make a dress?"

"Well," Cecil said, "what size woman do you want to cover?"

Regus was looking at him, a hint of curiosity in his mild face, but nothing of ridicule. "Bout this high," Music said, holding his hand out level with his shoulder. There was a ringing in his ears as though someone had fired a pistol off just over his head, but there was nothing to do but brazen it out.

"Yeah?" Cecil said. "And how big around?"

"I don't know," Music said.

"Ha," Cecil said, "don't tell me ye don't know no more about yer sweetie than that!"

"Mercy," Regus said softly and moved a few feet to the north to stand beside the bins of produce along the wall. He got out his plug of tobacco and his pocketknife.

"Say what?" Cecil said, turning to Regus and laughing.

"Don't mind me," Regus said. He cut himself a chew of tobacco, bit it off the knife blade, and talked around it. "I just don't want to be in the line of fire if you aim to keep showin yer bad manners."

Cecil flicked his eyes to Music and the butt of the huge Walker Colt. "Here now, didn't mean a single thing," he said. "It's just that I can't tell how much cloth to sell ye if I don't know what size the lady is."

"Not big," Music said.

Cecil rubbed his chin thoughtfully. "I reckon five yards ought to be aplenty." He brightened and took a yardstick from beneath one of the counters. "Hit's as pretty a cloth as I've ever carried in the store. Right expensive though. Cost you twelve cent a yard."

"That's all right," Music said.

Cecil flipped the bolt over half a dozen times and began to measure.

"I don't want that part," Music said.

Cecil blinked his eyes. "Say what?" he said.

"It's faded, and it's got coal dust on it," Music said.

"Christ, if the lady's goan wear it around here, hit'll have coal dust on it fore she turns around twice, and once she washes it and hangs it out on the line, hit'll fade out even," Cecil said.

"I won't have the dirty part," Music said.

"I can't just cut it off and throw it away without I charge ye for it," Cecil said. "I had to buy the whole bolt, and that's what I got to sell."

"All right," Music said.

"Take yer measurement from the other end," Regus said quietly.

"I'll have to unroll the whole damned thing," Cecil said.

"I expect," Regus said.

Mumbling and muttering to himself, Cecil unrolled the bolt, measured from the other end, and cut the material with pinking shears.

"You got any fine paper?" Music asked.

"Say what now?" Cecil said.

"Any colored paper, pretty paper?" Music said. Embarrassment, like anything else, he supposed, could be gotten used to. He looked Cecil straight in the eye.

"No, I don't," Cecil said. "Don't get no call for it."

"All right, have you got a nice box then?"

"I ain't got that either," Cecil said.

"All right," Music said, "do you have any ribbon?"

"I got some odds of hair ribbon is all," Cecil said.

"All right," Music said. "Wrap it up in brown paper and put a ribbon bow on it."

"I'll have to charge for the ribbon," Cecil said. "This here ain't my stuff. I cain't give it away."

"That will be fine," Music said. "That will be just fine."

Cecil wrapped the cloth and tied it first with string and then with ribbon. Music paid him, and he and Regus left together, but they got no further than the empty gallery, as though, having managed to buy the material and have it wrapped, Music's resolve would take him no further;

105

as though what he had already done were sufficient, an end in itself. He stood uncertainly on the gallery, staring off across the company street. Decorously, Regus looked up the highway toward Valle Crucis, chewed thoughtfully, spat thoughtfully, giving Music whatever room he needed to say whatever he wanted to say, or to say nothing at all. Music was grateful, although his ears were still warming the sides of his head. "I guess it wouldn't make much sense not to go on and give it to her," Music said at last.

"Sounds right," Regus said, calm and easy and without the slightest trace of irony.

"Ha, dammit," Music said all at once, "don't seem like much of a present now that I think about it. I ought to have bought her a dress, maybe."

"Nawh," Regus said. "I don't think you could have fit her. She'd as soon have the cloth, I'd vow." He turned his head and spat.

"Well," Music said, "I guess I'll go on then. I'll be back in a little."

"Take ye time," Regus said. "Grady says ole Hardcastle wants us to check in on Mink Slide to make sure they ain't no white faces ner strange niggers back in there. Wants us to take a look-see down to the Bear Paw, too, but it ain't no hurry."

"Well, I'll go on then," Music said, and he descended two steps and stopped. "Seems awful personal all of a sudden," he said. "Maybe I should have got some coffee or some grub."

"I think she'd as lief have the cloth," Regus said.

Music nodded, and after a moment, without looking back, started across the road. Look here, he wanted to tell her, I just jumped off a train down the road a piece. I got nothin to do with this coal company or any other. I didn't shoot your husband; don't intend to shoot anybody's husband. I been on the road nearly two years. I just want to get on back to Virginia, which I should have never left. I just want to make a few dollars and get on back home. That's what he'd tell her. He came up the hardscrabble path by her broken front porch and went around to the back door and knocked. His head hurt. He could feel the beard on his face, each individual hair of it, as though it were wire driven into the skin. The ancient Walker Colt under his coat seemed the size and weight of an artillery piece. Maybe the old woman would answer the door and he could give her the package and leave.

The door opened, and it was not the old woman. He fumbled in his head for what he was going to say. "Here," he said and held the package out to her. Her eyes were blue-grey, the color of smoke, and if they weren't so hard as they had been the times before, there was nothing else in them either, save, perhaps, curiosity. As though from a great distance, as though he were looking back on it from some future time when it no longer mattered so much, he saw himself standing upon the hard-packed, littered earth outside her back door, coal dust scumming over the small windows of the shack so that they resembled the dusky scales of a snake; smoke curling from the chimney; her eyes going from the brown paper she opened to his eyes, red-rimmed, a bit glazed with embarrassment; the badge on his coat; the pistol grip of the Colt sticking out over his heart like a pump handle; the package of bright cloth between them; and from that great distance he could see that she was only moderately pretty, the faintest touch of querulous lines already about her mouth, merely indeed, the female animal.

"I thought it might make a dress," he said.

Whatever there had been of curiosity in her eyes was replaced by something else he could not define, and all at once her mouth crumpled suddenly as though she would cry; and abruptly she shut the door in his face; although, before he had quite turned away, she opened it again. She looked at him a long moment—the material, the brown paper, and the ribbon crumpled against her waist—while she appeared to gain control of the expression around her mouth which had twisted it toward weeping. "I've got a little coffee on the stove," she said; "you can come in a minute if ye'd like to."

"I would," he said.

She abandoned the doorway, put her package on the table, and went directly to the cupboard for a cup and then to the small cooking range and poured him coffee from an enameled pot. He stepped inside and shut the door behind him.

"Who's come?" the old woman's broken voice asked from another room.

"You rest easy, Aunt Sylvie," the young woman said, as though it were a proper answer. She held the coffee cup in her two hands and didn't quite look him in the face. "Set ye down then," she said.

He sat down at the small table and she put the cup before him. "Won't you have some with me?" he said.

"No," she said, "I don't want none." She sat down across from him and folded her hands upon the table. After a moment she began to stroke the palm of one hand with the fingers of the other. "It's been right nice,

107

the things you brung," she said and gave a little laughing sigh. "County relief won't keep nobody much these days. Maybe a bag of flour now and again and a bar of soap. They seem awful anxious bout folks bein clean. Ye get more soap than ye can use." She gave a motion of her head toward the front rooms. "Course Aunt Sylvie's brother, over to Big Stone Gap, he sends us a dollar or two when he can. It's been right nice, the coffee and all," she said.

He didn't know how to reply. He took a drink of his coffee. She sat across from him rubbing the palm of one hand with the fingers of the other, her neck beginning to turn rosy, until, from one of the front rooms, came a sound as though someone were swinging a door back and forth on a rusty hinge. "Poor youngin," she said, "I got to fetch her," and she left the kitchen to return a moment later with the small child wrapped in a blanket.

"What's the matter with her?" Music asked.

"I'm scared hit's the whoopin cough, poor thing," Merlee said. "I thought she was goan drop off for a while, for she hardly slept at all last night. Poor babe," she said, "poor thing." She rocked the child against her breast while, with slow, puffy eyes, it looked at Music, its thumb in its slightly open mouth, its upper lip and nostrils wet and chapped. When the child began again to cough, Merlee held it tighter as though to brace it against the croupy, rusty-hinge sounds that wracked its body. "Now, now, now," she crooned.

"I use to come down with that a lot," Music said, "and my little brother worse than me. Momma made a poultice for us that helped, and sometimes gave us teaspoons of whiskey and honey she'd heated up. I've laid and watched her make that poultice many a time. I'll make her one."

"That's real kind," Merlee said, rocking the child against her breast; but then suddenly she stopped and sat absolutely still in her chair. "Look here . . . " she said, but her mouth and chin began to crumple, and she had to press her lips together to control them. When she looked him in the face, he saw that she was, after all, only a young girl, hardly grown herself; never mind that she had borne a child, that she was already a widow. Anger smoldered in her eyes, but even the quality of her anger seemed young, untaught. "Look here," she said, "I don't want to be beholden to no mine guard. I don't know what yer after, but ye won't get it!" She began to weep. Like a trick reflection of her, the child she held wept too, with the sound of a braying mule or the cawing of a young crow.

108

It was not at all funny. He had no notion why he was amused. "Excuse me," he said, "but seems like you could wait until I ask you and then tell me no." He got up from the table. "And the youngin's got enough trouble without you makin her cry. She can hardly get her breath."

"I don't want to be beholden to no company goon!" she said and began to rock her daughter again and shush her.

"I need a piece of wool rag, an onion, and some turpentine," Music said.

"I ain't got them," Merlee said.

"All right," Music said, "I'll go to the commissary and get them. I don't expect you got no whiskey, noway."

"No, ner any honey neither," Aunt Sylvie said, and Music looked up to see her standing just outside the threshold of the kitchen, her face all wrinkles and puckers and creases into which he could read any expression whatever, or none. "I'll git yore turpentine," she said, "and as fer onions, ye'll find one or two directly under the cupboard yonder."

"I don't want to be beholden to him," Merlee said, but the old woman, listing carefully from side to side and shuffling her feet, managed to turn herself around and move out of sight. "I'd as lief you'd hush awhile, myself," she said from another room.

While Merlee sat, red-faced and quiet, Music found the onions, peeled the largest one, and chopped it up fine on the sideboard. When the old woman returned, looking up at him from beneath her widow's hump, he could smell her. It was a strong but not unpleasant odor, like the den of an animal. "I recollect a granny woman use to doctor whoopin cough like this when I was a little bit of a gal," the old woman said, "but I disremember how she done it." She held a bottle of turpentine out to him in her warped and palsied hands. "Use hit as liniment fer my rheumatism," she said, "but hit don't hep much."

"Thank you, missus," Music said. "I need a cloth too, big enough to put on her chest and reach up her neck a little."

"Wool, did ye say?" the old woman asked and stood for a moment in thought, her head trembling slightly on her withered neck. "I don't know as to that, now."

"Any good cloth, I guess," Music said, and with a sudden, shameful inspiration, he took up the wine material where Merlee had left it. "This'll do all right," he said.

"No," Merlee said, and then blushing dark red, and in a softer, chastened voice, she said, "I'll find ye somethin."

Music didn't allow himself the slightest smile. "Yes," he said, "and

109

then if you'd get the baby's shirt off and lay her yonder on the table."

When the cloth was brought to him, he dampened it first with turpentine, wrapped the chopped onion in it, and with the heel of his hand brought his weight to bear on the cloth until it was soaked as well with onion juice. He dumped the onion out on the sideboard again. "If you put this in a tight jar, it'll get a little brown and slick and be better yet for your purpose," he said. "Now I need some lard or butter to grease her with. The poultice will burn her skin if you don't keep her greased."

Her round eyes swimming in tears, the child lay upon the kitchen table and looked up at him while, as gently as he could, he covered the silky skin of her chest and neck with lard. Except for the soft cawing of her breathing and one fit of her croupy, baying cough, which was brought on, it seemed, by the light pressure of his fingers, she was quiet and still, as though fascinated at being handled in such a manner by a stranger. He made two slits in the poultice rag with his pocketknife so that a portion of it could fit against her neck and the edges could lie flat across her thin shoulders. "You keep her good and warm, and she ought to breathe a little better before too long. I'll bring back the second part of the medicine this evenin," he said. He nodded to the old woman and then, in a motion almost as deep and formal as a bow, to Merlee. "I thank you for the coffee," he said, and before either of them could say anything at all, he let himself out of the back door into the cold, brilliant sunshine. On the way back to the power plant he scratched the stubble on his face, rubbed his tired eyes, and grinned; it had not gone so badly.

Even the filthy coal town seemed somehow acceptable. Out of the bright blue sky the sun shone on the broken pavement of main street, the commissary, the river, the black, hulking, noisy tipple wreathed in its cloud of coal dust. Hellkatoot, he thought, it's all in what a man gets used to. He was so tired his eyes felt stitched with wire. He felt weak and frail. But he was, he decided, almost happy.

Still, it was a hard mood to keep when he and Regus took a look around Mink Slide, where company shacks were merely two-room shanties with neither electricity nor plumbing, not even so much as a sink, and so poorly constructed there were cracks in the walls big enough for a cat to jump through, at least where they hadn't been patched with flattened-out tin cans and cardboard. As for the people, men, women, and children stood about before them like prisoners before their jailors, the silence so profound one would have thought there was to be an execution in the next moment. Perhaps it was the power of badges and guns that made the people seem to grow deaf, dumb, and blind in their presence.

110

Whatever, no question put to a group drew an answer. Regus had to call a man by his name to lift the spell. *Nawh, Cap'n, ain no white folks been up in dis place. Nawh suh, we ain seen no white man up in Mink Slide, is we? Sho ain, nawh suh.*

The Bear Paw camp at Tip's Creek was another sort of problem. It wasn't Hardcastle property. Bankrupt, derelict, it was not quite a ghost town, but a community of squatters. The Model T truck pecked slowly through town, from one end to the other.

"What the hell we supposed to be looking for?" Music asked.

Regus raised his eyebrows and shrugged. "Somethin that don't look right," he said. He spat out the window. "A car maybe," he said, "some feller without no holes in his britches, two or three people who don't look like they want to see us."

"Hellkatoot," Music said, "nobody wants to see us. How are we supposed to tell the difference?"

"Hit's the difference between mad and scared," Regus said and turned the truck around. "The one might stand his ground and give you the hard eye," he said and winked. "The tuther might play like he didn't notice us a'tall, or maybe he might try to ease outta sight."

"Yeah, well I don't want to catch no unionizer anyway," Music said.

"Yes, you do," Regus said.

"I reckon I don't!" Music said.

"Yes, you do," Regus said.

Music turned to look at him. Behind his grainy eyes, back in the sore, hung-over stations of his brain, anger flared. "Look," he said, "if it would suit you just as well, we'd get along better if you didn't try to tell me what I want."

Regus raised his eyebrows, gave his head a little sideways tilt. "Now and again, Bill Music," he said, "I get the feelin you ain't altogether sweet-natured." At the edge of Regus's mouth there was the unmistakable twitch of humor.

"Not when somebody tries to tell me what I think."

"How else are ye supposed to know?" Regus said, looking straight ahead through the windshield and swapping his quid from one corner of his mouth to the other in order to keep from smiling.

"Christ," Music said and fished out his cigarette papers and tobacco, "do you think we're going to have to find out which one of us can whip the other?"

Regus shook his head sadly. "You *are* bad-tempered, but I'd as lief put

111

that question aside till I tell you a story." He pulled the Model T to the edge of the road, where it chortled and pecked and shook. "If there's unionizers around here and we don't run em off, there's a good chance they'll organize them fools at Hardcastle, and if they do that, then one of these fine days a bunch of men is gonna show up shakin their fists, blowed up full of hot air, askin for a livin wage or some other such nonsense." Regus retarded the spark and throttle on the Model T and spat out the window. "I cain't tell ye what Kenton Hardcastle will do, for I don't know. He may bring in scabs and set you and me to tryin to keep the fool miners from shootin em. He may just put us to evictin any miner connected to the union. He may wash his hands of the whole damned thing and shut Hardcastle Coal Company down and run everbody off; but the one thing he won't do is let a union come in, which means, sure as hell, that some half-starved miner will be tryin to shoot our asses off, or us his'n, somewhere around six times a day." He took a deep breath, sighed a huge sigh, spat out the window again, and then after a moment turned and spat out his quid too, as though it had grown suddenly distasteful. "That there is why you want to catch a unionizer," he said.

For some minutes Music had been holding his head in his hands. "I wonder," he said at long last, "if you get tired of being right all the time."

"Yep," Regus said, "I do." He advanced the spark and throttle, and the engine began to cluck and peck faster, and in the next moment they lurched into the road again. Regus made a sound like laughing. "But while we're a-talkin on it," he said, "any unionizer we'd catch, we'd give over to the high sheriff in Valle Crucis, but them Burnside sons a bitches would likely shoot him; and as to which one of us can whip the other, I can whip you, Bill Music, but it would be a chore." He laughed again. "I'd as lief back down if I could."

"Stop at that shack yonder on the end," Music said. "I need to buy some whiskey."

"I would have thought ye'd had sufficient of that last evenin," Regus said.

"It ain't for me," Music said; "it's for Merlee Taylor's little youngin."

"Ha," Regus said, "do you aim to get her baby drunk? Don't see what good that would do ye, Bill Music."

"The child's sick," Music said, "and liquor's good medicine."

"Ha," Regus said, "sure thing; I seem to recall gettin doctored nearly to death with it last night." He pulled the Model T to the edge of the road. "I've heard it said hit was good for snakebite, and I expect that's true, too, if only a feller could find the snake that was going to bite him and pour it on the poor sucker."

Music did not reply. He got out of the truck, leaving Regus to amuse himself. Out of the tail of his eye he could see him laughing and shaking his head.

Before he had climbed halfway up the embankment to the first row of houses, he looked up to see the one-armed moonshiner standing on his porch, watching him, hat as absolutely horizontal on his head as if he'd checked the brim with a level, sleeve pinned to shoulder, hard, speckled eyes upon him without the least spark of friendship, or humor, or anything else in them.

"Howdy," Music said.

The one-armed man did not speak.

Music topped the embankment and the steps to the man's porch. "I'd like a pint of yer finest," Music said and reached into his pocket for his money.

"Hit's all the same run; doubled and twisted and good as hit gets," the one-armed man said with so little of either pride or conviviality that he might have been reciting the alphabet.

"Well," Music said, "it's good red-eye for sure; it's just that I ain't going to drink this here. I mean to make a whiskey and honey potion for a little baby in Elkin that's got the whooping cough," he said.

Of all the people he had confronted since he'd put on the Hardcastle deputy sheriff badge and the enormous cap-and-ball pistol, the one-armed man was the only one who never seemed to give them a glance, as though he didn't see them at all, or didn't find them worth considering, or maybe saw them absolutely without having to move his somehow impersonal, cold, pebble-colored eyes one iota from Music's face. But all at once Music found the one-armed man looking him up and down, as though mildly curious. "Dwight," he called, without so much as turning his head toward the house behind him, "bring out a pint of my own stuff," and Music was aware of movement behind one of the cloudy windows. "I don't tell no lies, mister," the one-armed man said. "Hit's some I set aside in oak barrels for my use. But I ain't so sure about you. Ye tole me oncet that ye was just a-passin through, and here ye show yerself a company goon. I give ye some advice, a-thinkin you a stranger.

113

I'll give ye better: don't come around my house no more for whiskey, for I'll sell ye none if you do. I misjudged ye oncet," he said. He looked at Music hard, and his expressionless face came very close to gathering into a frown. "Now ye cause me puzzlement again. If you want to buy the hooch I make, I'll sell hit to ye, but send me word by nigger. That way, if 'n I see you down here, I'll know ye've come on that son-of-a-bitchin Hardcastle's business."

"I didn't lie to you, mister," Music said. "I was only passing through." He made a futile gesture with the hand that held the money. "I got caught sleeping in a haystack, and instead of landing in jail, I landed in this job."

The one-armed man made no reply, merely continued looking him in the face until the front door opened and the boy with the strange cowlick sticking up from the crown of his head stepped out with a pint mason jar. He handed the jar to Music and took the twenty cents in return.

"If you have no further business," the one-armed man said, "I'd be pleased if ye'd take yerself off 'n my front porch."

Music wished somehow to explain, wished to say, *Look here now, I'm Bill Music from Shulls Mills, Virginia, electrician by trade and not one of your goddamned company goons.* He wanted to take out the revolver and say, *Look, it's older than me and you put together. What kind of a gun thug would carry a pistol like that?* But no such argument seemed very persuasive, and finally, flushed to the ears, he only nodded and took himself off the man's porch as he had been asked.

On the way back to Elkin, he sat in silence for the first two miles; then he unscrewed the lid of the mason jar and offered it to Regus. Regus shook his head, and Music took a drink and spun the lid back down.

"Thought that was for the little Taylor gal," Regus said.

"Ya know," Music said, "I thought I'd save up a little money and buy a car and have a dollar or two in my pocket when I went back home. Didn't want to come draggin in like a bum after all my big notions, after two years being gone."

"Yeah," Regus said, "a car don't cost so much, leastwise if ye don't mean a new'un."

"I don't know if it's worth it," Music said.

"I couldn't answer as to that," Regus said. "Anyhow, I don't know much about how a feller wants to look when he comes back home, since I either never had one or never left it. Sure," he said, "even when I got

114

married, I reckon I only asked Momma and Daddy to move over a little so's I could bring my young gal in."

"I didn't know you were ever married," Music said.

"Still am, I reckon," Regus said, "leastwise I ain't heard to the contrary."

"Hellkatoot," Music said, looking at Regus's calm, serious face, in which there was, even in that moment, the merest hint of humor. "You're full of surprises. Whatever happened to her?"

Regus sniffed through one nostril and arched his eyebrows. "I don't recall that the subject of my wife ever come up," he said. "But as to yer question, she never did much take to a coal camp. Hit was always as if she was moonin after another sort of place, thinkin on somewhere else; even when ye thought she was happy, you could feel that about her. And one evenin, when I come home outten the drift, she was gone. Youngins an all. Found out later she'd caught a ride with the mail truck into Harlan. You could give the mail carrier a dime and he'd carry ye with him into Harlan from Burdine." He took a deep breath and let it pass wearily through his nose. "When I got to Harlan, I found out at the train depot that her, or some young gal that looked just like her, a-totin two little youngins, had bought a ticket to Cincinnati."

"You go after her to Cincinnati?" Music said.

"No," Regus said, "I thought on it, but the train depot in Harlan was as far as I trailed her." He got out his plug of tobacco and, not bothering with his pocketknife, bit into it, twisting his quid loose as a dog might twist a piece of tendon from a bone. "Cincinnati is a right big town, and I didn't know where in it she might land up, but I reckon I could have found her one day, or another, or the next. I thought on it, but, finally, hit didn't seem the right thing. She never did like livin in a coal camp. I think she liked me well enough, though a man might not ken that sort of thing as well as he thinks. But she never liked the life." Regus turned his head and spat out the window. "I was born in a coal camp myself, so I don't know no better, but she wadn't. She was nine year old when her father, like so many other fools, decided he'd be a coal miner and make big money. She just had poor luck, I guess. She lost her daddy to the mines and her momma to consumption. Although I don't think she ort to have laid her momma's dyin to the coal camp, she seemed to." Regus made a sound like laughing and spat out the window again. "Course Ella Bone wasn't altogether happy about havin grandchildren she couldn't pet and

115

feed and fuss at, but you could hand Momma just about anything and give her time to turn it around and around, and she'd find its good side," he said and laughed. "She's long ago decided that it's a blessing her grandbabies ain't livin in the shadow of some coal tipple, just a-waitin to get old enough to clip a carbide lamp to their caps and go dig coal."

"Do you ever hear from your wife?" Music asked.

"No," Regus said, "not *from* her, but we've heard *of* her. Wasn't long after she left I found out from one of her woman friends in the camp that she had a sister in Cincinnati. And after her husband threatened to kill that poor woman, and after I swore with my hand on her Bible that I wasn't gonna go off and drag her back, the woman told me how to send word to the sister, and I did and said I'd take my wife back if she'd consent to come; but I reckon she'd made up her mind all right, or anyway that's what the sister wrote and told us. I still send money—for the youngins, don't ye know—to the sister, and ever once in a great while she'll send us some word. Momma begged about it until I wrote and asked for pictures of the boys, and two year ago, which I reckon was the last time we heard from Cincinnati, sure enough, we got us a picture of them, all dressed up nice and settin together on a sorta swing that's made to look like a half-moon. Stars hanging down around them. Shoot," Regus said and shook his head and grinned, "they looked real nice, and I expect that picture, which must have come from one of them fancy photographer places, was right dear to pay for."

Music looked out the window of the Model T. Jesus, he thought, Jesus Christ.

Regus laughed. "I expect if you'd been around when Vera ran off—Vera was her name—I would have sent all kinds of letters. Lord knows, many a time I thought of things I wanted to tell her, but hit took me near about all day to write some little ole no-account letter. Vera, though, she could read and write as good as airey schoolteacher you'd want to see. She was just gifted in that direction, I reckon. I was ever a little shy around her because of that. I nearly didn't write her a'tall on that account, but I thought to myself, if she was so good at readin, then she could make out the few things I scratched down well enough. Still, never did tell her about my name though," Regus said and laughed. "I reckon hit's both of us held somethin back, after all."

Jesus Christ, Music thought.

On the left they passed Mink Slide, and around the curve on the right, the Elkin school, where, as always, a ballgame was being played in the schoolyard. Distractedly Music was aware of the loud, woolly-headed boys and the little groups of shy, quiet girls, all in their ragged, hand-me-down clothes, but he did not see which one of them threw the rock that clanged against the side of the truck. He was so startled he nearly dropped the mason jar of liquor. "Christ!" he said.

Regus merely grinned, gave his head a slight jerk to one side, and sucked his teeth as though he were clucking to a mule.

"Even the kids are gunning for us," Music said and went on then to tell Regus how the one-armed man had behaved and what he had said, when twice before he'd been down to buy whiskey wearing both his badge and gun and had had no trouble.

Regus frowned, and, for once, there was no humor at all lurking anywhere in his face. They drove on through town, across the tilted plank bridge over the Switch, and stopped beside the powerhouse, where Regus shut the Model T down, and with a dying shudder it ceased to run. Regus sat looking through the vertical, grimy windshield, his large, chapped hands folded over the steering wheel. "That gal of yours, that Merlee Taylor," he said, still without the slightest trace of humor. "Ye'll have no trouble beatin my time with Vera. Merlee," he said, "she ain't never had nuthin." And then, as though he hadn't at all changed subjects, or as though he were merely finishing a thought he'd had earlier even though the time for it was past, he said, "I think we've got trouble. I suspicioned it at Mink Slide. Niggers ain't quite learned how to lie as good as white folks."

# 10

## THE FIRST SHOT FIRED

USUALLY WHEN HE stretched himself upon the hard little bunk, the noise of the power plant sung him to sleep and nothing disturbed him until Regus came and gave him a nudge to wake him for his shift. Big Cigar or Too Sweet scraping a coal scoop across the cement floor, flinging coal into the furnace, or clanging its iron doors shut, was no more to him than rain on the roof. But this night he could not sleep. Ella Bone had given him a haircut, and his neck was still a little chafed where she had scraped away at it with a razor, and he was wearing a new shirt she had made him which was still stiff with sizing, but his problem was not there. He did not require comfort in order to sleep.

Ella Bone had taken him over like a son, scolded him, fussed over him, sewed and cooked for him, and no doubt prayed over his soul, but it wasn't quite that either that kept him open-eyed, looking at the sooty underside of the corrugated iron roof over his bunk. Still he mulled his account with her: the shingles he had rived out and stacked in the barn to dry, enough to repair the rotting north side of the barn, the roof of the corncrib, and the springhouse; the morning milking he'd taken over from Regus; other chores. Regus was not a farmer, no matter that it was Ella's ambition to make him one. He milked down his shirt cuffs, into his shoe tops, and here and there around the bucket. He tried, did Regus, and he got two-thirds of the milk in the pail, but he made the cow nervous, and she would step around and switch about, and he never got all she had to give. Much of that would turn her dry. He'd showed Regus how to build rabbit gums, and they had set out four of them around the place and had caught a rabbit or two. "Don't they dress out just the prettiest, nicest things," Ella had said, "without no shot in em and all?" He'd found a bee tree, and he was going to get Regus a gum of bees, so that they might have honey. Not that any of that would make up for the way they had taken him in. No, nor was it what kept him awake, although he had mulled it over like an unpaid debt.

Too Sweet haunted the edge of his vision, bending over the belt to the turbine, an oilcan hanging from the end of his slender, limp arm.

But he was thinking about a time when he was seventeen and had hired out to help a man do his haying. He was thinking about the man's daughter, who would come to the fields where they sweated and swung their scythes, carrying two oak buckets of cool spring water with gourd dippers floating in them. A gangly, slue-footed, not quite pretty girl, who, while he drank and watched her over the edge of the dipper, had scooped her hand into one of the buckets and ladled water against her collarbones, which dampened her thin dress from the inside so that it clung to the slope of her breasts. "Whee, hit's a hot one though, ain't it?" she'd said, and as though it made sense or were somehow important, went on in a teasing voice to ask: "Ain't you the one that broke my brother's nose down at the Shulls Mills school some years ago?" "Yes," he'd said. "Ha," she'd said, "ain't nobody err deserved it more." And her father, standing some distance away, long and tall as a scarecrow, his widow's hump bent over the stoning of his scythe, said, "Pass that water on around, gal!"

And was it the next day or the one after when it was making up to rain and her father and the other two hired hands had taken a load of hay on to the barn to make sure of getting in that much, anyway, and left him cutting along the fringe of the woods, that she sneaked up behind him and dashed water on his back and caused him to start and kick his leg out and cut himself? She had laughed at the antic and his clipped curse. The cut across his shin had been shallow, and only the stinging of sweat and chaff made him hoist his britches leg to look. "I never meant you no hurt," she said. "Let me see." "Didn't get me much," he said. "Let me see," she said, but he told her he wasn't hurt, which was nearly true. "I just meant a little prank," she said. "That's all right," he said. "I just come down to see you. Them others won't be back for near a half hour; they're a-pitchin up into the loft."

He had begun to swing his scythe again, sliding his right foot forward

119

as he swung the scythe around to the left, sliding his left foot forward as he swung the scythe back for the next stroke, even his breathing somehow locked into the rhythm. "I expect they won't be back for better than a half hour," she said, and when he made no reply, she said, "You ain't real smart, are ye?"

It wasn't that he hadn't begun to suspect her meaning; he just didn't quite know what to do, or anyway, what to do first. But he was not a total fool and didn't plan to be taken for one. He turned toward her and leaned on the top curve of his blade. "I reckon I ain't the smartest fellow around," he said, blushing to the roots of his hair, "but if you're aimin to give lessons, I'll try to be handy."

"Ha," she said, "you come on into the shade."

When the big, cloud-colored Percheron plodded back down to the edge of the field with the hired hands and her father riding the wagon, he was back at work.

"Son," her father said, giving his head a shake and wrapping the reins around the stanchion, "don't appear you broke a sweat while we was gone."

He feared, unless he could think of a way to prevent it, the man would guess what he'd been up to. "Had a little accident," he said and raised his britches leg to show the folded crease of flesh across his shin, where, since it was so hot perhaps, the blood still oozed. He was thankful that it looked much worse than it was.

"Lord God, son," the man said, "how did ye get yore leg out ahead of you like that? You get on to the house and let the missus look to it."

"It's not so bad," he said. "I'd just as lief work."

"You climb up in this wagon," the man said. "I ain't a-sendin ye home with lockjaw."

He did as he was told, but as the man reined the big horse around, Music said, "It's not deep and it bled out clean. I just stumbled at the wrong time, is all."

"Well," the man said, "I'm shamed for thinkin you lazy. Hit's nearly time to quit anyhow. You clean it up and get a clean rag around it and get Mrs. Glenn to give you a glass of lemonade."

So at the house he got a clean rag from Mrs. Glenn and washed and dressed the cut himself in order not to give himself away, and sat on the porch in the shade and drank a glass of lemonade, the girl paying no more attention to him than if he were a barn cat.

In a little it began to rain and the others came in. Mr. Glenn stood on

120

the porch and watched it come down. "Well, son," he said, "maybe we'll cut no more tomorrow, but if hit dries off, will ye be able to work the day following?"

"Yes," he said.

"Hit must be four mile to yer daddy's place; I expect I'd better ride ye home in the wagon."

"No need," he said, "I didn't cut myself deep," and over the man's protests, he hooked his scythe over his shoulder and walked, and walked back that night as he had told the girl he might, and she met him in the barn. And there had been a dozen such nights over the summer, until she found herself a serious beau, which he was not, and threw him over. So.

He had puzzled more than once about how it was that Thelma Glenn and her brother, Russell, had both, in their separate ways, blooded him. There had been a time before Russell had up and left home, back when they were twelve and thirteen, he had fought the boy nearly every day, although he had never understood why Russell seemed to think that was necessary. He'd clearly whipped the Glenn boy only once, the last time; and even so, Russell was having the best of that fight too until he pulled a cheap pocketknife from somewhere and stabbed Music in the face with it. He had no notion what made Russell do it and him winning; he would never have thought to do the same. The blade had gone through his upper lip and wedged between his canine tooth and the front one next to it and broken off. But it was like getting a shot of pure power, for he had bucked the bigger boy off his chest in a fury and broken his nose and had to be dragged off him, still fighting. Both of them had been delivered up to an ancient country doctor, each as bloody as the other, but Russell had been easier to fix. The point of the cheap knife had broken off even with Music's gum and could not be drawn out, and so had to be pushed on through and taken out the back side, and his lip had to be stitched inside and out. Perhaps, he thought, Russell had known he would later deflower his sister. But no, that could not be possible, and anyway it had been the other way around. Someone had been with the sister long before he had.

Lord God, the warm, sweet center of her had taken hold of him like a hand, and for years after, thoughts of her would come suddenly upon him and make him burn.

And then there had been that redheaded woman in Chicago whose husband was off on the lakes, being a merchant marine. She was a wild one, wanting it done to her every which way while she yelled and took on and beat him with her fists. He never did get used to her and her odd ways; she would not take off her clothes, not any of them, or allow him to take off his, preferring to have them pulled and stretched aside. So.

Too Sweet, a white rag tied around his brow, swung the grating furnace doors open and shoveled in the coal, the scoop scraping the cement and swishing when the coal left it for the glowing innards of the furnace.

The child had gotten better. Whether through his doctoring or not, he couldn't say, but her fever had gone and her breathing had grown easier. He thought the poultice had loosened the congestion in her chest, and there was no doubt that the whiskey and honey had helped her sleep, or that she liked it, he thought, for she would take all she was given without the smallest wince or shudder. But she had lost her shyness of him too, which unmanned him.

Often now, when he came to visit, she would crawl to him and catch his britches leg in her tiny fists and pull herself up to stand at his knee, where she seemed to study him with her round, solemn eyes. "Miss Anna Mae Taylor," he would say, "and how are you?" But if she could speak, she would not do so. She would merely study him owlishly, swaying at his knee until she lost her balance completely and sat down with a thump. He knew nothing about babies, never having been around any, and he didn't know exactly what the child required of him. In fact, he was no better off with her mother. Nothing in his experience seemed to serve him. As the baby had grown less shy of him, Merlee had moved in the opposite direction. She was no longer harsh and insulting, but now and again she grew unaccountably quiet or seemed embarrassed for reasons he couldn't make out. He thought of himself as a man of some experience. He was not a virgin, after all. But when he looked for what he knew about women, nothing of value surfaced. He'd gone to a whorehouse once in Chicago. Would have gone more if he'd had the money. Still, but for that, the women he'd had anything to do with seemed to him merely to have come into season. Him being more or less handy at the time.

He swung his feet off the bunk and sat up, rubbed his face, rubbed the back of his neck. "Hellkatoot," he said. He got out his tobacco and papers and rolled himself a cigarette. "Hey, Too Sweet," he said, "what time do you make it to be?"

"I knows when de little hand's on five and de big hand's straight up, I got to blow de whistle," Too Sweet said. "An I knows I'm here till I see dat big nigger comin in de mawnin."

122

"All right," Music said, "where are the hands pointing?"

Too Sweet scratched his head and looked at the power plant clock Music could not see. "De little hand's nigh on to ten, and de big hand don lak much a' bein in de same spot," he said. "How come you ain sleepin, cap'n?"

"Can't quit thinking about one thing or another," Music said.

Too Sweet removed the rag from his brow, mopped his face with it, and tucked it in his hip pocket. He shook his head. "Lawd, I'd be a two-hundred-pound nigger, won't fur too little sleep and too much frogjaw," he said and laughed. "Ain nuthin but lyin awake with frogjaw keeps me so light; burns de meat plum off 'n mah bones."

Music grinned through the smoke of his cigarette.

"Yassuh, dat sweet hole, dat dark well—frogjaw'll melt a man down to mah size," Too Sweet said.

Music laughed. "I've been wondering," he said, "how you ever got a name like Too Sweet."

"You'ze zactly right," Too Sweet said, "thas the fust thing my momma say bout me the day I was bawn. Somebody come in de cabin and ask, 'Ida, how's dat baby?' and Momma say, 'Oh, he's jest too sweet.' Onliest name I ever had. Don't see no need to change it. Haw!" he said, "Won't fur de womens keepin me worn down so, ole Big Cigar Green hissef would run and hide when I come down de road. Haw."

Both Music and Too Sweet jumped when the door opened and Regus came in. "Never known you to be so purely anxious to get out on the job," he said.

"Wasn't sleepy," Music said.

"Tell me that when ye see me at two this mornin," Regus said. He took the watch from his watch pocket, gave it to Music, and slipped out of his jumper. The .38 rode with walnut and blued authority high up on his ribs beneath his armpit. Music himself slept with his coat on, wanting no one to get a good enough look at the cap-and-ball pistol to be able to tell what it was. "Quiet as hell out there," Regus said, "but I feel somethin. Somethin, by God, ain't right."

Music chuckled and slipped Regus's watch into his pocket. "What did you feel the night you caught that last unionizer in your haystack?"

"Ha," Regus said, "disappointment! I was a-lookin fer coon."

"I thought you told me Hardcastle wasn't big enough to draw any goddamned unionizers. The day I hired on, you told me some such thing, I remember it," Music said.

"Yeah, well . . . " Regus said and sat down on the bunk. He rubbed

123

the back of his neck, took a huge breath, and let it out. Ella had given him a haircut too, and his neck looked skinned and his ears stuck out. He flopped back on the bunk. "Yeah, maybe," he said and sighed. He looked thoughtfully at the ceiling a moment. "Yeah, I guess," he said. He knitted his fingers behind his head. "I'm tired, someway," he said. "When ye come around at two, try yer best to be late, will ye, Bill Music? My butt fits this sack just fine, even if yourn don't."

"Sure," Music said, "I'll be late just like Too Sweet won't blow me clean outta that bunk with that damned five o'clock steam whistle."

"Ha," Regus said.

Music let himself out and shut the door upon the noise of the power plant. On his right across the railroad track and siding, the hulking, black tipple loomed against the far greater mass of the mountain. A single light burned from under the roof of the tipple, two more along the conveyor, and another up the mountain at the drift mouth. Above the drift mouth the dark mountain reared against the stars, and somehow its great silence seemed to diminish and subdue the noise of the power plant behind him and even the sound of the river and the dim and occasional noise from the company shacks across the road; for the silence of the mountain was huge and not really silence at all, but an ancient and abiding sound that a man merely took for silence. A rushing. A sighing. A roar. He had no word for it. Sure, he thought, shoving his hands in his pockets and starting out toward the commissary, if Regus had been spooked by such as that, which he wasn't, then he would have listened to him. When he was prowling about in the middle of the night, that sort of quiet bothered him too, if only because he did not like the sounds he made over against it, the small, stealthy sounds of a man sneaking about where he didn't belong.

He decided he'd go look in on Merlee, then decided he wouldn't. He would walk down to Mink Slide and take a look around. If he went slowly, he could kill an hour of his four-hour shift with that. Maybe he'd even wander down to the Bear Paw. He crossed the river and came up by the commissary. There was no one abroad. Light from deep inside the commissary, back by the candy case, shone through the greenish glass of the front windows and out upon the empty gallery. It made the inside of the commissary look vaguely underwater, like the inside of a fishbowl. Hell, he thought, hellkatoot anyway—maybe she'd be up. Maybe she'd give him a cup of coffee. Before he could think better of it, he crossed the road and mounted the rocky path up to the first row of company houses. What if he knocked upon her door, and when she opened it, he bowed

124

and said, "Pardon, ma'am, Bill Music from the state of Virginia has come to seek the pleasure of your company"? Would she laugh? He had never seen her laugh, and it came to him that if he could see her laugh, he might be able to tell something about her, something he otherwise wouldn't know. He might even be able to discover, finally, his own feelings in this matter.

Merlee Taylor's shack, with the roof and floor of the small front porch collapsed and askew, seemed to have a light burning only in the kitchen. Good, he thought. Perhaps the old woman and the child were asleep. He looked in the window as he came around the side of the house. The rocking chair by the grate was empty, although a fire still burned—the nearly flameless, joyless fire of coal—and there was no one upon the ragged, broken couch, but faint sounds he could not identify came from the kitchen. He went around to the back to look in that window but discovered someone had hung a blanket over it and he could see nothing. He stood for a moment, undecided. Perhaps the little girl was sick again. Perhaps the old woman was up with her rheumatism. He went back around the house, and with his cheek pressed to the rough wood to one side of the window, he found that he could see a portion of the tiny kitchen through the connecting door. He could see half a galvanized tub, the wet sleekness of her thigh, the sharpness of her hipbone, her uptilted breast, and, when she turned away, the vulnerable dimples just above the swell of her buttocks. He yanked his cheek away from the house as if it had burned him. "You son of a bitch," he said, "you goddamned Peeping Tom." But his feet would not take him away. They grew into the ground like roots, and for twenty minutes he watched her.

Even after she had bathed and dried herself and pulled a ragged cotton slip over her head, he watched. Watched her drag the tub to the back door and open it and pour the water out so that it drained away under the house. Watched her step out of sight into the dark—his dark—where he could not see her anymore but where the sounds of her hanging the galvanized tub on the nail beside the door wallowed in the air around him. He watched her enter again, add coal to the fire, turn off the light in the kitchen, and come through the front room again in the dim wavering light of the fire upon the grate where she might have been able to look out the window and see his fool's face looking in, the inside and outside dark being, at last, nearly equal. And still he watched, even after she had entered one of the two small sleeping rooms and there was nothing more to see except the rough, bare floor and bleak furniture.

125

Nor was he exactly sure when he had quit the side of her house; he merely found himself between the depot and the school, hands in his coat pockets, head hung, feet moving south, thinking strange and disturbing thoughts. He had got beyond cursing himself for a Peeping Tom. Hell, that was what he was paid for. Fact was, he had been looking in windows for some time. Fact was, it suited him to do so. He'd seen nothing that was worth three dollars a day to Kenton Hardcastle, but he looked; and whether he watched a meeting of the Holy Rollers, a weary man slumped over a plate of biscuits and bulldog gravy, or Merlee Taylor taking a bath, he watched for purposes of his own. Hands shoved in his pockets, head bowed, he paused before the empty lot between the depot and the schoolhouse. It was rife with long grasses and dead weeds and cluttered with timbers for the mine. Somewhere an out-of-season cricket trilled, a crystal sound as if the creature were made of glass. Fact was, he spied on folks in order to get some clue as to what people did, as if he no longer knew, as if he were no longer one of them himself.

It seemed to him that his present mood was somehow unworthy and childish, but he couldn't shake it off. He had lost some proper sense of himself. How the hell did a man know who he was without knowing what he did or who he loved? He'd lost all command of such things, left them, somehow, all along his back trail since the day he'd struck out from Virginia.

He suspected he had lost a good deal more than money when those fellows had robbed him on Maxwell Street in Chicago. Yes, and before that, when the manager of the Embassy Hotel had talked him into paying three months' rent in advance in order to get a cheaper rate, and he had given the manager three months' rent one Monday morning and had come home Wednesday to find the hotel locked and barred and two uniformed policemen standing by to keep anyone from breaking in. He'd had an awful time even getting in to claim the few clothes he owned. That manager fellow had gypped nearly twenty people—old people, some of them—before he skipped out; gypped some folks bad if only because they had been able to pay six months' rent in advance for an even cheaper rate. Oh, there had been a bunch of suckers out on the street when the hotel was taken over by its creditors. But he'd washed dishes in an eatery; got pick-up work at the freight yards, loading and unloading cars at one, two, and three o'clock in the morning; and he'd got his diploma from Coin Electric; yes, and a job as a lineman. He'd made enough money to eat regularly, to buy himself a suit, to go to the picture show now and again, to go to a whorehouse. And who was he then? And when his partner had pulled the wrong fuse jacks and he'd gotten into twenty-three hundred volts and shook hands with the devil, who then? And when he'd gotten himself back on the street and could find no job, who stole clothes off clotheslines, stole food, ate from garbage cans with stray dogs and cats, carried the jarring ride of freight cars around in his bones for weeks at a time? And if he dragged up at this very moment and started back to Virginia, who would he be taking home? Unmanly as the mood was, he could not shake it, could taste it in his mouth like ashes.

The cricket, somewhere under the timbers in the vacant lot, made its crystal and intermittent trill, and on an impulse he was never to understand, he drew the Walker Colt from his shoulder holster, thumbed back the hammer, and took aim at the first target that caught his eye: the yellow light over the depot's empty platform. The pistol roared. A long tongue of flame leapt from the muzzle, and a nimbus of smoke and flame flared from the cylinder. The yellow light on the platform glowed untouched. He cocked the pistol again. He could imagine people in the company houses sitting bolt upright in their beds; he could imagine Regus snatching for his coat and rolling out of his bunk; Too Sweet immobile over his coal shovel, his eyes as white as porcelain knobs. He held the pistol with both hands, locked his elbows, and fired. The pistol roared. Smoke and flame fanned out in three directions. The yellow light stayed exactly where it was, but the cricket shut up. "Hot damn," Music said. He left the hammer resting on the nipple of the exploded chamber. Acrid, sulfurous smoke hung in a cloud around him. "Hot damn," he said, and feeling inexplicably better, he holstered the blackened, stinking pistol. If anyone asked, he'd say there had been someone walking the railroad track into town, and when he'd commanded him to stop where he was, why, the fellow had run away instead. "Decided I'd stir the gravel under his feet a little and help him on his way," Music would tell them. If Regus asked, he didn't know what he'd say. He started back into town; perhaps he'd think of something. He'd say he had taken some kind of fit. He'd say he'd seen Merlee Taylor taking a bath, and, just naturally, he had gone down to the depot and tried to shoot out the light. If Regus didn't want to believe that, then to hell with him, for it was as good an explanation as he was going to get.

As he passed the depot again, he could see a long, splintered gouge in the wooden ceiling over the platform; it wasn't more than three inches to the right of the light bulb. Damned good shot, he thought, for fifty or

127

sixty yards. He didn't know where the other .44 ball had gone and didn't care. There were faces in a few of the windows along the first row of company houses, but only one front door was open. A barefooted man in a union suit stood in it. He looked at Music and then turned his head owlishly to look up and down the street. "It's all right," Music shouted, "just some goddamned stranger, and I run the sucker off." The man backed up a step, took one more quick look up and down the street, and closed the door. Any moment Music expected to see Regus round the corner by the commissary, but Regus didn't show. And when he himself got to the edge of the gallery and stuck his head around to look down toward the power plant, the road was empty, merely a stretch of potholes and ruts, faintly polished with moonlight.

Music snorted softly through his nose. The reports of the Walker Colt had sounded to him like claps of thunder—hell, louder, like sticks of dynamite going off, one after the other. But Regus Patoff Bone was nowhere in sight.

He went on down to the power plant and opened the door upon the whir of wheel and belt and the deep hum of the turbine. Regus lay on the bunk, one arm flung up over his face, sunk into sleep like a stone dropped in a well. Too Sweet was busily rubbing beeswax into the leather belt to the turbine.

"You didn't hear anything?" Music asked.

"Nosuh . . . " Too Sweet scratched his head. "Yassuh, I thought I did, but didn't seem lak no business of mine if somethin want to go boom."

"Stranger wandered into town," Music said. He patted the Walker Colt under his coat. "I just helped him leave."

Too Sweet seemed to find nothing to say to that; the focus of his eyes—alarmed, thoughtful, furtive—shifted to one side of Music, to a section of the cement floor midway between them, to his can of beeswax.

"Just didn't want to wake up ole Regus there," Music said. "He's not fit to live with if he don't get his sleep." He let himself out and shut the door behind him again.

He was almost to Mink Slide before he realized he was walking like a man who actually had somewhere to go. That was the trouble with the job. There was nothing in particular to do, no place in particular to be. It made him nervous, gave him the willies, made the hair on his neck rise. No wonder he had taken a fit. Even without Merlee Taylor, he would have probably acted a fool sooner or later. He wondered: had that son of a bitch who had shot her husband just taken some sort of crazy fit? He wasn't so sure anymore. If you put a man on such a job and gave him a gun, was the silly bastard just going to use it sometime, whether it made any sense or not? Mercy, he thought. Jesus Christ. He was going to have to be careful. Watch for signs of craziness, and no matter how much he owed Regus or Ella, if he caught himself at any more funny business, he was going to have to drag up. Six months or so of riving out shingles and boards, six months of using a crosscut saw, of riding a sledge loaded with oak off Howard's Knob, of looking across some mule's ass at a furrow, would sweat all the craziness out of him, and maybe Chicago and a bunch of other places too, and he'd get right with himself. The thought comforted him a little, and casually, like a man taking a stroll, he went on toward Mink Slide.

But he didn't get far. He was no more than twenty yards up into the hollow from the pike before first one nigger's dog and then another began to bark and yap. Perhaps they heard him, but since such breeze as there was seemed to be at his back, they could as well have smelled him. Spent black powder was strong stuff, and the Walker Colt, warmed in the space under his coat, stunk like a fart in a paper sack.

It didn't matter, he thought; what the hell was there to see in Mink Slide? He went back down to the pike and walked a half mile or so toward the Bear Paw mine and then turned back toward Elkin again. It wasn't until a little past midnight that he did see something. He was standing under the shed roof of the old movie house when he saw it. A shadow moving behind one of the company houses on the second row. At first he thought it was some miner who had decided to use his outhouse rather than a chamber pot, but then, two houses up, he saw a second man come slinking down a path to another of the company shacks. He was still puzzling over that when he heard a third, or at least gravel being scuffed somewhere off to his right; whoever, or whatever, made the noise never came in sight. Music neither spoke nor stirred until, at last, coming down the mountain behind Bydee Flann's shack, he saw yet another man. The little preacher himself, to judge by his size, disappeared behind the shack with the simple wooden cross fixed to the porch roof, and he never came out.

For at least half an hour Music did not move, but he didn't see or hear anyone else abroad in the night. At last he let his back slide down the wall behind him until he was squatting. His hands were sweating. He had

129

difficulty rolling a cigarette, but he got it made and lit it. All right, he decided, at last, he would tell Regus what he'd seen. Right or wrong, he owed him. If he could do it without doing anyone harm, he'd stick it out until Friday, which was payday, but not beyond. He was no company goon. He'd read Ella Bone half the Bible if she wanted. Perhaps he'd cut the bee tree and at least rob it for them. Likely they wouldn't be able to deal with a gum of bees even if he didn't fuck up and drown half of them in their own honey, even if he could find the queen and get her in the new gum. He felt bad about it. He felt sorry, but he'd be damned if he was going to wind up pushing a bunch of half-starved miners around at the point of a gun. He'd have to tell it to Regus just that way.

# 11

## THE SECOND SHOT FIRED

BUT AT TWO o'clock he nudged Regus awake without making any mention of the men he'd seen slipping into company housing. Ten minutes later he was lying on his back, staring at the ceiling when Regus, still more asleep than awake, came back through the powerhouse door and stood looking down at him. "Gimme my watch," Regus said. Music handed it over, and Regus rubbed his muggy face and shook his head. "Hit don't make any sense," he said, turning away; "I'm wandering around outside with my eyes shut and you're a-layin in here with yourn wide open." He rubbed the back of his neck, shook himself all over like a wet dog, and went out of the door again.

Music was awake when Too Sweet blew the five o'clock whistle, and a half an hour later, when Tom Harmon came in to check all the dials and pressure gauges and, finding everything in order, got after Too Sweet for not keeping the place swept up enough. "You got to keep on a nigger," he'd told Music weeks before. "If you come in one mornin and fail to find somethin wrong, then the next mornin, they'll be somethin fucked up for certain; and if you don't say nuthin, then the next mornin they'll be two things fucked up." He'd given Music a friendly wink and grin. "If you want to work a nigger, you better find somethin wrong whether there is or there ain't."

The morning was misty and cold. Low clouds the color of smoke hid the mountaintops when Bert Maloney drove up at quarter to six and

131

parked. At that moment Music was pissing against the far corner of the powerhouse where men, like dogs, had marked the spot for so long the corrugated iron was rusting away. Maloney, always in a hurry, didn't seem to notice him. Maloney entered the powerhouse and almost at once came out again with a clipboard in his hand and Harmon behind him.

"Get that big buck on it," Maloney was saying. "Hell, I got a slate fall last evenin and track fucked up, and that's where my goddamned work crew's gonna be; you can put Big Cigar and Too Sweet both on it, but don't ast me to get you no coal in here today."

"If I do that," Harmon said, "who's gonna keep the boiler stoked?"

Maloney turned toward the other man. His eyes level with Harmon's chin, his voice womanishly high but with a hardness in it like struck steel, he said, "*You* are going to keep the boiler fired, goddammit! *You* are! And if I had the time, I'd come and watch you, just to see what you look like when you ain't sittin on yer ass."

Tom Harmon took a step backwards and raised his palms as though to hold Maloney back. "Okay, okay," he said, "Christ, Bert . . . " but the mine foreman had already started down the siding toward the tipple, where half a dozen men had collected.

Harmon turned to Music. "Now, does that seem right to you?" he asked. "Christ, all I wanted was some coal in here. I can't generate power without I got some shittin coal." Harmon went back inside the powerhouse. "You can set down that lunch pail, nigger, cause you ain't goin nowhere," Music heard him say.

Lean, in blackened work clothes, a few men were coming across the bridge like so many scarecrows slouching in from winter gardens. Up by the drift mouth, just beneath the belly of the clouds, a mine mule brayed.

Music stood by the corner of the powerhouse, his hands in his pockets, his arms pressed against his sides, his teeth close to chattering. But he was otherwise occupied and aware of being cold only in the most distant sort of way. He felt guilty, as if he were somehow personally responsible for Switch County and Hardcastle Coal Company, responsible even for the sulfurous stink of coal in the air and the chilly morning, gauzy with mist. Hell, he thought, hellkatoot, ain't none of this my lookout. *Regus*, he would say, *I can't make peace with it. I can't carry around this five-pound, god-awful pistol—folks expectin me to shoot somebody with it every minute. I'm goin on home.* And to Ella, who would be standing by, her head bent deferentially to one side, her gaze askew toward his shoe tops: *Ma'am, I appreciate you takin me in. I'm much obliged, for I've never been better treated, and I* . . . His jaw went suddenly rigid. He had twenty-two dollars in a tobacco sack hidden under the tick she had filled with hay for him. He'd leave fifteen dollars where Ella could find it. He'd put five dollars in an envelope and address it to Merlee Taylor, and he'd get his ass down the road. That would be as shameful as trying to explain himself. More. But at least he wouldn't have to listen to himself talk.

His teeth rattled for a second or two. Big Cigar Green was coming across the tilted bridge over the river. He was pitch-black, but not with coal dust; he was purple where the lining of his lips showed and where his arms bore old scars. He did not appear to be cold, even in the sleeveless shirt he wore. Behind him, rattling the planks on the far edge of the bridge, the Burnsides' Model A was coming. Cawood was behind the wheel. He blew the horn, but Big Cigar did not alter his pace even though the right front fender all but brushed him as he stepped from the bridge to the cinder and gumbo road. As the Model A passed him, Big Cigar touched his cap as though in answer to a pleasantry, as though someone in the car had said, "Good morning to you, sir."

Where the hell was Regus, Music wondered. He wanted to be on his way. He wanted to take the Walker Colt off and pick up his paper sack. It would have two extra shirts and a second pair of pants in it now, and he'd have two dollars and some change in his pocket. That was plenty. Hell, that was way more than enough. He could go halfway around the world on that.

Without really quite seeing them, he was aware of Grady standing with one foot on the running board of the Model A, lighting the stump of his cigar, and Cawood coming toward him, the straw skimmer sitting on the back of his head. But he was thinking of swinging up on a freight car, light as thistledown without the bulky pistol. No badge pinned on his shirt to tap against his chest like an accusing finger, to draw the eyes of everyone he met as if it were a printed sign saying: goon, gun thug, sworn son of a bitch. Just the idea of being free of those things raised his spirits and seemed to sweeten the air he breathed. He could see himself broke, humbled, but going home, walking the county road, say, from Shulls Mills to his father's farm, where anyone he might meet stood a chance of being a friend, or at least not an enemy. It made his eyes wet just to think of it.

"What?" he asked, for Cawood had said something or other.

133

"How long you been gettin in her britches? I said. Shit, boy, has it made you deaf?"

"What?" Music said, seeing, at last, Cawood's grinning face leaning close.

"I don't doubt a minute that's fine poozle," he said and laughed, "but what I hear is that it's terrible expensive. Now, I can put you onto a little nigger gal, ain't but thirteen, will fuck yer ears off fer a dime. Won't cost you no ten pounds of pinto beans ner five yards of dress material ever time you want to dunk yer wick."

For a moment Music studied Cawood's face. Except for the ageless glint of cruelty deep in the eyes, the face was nearly boyish, the nose pug, the cheeks round, the eyebrows sparse and colorless over heavy bones; and, oddly, what there was in Music of forbearance and good sense abdicated without warning. He took his hands out of his pockets slowly, or so it seemed to him; but Cawood was still leaning conspiratorially close when he knocked him out from under his straw skimmer: He tried to hit him again as he was falling but missed, the violence of his swing causing him to fall as well. "Whoa, Bill, goddammit!" he heard Regus say behind him and for a second felt a hand grab at his shoulder and slip away. Then he was on the ground with Cawood, both of them thrashing and grappling at each other. A blow on his ear made it ring and another chafed his forehead just above his eyebrow, but he had landed a wild, vicious blow of his own into Cawood's face and another upon his neck. Then Regus's boots, doing a kind of jig, got in the way between them, trampling both of them indiscriminately. "Whoa, shitfire," Regus was shouting, "you boys just let me git goddamn whoa the Sam Hill wait a fuckin no pistols you . . . " and then the boots flew up and away; and on the other side, Cawood, with bloody teeth and chin, was rising; and indeed Music could see the barrel of a pistol coming up like the sun over a mountain to shine on him; and there was nothing to do but roll on his shoulder right at Cawood in order to get in the lee of the muzzle. At the same time the explosion slapped a high-pitched ringing into his ears and seared the underside of his right thigh, he felt Cawood go over backwards again. He was trying to draw his own pistol, but the Walker Colt came out of the shoulder holster as slowly as if it were a three-foot piece of pipe, so there was no time left to cock it, and he merely brought it down across Cawood's skull exactly as he would have swung a length of pipe.

Cawood quit thrashing, and Music rolled up on the left cheek of his butt, since the bottom of his right thigh felt as though a hot iron had been laid across it. It made him breathe through his clenched teeth. "You stupid son of a bitch," he told Cawood through his teeth.

"I don't think he can hear you," Regus said.

Music turned toward the sound of the voice, trying to keep his right thigh off the ground. Regus had fallen some feet away and had his pistol drawn too. It took Music a moment to realize that it was pointed at Grady, who apparently hadn't moved at all. He still had one foot on the running board of the Model A. He was smoking his cigar thoughtfully and looking at them, looking with particular interest at the ancient Walker Colt, which, in the next moment, Music hid away in its shoulder holster as if it were something obscene and shameful.

"Are you all right?" Regus asked.

"I don't know," Music said. "I think I'm shot." For the first time he inspected his leg and the scorched holes in his pants; he didn't seem to be very bloody.

"Did you kill him?" Regus asked.

"I don't know," Music said, and without much preference one way or the other, looked to see. Cawood was breathing like a sleeping dog having a dream, his chest rising and falling irregularly and his nostrils fluttering. "Nawh, he's alive," Music said and began to make an effort to get up.

"Hold on," Regus said softly, "you're a smaller target settin down." Gently Regus flipped the barrel of his pistol up and down toward Grady. "What about you?" he said in a much louder voice. "You aimin to get into this?"

Grady did not speak a word; he merely wagged his head from side to side.

"Well," Regus said, "I don't mind callin it quits," and he got to his feet.

Music got up too and found that his right leg could bear his weight; there was merely a band of pain around it as though he'd backed into a hot stove. Out of the corner of his eye he could see Bert Maloney coming back down the railroad siding. But no one else moved. The men down by the tipple, the stragglers Maloney passed along the siding, Tom Harmon, Too Sweet, and Big Cigar Green, who, sometime or other, had appeared in the powerhouse door—all of them seemed to have taken root where they stood with their eyes locked open as though they could not blink. Only Bert Maloney was in motion and shouting: "Now what in tarnation was that all about?"

135

Music felt unable to answer. He didn't think he knew what it was all about. It had happened so fast, he felt he'd gotten there a little late and missed it himself. While he was puzzling over what to say, Regus spoke up.

"Aww, Cawood lyin yonder and Music had themselves a little misunderstanding," he said.

Bert Maloney came up, red-faced and puffing. "Who fired that fuckin shot?" he said.

Regus tipped his head toward Cawood.

Maloney considered Cawood a moment and then Regus, whose pistol was still pointed in Grady's general direction. "What about it?" Maloney said. "Are ye just about all done or what?"

Regus took one last look at Grady and holstered his pistol. "Sure," he said, "I never did quite git a leg in it noway."

"Here I got a contract for a little lump coal, and all kinds of hell comes along to devil me—fuckin slate fall, fuckin track fucked up." Bert Maloney withdrew a small, blunt pistol from behind his clipboard and dropped it in his pocket like loose change. He glanced at Music and then at Cawood, lying on his back, his arms and legs awkwardly misaligned as though he'd fallen from the sky, and a fierce red ridge beginning to swell from the middle of his forehead down the center of his skull as though he were a young rooster beginning to grow a comb. "Well, is anybody dead or dyin?" he asked.

"Bill Music is shot in the ham, I think," Regus said, "but he's standin. Cawood there, I don't know . . . " Regus shook his head and ran his finger back and forth under his nose. "If his skull ain't thin, he'll make it all right, I guess." Regus raised his eyebrows and looked at Grady, who had come to stand with them, his long, horse face regarding Cawood soberly. At last Grady's eyes and Regus's met. "But any man that pulls his gun," Regus said, "it seems to me it's his own lookout what happens to him by way of harm."

"That's right," Grady said in so dry and flat a voice Music realized suddenly that, of the five of them, Grady was the only one who hadn't had a pistol in his hand.

"Well," Maloney said, "you boys is some kind of half-assed law, and I reckon I don't give a hoot whether you want to call in the sheriff, arrest each other, or shoot each other. Whichever. Long as ye settle it and get to the business of keepin some bastard union off my back so's I can dig a little coal." He turned his head and spat. "I do think you ort to drag that idiot out of the road though, fore somebody runs his ass over." He looked at each of them in turn, spat again, and left them to go back toward the tipple and the men he'd left standing there. "You boys got so much money you can stand around and gawk!" he shouted to them.

"Well," Regus said to Grady, "you want to take an arm and a leg?"

Grady stooped and took hold of an ankle and a wrist, and Regus did the same, and they began to carry Cawood toward the powerhouse. Music collected Cawood's pearl-handled pistol and his hat and followed, limping more than was necessary in the hopes that people would think \the damages on both sides were nearly equal. Regus and Grady stopped beside the bunk, and Regus considered the situation. Cawood's head was hanging very low. "We're fixin to break his neck," Regus said. "Set him down and less us git him by the shoulders and feet."

When they got him on the bunk, Music limped over and laid the pistol and hat on his chest as if they were some sort of offering, lilies on the bosom of a corpse.

Regus looked at the clock. "Well," he said, "Bill Music, me and you is workin overtime. See you fellers in the mornin," he said cheerfully. He nodded to Grady and even to Cawood, who, with his eyes rolled up into his head so only slits of white showed and blood spattered upon his chin and chest, didn't look good. His lips were a deep shade of blue, but he was still breathing. All at once Music realized that Regus was letting himself out the door, and feeling foolish and vulnerable and almost forgetting to limp, he followed.

It was painful to sit on the truck seat, and Music propped himself on his left buttock, bracing one hand on the seat beside him and the other against the door. "Hellkatoot," he said after they had ridden across the bridge in silence.

Regus merely grunted and shook his head, staring with a kind of amazed stupefaction through the windshield.

"Where did you come from anyway?" Music said.

"I came down the railroad track," Regus said. He turned right at the commissary, grunted, and shook his head again. "How come you to crawl that big, ignorant sucker, Bill?"

Music thought about it, but Regus frowned, took a hand off the wheel, and waved the question away. "Hell," he said and gave a sudden snort of laughter. "Hell, hit don't matter. Ain't none of my business noway." Regus squeezed his eyes shut. "Ooowee, but you sure did swarm him," he said and laughed weakly. "I expect we ort to run you by the doctor, though. Are ye bad hurt?"

"No," Music said, "it's a little sore, but it's eased off some and don't seem to be bleedin much. I guess he nearly missed me."

"Momma's pretty good at doctorin," Regus said. "We'll let her take a look-see. If it's past her power, we'll go on to the doctor. I don't guess you're a-carryin the slug?"

"Nope," Music said, "there's two holes in my britches."

They said no more until they pulled up before the house, and Music was able to relax after the Model T had jounced along the washed-out wagon road. "You know," Music said, "I'd just as soon look after this myself, now that I think about it. I ain't got any underwear, and it's in a sorta unhandy place for your momma to doctor."

"Ha," Regus said. He got out of the truck and slammed the door. "I bleve it's more unhandy fer you, Bill Music. Hit's a little behind ye, son."

Music got out of the truck and tested the leg gingerly. The back of his pants were a bit wet and sticky, but not bad, and the wound, whatever its extent, was sore, but he could walk without a limp if he concentrated. "If I could have that piece of a shaving mirror," Music said, "I could see to it myself."

They mounted the steps to the open dogtrot, and Regus cocked his head to make some remark, but the kitchen door opened and Ella appeared. "I don't know what's throwed ye so late," she said, "but come in and eat and do yer chores after, fer hit'll git cold if ye don't."

"We got a little problem here, Momma," Regus said.

"Well, see to it after breakfast," Ella said. "I wadn't studyin on you boys bein late or I'da held off. But wash up and come on now," she said.

"Hit ain't bad, but Bill, here, got hisself shot," Regus said.

Ella Bone stopped short, and for the first time ever, she looked Music in the face, her reddish-brown eyes startlingly warm and handsome. "Lord have mercy," she said.

Music kept his butt to the wall. "There's nothin to it," he said. "The north side of my britches will require patchin if you've got the time, but I'll see to the other myself."

"You'll do what I tell you, boy," she said. "Let me see!"

"No, ma'am," he said and tried to keep his backside to the wall, but she caught his belt and turned him around.

138

"Lord, son, you're bloody as a hog. You git in the kitchen this minute and let me see to that," she said and steered him roughly through the door. "Now, you turn to the light so I can see, drop yer pants, and hold to that chair!"

There was nothing for it but to do as he was told. "Hellkatoot," he said under his breath.

"Well, hit ain't so bad as I feared," Ella said. "Looks a little like ye sat on a stub, cept yer kinda scorched. Regus!" she said. "Stop that laughin and get me some vinegar water to wash it off and some lard."

# 12
## HARD DECISION

WITH A SURE, firm touch, Ella cleaned, greased, and bandaged his wound, fussing and muttering to herself the whole time. She wanted to know why Regus hadn't looked after him better, but the moment Regus began to explain what had happened, she said she didn't want to hear about it. She noticed Music's ear, which was red and hot, and the slight swelling over his eye. She held his chin in one of her chapped, mannish hands while she looked at them, and shaking her head angrily, sent him off to change his trousers and bring back the shot-up pair for her to mend. While Regus and Music were eating, she patched the holes, her movements stiff, quick, and ill-tempered.

Music had eaten half his breakfast before he made his awful decision, put down his fork, and braced the palms of his hands against the table.

"Aire ye hurtin, son?" Ella asked at once.

"No'um," Music said, "I'm goin on home. I'm goin on back to Virginia."

Ella hesitated only a moment. "Yes," she said and adjusted the sewing in her lap and then adjusted it again. "Yes, well—this awful place—I don't blame ye. Not a bit, son. Not a little bit in this world. I reckon it eases my heart."

Music looked blindly at his plate, but he could feel Regus's eyes upon him. He could feel the question in them, the surprise, the embarrassment.

140

It took Regus longer to speak. "Well, Bill Music," he said at last, "I expect yer a-doin the smart thing after all. My notion is you've run a mean bluff on half the Burnsides, but a man don't never know. Ha," he said, and Music looked up into Regus's blushing face, "but ole Cawood cain't say he wadn't swarmed, no matter that he must have three inches and forty pounds on ya. Ha," Regus said and sucked his teeth and gave his head a quick jerk to one side.

"Cawood don't matter," Music said. "It was just dumbness that made me hit him. I don't like him, and he caught me at the wrong time."

Ella Bone looked at her lap. In Regus's eyes there was a small spark of relief, but puzzlement too, and still something of betrayal, which pained Music to see.

Music began to bob his head before he quite found the words to speak. "There is something going on, I think," he said. "Your feeling about it was on the mark. Somewhere between twelve and one o'clock this mornin there was a bunch of men sneakin down the mountain into camp." Music shook his head. "I don't think they'd been huntin, and that little preacher was with them, so I don't reckon they were out drinkin or raisin Cain."

Regus took a deep breath, tilted his chair back, allowed the front legs of the chair to plop down against the floor again, and let his breath out, his lips fluttering like the lips of a horse blowing into a watering trough. "Oh, shit," he said. "Yeah . . . " he said, but his voice trailed off. "Shitfire," he said at last.

Ella looked obliquely, thoughtfully at neither of them and made no remark about Regus's bad language.

"I can't make peace with that horse pistol and badge," Music said. "If those poor, ragged-assed miners was to show up with shotguns and pistols of their own, like you said they might, what the hell would I be supposed to do?" he asked.

Regus shook his head.

"I been livin under your roof and eatin at your table, and now I'm about to run out on you," Music said. "It makes me ashamed."

"Hush," Ella said. "Nobody here blames you, son. I, fer one, see no fault in what ye've said."

"Momma speaks for me," Regus said. "I'll not fault ye. You could do me a turn, though, if ye'd pull one more shift and help me collect those unionizers. It would give me a breathin spell."

Ella shook her head. "Ree, Son, ye've no right to ask it of him."

141

"I reckon Momma's right again," Regus said, "but I'd not ask ye to turn in a solitary Hardcastle man, and I'll give you my word they'll get the name of no miner from me. I know Kenton Hardcastle, and it'll go harder on ever soul in Elkin if a union comes in. Never mind Hardcastle, they ain't a minin operation in Kentucky that ain't fightin for its life, nor a one that would stand for a union. It might work some sweet day, but this ain't the time nor the place." Regus ran his finger back and forth under his nose. "Wasn't nuthin on earth that could teach my poppa that, rest his soul, but hit's a fact. And hit's far worse now than in his day."

"Ye've no right to ask him to go agin his conscience," Ella said.

"That's right," Regus said soberly. He looked Music in the eyes. "Ye'll have my hand, and no hard feelins either way, Bill Music."

"All right," Music said, "I'll help you collect the unionizers."

"I don't like this one bit," Ella said. "I can see in your face, chile, that you're persuaded otherwise, and I'd as lief you'd go on home. Hit ain't right for folks to go agin their conscience thisaway."

"Don't worry," Music said. He patted her rough, mannish hands. "I haven't thought of doing anything since the middle of last night that seemed anywhere near right. Longer than that," he said. "I'm going to go milk."

"I won't have it!" Ella said. "You set and eat yore breakfast! Regus'll do the milkin. He's not been shot and wallowed about so!"

"Regus can't hit the bucket," Music said. "He milks down his shirt cuffs. Let him chop the kindling."

"Ha," Regus said, "it's just cause that cow don't like me, and I didn't know nuthin when I bought her and let that feller sell me a cow with little-ole-nuthin tits."

Music got the buckets from the sideboard. "Wish I could at least teach him how to milk before I leave," he told Ella on the way out of the kitchen.

The cow blew softly into her trough and chewed with a slow, sideways motion of her jaws. For a long time no one came out toward the barn. They had things to talk about, he suspected. Ella would want to fuss at Regus, and he would want to explain. Maybe they had things to say to each other he could not imagine. Still, he was glad Regus had asked the favor of him. He had left the badge, shoulder holster, and the Walker Colt on the barrel top in his room, hoping never to put them on again; but pulling that last shift with Regus eased his conscience. Even Kenton Hardcastle would have less cause to complain. He didn't like it, and he

142

feared it, but maybe, after all, it would be better all around. Perhaps Regus was right about the union. Perhaps it would cause everyone grief and do no good; yet he saw no reason why men like Kenton Hardcastle should have it all their own way. There was no doubt in his mind that the working stiff ought to have a say in the matter too, that he ought to have an organization, a union, by God, to represent him. If there had been an electricians' union in Chicago, he might not have gotten burnt, might not have gotten fried like a piece of meat up there on that pole. The union would have seen to it that one man wasn't at the mercy of another who didn't know anything, some dumb son of a bitch the boss just felt like hiring who would pull the wrong fuse jacks and allow his working buddy to grab twenty-three hundred. Music snorted through his nose. Twenty-three hundred was what they sent through a man strapped in an electric chair, the dose they gave a murderer. "I done already paid," Music said. "I got a wide margin comin before I run through the balance. I got room to fuck up," he said and laughed miserably. He had no idea whom he was addressing or for what purpose, but it seemed to make him feel better. The cow moaned, shuddered her hide, rolled an ear in his direction. "Sawwh," he said to her, "sawwh, ole bossy."

Sitting with half his butt off the milking stool, he was comfortable. His leg felt much better since Ella had seen to it. He thought about Cawood Burnside lying on the cot in the powerhouse, that ridge swelling down the center of his head like the crest on a French soldier's helmet. Hellfire, he thought, damnation. He had made a mess, there was little doubt of that. He could have gotten people shot up, killed. As for himself, he supposed he deserved it, but he had a sudden vision of Regus sitting off to the side with his pistol trained on Grady, and the implications of that came home to him: when he left, Regus would have no one to back him, not even the Burnsides. The cow switched her tail, shifted, stepped around; and automatically, without even being aware that he had done it, he took the bucket away. It was three-quarters full. "Sawwh," he said to her. "Saawwwwh." He set the second bucket beneath her udder. "Sawwh now," he said and began again to milk. Regus and Ella could make it on the farm alone. They had a cow, some pigs, the chickens. They could make it better than any of the miners in Elkin. They wouldn't require much cash money. If he left them twenty dollars, it could run them through till spring. They needn't suffer a hungry day. After he quit, he'd hang around for a little while, cut down that bee tree, help get in a little more firewood, make another rabbit gum or two. Regus didn't want to be a mine guard, a company goon; surely he didn't. But whether he did or not, it wasn't the thing to do anymore, not after coming in on his side against the Burnsides, not after he'd held a gun on Grady. He'd screwed Regus up, there wasn't much doubt about that. Hell, he didn't even quite remember what it was that Cawood had said, hadn't heard more than the general drift of it. Anyway, it wasn't what he said that mattered. It was that he'd had the presumption to say it. It was that he would be the sort to conceive it, and take pleasure in it, and then have the presumption to say it.

Down at the house, the door to the kitchen opened and Regus stepped out upon the dogtrot. He looked up toward the barn, rubbed the back of his neck, and, trailed by Fetlock, stepped off the end of the open dogtrot and came on toward the barn. Music milked, a tinny spewing in the pail. "Sawwh," he said to the cow, who rolled her eyes and stepped around when the hound entered the barn. Regus leaned against the stanchion. "If you'd milk between your thumb and forefinger and not grab a teat like it was a hoe handle," Music said, "you might learn to milk as good as me. You might even amount to something."

But Regus wasn't having it. He got out his tobacco and his knife and cut himself a chew. "If we don't catch em tomorrow night," he said, "you get yerself gone anyway. I reckon I was tryin to work a wrinkle on ye, but Momma caught me out." He shifted his quid from cheek to cheek, spat, and tucked it along his jaw, where it made a knot the size of a walnut. "How many men did you see comin in last night?"

"I don't think there was more than three or four," Music said.

Regus nodded almost imperceptibly. "They just gettin started then. Wouldn't be surprised if they weren't at it ever night for a while, tryin to work up a decent membership."

"Well, why not try to locate the meeting tonight then?" Music asked. "Sawwh," he said to the cow and went back to his milking, for she was beginning to fidget and wouldn't stand much longer.

"All right," Regus said.

"If we don't catch up to them tonight, maybe we will tomorrow night." Music milked and Regus leaned against the stanchion, chewed, and appeared to think. Music had his forehead against the cow's side, but out of the tail of his eye he saw Regus shift, heard him spit.

"Dammit," Regus said, "you ain't bought in fer tonight or tomorrow night either if yer set agin it. I'll carry ye all the way to the Tug River and clean outten Kentucky if yer anxious to get on. I reckon I am tryin to

144

work a wrinkle on ye, Bill. You've no debt to pay with me, ner Momma either. Goddammit," he said. "Goddammit, Bill Music, ye don't feel that way, do ye?"

For some reason Regus's embarrassment made Music laugh, and once he got started it was hard to stop. The cow shied, but Music saved the pail of milk before she kicked it over. He had nearly milked her out anyway. "Hell, yes, I feel that way," he said, laughing still, and Regus began to laugh too.

"Good," Regus said, rubbing the back of his neck, "good enough."

"Why don't you turn the cow out and get Ella some kindling, and I'll strain the milk and get it in the springhouse," Music said.

"How's the leg?" Regus said, still giggling.

"Fine," Music said. "Just fine."

# 13
## UNION MEETING

AFTER THE CHORES were done, Music took out the Walker Colt and fired off the last three charges, which obliged him to explain to Regus what had happened to the other two.

Regus listened. "Sounds like you was a little tight strung last night. It's a shame somebody couldn't have warned ole Cawood."

Music was trying to disassemble the pistol to clean it before he recharged it, but he was having no luck. "I hate I got you into it with the Burnsides," he said.

"Weren't altogether your fault," Regus said. "I got a little overexcited." He scratched absently at the tawny hair growing out of the open neck of his shirt. "When I think back on it, I don't reckon Grady was going to mess in it a'tall. I get the notion he don't put his ass on the line fer nobody. And as for Cawood, you were handlin him all right by yerself. Fact is, I get the notion I nearly got you shot, messin betwixt and between you two like I was."

"Yeah," Music said, struggling with the plunger mechanism, "but the Burnsides ain't your buddies now, and that's no good."

"Ha," Regus said, "they never wuz friends."

"You know damned well that ain't what I mean."

Regus did not speak. Music struggled with the plunger mechanism. He could not remove it and hence couldn't remove the cylinder either. All at once he quit working at it and studied it instead. "Shit," he said, "I've broken your grandaddy's pistol in the bargain."

"What's wrong?" Regus said.

Music showed him. "I bent the goddamned plunger over Cawood's head."

Regus smiled and wiped his eyes. "I sorta wondered how that ridge down the middle of his head could be so long; I never thought about you wrapping that barrel clean around his skull."

With absolute seriousness Music sighted down the barrel and then held the pistol sideways at arm's length to squint at it. "No," he said, "the barrel looks all right; I think it's just the plunger."

"They couldn't make metal terrible hard eighty or ninety year ago, and I reckon the damned thang is that old. Hell, I know Grandpap had it way before the Civil War, cause he killed a man with it in 1846 down in Bristol, Tennessee." Laughing, Regus squeezed his eyes shut and shook his head. "Course, he didn't club hisn; he shot him, like the feller had a right to expect."

"Yeah, well," Music said, "I didn't have time to shoot Cawood. I would have had to cock the hammer and point the damned thing at him and pull the trigger. Seemed a lot easier to hit him over the head with it."

"I expect," Regus said, "yawl bein so tangled up amongst each other and all."

"I'm just as glad," Music said.

"I expect," Regus said. "But if ye bent it over Cawood's head, I don't see why we can't bend it back."

Music wasn't nearly so much amused by it all as Regus, but there was nothing wrong with his suggestion. He went off to the barn, where he had been riving out shingles, and got the froe and mallet. He set the blade of the froe between the barrel and the plunger and rapped the plunger on its high end with the mallet until it was straight enough to be removed. Regus wiped the cylinder and frame of the pistol clean with a rag while Music worked on the plunger with the wooden mallet, rolling it against the floor of the dogtrot and beating it straight. When Music put the pistol back together, it worked, if not quite so smoothly as before. He fired two rounds of caps on all the nipples to clear them and loaded five chambers of the Colt once again with powder, cornmeal, .44-caliber balls, and lard. At last he rested the hammer on the empty chamber and slipped the pistol snugly back into the gaudy, homemade shoulder holster.

147

Regus, sitting on the edge of the dogtrot, his arms folded across his chest, had watched the whole operation. He sucked his teeth. "I reckon I can see the virtue in whompin a man over the head with that sucker after all," he said. "Hell, if you shoot it, hit takes half the mornin to load her up agin."

"That's not going to bother me," Music said. "I'm not planning on shooting it."

"Well, if we're smart about it, if we plan her out just so, there shouldn't be any need."

"Shit, we don't even know where they're meetin. Whether it's up on the mountain someplace, or in Mink Slide, or where," Music said.

"Sure we do," Regus said. "They're meetin at the Bear Paw. They ain't goan meet on Hardcastle property if they can keep from it. That's askin to get caught; it's agin the contract the miners just signed; it's trespassin for the unionizers; hit's all kinds of things. If them unionizers set foot on Hardcastle property, they're bought and paid for, and they know hit as well as you and me. And shit, they ain't up on the mountain under no tree. Anyhow, Kenton Hardcastle owns that too."

"Well, they came down off the mountain," Music said.

"Sure, so would you. They ain't goan walk back by the road."

Ella came out the kitchen door then, and the two of them got quiet, as though their subject were, in some strange way, unfit for her ears. She carried buckets of water to the black iron washing pot behind the house. She built a fire beneath it and put clothes in it to soak, Music's newly mended trousers among them. She took down the galvanized washtub they bathed in from its peg along the wall of the dogtrot and filled that with water too. She cut a sliver of homemade lye soap into the black pot, and with a long-handled wooden paddle she stirred the clothes and soap around as though she were cooking a stew.

In subdued, chastened voices, they made their plans. In the afternoon they would drive to Valle Crucis, circle around the mountain on the west side of the Switch River valley, and come up on the Bear Paw coal company from the south. They would drive no closer than a mile, and like the miners the night before, climb the mountain and approach the Bear Paw housing from the woods above, where they would stay until after good dark or until they saw what they wanted to see. They would allow the meeting to take place. They would allow the Hardcastle men to leave, and then they would collect the unionizer and deliver him to the sheriff in

Valle Crucis. If no meeting took place, then they would try the next night; if there was no meeting the second time, then Music could take off his badge and gun and call it quits.

In grave, soft voices they agreed while Ella poked and stirred the clothes in the steaming pot, dipped them out on the end of her wooden paddle, and plunged them into the galvanized tub, where she rinsed them by hand. At last, paying no attention to the low, heavy clouds which had their vaporous beginnings at the tree line no more than three or four hundred feet above the barn, she wrung the clothes out and hung them on the line. She dumped the water from the black iron wash pot and from the galvanized tub, and when she brought the tub up on the dogtrot to hang it again from its peg, she said to Music, "You ort to rest yerself a little, son, and then I want to look at that leg again. I don't want it collectin fever on me."

"It feels fine," Music said, "but I reckon I could lie down for a little bit." He picked up the pistol and got to his feet, and indeed the leg didn't pain him much.

"Well," Ella said, "hit might grow proud if it ain't watched, is all."

"Yes'um," Music said, although he did not know what she meant.

"Proud skin that can't bear bein touched ain't fun nowhere," she said, as though she had read his mind, "but on a chap's bottom side, hit ain't no fun a'tall."

Regus chuckled. "Don't mind me," he said.

Ella didn't; she didn't even glance in his direction. "As fer yer britches," she said to Music, "I soaked em in the sink and I don't think the blood set, but I'm feared the patchin has ruined them for looks, and them nearly brand-new too. I'm right ashamed I'm no finer hand at sewin; the Lord just didn't mean these hands for makin things nice and purty."

"I'm grateful, missus," Music said.

Although he meant to lie down only for a little while, he slept until almost two o'clock, when Regus called to him from the dogtrot. Certainly he'd had no sleep the night before, but it was something else entirely that allowed him to sleep so peacefully: he could see the end of his job as a mine guard. Even his fight with Cawood, even their plan to pick up whatever poor devil was trying to organize a union, even the guilt he felt for leaving Regus and Ella—nothing could mitigate against the relief he felt.

"Are ye dead in the hull in there?" Regus asked from the dogtrot. "Momma's got some victuals set out, and I reckon she wants to inspect yer butt."

"Comin," Music said. He spied the flour sack Ella had spread over the barrel top and decided that a tablecloth was not what he needed.

In spite of the fact that his thigh was sore, he felt keen and rested. He ate a heaping plate of navy beans, corn bread, and side meat and washed it down with two scalding cups of coffee; and when Ella had cleared the table and commanded him to drop his trousers, he did so without any hesitation, revealing a flour-sack diaper with a large, rabbit-eared knot at each hip.

"Well, now," Ella said, "hit's swole up some but it don't seem to be no fever ner pisen in it. Ye hold still. I made up a batch of medicine." Music held on to the back of a chair and exchanged a look with Regus, both of them giving their heads one slight, identical, commiserating wag, as though they were mirror reflections of each other, while Ella got a saucer of black ointment from the warmer of the woodstove and picked up two yards of material, which, earlier in the day, had likely been a sheet.

She wiped Music's wound clean with vinegar, which caused him to grit his teeth and close his eyes. When he opened them again, Regus wagged his head exactly as before and grinned sheepishly. He was a bit blurred. Music felt Ella's broad finger spreading on the tarlike salve and tried to look down between his legs to get a glimpse of what she was doing. "Hold still," she said; "this'll take the pain of the vinegar off ye and help heal ye up."

"What is it?" he asked.

"Hit's chimney soot, lard, and sulfur," she said. "Hold still now while I wrap it. I want to wrap it kindly thin so's hit'll get some air." She started just above his knee and made a spiral wrap to the bottom edge of his diaper, pinning the bandage, top and bottom, with saftey pins. "There," she said, "that ought to do ye."

Quickly, Music pulled up his britches.

"We ort to get on the road," Regus said. "Hit's a ways around the back side of the mountain. Don't look for us till after midnight, Momma," he said to Ella, who was putting her saucer of medicine back on the warmer of the stove with another saucer inverted over the top of it.

"I ken more than I'd wish about what you boys are up to," Ella said. "But I don't want no shootin ner gettin shot, you hear me?"

"Yes'um," Regus said.

150

"Yes'um," Music said.

"Wait," she said, "hit's turnin off cold." She went into the front room, rummaged around, and came back with a thick grey sweater spotted with moth holes. "Hit belonged to Ree's daddy. Hit's a right smart too small fer Ree."

"Thank you," Music said.

"You put it on," Ella said.

Music pulled the sweater over his head and tucked it into his pants. It fit like a second skin.

"You git yore heavy jumper," she said to Regus.

"All right," Regus said. "Momma, now," he said, "we got us a good plan, and you've no need to worry."

Ella turned away toward her sideboard strewn with pans and dishes. "You ain't talkin bout no life I know, Son," she said. "I don't remember the day I didn't need to worry, cept maybe when I was a little bit of a girl."

Music and Regus looked at each other, neither of them with anything to say. Regus nodded toward the door, and they went out, Regus shutting it behind them. "We'll be on back," he said.

Music slipped his arms through the hangers of the shoulder holster and buttoned the flowered cummerbund around his middle. He pinned the badge to the inside of his suit coat, put it on, and met Regus at the truck. Only when they had backed out into the highway did they realize that Ella had come out upon the breezeway to look after them, her hands rolled into the top of her apron and her head to one side after her fashion, as though, even at that great distance, there was something about them she could not face directly.

They filled the truck with gas in Valle Crucis, took a hardtop road west, and after ten miles or so, turned south on a dirt road. Though rutted out, it wasn't so bad at first, but as they drove on, the small stream that ran beside it crossed the road more and more frequently, and there were long stretches where the stream and the road shared a common bed.

"I guess you don't come back in here if there's been a lot of rain," Music said.

"Or snow," Regus said, "or much of anything else. I don't guess you come back in here noway, unless it's home. I reckon this whole part of the country was just about like this till they started diggin coal and opened her up with roads and railroad spurs and all." The Model T pecked and growled along in low gear, and even though the ruts yanked the steering

151

wheel one way and another, Regus managed to hang on to it and cut himself a chew of tobacco. "I've heard it said that the entire assessed value of Harlan County was less than ten thousand dollars not much more than thirty year ago. I reckon hit's millions now. Shit," Regus said, "more than a man could count, I'd vow."

Fifty yards above them on the right there was an old log house. It was two stories tall and made of square hewn logs with a chimney of mud and thin flat rocks. Smoke curled from it. An old man in overalls and a denim jumper, but, oddly, wearing a dark, formal-looking vest under the jumper, stood on the porch and watched them pass. He had a white beard and leaned on a walking stick. Off to the left of the house there was a pole barn with a small, split-rail corral, and in it, two large, handsome mules rolled their foot-long ears this way and that in order to cipher and classify the sound of the Model T. As soberly as the old man had done, the mules watched them too. Both the house and the barn had settled into the earth and were leaning north, but they looked sturdy yet.

"Yeah," Music said, "too bad you couldn't count the empty bellies thirty years ago and today."

"Sure," Regus said, "but these is hard times. There's a depression on, if ye ain't heard."

"Shit," Music "the depression don't mean much if you never had any money anyhow. I bet if you asked that ole gentleman back yonder, he'd tell you he never had two half-dollars to rub together more than once or twice in his life."

"Ha," Regus said, "I bet he did. I bet he's still got em too."

"Maybe," Music said, "but likely he grows or makes what he needs and trades for the rest, or does without. And I'll bet he ain't hungry, and even if this depression goes on five or six years, I bet he don't get hungry either."

"All right," Regus said, "he might not. And them folks in Harlan thirty years ago might not have went hungry, but I wouldn't be surprised if about all the workin and thinkin they done was on that very subject."

"Not being hungry is enough for most folks to worry about, I guess."

"Sure," Regus said. He looked at Music, his eyebrows arched with humor. "But if that goddamned life is so fine, how come nearly ever sucker that had the chance throwed down his hoe and come a-runnin ever time some jerkwater minin operation got started?"

Music couldn't account for that; in his notion of the scheme of things there were areas he hadn't mapped out.

"Huh?" Regus said.

"Don't ask me," Music said. "Hellkatoot, I'm the feller that threw down my hoe and went off to Chicago to learn the electrician's trade."

"Ha," Regus said, "so you are." He adjusted the throttle and spark levers on the steering wheel, and the Model T growled and lurched ponderously at the rutted, steep pitch of the road. He turned his head and spat out the open crack of his window. "And while I'm askin," he said, "how come we're a-arguin about such as this?"

Music almost said he didn't know that either, but all at once he realized he knew perfectly well. "We ain't arguing anything," he said. "There just ain't no reason for you to be a mine guard. You got a cow, some chickens, a barn, a house, and forty acres. Ten or twelve of them acres lie pretty good."

"Hold up," Regus said; "I also got me a job that pays three dollars a day and I aim to keep it."

"You wouldn't starve without it."

"Maybe not," Regus said, "but I don't aim to find out."

"You could get you a shoat in the spring for two or three dollars. You could get a good mule for thirty."

"The way mines are going broke around here, I could pick up a mine mule fer less than ten, I bet."

"They ain't much bigger than dogs!" Music said. "But, all right, with no more ground than you got to break, maybe you could get by."

"Sure," Regus said. "Then I'd likely be in about the same shape as Lon Harmon was when he owned it and throwed hit over to start diggin coal; only he knew somethin about farmin, and I don't."

"Ella does," Music said, "and don't tell me she wouldn't like that better than you walkin around Hardcastle with pistols hanging off you. And don't tell me you like being a goddamned company goon."

Regus didn't answer. He looked straight through the windshield, bringing the Model T truck up over a rise where the left side of the road was the creek bed, no more than three feet across, and the right side was a bank tufted with grass, a foot and a half higher. The Model T struggled along, threatening from time to time to turn over.

Once they were over the rise, Music expected Regus to say something, but he didn't. He swapped his quid of tobacco from cheek to cheek and drove. They passed another log house, part of it one story and part two,

153

and again there was someone on the porch to watch them. A woman, maybe thirty, maybe forty, maybe fifty, years old, stood rigidly still with a small child sitting astride her hip and another half hidden behind her, holding on to her apron with one hand and sucking the middle three fingers of the other. There were also two young men—in their twenties, maybe—standing on the hard-packed mud of the front yard. At once attentive and shy, neither of them looked at the growling Model T truck more than a moment at a time, although they must have heard it coming for many minutes and had come out to confront and greet it. Music and Regus nodded, threw up a hand, and the men did the same. But curious as they must have been, they made no nosy inquiries as the truck— perhaps the only one to come by that year, perhaps the only one ever—growled and jounced noisily past.

Above, the road got worse. Twice they had to stop and carry stones to fill washouts they could not pass over. Once they had to drag a windfall aside. The creek grew smaller, wandered, returned, and vanished at last into the earth. Still, the truck seemed always tilted dangerously to one side or the other, and the woods closed in, so that branches constantly raked the fenders and body. Small trees an inch or two thick grew up in the center of the road, but these they rode down. It was three or four miles before they passed another homestead and the road began to get a little better, likely, Music thought, because the people who lived there traveled south to do their trading, rather than north toward Valle Crucis. He had begun to doubt that the road went through.

"If Hardcastle folds," Regus said solemnly, and as though half an hour of silence had not passed between them, "I reckon I can see if there's any farmer in me."

"Hellkatoot," Music said. "It only calls for common sense, hard work, good weather, good luck; and if you get all that, the ability to make peace with being broke anyway."

But Regus didn't so much as smile; he looked straight through the windshield and nodded.

Not long after they hit the hardtop road and turned north again, Regus swung the truck off to the left on what appeared to be grown-over skidway. Within fifty feet, the truck was hidden from the road.

"Well," Regus said, "we must have drove twenty-five mile to get four from home, but there won't be nobody lookin for us to come callin." He shut the Model T down, and after a moment of dying shudders and rattles, it ceased.

In the quiet that resulted, Music felt nervous. All at once he didn't like what he was getting into. It felt all wrong. When he did something foolish, he told himself, he did it in the heat of the moment. He didn't plan it out ahead of time. "Now that I think of it," he said, rubbing the back of his neck and frowning, "I don't understand just how we can arrest somebody when we ain't on Hardcastle property just cause he's talkin to some miners."

"Easy. Draw that horse pistol, lay back the hammer and say, 'Bud, you is under arrest.' " Regus pushed his door handle down, and the door squawked open. "We better git on. It bein cloudy, we ain't got more than an hour or so of daylight." He got out and the door squawked again and banged shut, seeming to startle the slash and brambles overgrowing the abandoned skidway.

Music got out too. He was not satisfied. "But that don't sound too square nor legal to me," he said.

"Hell, you're a deputy sheriff," Regus said. "If you say it, hit's legal."

Music came around the truck, and the two of them started up into the woods toward the northwest. Music lagged a step or two behind. "Well, it don't sound square at all to me," he said.

"Tell ye what ye do then," Regus said; "don't say nuthin, and leave me do the talkin." Suddenly Regus stopped, raised his face to the sky, and held up his forefinger. "Hell, I got the words for ye." Wrinkles of concentration sprang to his forehead. "Say, 'Yer under arrest for sedition and criminal syndicalism,' " he said and tucked his chin into his chest and smiled with satisfaction.

"What does that mean?" Music said.

"Hell, I don't know," Regus said, "but it's what they told my daddy the last time they took him to jail. I guess it means you can't have no union."

Regus started off again, and after a moment Music followed. All right, he thought, all right, I said I would do this thing, so I will.

And he resigned himself, following Regus down the skidway, then along an old logging road, and finally along a game trail through the woods. At last, above the Bear Paw, they found a hemlock blowdown which was yet alive and green, and they settled themselves under it to watch. His thigh pained him very little even when he sat on it, and he was surprised that Ella's concoction could work so well. He was grateful for the sweater too, for, as Ella had predicted, it had grown colder. Fitfully it began to drizzle, and here and there wet, heavy snowflakes fell, barely slower than the rain.

Regus had grown quiet and thoughtful and sat under the partial protection of the hemlock with his elbows propped on his knees. He watched the six or eight houses, among the many abandoned ones, from which chimney smoke struggled to rise, curled over the rooftops, and lazed away not far above the ground. Music turned the collar of his suit coat up, rolled himself a cigarette, and settled in to wait. He had been more uncomfortable; and at least until the hemlock got soaked and began to leak, it wouldn't be bad. Then, too, there was some hope that, his luck otherwise deserting him, the weather might turn grim enough to keep a union meeting from taking place.

Before long the rain turned to snow, and under it, in the failing light, the Bear Paw coal camp looked even more forlorn. The snow did not stick on the ground; still, the roofs of abandoned buildings turned white, and the architecture of briars and scrub and long grasses was rimed with it. And against such whiteness the contrast of the blackened tipple, the unpainted sides of buildings soiled with coal dust, the black outcroppings of coal seams along the railroad cut, even the dark, littered and trampled earth around the company shacks, was sad and sharp. Music had no idea why the look of it should remind him so strongly of home, but it did; and so, his shoulders hunched against the cold, he was soon adream and not aware of the men leaving the woods no more than thirty yards to his left until Regus touched his shoulder and pointed. Music counted ten of them, although he recognized only the little preacher and Worth Enloe. Somehow he had not expected the men to sneak into the Bear Paw from the woods, although it made perfect sense: they wouldn't wish to be on the road at the Bear Paw either. Music suspected Regus hadn't thought of that either, and only chance had kept the miners from walking right over them, or him from choosing just the wrong moment to light a cigarette or speak to Regus.

"Gettin an early start, ain't they?" Regus said.

"Yeah, and they damned near stepped on us too," Music said.

Regus jerked his head to the side and gave a wry smile. "One of us ort to have been smart enough to figure that," he said.

They watched the men pass down the grade of the mountain, through the stubble of a small cornfield and the remains of a vegetable garden someone had tried to scratch into the soil behind the leaning and dilapidated outhouses. If they spoke at all among themselves, no hint reached Music and Regus. At last the men filed into a house on the second row, where no smoke rose from the chimney and no lamp had been lit.

"Well," Regus said, "there them suckers are; already a half a dozen stronger than last night, if you seen the lot of them when they come home." In almost the same position as before, the inside of his elbows resting on his knees, his big hands hanging loose at the wrists, he shook his head slowly back and forth. "Shit," he said. He was silent for a moment as though deep in thought. "Well, Bill Music, we might as well go down and listen to that son of a bitch pitch em," he said. "We don't want to miss the show."

"What if there's men still comin that's late?" Music said.

"Yeah, all right," Regus said. He appeared to be embarrassed, undecided. He rubbed his hands together, got out his plug of tobacco, and cut himself a chew. "We ort not to commence till after good dark noway."

When he offered the plug to Music, Music took it, fearing to smoke lest someone at the camp see the flare of the struck match or even the glowing coal of the cigarette. Still, the chewing tobacco was not so calming as a cigarette.

"Yore daddy's always made his livin as a farmer, then," Regus said.

Music wasn't sure whether he'd been asked a question or not. "Well, sure," he said, "he fed his daddy and my mother and us three boys for as long as I can remember." Music laughed. "I sure didn't know the first thing about being hungry till I left. But he does other things. He makes shingles and sells em, and sometimes he'll even take the job of shingling a man's barn. He's a good wheelwright. I've known him to make ox yokes, a sledge. Once he built a wagon for a man. But he does those things for the cash money and because he's a good hand at foolin with wood. It's a mountain farm he's got," Music said, "mountain land, don't you know, and not the best for crops." Music spat and spat again and tried to collect the tobacco and keep it in one spot in his cheek. It seemed to cause him much more trouble than it caused Regus. "Most folks up around Shulls Mills have a hand in something else besides farming, even it's only doing a little trapping, or gathering ginseng to sell or something."

"Sure," Regus said.

"It's the farm that feeds them," Music said, "but if they want anything extra, or a little fancy, a few nice clothes, or a new cookstove, or something . . . "

157

"Sure," Regus said.

"But it's the farm that feeds them."

They sat for nearly an hour. Lamps had long since been lit in the occupied shacks of the Bear Paw, and they could even pick out the house the miners had entered, although something—a blanket, a piece of canvas or cardboard—seemed to be blocking the window that faced them, so only a dull, warm glow could be seen; and even that was so faint it teased the eye, lost itself in the dark and falling snow, and seemed to reappear always a little to one side of where it was expected. But the valley was losing definition, and at last the squares of yellow light from the windows and the planes and arches of snow floated on a pitch-black background.

"Okay," Regus said and got up. "Let's swing a little around to the south in case some more boys come to call from up to Hardcastle. I reckon they might have a lookout, too, so we ort to take it easy and slow."

"Amen," Music said.

They crept down the mountain. Their breaths and even their bodies steamed in the damp, chilled dark; and the intermittent snow was cold and slushy when it struck bare skin. In the deep shadow of one of the outhouses they paused for a long time looking and listening before they crept forward again.

The window had a gunnysack hung over it, but there was a little open space at either edge. Music knelt on one side of the window and Regus on the other. At the end of the room Music could see, there were two men who were strangers to him. One was short and dark and heavyset and appeared to be in his middle thirties; the other was medium tall and slight and looked no more than twenty. Music realized that Regus, from his angle, might not be able to see them at all, since he himself could see nearly nothing of the miners. He touched Regus on the shoulder and held up two fingers, and Regus nodded.

One of the miners was saying he didn't trust niggers, since they had come to Hardcastle, by God, as scabs.

"They were lied to," the young man said, "just the way labor always gets lied to. Nobody told them they were scabs. Nobody told them they were being sent up here to take the food out of your mouths."

"I reckon, fer sure, nobody told them they were goan get the shit shot out of them," someone else responded.

There was a smattering of grim laughter before the original voice

158

insisted stubbornly that a nigger wasn't to be trusted and nobody ought to say the first word to them about organizing.

"They broke your strike once because they were ignorant and they didn't have any choice," the young man said. "If you leave them out of this, you're just about forcing them to do it again, when they know better now. They've been here and they know."

"They've been slaves," the older, heavyset man said. He was leaning against a wall from which rags and tatters of wallpaper hung. He had his arms folded across his chest and looked impatient. "They know the truth."

The younger man nodded slightly to acknowledge the other. "They come from slaves anyway," he said, "but slaves were better treated than coal miners are. They were valuable property and could be sold and traded, and the man that owned them was wise to keep them fed and healthy. If one of them died, hell, he had to go buy another to take his place. But the coal operator don't care about you. He can get you killed, starve you out, work you to death, and it doesn't matter; there are other men standing in line to get your job when you're gone, maybe younger and stronger than you. The operator's got no investment in you; he don't care about your lives. He just wants your labor as cheap as he can get it. He's got no reason to pay you a living wage."

"That's right," someone said.

"He sure ain't doin it," another said. "If hit won't fer the county relief truck comin in and that one sack of Red Cross flour I got last month, I'da starved out. I drew less than two dollars in clacker all month, time they took cuts fer rent and lights and coal and insurance and doctor. I got enough powder to make maybe two more shots, and then I don't know what the hell I'll do. I ain't got the money to buy carbide, never mind powder."

"Ha," another voice said. "I didn't draw but thirty-five cent last month. I'd like you to tell me how yer a-doin so well."

"He loads more rock than coal; that's how he does it," someone else said.

"Well, I reckon I do a little better," said a calm, slow voice Music recognized: Worth Enloe, the one-eyed man who had talked to him weeks before.

"Yeah, you company suck," someone said, and there was the sudden scuffling of feet and the side of the building jarred. Music looked at

159

Regus, who merely wagged his head. "Well, how come he was brought here?" the voice asked, but it was strained this time and breathless. "You know damned well he'll turn us in."

"Shut up, Jesse," someone said, his voice tight as well, "you afraid you can't make it without yer thirty-five cent a month?"

"Don't tell me to shut up."

Again feet scuffled and thumped and the building jarred a little.

"I am tellin ya," the second voice said, sounding as harsh and ragged as the edge of a saw.

Like Regus, the heavyset man wagged his head. "That's right," he said, "fight each other like dogs. That's what this Hardcastle wants, so fat and fine in his big house; that's how he will like it, that you fight each other while he steals the bread from your mouths. Has he not always done so?"

Regus tipped his head toward the building. "Sounds like a foreigner," he whispered. "Is he a Welshman or a guinea or somethin?"

"I don't know," Music whispered back. "The Italians I ran across in Chicago put A's on the end of everything."

Regus duck walked around to Music's side of the window and looked in a moment. "Looks like a guinea to me," he said and duck walked back.

"I reckon I do a little better," Worth Enloe was saying in the same slow, calm voice he had used before, "but I give my workin life and one eye to the mines, and I got nuthin to show. And if I get turned out tomorrow, who will feed my youngins? Will you?"

"Yes," the heavyset man said. "It is about your children that we speak."

"And you don't want no dues?" Enloe asked.

"Have we asked for any?" the young man said.

"We want you to stand on your feet!" the heavyset man said.

"You see me standin," Worth Enloe said. The heavyset man smiled grimly, shook his head, and opened his mouth to speak, but Worth Enloe's voice took up instead. "You talk so good and so fine, but ye've yet to tell me how you are gonna make a union work when the United Mine Workers have tried for nearly fifteen years to organize Kentucky. They've throwed men out of jobs, got the mines tore up, made trouble, got folks shot. This last summer they wuz all over Harlan and Pike and Perry signin folks up and makin promises. And they called their strike, and they got it broke, and they got run out; just like they allus done

160

before. I'm fifty-two year old," Enloe said, "and I'm lookin at ye outten one eye, but I don't see nuthin new."

"I do," another voice said. "The U.M.W. had the sense to make a fuss in the summertime, where, if a man got evicted and lost his job, well, a tent ain't so bad, and he might gather a little poke greens and take a few victuals off the land."

The heavyset man made a farting sound with his mouth and looked disgusted, but the young one held up his hands. "We are better organized than the U.M.W. We've got the working classes up north behind us. Tell me the United Mine Workers tried to organize Hardcastle!" the young man said. "No, they didn't! They went after some of the big outfits and that's all. We're after everybody. We're not askin for dues because we know you don't have them to pay. We're askin you to stick. We're tellin you we'll bring in food and clothes. We're askin you not to put up with bein starved and cheated and maimed and pushed around."

"I don't see it," Enloe said. "Back when the mines were makin money, the unions couldn't do no good. These times is only worse. Mines goin broke all over. Hardcastle cain't be makin no money with the little ole contracts he gets, and when he lands one, he has to nearly give the coal away, so he still don't make nuthin. You come along and tell us we got to make him treat us right. Well, I tell you the old son of a bitch couldn't treat us right if he wanted to, not the way things is now."

"He is a suck, listen at him," a voice said from the other end of the room. "Shut up," said another. "You cain't trust no company man," said a third.

"No, no," the young man said, raising his hands, "the man is right as far as he goes. Probably Hardcastle Coal Company makes no money, and if it does, only a little."

"Ever one of ye knows how she works," Enloe said. "The biggest cost of gettin coal are the wages we men are paid. The coal operators bid for contracts, and the contracts go to the smallest bid. So our wages get cut to bring a contract in, and then they get cut again, and then another time, till finally the operators have underbid each other, till they ain't hardly nuthin left."

Against the grumbling and disagreement in the room, the young man raised his hands. "The system does not work. Not for you and not for them. If Hardcastle shut down tomorrow, he would lose his capital investment very quickly. There would be water in the mine without labor to pump it out. There would be cave-ins. The equipment would be

161

ruined and stolen, and soon he would have lost it all. It is cheaper for such a man to sell his coal at a loss than shut down. If he shuts down, and things get better, he can take no advantage."

"For money the swine have cut your throats, and now when there is no money, they cut their own," the heavyset man said with satisfaction. "That is what you must learn and what you must teach them."

"The operators have done this to you and to themselves because you have had no voice," the young man said. "Of course it didn't work," he said, "of course not. It's backwards. It's upside down." The young man smiled, laughed aloud. "The solution is simple. All of you must be paid a living wage for your labor. Enough to have the things you need, to raise your families, to live with dignity. You must set this wage, which cannot be traded upon or taken away. If all of you together say it must be so, then it must be so. The nation must have coal; you are the men who produce it. The controlling voice must come from the workers and no one else. You see that the other way does not work. The system can only be ordered from the bottom, from the worker. All you have to do is say that it will be done this way, and it will be."

"Great God, bud, where have you been?" Enloe said. "Sayin a thing is gonna be one way or the tuther don't make it happen. Not in this neck of the woods. I ken what yer a-sayin about bringin order from the bottom. It makes sense, but if ye think fer a minute that every poor sucker here won't be lookin at scabs and strikebreakers and gun thugs and all manner of things before we're all settin pretty like you say, why . . . why, boy . . . yer as dumb as a post."

The young man smiled his beatific smile. "Perhaps," he said, "but your children will thank you for your struggle when they have shoes to wear and food to eat and a house to live in instead of a sty; and if we all stand together—and we're organizing every mining operation we can find—perhaps not."

"But you are correct; the fight will not be easily won," the heavyset man said, looking, Music supposed, at Worth Enloe.

"Young man," another voice said, "I've listened to ye for three nights now, and I am willin to follow what ye tell us." Music recognized the voice at once. It was the preacher. The Holy Roller. "What do ye want me to do?"

Other voices agreed.

"I want you to bring us everybody you can trust, whether they are white or colored," the young man said. "And I want you and two others

162

to travel to Chicago for two weeks of training. I'll give you each ten dollars to keep your families in food while you're gone. You," the young man said, pointing to someone Music couldn't see, "I want you to go too."

"Hellfire," someone said, "he's been talkin agin you! Send me! My wife and chillun ain't seen ten dollar in better than a year."

"All right," the young man said, "you are the third. You three will meet me here in the morning, and Art will drive you to Cincinnati, where you will meet with other miners from across the state and be taken on to Chicago. There is a National Miners Union headquarters there, and after two weeks you will know much more about what the National Miners Union intends to do, and how it intends to do it."

"Do not forget the black man. He must be sought out," the heavyset man said. "We must all stand together as brothers and fight. Do you have questions?"

There was some muttering and comment, but no voice rose until the preacher's said, "I would like to pray."

"This is a time for men of strength to stand together," the heavyset man said. "It is not a time to pray."

"I would as lief ask the Lord's blessing," the preacher said.

Regus touched Music on the shoulder and motioned with his head that they should move around the corner, and Music could not hear how the unionizers responded. Whatever, when they were squatting at the end of the house, he could hear the little preacher's voice strike its praying cadence.

"Let them miners get all the way gone fore we make our move," Regus said. "There's a pistol or three in that bunch fer certain, and I don't want to be collectin them two in yonder with a couple of hotheads comin up on our blind side."

"What if the unionizers strike out too?" Music said.

"Hell, leave em go. We'll collect them in the mornin if they git gone and we cain't get no handle on them tonight."

After a while there was shuffling in the house, and finally the back door, which sounded as though it had stuck in the wet weather, shivered open. Footsteps and the sound of subdued voices spilled out into the night.

Music and Regus stayed where they were. The snow had turned again to a light, cold rain, and for the first time Music realized he was shivering steadily; that across the shoulders and down the center of his back, he was

163

soaked through; that his thigh, perhaps from squatting so long, was getting sore again. He wondered how many cylinders of the Colt would fire—if the threads of the nipples weren't worn, if the caps were firmly seated, all of them should—but he also wondered if it would matter.

After the miners had had more than enough time to reach the woods, they could still hear talking inside the shack. Finally Regus whispered, "Let's take a look-see," and cautiously they crept to the corner of the house and then beneath the window again. From his side, Music could see no one, but Regus was nodding and holding up two fingers.

The unionizers seemed to be arguing.

"The young one, yes, for he is angry. The man with one eye, maybe. But the preacher should not be sent."

"I studied for the ministry once myself," said the young man's voice with something close to laughter in it.

"I do not forget," said the other. "You think the struggle will be won with the head, but if it is won, it will be with passion and anger."

Regus tapped Music on the shoulder, held up his drawn pistol, and nodded toward the rear door.

"And I do not like the deception," the heavyset man was saying.

Music drew his pistol and stood up, and after Regus had duck walked beneath the window, he stood up too and went around Music to the door.

"And I do not like—" Music heard the heavyset man say, but Regus had opened the door. He had opened it gently, almost humbly, as though he were one of the miners returning. "Rest easy, cousins," he said.

Music went in behind him in time to see the change in their faces, in time to see realization drain their blood away. He himself, he realized, was not made for this sort of thing, for he would have yanked the door open wildly, and God only knew what would have happened.

Regus pulled his jumper aside and tapped his badge with one finger. "We goan take you boys to see the sheriff," he was saying.

The young man stiffened. The heavyset one seemed to sag. "And which one of them ran to you?" he said.

"None of those suckers told on ya, bud," Regus said. "You two just come to the end of yer string." Regus ran his finger back and forth under his nose. His face was red, Music noticed. So were his neck and ears. Well, anyway, Music thought, he's embarrassed, and he doesn't like it. "You fellers wouldn't have any guns on ya, would ya?" Regus said. "I don't want anybody to get shot."

"I don't," the young man said.

"Why is it the police are always on the side of the rich man?" the older one said.

"I've noticed that myself," Regus said. "Why don't you fellers turn around and face the wall and hold yer hands out behind you?"

When they had done as they had been told, Regus slipped off his belt and held it out to Music. "See if them birds are carryin anything to shoot with and tie two of their hands together. I'd feel better if they were yoked up, since we've got a ways to walk."

"And you," the heavyset one said while Music was patting his partner around the chest and pockets, "are you happy to be an oppressor of starving coal miners?"

"No," Music said.

"Then why do you do it?"

"Shut up, willya?" Music said. He began to search him and found a large automatic in his coat pocket. "Jesus," Music said and passed the pistol back to Regus.

"A feller told me once that guineas liked these big ole automatics," Regus said.

"My name is Arturo Zigerelli, and I am an Italian," said the unionizer.

"I thought you sounded like a foreigner," Regus said.

"I speak English better than you," Arturo Zigerelli said.

"Yeah," Regus said, "but this here's Kentucky."

Music had holstered the enormous Walker Colt and tied the inside wrists of the two men together. When he stepped back, Regus offered him the automatic. "You want this'un?"

"No," Music said, "I'm use to the Colt."

"Well, I'd feel better, Bill Music, if ye'd keep the damned thing out where you can wave it around."

Music drew the pistol again.

"Boys," Regus said, "if ye'd just go ahead of us out the door and walk kindly nice and easy, we'll all get along fine."

But when the young one realized they were being taken south, he stopped short. "There isn't any town for miles in this direction. What are you going to do with us?"

"Like I said, you boys are going to see the sheriff," Regus said. "Get along."

"Perhaps they will beat us, and perhaps they will shoot us," Arturo Zigerelli said.

"No, we won't," Music said. "We have a truck parked down the road,

165

that's all." He took hold of Regus's arm so that the two of them fell back a pace or two. "Goddammit," he whispered, "let's turn the poor bastards loose."

Regus snatched his arm away. "After we gone to all the trouble to catch em? If we let em sell that snake oil, they'll raise more hell in a day than a mine guard can beat down in a week."

"Come daylight, I ain't gonna be a mine guard," Music said, "and, shit, you ain't never been, if you'd stopped once to notice."

But Regus merely spat and caught up with the unionizers. A moment later, in a bitter, sarcastic voice he asked, "What I'd like to know, Mr. Zigerelli, is how come you to travel all the way from Italy to Switch County, just to make trouble?"

"I come to this country more than ten years ago, Mr. Officer of the Law; and I did not come to make trouble but to pick up gold from the streets," Arturo Zigerelli said. "I did not find it."

"I expect not," Regus said.

"I pick garbage from the streets in Philadelphia and I pick fruit in California and I eat them both to line my stomach, and I am a citizen of this country like you. But I do not sell my honor to the capitalist like you, or make the poor miner carry me upon his back."

"Be quiet," the slender one said and jerked their bound wrists.

"It will not matter," the Italian said.

"What's yore tale?" Regus said to the other one. "Ye sound a little closer to home."

"I was raised in Memphis," the young one said. His voice was shaky, but he seemed to struggle to put some iron in it. "I went to Vanderbilt Divinity School because I wanted to be a minister and save men's souls."

The Italian laughed.

"But . . ." the young man continued, "but when I got a little smarter, I thought I'd better try to save something I could see."

"Sure," Regus said. "Cut down the hill toward the road; hit's easier walkin."

"They sent me here because, like you say, I sound closer to home," the young man said.

Suddenly the Italian laughed again. "And I do not speak Kentucky," he said.

They were perhaps a hundred yards below the Bear Paw camp on ground that had once been cleared, although Music could not think for what purpose. Perhaps, he thought, to build more shacks. But it had long since grown up in scrub and briars, and the walking was very difficult. The slushy snow that lay upon the slash was falling off of its own weight in the rain, and what remained fell when they brushed against it. He was soaked to the skin, even through the bandage around his thigh. He holstered the Colt in spite of Regus. He was tired of pointing it at the unionizers' backs.

At last they floundered down a slick, steep cut into the roadbed, and, all four of them steaming like horses in the cold rain, they went on south.

Presently, the sarcastic edge still in his voice, Regus said, "Why don't you boys own up and tell me just what in the hell you git outten this?"

"Satisfaction," the young man answered in his tremulous voice, "and we get peace and hope for the future."

"Ha," Arturo Zigerelli said, "hope, maybe; but mostly we get only the harsh treatment we have in this moment, or worse."

When they had walked another fifty yards, Regus's pace began to falter. "Shitfire and damnation," he mumbled and shot Music an accusing and confused glance before he stopped dead in the road. "Hold it right there!" he shouted in so loud a voice the backs of both unionizers stiffened as if they'd been struck.

"Ahh," the Italian said, "now it comes."

"Just gimme my goddamned belt," Regus said.

"So," Arturo Zigerelli said, "will you shoot us now after all?" and he turned to face Regus and Music, pulling the younger man around too, who stumbled and tried to raise his hands.

"Goddammit," Regus said, "gimme my goddamned belt and get the hell away from me."

Hellkatoot, Music thought, and in the next moment the young man came to life and began to fumble and claw at the belt with his free hand until, at last, he untied it and extended it toward Regus.

Arturo Zigerelli had made no move to help him. "You are letting us free?" he said.

"Walk, goddammit," Regus said.

Arturo Zigerelli hesitated. "Can I have first my weapon?" he asked.

"What, so you can shoot me and Bill with it?"

The Italian made a curious little bow. "But you did not shoot us."

Regus jammed his hand in his jumper pocket and thrust the automatic at the Italian, who took it.

167

"You will not give us away?" he asked.

"If I meant to give you away," Regus said, "I'd still be marchin ye down the road."

"We will continue in our purpose," Arturo Zigerelli said.

"Do what the hell you want," Regus said. "By this time tomorrow I'll be a farmer, God help me, and ye'll be no concern of mine. Come on, Bill Music," he said, and snatching his belt from the young unionizer, he brushed past him.

It took Music a dozen strides to draw even with Regus, and oddly, by that time, all the things he'd had in his head to say seemed not quite equal to the occasion. As for himself, he couldn't remember when he'd last felt so free and unburdened—yes he could: it was the day before he'd hired on at Hardcastle. He felt square with the world for the first time in weeks and would have said as much to Regus but for the black mood that seemed to haunt the space around him. You're an odd fellow, Regus Patoff Bone, Music thought, for it was clear that Regus had been in a better mood when he caught the unionizers than when he turned them loose. And so he couldn't think of a single thing to say all the way back to the truck.

Finally, when Regus had backed the Model T out of the grown-up skidroad into the highway, Music said, "By God, you'll make Miss Ella happy anyway."

"I expect," Regus said, staring grimly through the drizzle and down the highway.

When they had driven only a little way, Music glimpsed the two unionizers duck out of their headlights and vanish like rabbits into the ditch. "There they are," he said.

"I saw em," Regus said.

"You think we ought to give them a ride back to the Bear Paw?" Music said.

"Hell, no," Regus said, "let the sons a bitches walk."

# 14

## LAST TRIP TO THE
## COMPANY STORE

THE NEXT MORNING was cold and clear and still as held breath when Music stepped off the end of the dogtrot on his way to milk. The high ridges and knobs of the mountains were white with snow, but the valley had merely been washed and frozen. Here and there in low spots and swales, patches of ice shone like glass, and the clothes Ella had not taken off the line to dry by the stove were stiff as sheet metal.

On the lowest limb of the black walnut tree a rooster beat his wings, stretched his neck, and crowed as he might have done in Shulls Mills, or anywhere. In her stall the cow moaned. And Music felt brand-new. So, he was certain, did Ella, who had been going about all morning with a bright, unusual spark in her eyes. Only Regus seemed to keep his black mood of the night before.

Nor did he give it up even after the chores were done and the three of them were sitting around the breakfast table.

"I don't know, but hit seems like we ort to lay in some stores with this last money," Ella said. "I figure ten pound of coffee, twenty-five of sugar and salt, and fifty pound of flour. And maybe a little side meat while yer a-gittin and a couple of sacks of dried beans."

Regus neither nodded nor spoke. He forked half an egg into his mouth and chewed, the muscles in his jaw rippling as though the egg were tough as harness leather.

"We might cut that bee tree I found across the branch too," Music said. "Wild honey is strong and dark and a mixture of whatever has bloomed all summer and fall, but I've always liked it. Might get ten, fifteen, twenty pounds of it."

"Ye'll git stung is what ye'll git," Ella said and laughed.

"Ha," Music said, "I'm counting on it."

Regus ate, took a drink of his coffee, and ate some more. He did not eat as though he were hungry, but mechanically, as though eating were only another chore to be done.

Music rubbed the back of his neck. "We ought to knock together another couple of rabbit gums too; fresh meat is always handy, even if it's only rabbit."

"I thought you wuz all fired up to git home, son," Ella said. "You seem to be laying out a big bunch of work fer a feller that's leavin."

"I ain't in such a rush now that I don't have to walk around with that deputy sheriff's badge pinned on me and carrying that big horse pistol," Music said.

Regus looked at him then. He was blue under the eyes as if he were hung over or hadn't slept, and the skin over his cheekbones looked strangely thin. "You can take off yer badge, all right," he said, "but if ye think there's no need for that pistol, yer wrong. Me and you didn't say good-bye to trouble, cousin; we just changed sides." He picked up his enameled tin cup, drained the coffee in it, and set it back on the table. "I'd give a little more thought to gettin on back to Virginia if I was you."

"I think I am not ready to go," Music said, "unless, by God, you're telling me to leave."

Regus pursed his lips and nodded his head. "Suit yerself," he said. He pushed himself away from the table and got up. "We got people to see," he said and let himself out upon the dogtrot.

Music and Ella sat where they were for a moment. Music sucked his teeth and shook his head, and Ella said, "He done right last evenin when he turned them fellers aloose. And I reckon, some way or other, he knows it. He just ain't made peace with hit yet."

Music nodded.

"He fears he cain't make a livin outside of coal, I'm thinkin," Ella said. "And I know he holds the unions to blame for all the world before his daddy died. He's just mixed up in his head. He ain't down on you and me."

"Yeah," Music said, "if I ain't steered him wrong."

Ella threw up her hands. "Lord, son, cain't nobody steer Regus one way or the other," she said and laughed. "Don't you worry on that." Ella stood up and brushed at her apron. "Did you wrap a clean bandage around that leg last night like I told ye?" she asked.

"Yes," Music said.

"Well, let me take a look at it and see how it's farin."

"There's no need," Music said, and he got up too. "It's not even hardly sore."

"Well," Ella said and nodded, "well then. But make up yer mind that I'm goan see it before this day is done."

"All right," Music said.

In his room, after trying to put the Colt in his coat pocket—where it wouldn't fit—and sticking it in his belt—where the weight of it made it hard to keep his pants up and the barrel ran to the middle of his thigh—he put on the shoulder holster again. The badge, at least, he could drop in his pocket like bad money. When he went outside on the dogtrot, Regus was just folding his knife blade away and tucking a quid of tobacco the size of a walnut into his cheek, and Fetlock was rising to stretch himself and wag his drooping tail in anticipation of some word or a rough, clumsy pat on the dome of his skull. But Regus only spat some small shreds of tobacco from his mouth and went off toward the Model T truck, and Music followed.

The moment they turned toward Hardcastle, Regus said, "I don't know but what it might be smart not to say nuthin to the Burnsides except that they got a long shift to pull. I'd like to get my pay and Momma's stores and get the hell outten Elkin lest somebody take a notion to try and hold up our money, say, or help us out of town like a trespasser. Cawood's a little crazy, and I wouldn't want nuthin cute to enter his head." Regus spat out the window. "If he ain't still stretched out on that cot like a goddamned butchered hog."

"All right," Music said.

But Cawood was not stretched on a bunk. He was sitting in a split-bottomed chair on the gallery of the commissary, albeit his straw skimmer was hanging on the chair behind and not cocked on the back of his head. Grady was there too, the sole of one boot and his shoulders propped against the wall and, as always, half a cigar in the corner of his mouth.

"Shit," Regus said, "I was hopin to get our tradin done before we run into them suckers." He turned in beside the commissary as though to drive up beside the powerhouse, but once he crossed the river, he turned the truck around, drove back to the commissary, and stopped with the truck pointed toward Valle Crucis. "Was Cecil in there?" he asked.

"I think so," Music said; "there was more lights on than just the night-light."

"I like a man who loves his job," Regus said. "Let's get our pay and tucker."

When Music reached for the door, his knees turned weak. His stomach, too, was cold and jumpy, and he realized, all at once, that he dreaded the Burnsides. In the next moment he realized he had always feared them, even from the first moment he'd met them. He would never have jumped Cawood if he'd had time to think; he was satisfied of that. But now that Cawood and Grady were the law, and he and Regus were merely themselves, he dreaded them even more. Strange how that works, he thought; any asshole with a badge has got an edge on you. The insight brought an odd smile to his face and made his hand shake when he opened the door of the truck, but he got out and walked around the hood to climb the steps with Regus.

"Mornin, boys," Regus said. "How's yer sore head this mornin, Cawood?"

"That ain't funny," Cawood said.

"I can see it ain't," Regus said.

There was a large blue lump running from the center of Cawood's forehead back into his hair. His left eye wept and had all but disappeared in the thick folds of his eyelids. His upper lip, too, was puffed toward his nose; but even as Music looked at him and his stomach chilled, he could not get the silly smile off his face.

"They had to fetch a doctor to me last night!" Cawood said. "The son of a bitch charged me three dollars just to tell me I got a concussion!" Cawood pointed his finger at Music. "You gonna pay for sucker-punchin me, buddyroe," Cawood said. "You gonna pay!"

Music couldn't think of a single comment to make, nor could he stop smiling.

"I've talked to him," Regus said, "and I've told him that a feller who pulls a gun on him has a right to get shot and not whomped on the head like a steer. I don't blame ye a bit for gettin mad." He opened the door and motioned Music inside. "Not a little bit."

"Goddamned right," Cawood said and nodded, although, in the next moment, his lumpy brow wrinkled with puzzlement.

Halfway down the aisle of the commissary Regus said, "Long as Cawood keeps talkin, I expect we're all right; he ain't got enough brain to run his mouth and anything else at the same time." Regus glanced at Music and then glanced at him again. "What the hell you smilin at?" he asked.

"I don't know," Music said and wiped his sweaty palms on his britches legs.

"Well, Cecil," Regus said in a much louder voice, "it's payday. Gimme ten pound of coffee, fifty pound of flour, twenty-five pound of sugar and salt, and . . . " Regus turned to Music. "What did she say?"

"Some side meat," Music said, "and a couple of sacks of dried beans." Thinking of the bee tree, Music ordered two cartons of quart mason jars, and remembering Ella's promise to inspect the back of his thigh, he picked up two pairs of undershorts.

Cecil protested that he wasn't even open yet, but it did him no good, for Regus collected half the order himself and bullied Cecil into setting the rest on the counter and paying them the remainder of their wages in cash money.

On their first trip to the truck the Burnsides merely watched them, which made Music uneasy since both he and Regus had their hands full. The second time Music came through the door, he carried the fifty-pound sack of flour over his left shoulder so that, if he needed to, he could get at the Colt, although the very thought of it made him despair, for he knew, without having to try, that drawing the long cap-and-ball pistol out of the homemade holster would be like dragging a gopher out of its hole. But to his relief Grady was nowhere to be seen, and Cawood was occupied, hat in hand, with easing down the steps, holding on to the wooden railing.

"Where's yer partner?" Regus asked, coming out upon the gallery with his back bowed over a terrific load of goods.

"Gone to get the goddamned car," Cawood said.

"Ever step I take jars my head and pains me terrible," Cawood said when Music passed him on the steps. "I ain't forgettin it," he said, his voice as peeved and querulous as an old woman's or a child's.

"Cawood," Music said, "you shot me in the leg."

Cawood's lumpy face brightened. "I thought I missed ye," he said and straightened and puffed out his chest. "I ain't sorry."

Music looked at him for a moment, realizing, at last, that however dumb he had supposed Cawood to be, he had overestimated him. The knowledge didn't make him happier. He shook his head and went on down the steps and loaded the sack of flour in the bed of the truck where Regus, too, was unburdening himself.

"Yer lying to me," Cawood said behind him. "If I shot ye, how come yer walkin around? Next time I'll fix yer hash. I'll shoot yer fuckin lights out, Bill Music!"

Regus and Music got in the truck. When Regus had cranked it and the Model T began to chortle and shake, he stuck his head out the window and spat. "Cawood," he said, "you tell Grady that yer gonna have to pull a double shift, cause me and Music ain't got time." Regus gave his head a little jerk to one side and smiled. "Hit'll give ye a chance to earn that doctor's fee back." Regus pulled his head in and, with a bitter laugh, let out the clutch; and the Model T lurched away toward Valle Crucis.

# 15

## MERLEE

A FEW YARDS from the northern edge of company housing there was a ditch choked with a low growth of sumac, and that was where he knelt. For a quarter of an hour he watched the worn footpaths of Hardcastle, but there was no sign of a mine guard; and at last he stood up, stepped into the open, and walked to Merlee's shack as casually as he could in the hopes that, if he were noticed, he would seem to be only another miner, confident of his right to be there and so in no hurry whatever. Still, when he knocked on her back door, he was giddy and his palms were damp; but it was much more a consequence of excitement than anything as simple as fear.

He had to knock a second time before the old woman opened the door. White hair straying from its bun around her face and the odor about her of dead leaves, she seemed to look him over for the gift of food he usually brought, until Merlee appeared behind her and said, "Aunt Sylvie, git outten the door and let him in! Quick! Quick!"

"Don't rush me, chile," the old woman said. "Hit ain't no quick left in me." She shuffled aside, and Music entered, but as she was about to close the door, Merlee pushed in front of her and closed it herself. "Mercy," Aunt Sylvie said, "ye'd knock a feller down if he wadn't a-watchin."

"I'm sorry," Merlee said and patted one of the old woman's warped, arthritic hands, but Aunt Sylvie only muttered, "Yes, ye would now; ye'd knock me to the ground," and she went off into the front room with her chin trembling.

175

"She's not feelin well," Merlee said, "and I've been too scared to pay her any mind. I heard ye had a terrible fight with Cawood Burnside."

"Yes," Music said, both surprised and flattered. He could read the alarm in her eyes before she made some useless gesture with her hands and looked away from his face.

"And I heard ye quit yer job and ain't a mine guard no more," she said.

"Well," Music said, "that was what I was anxious to tell you. News sure travels around here; I only just quit this afternoon."

She looked at him again, and then just as quickly at the floor. "Ain't much that won't be all over Elkin in an hour," she said, "anyway if anybody sees it, or that nasty store clerk hears about it." She shrugged after the manner of a small girl. "I reckon ye'll be off to Virginia then," she said.

"Yes," Music said. "Well, one of these days, but not for a while yet. I need to help Regus some before I go."

"He quit too, I heard," Merlee said.

"He was a miner himself for a long time," Music said. "He didn't like being a mine guard."

For a moment Merlee stood before him, smoothing her dress along her thighs. "Would ye like to sit down then?" she asked him. "I can make some coffee if you want?"

"Ahhh," Music said, "that would be handsome."

Merlee shook down the ashes in the stove, poked up the fire, and put on a lump or two of coal. "We've still got a lots of coffee from what you brung," she said as though merely to fill up the quiet. She dipped water out of a bucket on the sideboard and poured it into the coffee pot, but then she jumped suddenly and rushed to hang a dishtowel over the tiny kitchen window. "Mercy," she said, "what if Cawood Burnside was to prowl by and see you? Hit ain't safe fer no outsider in Elkin, but him with a grudge agin ye—he could shoot you down dead, and the law wouldn't do a thing to him!"

"I wouldn't worry," he said. "I don't think Cawood will be on the prowl tonight; I understand he's not feeling well." But there's nothing wrong with Grady, he thought, and in spite of himself he felt a little buzz of fear.

Merlee went to the sideboard and measured coffee into the pot, and with her back to him and in a strange small voice, she said, "I heard today that Cawood had already shot you when you and him fought, and I nearly died." She cleared her throat and wiped a strand of hair back from her forehead. "But then they's another woman that said it wasn't so, fer she'd seen you this mornin outten her window and ye looked in fine fettle and carryin a big sack of flour over yer shoulder."

"Well, he shot me a little bit," Music said. "While we was thrashing about and all, he sorta creased the back of my leg. But Ella Bone has doctored me fine."

"I wish you'd killed him," she said. "He ain't nuthin but mean; just a big mean company goon is all he is."

"Yes," Music said.

Merlee brought two coffee cups to the table and sat down with him. She was deep red around the neck and ears.

Music smiled to himself—mother and widow aside, he thought, she's still only a young girl and sometimes shy—but he tucked the smile quickly away. "How's the little one?" he asked.

"Oh, she's fine. She's takin steps, she is. She'll be runnin all over before long." Merlee ran her finger around the lip of her empty coffee cup. "She's asleep; I put her to bed about an hour ago. I think she's been a-wonderin where you're at. She likes you," Merlee said, and the blush around her neck and ears seemed to creep into her jaw, to spread faintly toward her eyes the way a sunset diffuses into the sky; and she seemed on the verge of some sort of confession, but she rose abruptly and went to the stove, for what purpose, Music couldn't tell, for she only moved the coffee pot an inch or two one way and then the other before she came back to the table and sat down again. "I'm right ashamed that I've treated you so poorly," she said at last, "and you bein so nice to us. And now you gettin ready to leave and all. It might not none of us around here git to see you again."

"Well, you did call me a company goon once," Music said, enjoying her admission and embarrassment more than he knew he should.

"I'm shamed by it," she said, "and I'd be obliged if you didn't remember it of me."

"I won't," he said.

"I don't know what would have become of Anna Mae if ye hadn't doctored her. And all the things you brung to us, and that purty cloth. I'm a-makin a dress, but I'm scared ye'll be gone outten Switch County before I git done with hit."

"I'll make it a point to stay until you finish, so I can see you in it," Music said.

She rose from the table again and moved the coffee pot around on the stove and brushed the hair off her forehead with her palms. "I don't think

177

hit's ever gonna boil," she said. She started back to the table, but then stopped and gave him a look he couldn't fathom before she went into the front room and disappeared. When she came back, she was flushed to the eyes again. "Aunt Sylvie's gone to bed too," she said. "I reckon she ain't asleep, but she's nearly too deaf to hear hit thunder."

"Well, that's a shame," he said, "but she's right old and . . . " Merlee was standing just inside the doorway with her head hung, fairly glowing with embarrassment. The back of his throat went dry, and in some remote chamber of his brain he told himself in a quiet voice: You are a fool, Bill Music; you have always been a fool and you will always be a fool. He accepted the pronouncement without quarrel, and in the next moment put the thought away as not even important enough to be regrettable.

"If ye want," Merlee said without looking up at him, "I'll be yer woman until ye leave."

He held out his hand to her. "Hush now," he said, but whether to her or to the voice inside his head, he couldn't tell.

Man of experience though he was, he was humbled that he had never actually held a woman, not with his cheek resting on the crown of her head and her breath against his neck; nor had he ever thought of doing so. And since he had reached his majority, no woman had ever held him. He had been hugged. He had been squeezed. He had resided for a time in the warm cradle, the sweet scissors of their legs, spurred by their heels, clutched by their hands, urged by the breathless and urgent sounds they made. But he had not been held. There was nothing wrong with what he had experienced, he decided. It was fine. It was a hell of a lot better than fine. But somehow it was also irrelevant to Merlee, who had said she would be his woman and then came to him to be held and to hold him so that he could feel the beating of her heart like some small animal he had caught in a trap or a snare and would likely kill. The other women were exciting. The memory of them made him burn. But even as she withdrew from his arms and gave him another brief and mystifying glance and went off into the other rooms of the shack and came back with a worn and tattered quilt and spread it at his feet and drew her dress over her head in one smooth and graceful motion, even then, he was sure he wouldn't remember this moment with so much heat as the others, but with another sort of feeling he didn't yet understand. It was all very curious and sobering.

At a little past midnight Merlee turned out the light in the kitchen so that he could pass from dark to dark, and he slipped out of Elkin. But he hadn't much more than scuttled across the ditch and gained the grown-up pasture on the other side before he began to puzzle over what had happened. It seemed to him strange that he had been so calm and detached, as though a part of him had been standing back and looking on, a part capable of setting the coffee pot aside and—when he took off his clothes—capable of leaving his coat in such a manner that he could reach Regus's little chrome-plated derringer, which he had carried with him instead of the huge Walker Colt. It wasn't like him to be so calm and distant, and he wondered what was wrong with him until he thought better of it.

Women had always been able to play him like a fiddle, and Merlee herself had set the style of their lovemaking. It was curious. The holding and the gentleness was new to him, but there was something missing too, something held back. He paused among the broom straw and locust of the overgrown pasture to ponder it, and he had such a sobering thought he had to sit himself down to let it sink in. She hadn't, he realized, given him her pleasure. She had been so resigned about it all and, in spite of her shyness, so determined.

The first notion that came to mind made him angry. Hellfire, he thought, was she just paying him some way or other for the things he'd brought by, for doctoring the little girl? He thought of turning around and going back and getting that straight with her. She'd said she was shamed for treating him so poorly. She'd said that. He did not wish to think she was only trying to make it up to him. No, he thought, somehow there seemed more to it than that. If nothing else, there was the way she'd been so still in the circle of his arms, the way she did not want him to leave.

He sat and pondered it until the frosty earth had wicked his heat away and he was so cold and stiff it was hard to rise. Well, all right, he told himself in frustration, you have already admitted you're a fool, and women are too big a puzzle for a fool. But it didn't help, for he was in no mood to kid himself with easy conclusions. After all, he could still smell the warm musk of her upon his body. He looked around the grown-up pasture under the high, sailing moon as though to seek its counsel. He scratched his neck, tried to rub some circulation back into his buttocks, and, finally, he started out again toward home, hoping he had invented the whole problem. But he knew he hadn't.

179

# 16

## FREE MEN

MUSIC SQUATTED IN a litter of shavings and sighted down the trigger stick he was making toward Regus, who was supposed to be working on the door; but though Regus had the board which would make the sliding door of the rabbit gum clamped between his knees and the drawing knife in his hands, he wasn't doing anything. "I'd hate to be paying you by the hour, cousin," Music said. He shook his head and made a noise in his cheek as if he were clucking to a mule.

"Yeah, well, you ain't," Regus said, but after he'd given Music a long, hard stare, he turned his head and spat and began to use the drawing knife.

He was, Music figured, still bothered by quitting his job, and more than that, he guessed, by the way Kenton Hardcastle had dressed the two of them down. He himself hadn't been much shaken by Hardcastle, since he'd taken what the old son of a bitch had to say as the ravings of a man who was used to having his own way, all of the time, under all circumstances—a rich man who had glimpsed the shitty possibility that he might lose what he'd spent his life getting and wind up no better off than, say, William Music or Regus Patoff Bone.

As before, they'd gone around to the back of the enormous house and been confronted there by the splayfooted, tired-looking black woman. But this time, after she'd consulted with the master of the house, she came back and guided them through the musty rooms to Kenton Hardcastle's office, where he greeted them heartily and had them sit down. Well, he had style, did Hardcastle. Likely he'd have gotten around to asking them why they'd come sooner or later; asking them what he could do for them, perhaps. But first, as though they were equals and partners, he told them about the little coal contract he'd won. Then, as if Music and Regus were responsible, he plucked a newspaper off the corner of his desk and showed them where it said that two organizers for the National Miners Union had been jailed in Whitesburg, and a third in Pikeville. "We got them on the run," he'd said, and he'd been generally full of gruff, false cheer, Music thought, at least until Regus told him that he and Music had come by to quit. But then, with no warning whatever, an awful stillness fell upon the old man; he turned pale and his lips trembled. "You say what?" he asked, his voice deceptively weak and mild as though, indeed, he might not have heard correctly.

Regus looked a little stunned himself. "I thought I might try my hand at farmin," he said and stared blindly at the floor between his feet.

"You sit there and tell me you're quitting when my back's against the wall?" the old man asked. "When the goddamned Reds are crawling all over the state of Kentucky! What the hell you think you're doin?"

Regus shook his head as though he wondered.

"I've paid you good money! Hell, I'm losing my ass all the time, but I paid you, didn't I? I treated you right, and you let me down like this! Goddam!" The old man's fists were clenched and his jowls were trembling.

"You can call the sheriff," Regus said, his voice humble, reasonable, subdued. "He'll have you two men down to Hardcastle by tomorrow, I'll vow."

"You goddamned right he will," Kenton Hardcastle said, "and let me tell you somethin: you ain't quittin; you've been fired, Mr. Bone! You let me down. You let me down when my back was against the wall. Now, I'll tell you what that means, mister," he said and pointed a trembling finger at Regus; "you'll never hold another job of any kind with my coal company; no, nor any other in this county, not as long as I draw breath. Now, you and that damned scoundrel there," he said and included Music in the shaking arc of his finger, "you get the hell outta my house."

Flushed to the eyes, Regus got to his feet, and for a moment Music thought he was going to make some reply; but, at last, Regus only nodded, and he and Music left as they had come, trailed by the splayfooted black woman, who scuffed along behind them in an old,

181

cracked pair of men's shoes—likely, Music thought, Hardcastle's. She let them out the back door and shot the bolt behind them.

"I guess you don't get no cigars when you quit," Music said, but the joke seemed weak even to him. Regus, who was beyond the reach of humor, didn't reply; he merely went on toward the Model T truck sitting static as a derelict on the pea gravel of Kenton Hardcastle's driveway.

As before, too, the sheriff had been called and was waiting with his hand out when they walked into his office. "Let's have em, boys," he said.

Music couldn't say, nor did he understand, why Regus had been so subdued with Hardcastle, but whatever, Sheriff Hub Farthing didn't get the same treatment. Regus unpinned the badge from his shirt and flipped it skittering across Farthing's desk. Music, who already had his badge loose in his pocket, slapped it down in the sheriff's hand. Farthing, his eyes narrowed and glittering with offense, looked from Regus's badge to Regus. "I don't like a man on a high horse, bud," he said. "Just who do you think you are?"

"Beats me," Regus said and raised his eyebrows. "Who do you think I am?"

The sheriff pursed his lips and declined to answer. He looked at Regus for a long moment. "I'll tell you this," he said. "I don't like a man what ain't a deputy of mine carryin a concealed weapon. When you give up the badge, you give up the right to that."

Regus looked at the sheriff and nodded his head. "Sure," he said. "Sure thing." He drew his pistol from the shoulder holster and jammed it in his belt just behind the buckle. "How's that?" he said.

Regus pulled the drawing knife toward him, wood curling up ahead of the blade. He took a halfhearted sighting down the edge and fitted the door into the slotted front of the rabbit gum. It slid shut. Music stopped whittling on the trigger stick and picked the door up by the bent nail ring in its top and let it slide shut once and then a second time.

"It's too tight," Music said.

"It drops shut slicker than shit," Regus said.

"Sure," Music said, "but the wood's dry. When it sets out on the ground, when it snows, when it rains, it won't drop slicker than shit." Music pulled the door out of the slot. "Take a little more off here," he said, running his thumb down one edge to illustrate, "and here and here too."

182

"Well, goddam," Regus said and yanked the board back.

Music watched him set his jaw and work on the board with the drawing knife. Building a rabbit gum ought to have been a pleasure, Music thought, a good chore, easy and interesting; he shook his head and went back to cutting a notch on the trigger stick. He himself had always enjoyed such things, but it was clear that Regus didn't. He wasn't even sure that, after watching him build four of them and helping on two, Regus could knock together anything that would catch a rabbit by himself. Well, of course, if he used one of those they had already made as a model, he could, Music told himself.

"Hit would be a hell of a lot easier and more fun to shoot the goddamned rabbit," Regus said.

"Well, sure," Music said, "if a man can afford to run out and buy shotgun shells any time he wants."

Regus gave him a quick baleful look, turned his head, spat, and dropped the door once again in the slot. It was not a smart thing to have said, but it was getting difficult to steer around Regus's touchiness. Still, he tolerated it, suspecting, oddly, that last evening with Merlee had somehow made him mild. He stuck the trigger stick through the slanted hole in the top of the gum until it struck the floor toward the center of the box, picked up a second stick, inserted it through the ring in the door, propped up the middle of it with a short notched board which was to stand up halfway down the top of the box, and carefully slipped the end of the second stick into the notch of the trigger stick. He took his hands away cautiously lest the mechanism collapse and the door drop shut. Everything held. "Reach in and poke the end of that trigger stick," Music said, "and let's see how she works."

Regus did as he was told and the door dropped on his forearm.

"How hard was it to trip?" Music said.

"Hell, I don't know," Regus said.

"Well, you set her up and let me see," Music said.

The two of them changed places, and when Regus got the mechanism set up, Music reached inside and fingered the stick. After two or three nudges, the door fell on his arm. "It's a little coarse," Music said; "the damned rabbit would have to lean on it." He withdrew his arm and made the notch in the trigger stick a little shallower. Regus had some trouble getting the trap to stay set the next time, but when Music gave the trigger stick the slightest tickle, the door plopped down on his arm. "Ahh," he

183

said, "that's a rabbit gum, by God." He looked up at Regus and winked. "It's nearly too good. I think it might catch a field mouse, but let's set her out."

Regus nodded without enthusiasm, and the two of them picked up the gum and carried it out of the barn, across Regus's field, and into the grown-up pasture Music had traveled through the night before. Even after dark it had looked good, but when Music had gone back that morning, he'd found it laced with rabbit runs and droppings. "It's a hell of a good year for rabbits, ain't it?" Music said as he got his end of the rabbit gum over the sagging fence at the end of Regus's field.

"Ain't but so many of them suckers a man can eat, though," Regus said, carrying his end and stepping over the fence effortlessly with one long-legged stride.

"Sure, I reckon," Music said, "but a man might be able to sell them in Valle Crucis if they was all dressed out pretty and clean. And next year—you can't tell—a rabbit might be hard to find. It seems to go that way. My grandfather use to tell me that if there were too many rabbits, they'd come down with rabbit fever for sure, and then they'd die back to nearly nothin, and the whole thing would start all over again."

"Can a man catch that from them, that rabbit fever?" Regus asked.

"I never knew anybody to have it," Music said, "but my old grandfather seemed to think so. He taught me to slit the belly and then sling the guts out on the ground so as not to have to touch em; and if the liver was red and smooth, not to worry and take it on home; but if the liver was lumpy or spotted, to drop the rabbit and leave it lay. Ha," he said, "I never thought to take exception to anything he told me, I guess, for that's the way I do it."

They wandered over the grown-up pasture, each with an end of the rabbit gum, looking for a place to put it. "Jesus, right there by them little cedars," Music said at last. "Look at all the rabbit shit, for Christ's sake."

While Music positioned the gum and set the mechanism, Regus squatted on his haunches. "Do you reckon a man *could* sell the damned things?" he asked.

"Can't tell," Music said. "If we git up a batch, we might carry them into Valle Crucis and see."

Regus shook his head and sighed and looked off at the horizon. Music stood up and backed away from the rabbit gum with the fingers of both hands spread lest the trap be sprung, and Regus stood up too. "I don't see why ye don't bait the damned things with somethin, a piece of apple tied to the trigger stick or somethin."

Music shook his head. "Rabbits ain't real smart," he said. "I think they go in just to look around, maybe to see if it's a good place to set up housekeeping. You might try using a piece of apple or something like that, but if you caught a skunk, then the gum wouldn't be any account for a long while."

Regus nodded thoughtfully and spat.

"Well," Music said, "we got two traps at the edge of the cornfield by the branch, two up in the elderberry bushes on the other side, and two in this here pasture."

"And a couple of them damned bunnies already skinned out in the springhouse. I've lost my taste for them already," Regus said. "But I got an awful notion that the time for serious rabbit eatin ain't come yet."

"Ha," Music said, "you might grow fond of them."

But Regus made no answer to that, and the two of them started back toward the house.

"You reckon them silly, softheaded miners have got to Chicago by now?" Regus asked after they had walked a little way.

"They only left yesterday morning," Music said. "I wouldn't think so."

"Yeah," Regus said, "Chicago's a ways off, I'll vow; they wouldn't be there yet. Tomorrow, do you reckon?"

"Maybe tomorrow," Music said, "if they've kept at it and made good time."

"Yeah," Regus said. "I expect all hell's gonna break loose when them idiots get back."

"Well, it ain't any skin off you and me. You don't even have to think about it."

Regus turned his head and spat, then kicked the spent quid of tobacco out of his mouth with his tongue and spat again. "I'm a man without any goddamned work," he said. "What the hell else I got to think about?"

"Well," Music said, "I thought we might cut that bee tree this afternoon and then try to get the honey tonight after dark. You can think about that."

"Buildin rabbit traps, cuttin down a tree with some goddamned bees in it . . . shit," Regus said. "What the hell kinda work is that? And what we gonna do then?"

"Buddy," Music said and stopped, "I don't think you've got a proper grip on the things that need to get done around here."

Regus stopped too. "I expect yer right about that," he said. "Why don't you just go ahead and lay out fer me what the hell I've got to do on a little shirttail piece of land like this?"

"All right," Music said. "You need to build a pigpen."

Regus's eyebrows rose and he colored. "I ain't got no goddamned pigs!" he said.

"You got to get some," Music said, "and then you'll need a place to keep em. And you need to put a stall in the barn for a mule."

"I ain't got a mule either!" Regus said.

"That's right," Music said. "You got one old rusty plow point, but you ain't got a plow. You ain't got a singletree, if you had a plow. And you ain't got but about half a harness. You need to get some lumber and put a hayloft in that barn. When the shingles I rived out dry, you got to put a new roof on it and reshingle about half of the north wall. Goddamned near all your fences are down, and—"

"Wait," Regus said. He waved his arms around in frustration, a pained and despairing look on his face. "Just wait a damned minute; yer not more than a year ahead of me."

"Not me," Music said, "but this here place is. If you hope to make a decent living from it, you got all kinds of work to do, little and big. In the meantime you got to lay in food where you can, and while you're doin that, you got to figure."

"Shitfire," Regus said and looked Music up and down as though he suddenly found him both incomprehensible and very aggravating, "figure me how I'm gonna get the money to pay for pigs and a mule without no job, why don'tcha?"

"Well, you might sell that purty little pistol you loaned me last night, say."

Regus snorted. "I'd be lucky to get three or four dollar fer it in these times, maybe not that much," he said.

"Sure," Music said, "but you might swap it for a shoat."

"All right," Regus said, "and what the hell am I supposed to swap for a mule?"

Music pursed his lips and shook his head. "I don't know," he said. He thought about it, shook his head again, and started off around the gone-by kitchen garden toward the house. "Your truck, maybe," he said over his shoulder.

"I need that truck," Regus said, coming up beside him.

"Not as much as you're going to need a mule," Music said.

"That's just what the hell you say," Regus said and caught Music by the arm and swung him around. "How the hell do you know so much about it? I picked ye outten a haystack not so long ago, cousin," Regus said, "and nearly starved out, you was, too."

"That's right," Music said, and he and Regus looked at each other. Regus's eyes had a distracted, wild look in them, and his jaw was as rigid as a shovel. Although Music was not prepared for anger, the look on Regus's face made him lose his temper too; and as if anger were a disease that could be instantly caught, Music said again, "That's right!" and yanked his arm free.

"Don't tell me I gotta sell my truck, like you wuz some kinda head knocker around here!" Regus said with his eyes blazing.

"I didn't tell you that," Music said. "You ask me to figure!"

Regus stared at him a minute and then seemed to sag. He wiped his face with a sudden vigor, as though he'd stepped into a cobweb; he looked off toward the house and barn. "Yeah, well," he said, "ye take too much on yerself, Bill Music."

"Maybe you're right," Music said. "I'll keep my advice to myself."

"I'm a coal man, goddammit," Regus said. "I don't know my ass from my tits when it comes to a farm."

Music didn't know what to say to that, so he didn't say anything.

"But I reckon I don't like bein told what to do on my own place. I may need it, but I don't like it," Regus said.

Music's anger began to ebb, even though his ears still rang with it. "You'll catch on," he said, which was as generous, at that moment, as he could be.

"Well," Regus said, "less us go on to the house and get some grub. Long as hit ain't rabbit, I reckon I'm hungry."

And they went on.

Ella brought out a washpan of hot water and a clean flour-sack towel, and they rolled up their sleeves and washed, but there was an awkward sullenness between them he knew Ella sensed even before they pulled up to the table to sit down. Still, she did not ask about it. Her head hung deferentially to one side, as though she heard only the sound of her own footsteps, she served them. But Music knew better; she was watching and listening to cipher what was wrong between them, to judge and weigh it.

Music wondered if he ought to stay. His pride and what remained of his anger made him want to drag up. He had the twenty-two dollars, plus the twelve he'd been paid for the last four-day shift, less what he'd spent for mason jars and two pair of undershorts. It was not impossible that he could find a pretty good little coupe for twenty-five dollars, and, hell, two dollars' worth of gas would more than get him home. He mulled the possibility over until it showed all its shameful and disappointing edges. Fact was—though it was a sad thing to admit it—he wasn't sure who he would be if he were home. All the things he had done, worthy and unworthy, and the places he had been—all that had changed him; and he knew would appear to have changed his family too; so that, when he went home, they wouldn't seem quite like his family any longer, but strangers who would be polite to him for his family's sake. It seemed to him passing strange that, when he was down or hungry or beaten, his memory of home was sharp and clear and full of great sweetness; but in this moment he could not even call up a picture of his mother's face, who had borne and reared him, or the face of his good father, or the faces of his brothers. But Ella Bone, she was right there before him. And Regus, the difficult son of a bitch. And Merlee, who was only a bit more than a mile away, and who, however mystifying, had lain with him the night before, and who had said she would be his woman. He did not wish to leave.

But even as the realization came, anger surfaced in him again. Regus was even dumber in some respects than he advertised himself to be. Just naturally and as a matter of course, if a farmer were going to make it, he not only had to be able to sow his fields and get his crops to grow, but he had to be a carpenter, a mechanic, a veterinarian, a blacksmith, a butcher, a damned smart man in a trade, a man who could cure meat, mow hay, set a fence, patch a harness, make a proper potato or cabbage mound so such things didn't rot or freeze and would last the winter out, and do a hundred other things. Regus had a hard time milking a cow or making a nest a hen would lay in. It wasn't very long ago that he'd thought Regus was the rare sort of man who could take anything in stride, anything that came along, and make peace with it. He was afraid he had misread him. There was in Regus, like any other, the possibility of turning sour, the possibility of making an alliance with failure before it was forced. Well, buddyroe, Music thought, you'll have to pull against me.

They had eaten half the meal in silence before Ella seemed able to weigh their bad humors and decide to speak up. "You boys," she said at last, as though she had decided that their anger was not as serious as her

188

own, "I want you to treat each other right!" and she gave each of them a whack on the head with a wooden stirring spoon, which splattered them with gravy and so startled them, it might, under different circumstances, have caused Regus and Music to go for each other's throats like two dogs, hackles up, joints stiff with tension, springing at each other just because some onlooker had scuffed the ground with his shoe or clapped his hands. "Hit ain't right fer you boys to be ill with each other," Ella Bone said, coming back to the table with the coffee pot, "and I won't have it!" She filled each of their cups. "I been seein it in my dreams: they's hard times comin, and we got to stick close," she said. "Hit ain't time fer nonsense." She put the pot back on the stove and tossed each of them a rag from the sideboard. "Clean that gravy outten yer hair," she said. "Yawl look like hogs at a trough."

And through the afternoon and evening—although they were a bit awkward and self-conscious—Music and Regus confronted each other with something like their old good humor and tolerance. The cutting of the large, black-gum bee tree did not go well, and Music didn't know whether that had anything to do with the slow return of Regus's good spirits or not, but if it did, Music told himself, then maybe, by God, it was worth it.

There was trouble from the beginning, probably because the day was fairly warm and the bees were more active than he'd hoped; so much so that, when they had decided which way they wanted the tree to fall and Music had given the black gum three or four good licks with the ax to make a notch, Regus called out that there was a bunch of damned bees beginning to swarm all over hell up toward the top of the tree. Regus himself was sitting some distance away with the bucksaw resting across his knees and his hands folded behind his head.

Music looked up at them and said yeah, the ax was probably jarring them a little, but honeybees weren't like hornets; they didn't find you right away. Having said that, he took just one more swing with the ax before the first bee stung the back of his neck and he jumped and swore.

"Say what?" Regus asked him.

But Music merely left off chopping and stepped around the back side of the tree. He looked up at the bees. There was a good deal of activity going on up there, but it seemed to him to be mainly formless and random.

"Just a stray," he told Regus; but when he'd gone back to work on the notch again, he had taken no more than a half dozen swings when honeybees began to drop like rain, and he was stung on top of the head, on the cheek, and arm, and neck again, the last two bees popping him while he ran, swatting at them, past Regus and across the branch into the cornfield.

"Hey, bee man," Regus called after him, "are ye sure them things ain't hornets?"

Music bathed his stings in the cool water of the branch before he came back to where Regus was sitting in quiet amusement watching the small cloud of honeybees slowly thin and disappear back into the black gum. It seemed a good time to admit that he hadn't actually ever cut a bee tree himself, but only seen it done. There had been a real bee man in Shulls Mills, he told Regus, who had many hives of bees he had captured and made his own; and he'd watched him cut a bee tree and rob it. The bee man had always taken both the bees and the honey. He'd always had a new hive with him, and he'd cut some honeycomb and put it in the hive he'd made, and he'd find the queen and urge her into the hive, and the other bees would follow. And after dark he'd come back and plug the hole in the new hive, pick it up, wild bees and all, and carry them home.

Regus wanted to know why they hadn't built a hive then, if that's the way it was done. But Music said it was the wrong time of year, and they'd have to feed the bees through the winter, and anyway, he wasn't so sure he could find the brood chamber and the queen, even if the damned big-assed tree falling didn't kill her. Also he'd already been stung enough to suit him, and he didn't have a head net or gloves; and when he got the bee tree down and split, he wasn't going to paw around in there any more than he had to.

For a while then they talked quietly about the easiest way to get the honey, deciding, at last, to fell the tree and run and come back after dark when the bees had settled. They would bring torches and deal with the bees as they came out. It seemed a shame to Music, somehow, to burn honeybees, but he could see no way around it if he wanted Ella and Regus to have honey. The bees would die in any case, if they were robbed so close to winter.

When at last the bees had quieted, Music and Regus crept down to the tree and used the bucksaw like a crosscut. It was not so disturbing as the blows of the ax had been. They took very slow, even strokes, and there was little commotion above them until the great tree popped and groaned. But when that happened, the black gum seemed to sigh a cloud of

190

honeybees from the hole near the top, and Regus let go of his side of the bucksaw and ran like a thief. Music stayed long enough to give the bucksaw three more strokes and to get stung once again just as the great tree started to fall, and then he pounded after Regus through the slash and second growth, across the branch and into the cornfield.

Back at the house they made torches of rags tied with wire around the ends of long sticks. They cleaned out the washtub and put a grain scoop and a half-gallon can in it to carry back to the tree. They got two wedges and a mall from the barn so that they would be able to split the hollow part of the black gum to get at the honeycomb. The ax and the bucksaw had already been abandoned at the site and were, therefore, waiting on them. Finally, after they had eaten their supper and Music had read the Bible to Ella, they soaked the bulky heads of the torches in kerosene and nervously and with many misgivings went off to rob the bees.

It was a long, difficult, sticky, painful process. Mostly from honeybees that had had their wings burned away but were not dead, Music got seven new stings and Regus got four—wingless honeybees crawling to the attack, sometimes even up inside the legs of their trousers. And when at long last it was over and they were home again, they had a washtub a little more than a third full of honey, although even that was littered with broken comb, bits of wood, and drowned bees. Still, Ella Bone was so surprised and happy with it, she clapped her hands and whooped. And the following evening—after she had cleaned the honey as best she could and put it away in quart mason jars—Music got to take a jar of it to Merlee, and one of the dressed-out rabbits, too, which had been soaking in slightly salted water in the springhouse and was consequently bleached almost as white as snow.

# 17

## THE YOUNG UNIONIZER
## KILLED

THE NEWS HAD gotten out that he and Regus had turned the unionizers loose down at the Bear Paw. Merlee had heard it, she told him; and if she knew about it, then it wouldn't be long until Kenton Hardcastle and his gun thugs knew, if they didn't already. She had been afraid and would not be consoled or comforted. She did not want him to sneak into the coal camp and see her ever again. "I don't want ye shot," she'd said, "and if you come here again, I won't lie down with ye another time. I swear it!" She would come to him, she told him. She knew where he lived, for she had seen Regus's place many times on her way to Valle Crucis. "Aunt Sylvie can look after the baby. Listen," she'd said, "I can whistle for you. I'll come and hide outside yer house and whistle like this," and she'd folded her hands together as though she'd caught something small and precious in them; and while he looked on amused with her great seriousness, she'd pressed her lips to her thumbs and blew, lifting the fingers of one hand and closing them down again so that a soft, two-noted sound, such as a mourning dove might make, stirred the dark kitchen where they stood. "I can do it loud," she'd said.

"So," he'd told her, "you aim to treat me like an old dog then. You won't let me in the house, but you expect to whistle me up any time you care to."

But she would not be teased about it, and he knew she was right. Regus had already warned him that if he were caught, she could suffer for it too.

And now that the word was out on him and Regus, it could only be worse. Even if he were seen coming out of her house, they might evict her. He himself had made her sign the contract which threatened it. And so, even though he had been smarter the second time he'd come to see her and hidden in the ditch until the new mine guard passed the commissary on his way to change shifts, he agreed not to come again. It had been five minutes until ten o'clock when the new guard had passed by; a ragged man in overalls he was, carrying a shotgun cradled across one arm like a hunter. At three minutes before two in the morning, when both mine guards were most likely in the powerhouse, Music had crept out of the camp, having spent six hours in Merlee's shack with no more light than the fire on the coal grate could cast.

The next morning when he returned Regus's pocket watch and derringer, he told Regus what Merlee had heard.

"Well," Regus said, "I knew it would get out; I reckon there wasn't never any doubt of that." He pursed his lips thoughtfully and shook his head. "I did think hit might take a week or two though. Well, now," he said and scratched absently at the tawny hair rising from his shirt collar, "well, now, I guess they ain't much way to tell what Kenton Hardcastle will do when it gets to him. I wouldn't be surprised to see some kind of visit though," he said, and although Music couldn't think why, there seemed to be light in Regus's eyes at the prospect, and even the hint of a faraway smile on his lips. Regus walked to the end of the dogtrot and looked down at the highway. He snorted and shook his head. "I guess my poppa reared him a fool after all."

Fetlock, roused by all the talk or the walking over his head, eased himself out from under the dogtrot in one long, smooth motion. He looked up at Regus, yawned, and, stretching first one hind leg and then the other out behind him, came over to Music to be petted.

Regus rubbed his palms on the thighs of his britches. "I don't know," he said, turning toward Music, "I may be blowin smoke, but if ye aim to hang around here, my friend, it might be a good idea to strap that horse pistol back on. I'm not sayin ye'll need it, mind you, but I'd take it as a favor if you kept it handy."

"Sure," Music said, puzzled that giving Regus bad news seemed, in some strange way, to cheer him.

Wearing his shoulder holster once again and the blue having all but vanished beneath his eyes, Regus looked much more like himself by the time Music had finished milking and come in for his breakfast.

"Then why do I have to look at that fool contraption first thing in the mornin?" Ella was saying.

"Now, Momma, I expect yer right," Regus said. "Likely when old Kenton Hardcastle finds out me and Bill turned them fellers loose, he'll be interested in them and not us. But there's a chance he might think he owes us a lesson." Regus blew into his steaming coffee cup and gave Music a look across the brim of it. "I ain't sayin it'll happen, but if one of his goons was to show up with a stick of dynamite to pitch at the house, I wouldn't want to have to look for my pistol."

"Lord help us," Ella said.

"Now, now, it ain't like the old days with Poppa," Regus said. "We ain't on strike. We don't work for Hardcastle Coal and ain't demandin nothin of them. We ain't joined no union. Fact is, we fixin to build a hogpen today, ain't we, Bill?"

"That's right," Music said. "We're going to start anyhow."

"It's just that I wouldn't like bein took by surprise," Regus said. "That's all there is to this, Momma," he said and patted the pistol butt hung just forward of his armpit, "all in the world there is to it," and he sucked at his scalding coffee.

It was hard for Music to believe that the frail, trembling old man he had last seen would pay someone to throw a lighted stick of dynamite through Ella Bone's kitchen window, never mind that he had been angry. At least that was the way Music felt when he and Regus went out to carry in Ella's stove wood, but perhaps it was only because such thinking seemed out of place under the bright, guileless, morning sun in a barnyard where chickens clucked and pecked and the frost was retreating toward the shadows. "He might sic the sheriff on us for some damned thing or other I never heard of, but the son of a bitch wouldn't try to blow us up, would he?" Music said.

"I couldn't tell you," Regus said. He sucked his teeth thoughtfully. "The old bastard might only damn us to hell and forget about us. Hit ain't like it was with Poppa. This here is my place, not hisn. He cain't, by God, evict us, can he? And I reckon, if hit comes to that, I can shoot a trespasser same as a coal operator can. Maybe that's the way he'll figure it too."

Music split one last piece of kindling and left the ax in the chopping block. He gathered up the kindling while Regus stood by with an armload of stove wood. For some reason he could not keep himself from blushing. "I'd appreciate it if you didn't shoot Miss Merlee, though," he said. "She's going to come out and see me this evenin."

Regus's eyebrows arched. "Ha," he said, "ye don't say so!"

"Yes," Music said. "She told me she would hide and whistle for me."

Regus laughed, and in his face Music saw the old lines of humor and tolerance. "Ye've got me thinkin, Bill Music, that it ain't entirely Momma's cookin that's kept ye so long in Switch County; no, ner us bein buddies either. Couldn't be that I ken ye a little better than I did a while ago, could it, Bill?"

Music did not answer if only because in some small corner of his brain he thought he was beginning to understand Regus Patoff Bone a little better too: he was indeed cheered by the possibility of trouble. He was a coal man, just as he had claimed to be; and if he was afraid of anything, it was that Kenton Hardcastle might forget him, that the coal miners might forget him, that he might have to spend the rest of his days being merely a farmer. Coal was, Music feared, not only all Regus knew, but all he wanted to know.

"It makes a little sense," Regus was saying as they came up on the dogtrot, "for a man to work fer no pay, to get himself bee-stung, and Lord knows what else, if only ye get the right angle on it."

Having the lighter load, Music opened the door to the kitchen, but he went on in rather than stepping aside for Regus. And no matter that her glance was as oblique as ever, Ella Bone got a look at his face and abruptly set her hands on her hips. Regus dumped the stove wood in one end of the woodbox and Music dumped the kindling in the other. "Ree," Ella said all at once, "have yawl been devilin each other again?"

Regus laughed. "Don't hit me with nuthin, Momma," he said. "I've only just been guyin Bill a little about his sweetie."

"Well," Ella said suspiciously, "I reckon if that's all yer up to . . . " She cast Music a glance out of the corner of her eye. "I reckon that's all right."

"No, it isn't," Music said. "Go ahead and hit him."

Regus tossed his head and laughed, but because of his recent and complicated understanding, Music could not. "All right," he said, "all right, do you want to get at building a hogpen or not?"

"I'd just as lief," Regus said.

"Then let's do it," Music said.

Without regard for Regus's preferences in the matter, Music picked a spot thirty paces to the southwest of the barn, which would not be too close to the barn, the springhouse branch, or the house. Regus merely bobbed his head. "What do we do first?" he said.

195

"We can dig or we can cut posts," Music said. "Some critters can't change their natures," he said and looked Regus in the eye, "and it is the nature of a pig to root. We'll need to go down three feet, anyhow, if we hope to keep them up. If we're going to do it, then we might as well do it right and put down locust posts set close enough together so they can't get between them."

"All right," Regus said. "I can use a pick and shovel. You get the posts. I'll dig."

When they went back to the barn to get pick and shovel, bucksaw and ax, Regus said again that he would take it as a favor if Music would keep the old Walker Colt handy; and without arguing, Music went back to his room and strapped it on over the moth-eaten sweater that had belonged to Regus's father. No one was going to show up in bright daylight to cause trouble; he was convinced of it. Therefore, it made little difference that, after the soaking the Colt had gotten when they caught the unionizers, the chambers might not fire. He would worry about that later. "Hellkatoot," he muttered to himself, struggling to fasten the big yellow buttons and adjust the flowered belly strap. He had been a long time without much to eat when Ella had first made it for him, and over the sweater it was a very tight fit. "Hellkatoot," he said again, but cumbersome as the rig was and ridiculously unthreatening as he supposed it looked out in the open rather than half hidden under a coat, he set his jaw and went out.

All through the rest of the morning and afternoon, he worked hard among the locust growing down from the edge of the woods toward Regus's cornfield. Although the day was cold, it didn't take him long to shed the sweater and the pistol as well, for he was soon wet with sweat, and the pistol was a clumsy thing to have strapped across his chest and under his arm when he was trying to use the bucksaw or the ax. His hands began to blister and a network of pain spread across his shoulder and even into his arms, for he was no longer accustomed to such work. But the labor comforted him and even gave him a grim, illogical pleasure, as though by working hard he could force Regus to work hard as well and, thereby, punish him somehow for being cheered by the possibility of trouble—perhaps teach him, by God, that doing the labor of a farmer was not a thing to sneer at.

He cut the locust posts in what he figured were eight-foot lengths, and when his back and arms were burned out beyond doing any more limbing or sawing, he would slip into his shoulder holster—although he left it loose and flapping—and carry the posts down to the site of the hogpen in order to rest himself. He could not carry many at a time, for the locust was green and heavy as iron, but it was a hard and durable wood and would not rot for many years, even buried in the ground. When Ella called them in to eat at noon, he carried two posts down and hunched them from his shoulder beside the ditch where Regus was swinging his pick. "I don't know, I reckon coal miners don't have to dig too hard to make a living," he said, considering the trench Regus had dug where one side of the hogpen would be.

Regus took one more swing and turned his head and spat. Whatever had been in his face when he first looked up at Music changed. He ran his finger back and forth under his nose. "Well," he said, "I reckon they don't try to work the mine out in one day, for a fact." He leaned on the butt of his pick, giving Music the once-over and grinning. "I reckon they figure they might have to work the next day too."

Music tried to stand a little straighter. "I'll be here tomorrow," he said, "and the day after, and the day after that."

Regus kicked the quid of tobacco out of his mouth with his tongue and spat two or three times after it. "All right," he said. "I won't argue with ye. Not, anyhow, until I can figure what it is we're arguin about." He stepped up out of the ditch and dusted his hands on his trousers. "Less us git some grub; I'm h-a-w-n-g-r-y," he said, drawing out the word and mispronouncing it for the pleasure it gave him.

The homemade lye soap was painful where the blisters on his palms had broken, and when he ate, handling such small items as biscuits, fork, and cup seemed to make his hands creak in joint and flesh. Although it would be slower, he realized he was going to have to limb the posts with the bucksaw if his hands were to last out the day.

Still, all through that afternoon he set his teeth and labored, and by that evening he had a great, ungainly pile of locust posts laid out where the hogpen would be built. Regus paused in his digging from time to time to watch him and shake his head. Halfway through the afternoon, when Music struggled down from the edge of the woods to dump a load of posts from his shoulder, Regus said, "Look, Bill, hit ain't no reason in the world to kill yerself." But Music merely turned away as though, by that time, his stubborn determination had locked him in, even past the point of talking. When Ella came out on the dogtrot and called them in to supper and Music—having just dumped a load of posts from his shoulder—started back up toward the hillside for another, Regus climbed out of the ditch and blocked his way. "Ye've done the work of three men," he said.

197

"Now that's enough." Regus looked at him and slowly shook his head. "Ye've taken some sort of fit I can't decipher," he said, "but I reckon yer a-tryin to shame me."

Somehow hearing it said, straight out, humbled him, and he unbraced just enough to provoke the great knot of pain which seemed to bind his shoulders to the rest of his back.

"I guess I don't understand ye so well, Bill Music, but if it's about Miss Merlee that you're peeved, I meant no harm." Regus's forehead creased with thought, and he colored around the neck and ears. He stuck out his hand. "I'll ride you no more about her; I'll give you my hand on it. But if it's something else ye got against me, then you'll have to tell me, for I'm an ignorant man and slow to ken how I've wronged ye."

The sweat began to dry and turn sticky at Music's temples, and every muscle he owned seemed to stiffen and creak with pain. He had not been wronged at all, he realized. Wisdom, he decided, came to him, if it came, in very small portions. He had been peeved; Regus was right about that. He had been trying to shame him; he was right about that too. But in a moment of understanding that his labor seemed to have paid for, he realized how witless it was to be angry with Regus. It was in no way smarter than being angry with winter because it was cold, or summer because it was hot. All his labor had worn out more than his body; his anger, too, had worn thin. He tried to laugh and made a reasonable facsimile of it. He caught Regus's hand and shook it. "You're right," he said, "I took a fit. It's been about a year since I had any real work to do, and I guess I thought I could make up for all that in a day."

Regus looked relieved and gave Music's hand a single strong, hard pump.

It was as close to honesty as he could come, for if he had had no right to his anger, then he had no right to be honest about it. He tried to stand easy, to put a comfortable set to his shoulders, but no such thing was possible. He grinned and blushed a little himself. "And you can ride me as much as you like about Merlee," he said.

Ella had fixed rabbit again for supper, but it wasn't the rabbit that made Music pick over his food. He had, he realized, worked not only past his motive for working, but past his appetite. He tried to make a show of eating, but he didn't fool anyone. Ella asked if he felt like he was coming down sick. Regus speculated that there might be too much rabbit showing up on the table, to which Ella replied that she wasn't about to see good food go to waste. Music, honest at least in this, said he was merely a little

198

more tired and sore than he was hungry. Regus said he could understand that, all right, and would do the milking, since he hadn't tried to kill himself like Music and didn't have a lady friend to entertain like Music. Even his soreness of body, even his new humility, couldn't keep Music from getting up to take the milking buckets off the sideboard, but they did keep him from arguing when Regus beat him to them.

Instead of doing the milking, Music got down the galvanized tub and set it out by the north corner of the house and filled it with piping hot water from the stove; and in the last tarnished light of day, he bathed. He was pale against the darkness, and he and the tub of hot water smoked like a fire of green wood. He knew how visible he must be. If he should hear Merlee's soft, dovelike whistle, he was too weary to consider what he would do. If he should see one of Kenton Hardcastle's goons sneaking toward the house with a stick of dynamite, well, he supposed he'd yank the old Colt out of the holster hanging from the rough corner of Regus's windowsill and simply—without worrying about it one way or the other—shoot the son of a bitch. But neither of those things happened. While the hot water seemed to reach into him and take some of the soreness from his muscles, the cold air seemed to penetrate no deeper than the surface of his skin and so refreshed him.

By the time he was back in his room, he was feeling oddly content and happy, although he was certain such feelings could not bear close scrutiny, since they were at least as suspicious as Regus's own change of mood. Humility, he decided, suited a man of his principles a good deal better than self-righteousness.

He put on the clean shirt Ella had recently made for him and a new pair of undershorts, taking stock of the all-but-healed wound where Cawood had shot him and Ella had doctored him. There was a thin scab down the middle, which itched like hell, and a very dark scar on either side, where the chimney soot in Ella's medicine had been absorbed by his flesh and would, he suspected, remain with him until the end of his days.

He had dumped out his bathwater and was hanging the galvanized tub on the wall of the dogtrot when he heard her whistle. Never mind that he had heard it before, it took him a moment to recognize it, the sound seemed so natural and proper, at least until he asked himself what it could be. Even though it lingered in the darkness, he had no notion of its direction or how near or far it was until he heard it a second time and realized it was coming from the pasture somewhere around the haystack where Regus had first discovered him. Even Fetlock, curled nose to butt just to one side of the kitchen door, paid it no attention.

He stepped off the dogtrot and paused a moment in the light coming from the kitchen window so that she might see and recognize him before he started in the direction of the haystack. Still, he hadn't gone far before she whispered to him from the ungainly jumble of locust posts, closer and far more to the west than he thought she could possibly be. When she came out to meet him, he cupped her face in his hands. "Come on," he said, "I want you to meet Mrs. Ella Bone, and I want you to meet Regus when he ain't got some damned contract in his hand for you to sign."

"No," she said, "I cain't. There's a curfew on everybody in the camp, and I got to be back by seven."

"Well, it can't be much past six, and how come—"

"Hit's a bad thing that's happened," she said, putting her fingers on his mouth to stop him. "The mine guards killed a young white man in Mink Slide last night, and they know what you and Regus done."

"Killed a man?" Music said.

"Yes, and they's another, a nigger man that might die too, for he was bad shot."

"Come on," he told her; "we'll get you back to Elkin quick, but you've got to tell Regus everything you know," and he took her off to the house.

But there wasn't much she could add. A miner, a fellow named Floyd Lewis, who had been at the union meetings down at the Bear Paw, had given the whole thing away. He had known that one of the unionizers was going to hold a meeting at Mink Slide and he made a special trip to tell Kenton Hardcastle. He had told about the men who had gone away to Chicago, about Music and Regus catching the two unionizers and then turning them loose, and all the rest of it. He had also, since the shooting, disappeared.

"Sure," Regus said, "I expect he has, for one of those miners he told on would likely settle it for him. Was it that damned Eyetalian that got hisself shot?"

"I don't know," Merlee said. "I heard they carried his body over to Valle Crucis, but I never heard what country he came from."

"The Bible's bein fulfilled," Ella said. She had been standing just inside the door to the front room, where none of the three of them had taken any notice of her. "The Lord said there'd be a famine in the land of plenty. He will destroy a sinful nation and raise up another that will serve Him."

It was as though none of the three of them knew what to make of that. At least none of them could knit it into the conversation, since, for a long moment, no one spoke. Still, Ella stood where she was, her head bent humbly to one side and her face composed and calm as though she had merely been thinking aloud. "Chile," she said, as if, all at once, she'd entered the present moment, "I've got food in the cupboard if you be hungry. Won't take me but a minute to heat it up."

"No'm," Merlee said, "they's a curfew at the coal camp, and I thank ye, but I'm scared to stay another second."

"Well, you are a pretty chile and sweet," Ella said, as though she had dismissed all trials and tribulations with one pronouncement from the Bible and could go on to the more important matter of treating Music as if he were a son who had brought his young woman home for approval. "I hope you'll come back when ye can tarry."

"Yes'um," Merlee said.

"I guess I better get you on back to camp," Music said.

"No," Merlee said. "Hit ain't safe."

"Me and you wouldn't be popular down there fer certain," Regus said.

"Then I'll walk you partway," Music said.

"You come back, chile," Ella said. "I hope to see a lots more of ye from now on."

"Thank you, ma'am," Merlee said, but the moment the two of them were outside, Merlee stopped and faced him. "Please," she said, "I don't want you to go with me."

"How can you prevent it?" Music asked.

"Please," she said, "don't joke with me, not if ye want me to come again. And I will. Not tomorrow, but the next day. I'll be a-walkin to Valle Crucis to the county relief office, and I'll stop."

"All right," he said, "I'll take you to the end of the pasture and no further."

She did not argue and they walked together, but they didn't touch or speak until they reached Regus's sagging, half-down fence, where Merlee turned to him again. "If you went on to Virginia, you would write to me sometime, wouldn't ye? There'll be more killin here," she said; "I know there will be."

201

"I'm not ready to go just yet," he said.

"But you ort to go home where there ain't such craziness, and if you'd write me, I'd write ye back."

He laughed softly. "How do you know I can write?" he said.

"Well, you could tell someone else the words and they could put them down. Or if you could just tell me where, I'd write to you; only it would be better if you could answer me back someway, so I would know ye were there." Abruptly she jerked her head to one side. "Ohhh, but I'm crazy too," she said in a small, broken voice; and, before he could so much as stretch out his hand, she lifted her skirt, and stepped across the sagging fence, and hurried away.

He watched until she had disappeared in the darkness, and then he followed. Once or twice he caught sight of her again and shortened his stride or stopped completely. Just before he got to the overgrown ditch bordering the rows of company shacks, he turned uphill, and moving as quickly and as quietly as he could, he found a hidden vantage point from which he could watch as, furtive and hurried, she crossed the wide, hardscrabble patch of earth between the ditch and her shack.

But even after she had entered her house uncontested, he did not leave. He remained crouching where he was, and for a long time he had no thoughts whatever, as though he had merely caught up to himself, somehow, and could do no more than simply wonder. It seemed unlikely that a man he had seen only a few days before had indeed been shot and killed; that the man's life was all used up, gone. Nor was he convinced that there should be, in all the sorry world, such a sorry place as Switch County; or that he, by whatever accident or turn of fate, should have landed there. He stayed where he was for a long time, not so much thinking as pondering, until, at last, without having made the slightest peace with any of those things, without having found even one of them right and proper and, therefore, believable, he realized he knew only one thing for certain: the time when he could have picked up and gone home had passed him by.

# 18
## EVICTIONS

THERE WAS JUST a dusting of snow, no more than half an inch, but it bleached the darkness so that he could see, even though the first sign of dawn was likely an hour away. He awoke sore as hell and restless beyond any hope of further sleep, but he hadn't realized how early it was until he had dressed and made a trip to the outhouse. From Ella's room, from Regus's, the silence was as deep as held breath; and outside, too, the night was dense as stone and deep as a well.

Since he did not wish to wake anyone and couldn't abide the thought of stretching himself out on his tick to wait for morning, he decided to make the rounds of the rabbit gums. By the time he'd done that, Ella might have risen, and he could get himself a cup of coffee before he did the milking. Behind the barn he broke ice in the springhouse branch with his heel and washed his hands and face. The night was bitterly cold, and the water stung his face and paralyzed his fingers. He dried his face on his coat sleeves and his hands on his britches legs, but before he was halfway to the first rabbit gum, his fingers began to ache so fiercely he had to keep his hands in his pockets, where they drew heat from his thighs and chilled them too.

Snow or no snow, he couldn't see into the elderberry thicket across the branch where the first gum was set, and he had to jump the tiny stream, which caused all his sore muscles to sing with pain. But even on the other side he could not tell that the trap was open wide and unsprung until he was close enough to touch it. The next trap, about thirty yards up the hill, was also just as he had left it; but the third, set toward the head of the spring branch, had been tripped.

He set the gum on end, hearing the light scuffling of an animal inside. Not much liking the idea of reaching blind into the trap, he struck a match on his thumbnail so that he could take a look when he slid the door open. Whether or not the lighted match caused it, he couldn't say, but he had the door no more than halfway open when the rabbit made a leap for freedom, and he had to let the gum fall and grab the scruff of its neck. He snapped the match away, caught the rabbit's hind legs, and gave it a blow to the base of its skull with the side of his hand to break its neck. He pitched the rabbit aside and struck two more matches in order to find the various parts of the gum and set it up again. When at last that was accomplished, he picked up the small, limp, incredibly warm body and carried it some distance away before, carefully, he slit the belly and flung the entrails upon the ground. In the light of another match he saw that the liver was bright and unblemished.

He rolled himself a cigarette then, and smoked it, and tucked his hands under his arms to warm them. While he squatted in the darkness, thoughts of the dead unionizer came to him unbidden, and soberly he pondered the nature of death as though trying somehow to understand its specific gravity. He shook his head. He had come very close to dying and had not found it especially hideous, but then again he had drawn back at the last moment, too, and therefore had not pulled aside the final curtain. He shook his head again. He supposed, for all his narrow escape, he knew no more than any other man. What could he know, after all, about the one who had died except that at this moment he was deprived of the sharp, raw bite of the cold that he, himself, could feel; that he could not smoke a cigarette or look forward to a steaming hot cup of coffee. Perhaps that's all there was to death: merely the giving up of things both good and bad. And maybe, indeed, it wasn't the worst thing that could happen, but only the last. And even if that was not all that could be said about dying, he saw no reason why a man should take the matter further. He smoked his cigarette until the coal began to burn him; then he plucked it from his lips and snapped it away into the darkness.

The next trap he found was sprung, but mysteriously empty. By the time he reset it and made his long way back to the grown-up field where the new traps were set, the rim of the mountain was visible against the eastern sky. Both new traps were sprung, and both had rabbits in them.

The second rabbit, however, unnerved him by crying in a thin, bleating voice when he reached in to grab it. Almost always rabbits suffered their fates as silently as if they were mute, but this one bucked and struggled and set up such a keening that he struck it too hard with the side of his hand and sent its head flying through the broomstraw; and for a moment, though headless, it continued to buck and jerk as it dangled from his grasp about its hind feet and, consequently, covered his britches leg with blood. Even when he shucked out its entrails to steam and crawl upon the earth, he was still unnerved and trembling, although he made no conscious admission that death might have dimensions besides those he had conceded.

There was no doubt, however, that when he started back toward the house, he was comforted to see a soft yellow glow of lamplight coming from Ella's room. Still, he went on to the barn and dressed out his rabbits before he delivered them into the warm sanctity of her kitchen.

"Oh," she said when he came in with them, "ain't they just the cleanest, purtiest things? I'll rinse em and carry em right on down to the springhouse; but I wish you'd tell me, son, just what yer a-doin up and about so early in the day. I thought you boys had set them traps all over tarnation."

"Just couldn't sleep," he said. He fidgeted, scratched the back of his neck. "You don't suppose a fellow could get an early cup of coffee before he went out to milk, do you? I got a little chilled, someway."

"Why, course ye can," she said. "Set ye down and I'll fetch you one in just a minute."

He did as he was told, and before long he held a steaming cup of coffee between his cold hands. To whatever degree he had been chastened by the morning, he felt also blessed by Ella's kitchen, and as he listened to Regus beginning to stir across the dogtrot, he tried to forget everything in favor of the simple and comforting anticipation of the work they would do.

The day warmed and the snow disappeared, and with it, the dusty, cold odor of winter. He could smell the earth they dug in, dead grass, leaves, the odor of wormy, worthless apples from a nearby ancient tree, apples many times frostbitten but warming in the sun. Lucky' for him Regus did not push hard and seemed amused by his slowness and the groans that escaped him from time to time. And by the middle of the afternoon, Music's back and arms were beginning to loosen up from the previous day's abuse. The two of them, switching off with pick and shovel, finished the ditching and even had a few locust posts seated along one end of the hogpen when the tan Dodge coupe turned off the highway, and jounced up toward the house, and the last person either of them expected to see opened the door and got out.

"Damned if hit ain't that Eyetalian," Regus said. "I reckon I just took fer granted it was him that bought it."

Music bobbed his head. "Me too," he said.

"He sho seemed to expect it," Regus said, "seemed damned near to count on it. Hmmm," he said, "so it was that little sucker from Memphis, then, that said he'd started out to be a preacher. I'll be damned." Regus turned his head and spat. "I reckon we ort to see what he's got on his mind," he said and plucked his jumper off the pile of locust posts beside him. He did not put it on but merely hooked the forefinger of his left hand in the collar and carried the jumper across his shoulder, which left the .38 in the shoulder holster unencumbered and visible.

Fetlock came out from under the breezeway to bark at the stranger in his nonthreatening, croupy hound's voice, and Ella, too, came out of her kitchen to see what all the fuss was about.

Music collected the Colt, slipped his arms through the hangers, grabbed his coat, and caught up with Regus, who was only a step ahead of him.

Standing by the left front fender of his car, Arturo Zigerelli hadn't moved since he'd gotten out except to take the cloth cap from his head and give Ella Bone a stiff and formal little bow when she'd appeared on the dogtrot. As Music and Regus came around the southern end of the house, he still held his cap in his hands as though, once having removed it, it would be bad manners to put it back on his head. "Mr. Bone and Mr. Music," he said, "I have come to ask a favor of you."

Regus spat and looked the Italian up and down. "I think we done you a favor some nights back," he said. "If we'da carried ye on to jail, I reckon there'd still be two of you."

"Yes, perhaps that is so," Zigerelli said. "But where is the blame when you cannot see into the future?"

"I don't know," Regus said, "but I ain't sure, either, how many of my favors the likes of you and me can afford." Regus ran his finger back and forth under his nose. "To tell ye the truth, I was certain you was already shot."

"My comrade was a foolish boy," Arturo Zigerelli said. "I tell him not to go on the ground of Hardcastle, but he would not listen. However, he had conviction. Perhaps he thought that all mine guards would turn him

206

free as you did. Still," he said, "even in death he will accomplish very much. His body will be taken to New York City. It is already on the train. And when he gets there, a big meeting will happen and there will be many speeches, and the people will walk in long, long lines past his coffin and leave the money they can spare to help the coal miner. They will give a great deal of money because he has given his life." The Italian passed the rim of his cap around and around through his hands. "It is a strange lesson, is it not, that one who carried so great a burden of foolishness could help the struggle against the oppressors so much?"

"Sure," Regus said, "but it ain't all that clear to me just who has been helped."

"Why, you have," the Italian said at once, "and Mr. Music, for you turned your back on the capitalist swine and said to him he could not buy you with his money."

"Sure," Regis said, "and you come by to give us some more of that kind of help, I reckon."

"You have humor, Mr. Bone," Arturo Zigerelli said, "but it is true; I have come to help you again, and to allow you to help your brothers."

"Great God," Regus said and cocked an eye at Music. "What do you think, Bill? I think this feller would try to talk the fleas off a dog." Regus chewed thoughtfully and looked at the Italian. "I don't reckon Momma ever seen a foreigner before," he said, "never mind heard one's spiel. Less us go on up to the house, for I wouldn't want her to miss it."

"Thank you," Arturo Zigerelli said.

But if Ella Bone was surprised or thrown by the Italian and his elaborate manners, she did not show it. When he gave her a deep bow and called her Madame Bone, she nodded with perfect dignity and told him, "Howdy"; and, as she would have done with anyone, when she had given the three of them coffee to drink, she told Arturo Zigerelli if he was hungry, it wouldn't take her but a minute to warm him up some victuals. The Italian said he was honored, but, many miles away, men would soon be waiting for him, and therefore he was not free to accept her hospitality.

Finally, his dark, sharp face gathering into a frown, he said, "If you will excuse me, I would tell you now my purpose that brings me. In another state, but very close, there are tents, clothing, blankets, and food for the miners of Hardcastle; and it would be of important service if you, Mr. Bone, and you, Mr. Music, in your truck, would bring these supplies to the Bear Paw."

Music felt the matter wasn't much of his business and certainly not his decision to make; still, he couldn't keep from asking why the folks who had brought the things wherever they were couldn't bring them the rest of the way.

Arturo Zigerelli said if the two of them did not help him, they would attempt to do it just so, but that a strange truck bearing the license of another state would attract much suspicion and might be stopped and the stores lost. Even if the two of them consented to do this thing, he feared there would be risk, but the risk would not be so great.

"I don't think it would be a good idea to go off and leave Ella by herself," Music said, looking at Regus, who was leaning back in his chair with his fingers knitted across his stomach and a deep frown on his face. Since he had missed his chance to keep quiet, Music saw no reason not to say what he felt. "Anyhow, if you think Hardcastle might be thinking about getting back at us," he said.

Regus, having merely tucked his quid of tobacco away in his jaw, even when he drank his coffee, moved it from cheek to cheek, chewing thoughtfully. Finally he got up from the table, opened the door to the dogtrot, and spat his quid onto the hard-packed earth and scrappy grass of the backyard. "That's right," he said, "I ain't gonna leave Momma by herself to make no trip."

"You think Hardcastle will attack you for letting us go?" Arturo Zigerelli said.

"He might," Regus said. "I don't know."

"Then I will ask some of the men who have joined us to guard this dwelling while you are away. There was the Floyd Lewis who ran to Hardcastle, yes; but there are others who are young and have conviction and hot blood who will be eager to defend your house while you go for supplies. They would guard what is yours for the thing you have done already." Arturo Zigerelli turned to Music and smiled. "You are much admired, Mr. Music, that you beat this murderer, Cawood, who shot my comrade and the black man, who—it is a great pity—died this morning also."

After a moment Regus said, "When would you want us to make the trip?"

"You will do this then?" Arturo Zigerelli asked.

Regus looked at Music and raised his eyebrows quizzically. "Do you think we ought to do her, Bill?"

"No, I don't think so," Music said.

"I reckon," Regus said and scratched his jaw, "but will ye ride along?"

Music frowned. "Yes," he said, "but I'll be wondering why you changed your mind about unions."

"I ain't changed my mind," Regus said. "I never seen one come in that didn't make a mess, but this one's already here." He sucked his teeth and shook his head. "Ain't never quarreled with the notion; only the goddamned unions never seem to work."

"Don't you take the Lord's name in vain, Son," Ella said quietly.

But for once Regus seemed to pay no attention to her. "Hell," he said, "hit ain't likely to be much middle ground around here anyway. I expect a man might as well go on and pick him a side."

Arturo Zigerelli had been looking from one of them to the other. "Is it agreed then?" he asked.

"Sure," Regus said, "only I think it would be a good deal smarter to bring yer stores here, for hit won't matter whose truck stops at the Bear Paw; if the wrong man sees it get unloaded, he won't be fooled. We'll have goons and the law and whatever else Hardcastle can muster down on us. Nawh," Regus said, "folks can tote the goods from here, maybe, a little at a time, and up through the woods, and get by; and we can leave my place and come straight back and have a strong chance of keeping clear of trouble, but I don't like the idea of pullin into the Bear Paw and tryin to unload."

Arturo Zigerelli appeared to think only a minute before he nodded. "Yes," he said, "you are wise."

He told them they were to pick up the goods in Bristol, Tennessee, the day after tomorrow. He wrote down the street address for them and put a dollar on the table so that they could buy gasoline. He told them that there would be a great need for the supplies, for already today the mine guards and the sheriff had come to Mink Slide and loaded the meager possessions of eight families upon trucks and dumped them off on the side of the road just beyond Hardcastle property half a mile from the Bear Paw coal camp. There had been nowhere for the people to go for shelter except into some of the abandoned shacks of the camp, many of them without panes in the windows or a proper roof. There were two families in the old power plant, and one family had even occupied the drift mouth of the mine. Tomorrow, he told them, some of the white families of the Elkin camp would suffer eviction as well, and therefore the things waiting in Tennessee would be doubly needed.

At last Arturo Zigerelli rose from the table and took one of Regus's hands in both of his and shook it warmly. He knew they would help in the struggle against Hardcastle, he said, taking Music's hand and shaking it as well, for Hardcastle was a swine who would take even the shelter from his worker and cast him, together with his children, beside the road like garbage. He knew they would help him, he said and smiled, because he had always had a rare gift in the judgement of men, which had been given to him at his birth. He took two cards from his inside coat pocket and placed one before each of them. He turned to Ella Bone and gave her a formal bow. "I must be quickly gone," he said, "but I will see you soon again," and he let himself out of the door.

Music and Regus sat looking at the National Miners Union membership cards, their names already written upon them in a bold, flowing hand.

"Well, he was a friendly sort of feller," Ella Bone said at last.

Neither Music nor Regus made any move to pick up the union cards. "I don't remember saying anything about joining a union," Music said. He laughed a short, incredulous laugh. "And a coal miners' union; hellkatoot, in all my life I've never done more than walk past a coal mine and look in."

"I hope that's as close as ye'll ever come, chile," Ella Bone said.

Regus took a deep breath, let it whistle out through his nose, and shook his head. "I don't know," he said, "we may be sorry yet we didn't shoot that durned foreigner, or at least carry him and that dumb kid on to the sheriff. Ain't much doubt somebody's gonna shoot him anyway, just like they done his buddy, only it'll likely be too late to do any good."

"He was right friendly though," Ella said.

210

# 19

## SQUATTERVILLE

THE COOKSTOVE BEING dumped beside the road made a noise like distant thunder. Bedsprings came over the side of the truck next and made a windy sound when they struck the earth and again when a mattress landed on them and bounced half off. Bed boards clattered into the ditch like a brief clapping of hands. There were four men working, and three of them seemed to make an effort toward handing things down, but the fourth simply flung whatever he could pick up from the side of the truck. And in no time at all the truck pulled up into Regus's washed-out road, backed around, and went south again toward Hardcastle.

"Judgement Day," Regus said, looking down toward the jumbled belongings strewn by the side of the road.

Both of them had stopped setting the locust posts the moment the truck had growled to a standstill down on the highway.

"Where are the folks who own those things?" Music asked, but Regus merely shook his head.

As if by mutual consent, they left off work and went down to the roadside, but not a soul was in sight.

For a long moment they stood among the possessions as though embarrassed by them. There weren't many, and however shabby they might have looked in the Hardcastle shack where they belonged, scattered beside the road in the bright, mild warmth of the November sun, the few simple articles of living looked as forlorn and ragged as abandoned idiot children.

"Sons a bitches," Regus said, gazing around him at iron bedframes and stained mattresses, a washtub full of half-broken crockery and kitchen utensils, a heap of bedding on a soiled couch. All at once he swung his foot and kicked the metal headboard of a bed propped against the couch so that it went over noisily into the ditch. He shoved his hands in his pockets, and glancing at Music and flushing red as though he'd just been caught in some shameful act, he opened his mouth to speak, but had to clear his throat before anything came out. "Maybe a man can be only one kind of fool or another, but we done right when we quit Hardcastle. I'm obliged to you that you seen it, Bill Music."

But Music wasn't so sure. He began to struggle to right the cookstove, which had been allowed to fall forward on its front. Regus helped him, and they set it upright, closed the slightly sprung oven door, and replaced the lids. Except for the oven door, no serious damage had been done; still, setting it upon its legs seemed a futile gesture.

Music's hands were marked with soot from the stove lids, and he wiped them upon his trousers.

"Well, yonder they come," Regus said, his pale, bleak eyes staring into the distance down the road, and Music turned to look at the figures moving slowly around the bend; a man and a woman and three children, all of them laden. At first Music thought the man was carrying a barrel such as pickles come in. He watched him set it down and rest while the woman and the children came on.

"What the hell's he totin?" Regus said.

"A barrel of something, I reckon," Music said.

"Maybe," Regus said. "Hit's three or four times the size of a keg of powder for sure."

The man caught up with his family and went ahead of them perhaps five yards before he set his burden down again.

"It's a goddamned radio," Music said, seeing it clearly at last.

"Ha," Regus said, "even back when money was good, he likely gave a month's pay fer it." He shook his head and spat. "Just what a man needs who's fixin to settle his family in a fuckin ditch."

Again, as if by mutual consent, they started down the road toward the ragged line of people. The man was just coming abreast of his family once more, carrying the radio hugged against his chest, although his arms failed to reach much more than halfway around it. They could see, as they drew closer, that he was sweaty and wild-eyed with fatigue. He staggered when he was perhaps ten yards ahead of the others; his knees seemed to give way all at once, and he set the radio down in the road and rested his forearms on its top.

"Let me give you a hand?" Music said when he reached him.

"I ort to have shot em," the man said. "Them sons a bitches chucked my stuff on that truck like they was a-loadin lump coal. But I wouldn't let em touch my radio, by God, for hit's a good'un. Do you blame me? Do you blame me for that?"

Regus took the woman's burden, which seemed to be clothing bundled in a sheet, and the two of them and the children passed Music and the man by. The larger of the two boys carried a single-barreled shotgun and a sack which smelled sharply of side meat; the smaller boy carried a mop over one shoulder and a broom over the other; and a little girl carried two framed pictures. And all the while Music looked into the man's stunned, wild eyes.

"I ort to have shot em, and I would, only they was five of the sons a bitches, and it wadn't but three shells in the house. Do you blame me?" he said.

"You take one side," Music said, "and I'll take the other."

"I'd as lief have shot the bastards dead if I'd had the shells to go around," the man said, but when Music bent and began to lift the radio, the wild-eyed man did the same.

When at last the two of them drew abreast of the man's possessions, the woman and the little girl were sitting on the couch with the empty expression of two people in a depot who had missed their train. "Git up from there, Dora Dean," the man said, "and git that youngin up!" Although he had no idea why, Music realized the man intended to put the radio on the couch, and in order to keep from dropping it, he was obliged to help him do so. He managed to exchange a look with Regus, who shook his head.

"Missus," Regus said, "why don't you and the little chaps go on up to the house and rest yourselves. I expect Momma will have some milk for the youngins and a hot cup of coffee."

"Yer right kind," the woman said listlessly, but she made no move to go; she merely looked off in the distance toward Hardcastle.

"Son," Regus said to the boy holding the shotgun and the rancid sack of meat, "set them things down and take yer momma on to the house so she kin rest."

213

The boy did as he was told and the other children followed.

"My daddy was born on that creek fore err Hardcastle Coal Company was thought of, and I was too. They can't treat me thisaway," the man said.

"I reckon things will turn out," Regus said.

"Sure," Music said, "the top dog don't stay on top forever."

Like his wife, the man looked down the road toward Hardcastle, but this time there was something to look at, for the truck was coming back. As it drew closer, Music could see that Sheriff Hub Farthing was driving. He recognized none of the other men, but two of them appeared to be deputies and two, he guessed, were the new mine guards. "Yer a-wearin guns," the man beside him said in a broken, shaky voice. "Hep me, and we'll shoot them goons off that goddamned truck." Music turned to see him ram his hand in his pocket and come out with two shotgun shells—one of which he fumbled into the ditch—and reach at the same time for the shotgun the boy had left atop the cookstove. "Whoa," Music said and grabbed his arm. "Turn me aloose!" the man said in his broken voice and struggled to take up the shotgun. "If you won't hep me, I'll kill the sons a bitches myself!" "Whoa, now," Music said, restraining the man easily, for he seemed no more substantial than a loose collection of bones covered with ragged clothing.

The truck pulled up beside them and stopped. "Have you got that idiot?" the sheriff asked. "Cause if you ain't, one of us can lay him across the head and carry him on to jail."

"I've got him," Music said.

"See that you do," the sheriff said. "We're doin our legal duty, and I don't intend to be interfered with."

The man merely shook in Music's grasp, and after considering them a moment, the sheriff looked at Regus. "Well, now," the sheriff said, "it's a fine day for it, ain't it?" The sheriff pushed the brim of his hat up with his forefinger and smiled; or at least there was something about his face to suggest smiling, even if Music could not isolate exactly what it was. "I'm afraid you're about to have a squatterville on your land here," he said. "And if you don't like bein up to your ears in these here damned troublemakers, I reckon you can drop by the courthouse and file fer an eviction notice. Course now, that's likely to take some time, since I don't reckon you had the foresight to make em sign a legal document like Mr. Hardcastle done." The sheriff gave his eyetooth a suck and appeared to think a moment. "I figure I better warn you that I don't want to see a single one of these damned scarecrows parked across the road, for that's still Hardcastle property." He and Regus looked at each other. "All right, boys," the sheriff said, the suggestion of a smile still on his face and his eyes never leaving Regus's, "throw that junk off so we can go back and get another load."

"Don't throw it," Regus said. "You hand it down, and we'll take it."

"Why, sure," the sheriff said. "It's neighborly of you to help us out." He pushed the brim of his hat up another inch with his forefinger, lit himself a cigarette, and settled comfortably behind the steering wheel.

Regus turned to Music. "Is he all right?" he asked. "Do you think you can turn him aloose?"

"What about it?" Music asked the man he held.

The man merely trembled in his grasp and made no reply.

"Why don't you give me the shells you've got. I'll give them back after a bit. You don't want to get yourself killed or thrown in jail." Music turned him loose and held out his hand, and the man put a shotgun shell in it, withdrew another from his pocket, and reluctantly, clumsily, gave that one to Music too, his fingers, as they brushed Music's palm, feeling as stiff and insensitive as the talons of a bird. Music picked up the shell in the ditch and pocketed all three. And he and Regus and the man began to take items handed down to them from the truck and place them as carefully and neatly as possible beside the road. Frail almost to the point of collapse as the man had seemed, he made as many trips from truck to ditch as Music or Regus, and when the three of them had to carry something heavy, he held up his end, although Music would have sworn he did not have the machinery to do so.

By midafternoon the belongings of ten or more families cluttered nearly fifty yards of roadside, and there were many helping hands for the unloading. As more and more people straggled in, the spirit of the ragged group gathering on Regus's land seemed to rise. Now and again among the evicted miners there were sour jokes and grudging laughter, almost as though everyone had gathered for a picnic that had been rained out. Gangs of children played games in Regus's pasture. Lines of men carried articles which might otherwise be damaged if there were bad weather into Regus's barn. And Ella Bone, helped by more women than could handily move in her small kitchen, had used all the rabbits in the springhouse and two chickens besides. She made bushels of biscuits and corn bread and gallons of gravy and saw to it that almost everyone, as

215

they arrived, got at least a little something to eat. Her head hung obliquely to one side, her face flushed far more by their warm regard than by the heat of her wood range, she was, Music realized at once, a content and happy woman, and he began to understand how completely cut off and alone she had been, and how much Regus's job had cost her.

And as for Regus and himself, what Arturo Zigerelli had said was true: the citizens of squatterville held them in high regard. People came up to apologize for thinking poorly of them in the past, and more than once men shook Music's hand for having laid Cawood Burnside out cold, even though one or two of them regretted he hadn't killed him. Still, their admiration made Music almost as uncomfortable as their thinly disguised hatred had once done. He felt he deserved the one no more than the other, and he wanted neither. Although he could not quite think it into words, he wanted only his anonymity. In the years since he'd left home he'd grown accustomed to it, ridden the rails with it, visited strange cities wearing it like a cloak of invisibility. It had become in part, a definition of himself, which he had assumed nothing, least of all the depression, could take away. The warm regard and admiration of the miners made him feel a little high, there was no doubt of that, but beneath the gloss he was uncomfortable as hell, and he didn't like it. And he didn't like the union card in his pocket with his name on it.

He was helping to dig one slit trench and directing the digging of another when Merlee appeared as she had promised. He saw her standing by a jumbled heap of belongings, looking along the outstretched arm of a miner who was pointing him out. "Here," he said and gave his pick to the man beside him. "Since we have to get it sorta wide to get it deep, it probably wouldn't be a bad idea to sink a post on either end and run a pole between so a man can have something to lean against and won't fall in when he's trying to take a crap."

"Ha," the man said, "we'll do her, Mr. Music."

"There's some posts already cut up yonder a little south of the barn."

"All right," the man said.

"And maybe you could set up some sort of a blind so folks could have a little privacy; leastwise around the women's trench," Music said.

"All right," the man said.

Music wiped the sweat from his brow with his shirt sleeve, slapped some of the dirt from his britches, and went to meet Merlee.

"Lord." she said, "ain't it awful? Seems like they've moved half the

216

people in Elkin out today. What they gonna do? Where in God's world are the poor thangs gonna sleep?"

Music shook his head. "In the barn, on the breezeway. We've got pallets for some of the old folks and little children in Regus's room and mine and in with Ella."

"Then where you gonna sleep?" Merlee asked.

"Well," Music said and smiled down at her and stroked his chin.

"No, you ain't," she said, backing away from him. "You ain't either, Bill Music. I'm sick to my soul I'll hear ye've been up to some foolishness and got yerself killed. If ye own any love fer me or any mercy, ye'll not set foot in Elkin!"

"Shh," he said, embarrassed that such a small and private subtlety could have provoked so much. And Merlee, aware at last that she'd caused people nearby to gawk and stare, bloomed red as a rose. "Yawl could mind yer own business, seems to me!" she said and stamped her foot.

"Ha," said a man squatting with two companions by the litter of.their belongings, "maybe Cawood wadn't so tough, but I ain't sure he can strap on that little gal yonder." The other two guffawed.

"Come," Music said, his ears warming the sides of his head, "walk with me." And Merlee, giving the squatting men one last hot look as though considering whether or not to do violence, fell in beside him, and they walked up past the house and barn. A few yards into the woods there was an old bull pine, which had covered the ground with generations of warm, fragrant needles, and he led her there.

He sat down with his back propped against the rough, pitchy bark and considered her. She sat with her legs folded beneath her, still, it seemed, a little flushed around the neck and ears. He wiped his eyes and smiled. "Well, I reckon you ain't the most even-tempered gal I ever seen," he said.

"I never said I was," she responded.

"I guess you never, at that," he said mildly.

"Men ain't got the sense of mules," she said, looking at him as though she wished to slap him, pull his hair, claw his eyes. He had no notion what he had done to provoke such craziness. "My husband got hisself killed over a head scarf! Did ye know that?"

He knew, but he didn't know how to respond.

"He was goan steal hit cause he didn't have no money to pay," she said, her eyes absolutely dry and fierce. "A kerchief fer me to wear!" she

217

said. "Fool that he was! And you ain't no better. You ain't one bit better. You'd dare gettin killed for sport, to tomcat around!" Suddenly her mouth crumpled and she pulled up handfuls of pine needles and flung them at his face. "You want to do it to me?" she cried. "Do you? Do you?"

He had no idea what to say or do. He tried to laugh. "Well, I did a minute ago," he said. She flung pine needles and the damp, musty earth beneath them at him until he held up one hand to protect his face and reached for her with the other. She came to him fighting and slapping, but he contained her. "I only meant to tease you a little," he said.

"No, you didn't," she said and struggled against his chest. "You're a fool. Ye'd have come if I'd said to. Wouldn't ye? Wouldn't ye?"

"Yes," he said.

"See?" she said and began immediately to weep.

He rocked her, feeling helpless and befuddled.

"Turn me aloose," she said and tried to push away from his chest.

"No," he said and held her in spite of herself. "I think you're a little bit crazy," he told her.

For a long time she didn't move, and if it hadn't been for the hot, wet vapor of her breath against his chest, he might have wondered if she were still breathing. "Yes," she said at last, "I am crazy." She seemed to shiver for a moment. "Do you know how long a body can live on spite?" she asked him.

"No," he said softly.

"A long time," she said. "I thought I could live on it till the end of my days." There was a damp explosion of air against his chest, but whether of laughter or crying, he couldn't tell. "Don't anything scare you when ye got nothin but spite in yer heart," she said. She shuddered and seemed, suddenly and mysteriously, to fit the circle of his arms, as though her bones had grown soft, pliant. "Didn't think I'd own anybody in my life, ever again, Bill Music," she said. "Didn't think I'd care to."

He knew her meaning; he knew it was only a mountain girl's way of saying she never thought she'd admit having someone else to love, but the possessiveness of it caused him a little fear. She leaned away from him and looked into his eyes as she had never quite done before. "I'm sorry," she said. "I didn't mean to act such a fool." With her fingertips, she brushed at his hair, his eyebrows, the corner of his mouth, to clear away the pine needles and dirt she had flung in his face. Then she lay down and drew him after her.

There was a change in her, as though she had the power to become younger and more beautiful than he had ever seen her, and that caused him a little fear, too, if only because on some deeper level he understood it. She had become new for him, and he could match no such trick as that. Perhaps no man could do such a thing; he didn't know. But, for his part, he couldn't even quite manage to shut out the distant hubbub of squatterville while they made love.

# 20

## FIRST NIGHT IN SQUATTERVILLE

HE TOOK HER to Valle Crucis in Regus's truck and then to the northern edge of Elkin, where he let her out as he had given his word he would do. While the Model T pecked and chortled, he watched her turn off the highway up the path that led to her shack, her spine bent humbly over the sack of Red Cross flour the county relief office had granted her. She paused to look at him before she disappeared, this female who had singled him out for purposes of her own, and he had no idea whether he wished to weep or sing or draw his pistol and ride through the coal camp shooting out lights.

But he did none of those. He merely watched her until she was gone. Then, for a moment, he gazed at the coal camp. It looked exactly as it had the first time he'd seen it: a grimy derelict of a town, a smear of coal smoke floating like a veil a few hundred feet above it; the lights of its dwellings, of the commissary, of the tipple and conveyor and drift mouth, giving it an oddly festive, almost carnival, atmosphere. He could smell the sulfurous stink of burning coal. Yet the sight and smell of the coal camp did not fill him with revulsion. God help him, God help them all, there was about the place a grim and sad sort of beauty, as though, such as he was, such as the miners were, they might wish for no better place to call home. Hellfire, he thought, no doubt rats felt the same way about a city dump. He let out the clutch, and Model T lurched across the road and back toward Regus and Ella and the others.

There were three or four small fires burning and people squatting or standing about them when he pulled off the highway. The truck growled slowly up the wagon road, and he nodded or spoke or threw up his hand to those who greeted him, although he recognized very few of them.

Even though it was not yet dark, the dogtrot was already littered with people who had chosen a spot for the night; and he entered the kitchen to the thin, tired weeping of an infant. The mother was sitting at the table, holding the child against her shoulder and jiggling it, while it cried, somehow mechanically, as though it were saying a psalm or reciting the alphabet.

"Bill," Ella said, "have ye seen Regus?"

"No, ma'am," he said, "I just got back."

"Well," she said, "you boys is gonna be on short rations tonight, but I saved a little somethin out." She handed him a small, brown paper bag, folded around itself and spotted with grease. "This will have to do ye both, and mighty sorry grub it is too; but if I don't give hit to ye now, Lord knows, hit might not be here the next time I see you."

"I wouldn't worry," Music said. "When we get back from Tennessee tomorrow, there ought to be enough to go around for a while."

"Sure," Ella said. She shook her head wearily and wiped a strand of hair away from her face with one of her broad, mannish hands. "They's so many little tykes here that ain't et good in an age. You can see it in their eyes, don't ye know. I'll give em a cup of milk to drink, and some cain't even finish hit, like as if their stomachs had drawed up to nearly nothin. Lord help us," she said. "Lord help us. Stick that paper poke in yer pocket and milk that cow fer me, if you will."

"Sure," Music said and got his buckets and went off to the barn.

Regus wasn't out there either, but others were. Blankets were hung here and there, and women and young girls fussed about with bedding. The barn, he decided, must have been declared women's quarters, at least except for a very few small boys.

The cow was not happy with the company and rolled her eyes and ears and stepped about and lowed, and although he crooned to her constantly and rested his forehead against her belly, she wouldn't quite settle down to eat from her trough or stand for long. Still, at last he got her milked. But when he carried the buckets into Ella's kitchen, there were a dozen children waiting on him, and Ella rounded up others soon after; so finally there was little more than a quart left to carry down to the springhouse.

221

Just as he dropped the latch on the springhouse door behind him, he saw Regus standing before one of the fires shaking his head, while a young, broad-shouldered man just on Regus's right threw up a hand in an exasperated gesture. "Goddam! If the mine guards didn't get outten the way, I'd be happy to shoot em!" the young man was saying.

Regus pursed his lips and looked at the young miner. "Ye'd be happy too, I reckon, to get hung for murder," he said, just as Music came up beside him.

"Shit," the young man said and looked away into the darkness.

"Well," Regus said, "when you hot bloods decide to walk into the commissary and take what you want, you be a-lookin for the state militia and the army, too, for them's the fellers ye'll see next."

The young man did not reply; he merely looked away, sullenly, into the night. The other miners standing about the fire, their faces brooding, didn't speak either, as though their earlier false cheer had faded with the light of day, as though they had begun to see themselves as survivors of some great natural disaster such as a flood or an earthquake.

"If yer wife and babies were starvin now," Regus said, looking into the fire as though he, too, were adream, "maybe you wouldn't care to consider what some judge, or governor, or president would decide to do. Sure," he said, "sure, I reckon I'd be treadin on yer heels when you was breakin down the door in such a case as that." He looked at Music without any sign of recognition, but then, all at once, his face seemed to brighten and his vision to snap clear. "But me and Bill is supposed to bring back a whole truckload of grub and tucker tomorrow," he said. "Maybe we ort to save the commissary till times get rough."

"Ha," one of the miners said.

"Sure," said another and guffawed, "we got no houses, ner jobs, ner money; but hit might not always be the easy life hit is now. Hell, times might git hard."

"Fools," the young miner said and stamped away into the darkness. The others looked after him, somehow disappointed in him, somehow chagrined.

"Well," Regus said and spat thoughtfully, "I reckon he's got us there."

Music caught Regus's eye and made a motion with his head that Regus should follow him, and, nodding to the men around the fire, the two of them went off toward the springhouse.

"I was just thinking," Music said, "if you really suspect Hardcastle might send some night riders to visit us, maybe we ought to post a guard."

"I thought of that," Regus said, "but three or four of these fellers is fixin to camp down by the pike. They think somebody might run off with their stuff, I reckon. But they're so poorly set up fer sleepin, I'd be surprised if anybody could show up when it wadn't at least two of them awake and shiverin."

Music nodded and after a moment took the paper bag Ella had given him from his coat pocket and handed it to Regus.

"What's this?" Regus said.

Music found himself a hummock of broomstraw and sat down. "It's our supper," he said.

Regus sat down beside him, opened the bag, and looked in. He seemed to stare at the contents incredulously for an instant; then, giving his head a shake and sucking his teeth, he got out one of the biscuits and passed the bag to Music. "Well," Regus said, "I don't reckon I'm all that goddamned hungry noway." He turned the biscuit this way and that as though he had never before seen one, sighed, and took a bite. "She run through all the grub on the place in just one day?" he asked.

"I guess she did," Music said.

For a long time they sat with their arms propped on their knees and considered the fires, the dim piles of belongings, and the shadowy figures of the evicted miners strung out along the edge of the highway. They ate slowly, for the biscuits were very dry and the side meat in them was tough.

"What was that young fellow so worked up about?" Music asked at last.

"Aww," Regus said, "he wanted to save you and me the trouble of going down to Tennessee. Thought it would be better all around just to walk into the Hardcastle commissary and unload the place."

Music nodded.

"Sure," Regus said, "he's a little crazy. But I seen his wife this afternoon: pale as milk, except for little spots of red up on her cheekbones; got them dark, shiny, kinda slick-lookin eyes. She's got consumption, that woman, and I guess he fears she ain't gonna last." Regus plucked a piece of broomstraw and stuck it in his mouth. When he talked, the broomstraw flipped up and down. "Nawh," Regus said, "he just didn't take to being throwed out of his job and having his wife and babies throwed out on the side of the road." He cocked an eyebrow at

Music and shrugged sadly. "Sure," he said, "the man's mad as hell, and he wants some satisfaction."

Music merely shook his head, wondering whatever made him think he had any right to argue about unions with Regus Bone. Wondering whatever made him think he had a right to an opinion, even if he kept it the hell to himself. His mouth was dry.

Regus spat out his broomstraw. "You reckon that guinea's gonna show up fore we go to Tennessee?" he asked.

"I don't know," Music said and got up to get himself a drink of water from the springhouse branch. He got down on hands and knees and drank from the branch like a horse. The water was so cold his teeth were aching before he rocked back on his haunches and wiped his face on his sleeve. "When do you think we ought to leave in the morning?" he asked.

"Early," Regus said. "Hit'll take most of the day, I'd guess."

Music drew the cap-and-ball pistol and looked at it doubtfully. "It's just that I ain't sure this thing will fire since it got so wet down at the Bear Paw. I don't want to try to shoot it around all these folks tonight though; God knows what they'd think was happening. But this sucker ought to have fresh loads before we go off to Tennessee."

"We shouldn't have no trouble on the way over," Regus said. "Bring yer powder, ball, and caps, and we'll stop and empty it beside the road somewhere." Regus watched Music holster the pistol and shook his head. "I wish I thought that goddamned thing was half as dangerous as it looks," he said. "We ort to have got you a real gun. Hit ain't too late yet, I reckon."

"I don't know," Music said; "it's as good as any other pistol, long as it goes off, and money's gonna get a lot more scarce than guns around here."

"Well . . . " Regus said, but the sound of a vehicle coming down the highway from Valle Crucis stopped him, and a moment later headlights probed around the curve and a car appeared, slowed, and swung into the washed-out wagon road below them. "Ha," Regus said, "if ye speak the devil's name, he'll show up, they say." He looked at Music and raised his eyebrows. "We might not have faired so well on supper, but I'd bet we'll not run short of bullshit and promises."

Yet, when they descended the hill, they found the Italian standing with his hands in his pockets while the ragged men, gathering around, harangued him, interrupting each other to tell him what he knew

224

already: that they had lost their jobs and been evicted, that Hardcastle had promised to blackball them, that it was the middle of the goddamned winter, that they hadn't been able to voice a single grievance or make one solitary demand before they were turned out like dogs. And all because, by God, they had listened to him. But if the Italian's hands were in his pockets, it was because they were cold or because it was his habit to keep them there, Music thought, for he wasn't shuffling his feet in the dust and his head wasn't bowed. There was nothing hangdog about him. He looked each man who spoke in the eyes. And at last, perhaps because the Italian had said nothing, perhaps because his black eyes had about them something not merely unyielding but fierce, the miners grew quiet and sullen.

Arturo Zigerelli looked from one of them to the other. "Yes?" he said. "Yes, yes, go on. What you say is true. But haven't you forgotten the black man who has already been killed, and my comrade too, in your filthy Mink Slide? Haven't you forgotten they were betrayed by one of you? If you wish to tell me your troubles, why do you not tell me all?" he asked and thumped himself violently on the chest. "I should not have to tell you how many are your enemies and how few your friends, but maybe you have forgotten. Maybe I should remind you that it is not only Hardcastle and mine guards and the sheriff but your own weak comrades, who will not stand firm, that you must fight against. I come here and you show me your anger," he said, "but I did not betray you." He folded his arms and looked into the faces of the men standing around him. "Yes," he said, "I see that you must be reminded of your troubles before we can go forward, for I think they have grown dim in your memory. You must be reminded that there is no one to help you but yourselves. You!" Zigerelli said and pointed at the young miner who had been so angry with Regus. "Where would you go to seek help if you were starving and your children had no clothes to wear?"

The young man did not answer.

"Well?" Zigerelli said impatiently. "Do you have a Red Cross in the place you call Valle Crucis?"

"They's a county relief office down by the depot," another man said.

"Ahh," Zigerelli said, "places where the poor, the hungry, can go and receive help, mercy, a little bread. Yes? Is it not so?" he asked them.

No one made him an answer. Sullenly they looked at the fire, or off into the darkness, or at nothing at all. Here and there a man turned his head and spat upon the ground or rolled his shoulders uncomfortably as though to loosen the grip of anger.

"Ha," Zigerelli said scornfully, "if there is one among you who thinks there will be mercy, let him go to the county relief office tomorrow. Tell them that your children cry with hunger. Ask for a sack of flour. You will get nothing! The sheriff will have given them a list of the outlaws he has evicted, or your fine Mr. Hardcastle will have done so. They will have no charity for striking miners or those who have been fired for joining a union. You are outlaws. Yes? Yes? You are criminals because you fight the coal operator, who is the first citizen of Switch County. You are prisoners of the industrialist and the government. You know these things, and I should not have to remind you. I know them too," he said and smacked himself upon the chest. "We know because they have happened already many times in Kentucky. Yes, and they have happened in California, where I fought beside the men who pick the fruit. There is no charity for those who reject a starving wage. Charity is saved for the meek, for the good ones who have no job but would gladly accept slavery to get one!"

Music leaned toward Regus's ear. "Is this the bullshit or the promise part?" he asked.

"Damned if I know," Regus said. He cut himself a chew of tobacco and bit it off the blade of his knife.

Bleakly Arturo Zigerelli looked into the fire, sighed, and shook his head. The firelight played on the bones and planes of his face. "Does the slave love the master?" he asked, as though he were speaking to the fire itself. "Perhaps," he said. "It is a thing the master always tells us, as he will tell us the slave loves his condition and will be happy in no other." He looked into the fire and wagged his head from side to side. "Perhaps it is true after all. It is impossible for Arturo Guido Zigerelli to understand this world without such madness."

"I ain't right goddam sure I understand you," the angry young miner said. "Maybe ye ort to trot all that by again, right slow, so I kin see do I like it any better."

Arturo Zigerelli looked at the young man, his head to one side, his voice calm, reasonable. "Your Mr. Hardcastle has thrown you out like unwanted children. He does not love you," the Italian said. "Yet you, all of you, are angry with me. Why is this? It is a puzzle, no?" he asked and shrugged his shoulders.

"Just don't ye call me no slave," the young man said. "And don't tell me I love that son of a bitch Hardcastle! I'd kill him quicker than you could spit!"

"Are you a married man?" Zigerelli asked.

"I don't ken what my wife has to do with this," the young man said, his face pale, his lips blue, even in the firelight.

"If she were unfaithful, would you kill her?"

"Well, I might," the young man said, "and the son of a bitch that bedded her too."

"Forgive me," Zigerelli said. "I am only an ignorant man, and I am trying to understand. But I do not think I am as ignorant as you. For this time I do not require that you kill Mr. Hardcastle—one day, perhaps, it will be necessary—I require only that all of you stand firm and fight him as an enemy; for he is your enemy; he is not your father and not your lover."

Beside Music, Regus shifted, ran his finger back and forth under his nose. "Mister," Regus said, "I think you are about to let yer mouth overload yer ass. You tell these boys straight out what you think we ought to do and have done with it."

"I do not understand this thing you say, Mr. Bone," Arturo Zigerelli said, a puzzled half-smile on his face. "Please explain. And tell me also, if you will, how your friends have become unmanned, for it is a mystery to me, although I have seen it many times before."

"I ain't interested in yer mysteries," Regus said. "These folks here, sleepin on the ground and on my dogtrot and in the barn, likely ain't interested either." Regus stepped into the circle of men around the fire and hitched up his pants. "Since ignorance seems to give a man the right to ask questions, I'll claim it myself. I'd like to know what the National Miners Union has on its mind to do. Let me hear you talk on that, Mr. Zigerelli."

The Italian looked at Regus for a moment as though puzzled, as though he had never quite seen him before; but then his dark eyes seemed to glitter, and he smiled as though, perhaps, just maybe, he did know this man after all. At last Arturo Zigerelli laughed aloud. "Yes," he said and gave Regus a short and formal bow. "I ask your pardon," he said, and while the men stood about the fire to listen, he began to speak in a different voice, a voice that was soft and sad, if somehow more resigned. "The news is not good," he said. "At many mines, because we were clumsy or because of informers and spies, we have been discovered. Many of our field workers are in jail at this moment; others have been beaten,

227

some tied to trees and whipped until the skin was gone and they could not stand; and many miners have been evicted." For a moment Arturo Zigerelli stopped speaking, his eyes focused on nothing, and in that moment Music realized how strange and out of place the Italian was. It wasn't simply a matter of his queer cloth cap and his striped woolen suit, which, no matter that it was baggy and soiled, did not belong in Switch County, Kentucky; the Italian's body seemed built to finer tolerances and his features were somehow more delicate than the miners', who, in both body and face, seemed long-coupled and angular and rough-hewn, as though they had been made with an ax. The Italian was quiet only a moment, but somehow Music believed he had caught Arturo Zigerelli's own thought: the strange, small man was wondering, himself, what in God's name he was doing in Switch County. Still, the Italian merely wet his lips and went on. "To continue in secret to organize is not possible," he said. "There is no longer any secret. Therefore, in Kentucky we will call a strike of all members of the National Miners Union on the day after tomorrow. Everywhere will be picket lines. Everywhere we will call upon the scab to join us so that we will become stronger and stronger, until we can break the capitalist coal operators and bring them to their knees. Yes," he said and licked his lips and nodded. "We have asked for a checkweighman to be elected by the miners to see that they are not cheated on the coal they have mined." Arturo Zigerelli looked from one to the other of them and smiled. "This checkweighman is a right you have already; it is a law of the state, but the operator does not allow it," he said, tilting his head to one side and shrugging his shoulders. "Also we have asked for many other necessary conditions so that the worker may live with dignity." He wet his lips and nodded. "You must, all of you, learn these demands that we have written down and say them to each other and to the world and, most of all, to the scab who passes you in the picket line to sell his labor and his life so cheaply. He must be taught that you are right and he is wrong. He must be taught that you are his brothers and only together can either of you live like men. Is it not true?" he asked. "Yes? Yes?" he said and looked from one man to the next.

The faces of the miners were grim and thoughtful, Music thought, but they nodded.

"We have not been beaten," Arturo Zigerelli said, as though he had seen what Music had seen. "The tocsin of war has only now sounded," he said and smiled. "Ha, it is only necessary that we be men of steel, because once the capitalist sees that we will not be beaten, that we will have the final victory, he will fight more desperately than he has ever fought before. So" he said and smiled and drew his shoulders up toward his ears in a gesture that was almost comical, "be of good cheer." All at once he took hold of the miner nearest him and shook his hand with both his own, and then passed among the others, giving each man's hand a single firm shake. "Have cheer," he told them. "Mr. Music and Mr. Bone will bring food and supplies tomorrow. Next week your comrades in Chicago will return full of knowledge and courage with which to fight your enemies. And we will win. Yes? Yes?"

Little by little the faces of the miners seemed to brighten, and on one or two Music could see even a faint, wry smile, as though the enthusiasm of the Italian, or perhaps his very strangeness, his queer speech and behavior, had begun to lift their spirits.

"You," the Italian said to the angry young miner. "I have seen that you have hot blood. To you goes the honor of giving into Mr. Hardcastle's hands the list of his crimes, which he must correct." He led the young miner to his car and handed him two papers. "One is for the swine Hardcastle and one is for yourselves so that you can see the new life your victory will bring."

The young miner looked at the papers in his hand as though he didn't quite know how they got there. He shook his head. "I cain't read," he said. "Why don't you give em to the son of a bitch yerself?"

"It will be a little dangerous for you to give these papers to Mr. Hardcastle," the Italian said, "but for me it would be many times more dangerous. It does not matter that you cannot read. Mr. Hardcastle can read, and you will see in his face what is on the paper. Take one or two friends with you and go to his house. It will give you pleasure, I think. Yes?"

The young man nodded at last. "I'd like it better if I could read it to him and make him sign the goddamned thing in the bargain."

"Ha," the Italian said and gripped the young man's shoulder briefly. "Someone here can read it to you, and perhaps you can learn it by heart and recite it to Mr. Hardcastle. And someday, my friend, you may be sure you will force him to sign away his power.

"Now," the Italian said, "I would speak a moment to Mr. Bone and Mr. Music," and while the young miner showed the documents to the others, who squinted in the firelight to decipher them, Music and Regus and the Italian walked a little way apart. "My talk of the slave loving his master has offended you, I fear," Arturo Zigerelli said to Regus.

229

"It came right close," Regus said, his arms folded across his chest and both his voice and his eyes cold and bleak.

"I regret it," the Italian said. "Sometimes it is even possible for me to forget that we will win. I have learned how hard the enemy will fight, and this does not weaken my spirit, but the men do not stick to our organization. Their resolve is weak." He cocked his head to one side. "And everywhere, it is true, our organizers are being found out and beaten or arrested."

Regus pursed his lips and nodded. "I'm right surprised that you're still runnin around loose, come right down to it," he said. "Kenton Hardcastle might not have the money or the backin that some of these sons a bitches got behind them, but he's a hard case; make no mistake."

"Yes," Arturo Zigerelli said. "I have not spoken to him, but I have spoken to the sheriff."

"And you ain't in jail?" Regus said.

"I make arrangements with him for the body of my comrade," Zigerelli said, "but I also have the help of the smartest of our lawyers, who brought the charge of murder against this Cawood Burnside. And, I think, brought caution to your sheriff."

"Will they get Cawood for murder?" Music asked.

The Italian shook his head. "No, my friend. The grand jury has already let him free; but the lawyer of the National Miners Union has frightened the dogs a little, I think, and they are not sure if they dare to shoot Arturo Zigerelli also, for they have been told I will not be found on the property of Hardcastle. Even my pistol, now, I do not carry any longer." The Italian looked at the ground and rocked from toe to heel and back. "It is rare, is it not, that in death a man can do so much? My comrade has raised many thousands of dollars for the miner, and in death he protects me also. But he cannot protect you tomorrow. Two of our trucks already have been attacked. Both were burned, and the stores were lost."

"What about the drivers?" Music asked.

"Of one truck, he was not harmed, but only cursed and threatened," the Italian said. "But of the other, we do not know, for he has vanished."

Regus turned his head and spat into the darkness.

"If you drive to Bristol, you must be watchful, for there is danger now, not just in Switch County, but everywhere," Arturo Zigerelli said.

"We already told ye we'd fetch them things," Regus said.

"Do you have still the address where the supplies will be waiting?"

"Right here in my pocket," Music said.

"Good," the Italian said. "I give you my hand and I must go."

As he had done with the others, he took first Music's hand and then Regus's in both his own and gave them each one single, hard pump before he turned on his heel, stopped a minute to speak to the miners around the fire, and got into the Dodge coupe. A moment more and he had backed around and disappeared up the highway toward Valle Crucis.

"Well," Regus said, "I guess you and me ort to think about gettin some sleep."

"I guess," Music said, and while Regus went off to give good-night to the men who were going to pass the night guarding the belongings down by the road, Music went up to the house to get his quilt, for without quite knowing when he had decided it, he had made up his mind to sleep under the big bull pine where he and Merlee had made love. But when he gathered his quilt under his arm and stepped carefully across the dogtrot among the bundled drowsing bodies to tell Ella where he would be, she wouldn't hear of it.

She had found herself a baby to hold and was sitting in her rocking chair, the sleeping infant's smooth face against the coarse and weathered skin of her neck. Music suspected it was the child who had been crying in that tired, mechanical, almost obligatory fashion when he had been in before, if only because the woman sitting at the table seemed to be the same one, seemed, in fact, not to have moved. Her dark, glittering eyes and the strange spots of red at her cheekbones made him wonder if she weren't the wife of the young, hotheaded miner who had been arguing with Regus.

"Why, chile," Ella said when he told her where he was going, "hit's cold as Christmas! I won't have ye a-layin out on the ground. Why, that's crazy. Ye'll catch yer death!"

"No'um," he said, "I'll be fine. When I was a boy and off hunting, I use to stay out in far worse weather and call it fun; and there's folks on the dogtrot or some of these little children that can put my straw tick to good use."

"No," she said, "I won't hear it!" The child on her bosom stirred and turned its face away from her neck, dragging its lower lip half wrong side out in the process, but it did not wake. Ella's hand went up to its back, her fingers against the nape of its neck and the fine, downy hair which curled there, and such an abstracted look of pleasure came to her face Music

231

knew he was forgotten and could have left without another word if Regus had not come in at that moment and brought her attention back. "Ree," she said, "tell this youngin he ain't to go out and sleep on the ground and it wintertime and cold as kraut."

Regus looked at Music with the quilt bundled under his arm and cocked an eyebrow. "Well, Momma," he said, "first time I ever laid eyes on him he was a-layin on the ground and sleepin like a rock. I don't think he's altogether housebroke yet."

"Nonsense," she said.

"I sleep better when I'm off to myself," Music said. He nodded to Regus. "I guess I'll see you about daylight in the morning."

"Mercy," Ella said. "Honey, dip him up a cup of that broth before he goes. I saved all the chicken and rabbit bones and sorta broke em up, so you look out you don't get no splinters in yer throat. I'll have to strain hit fer these youngins," she said, caressing the downy hair of the child sleeping on her bosom.

The woman at the table rose, dipped a tin cup into the pot simmering on the woodstove, and handed it to Music. She was bloodlessly pale except for the spots of red on her cheeks, and her great, dark, glittering eyes made Music instantly ashamed of his own good health. "Thank you, ma'am," he said, and feeling awkward and guilty, drank the broth off as quickly as he could despite the fact that it was piping hot and scalded him all the way down to his stomach. The pieces of bone, which were indeed in the broth, went down like gravel and broken glass, but at least they didn't stick in his gullet. He nodded good night to them all and let himself out upon the dogtrot.

He spent half an hour raking up pine needles, rolling himself into his quilt as though it were a cocoon, and covering the quilt over with a great mound of pungent needles from his feet to his waist. Finally he drew his left arm inside and, one-handed, finished the tedious process. Except for his face, which was stiff with cold, he was quite warm and comfortable, and he looked up through the pitch-black arms of the pine and the tufted clumps of needles to the stars. They seemed so brilliant and pure and remote they reminded him of his former life with its simple ambitions. Of his present life he seemed to understand nothing, as though, having so recently been born into it, he could get no proper perspective. He needed to think about it, about the nature of his obligations. It seemed to him he must see them through before he could pack up and leave, but it was difficult to imagine any exact moment when they would be satisfied, nor was he sure that obligation was exactly what bound him. In the circle of his arms Merlee had said, "I didn't think I'd own anybody in my life ever again, Bill Music." Was there a time, then, when a person ceased to own himself and was claimed instead by people and circumstances? He remembered when he'd thought he owned himself, and the memory was sweet.

He would have puzzled over it further if he hadn't suddenly heard a noise and realized that something was approaching and in the starshine seen the thin, slinky figure of the hound, tracking him to his bed as he had done that first night. "Fetlock, you knothead, all them people run you off too?" he asked.

The dog stopped short, startled, and Music got some sense of how the hound must feel, being addressed so abruptly and apparently from the very earth, no erect man-shape anywhere in sight. The hound circled warily. "Ha," Music said, "it's me. Come on here. Come on." Nervous, close to the earth, the dog circled in, and finding, at last, Music's face at one end of the pile of pine needles, went into a half-relieved, half-puzzled fit of tail wagging and whining and face licking. "Stop, you son of a bitch," Music said, for the hound seemed to think he needed digging up, as though he were a landslide victim or a favorite bone. At last Music had to free an arm and settle Fetlock down, scratching the hound's head and long velvet ears until he lay down with his head on Music's chest.

That was good. The dog's warmth seeped down to him, and his only problems were his face, searingly cold where the dog had licked him, and his bladder, which wished to be emptied even though he had already emptied it before he ever got to the bull pine to make his bed. Must be the broth, he thought; it went straight through me.

Nevertheless, he made up his mind to pay no attention to either problem. He didn't. And he slept straight through till morning.

# 21

## THE BRISTOL RUN

EVERYTHING WAS RIMED with hoarfrost. The very air seemed frozen stiff. And the Model T didn't want to start. Both Regus and Music took half a dozen turns at the hand crank. Still, the motor finally kicked over and caught, the handle of the crank tearing itself from Music's grip with nearly enough force to break his thumb. Regus adjusted the spark and throttle and stuck his head out of the crack of the open door. "Aire ye hurt then?" he asked.

"No, the mulish son of a bitch!" Music said, and wagging his hand on the end of his arm as though he were drying it, he got in the truck, and they backed around and started off toward Elkin.

It was about the time of day when they had formerly gone to work, and sure enough, as they passed the commissary, Cawood and Grady Burnside were lounging on the steps. Regus, who had appeared that morning wearing his old miner's cap as though it were a twenty-dollar Stetson, tipped it grandly as the Model T clucked past.

Music rolled himself a cigarette and lit it. They were well past Mink Slide and the cigarette was half gone before he spoke. "I didn't think you were the sort of man who would poke a snake for no reason," he said.

"I been a paid son of a bitch for a long time," Regus said. "What makes you think I ain't got a reason?"

"Well," Music said, "you seem to take my meaning anyway. I guess you think we've got as fine a chance to get to Bristol and back with you wearing that cap as we would otherwise."

Regus stared straight down the road, no expression whatever on his face. Finally he took off the cap and pitched it on the seat between them, and no more was said about it. But in some corner of Music's brain it seemed significant and worrisome.

About a mile below the Bear Paw they pulled off the road, and Music fired the Colt. Much to his surprise, all five loaded cylinders went off without so much as a hangfire, and the stone he was aiming at—somewhat smaller than a dinner plate and around thirty yards distant—bore the marks of five .44-caliber balls. With the smoke hanging in the frigid air and his ears still ringing, he sat on the running board and recharged and recapped the pistol, resting the hammer, at last, on the nipple of the empty chamber. "A man couldn't want a better pistol than that," he said, when he climbed back in the truck. He set the musette bag containing powder, balls, caps, cornmeal, lard, nipple wrench, and nipple prick down directly on top of Regus's miner's cap.

"Absolutely," Regus said, "so long as you're a-shootin at rocks." He sniffed. "They mean you no harm, wait while you reload, and hold right still while ye chew yer tongue and take aim."

"Ha," Music said.

After about an hour they passed through a community called Saltlick and then another called Fivemile, where two men armed with shotguns waved them down.

One man held his shotgun leveled at the cab of the truck, and the other came up to Music's window, propped his foot on the running board, touched the brim of his hat, and asked, "Where you fellers bound?" He had a gold tooth and held his shotgun casually beside his leg and pointed at the ground.

"Over Tennessee way," Music said. "Hope to buy a hog or two."

"Ain't they no hogs in Kentucky?" the man asked.

"Sure," Music said, "but my uncle don't own em. He's got two he didn't butcher and don't want to feed em over. Wrote and said I could have em fer three dollars apiece and them pretty good-sized." He hoped to hell he sounded like a Kentucky farmer. The man with the gold tooth flicked his eyes from the pistol butt sticking out of Music's coat and the lump it made against his side to Music's face, to Regus, and back to the pistol. Regus's .38, luckily, could not be seen beneath his jumper.

"Yer right well armed just for buyin a pig," the man said.

"Lord," Music said, "I'd like to get home with it. Damned coal miners all makin a fuss and trouble, and people up to meanness. If I pay for a couple of hogs, I aim to get back home with em."

The man's eyes covered exactly the same ground as they had a moment before.

"It's gettin to where a poor farmer cain't hardly even travel the road," Music said.

The man appeared to think about it and then abruptly swung his head for them to move on, saying to his partner across the road, "Let em pass."

When they were a little way distant from the armed men, Regus cut his eyes around to Music without quite moving his head. "Well, well, well," he said. "Who would have thunk ye'd show such a talent for lyin." Regus tasted the inside of his mouth and grinned in a way that sent a little buzz of anger through Music. "A feller just don't know who in hell to trust anymore."

Music was himself surprised at what had come out of his mouth. "I intend to get to Bristol, and I intend to bring them damned supplies back," he said and began at once to take off his coat so that he could get rid of the shoulder holster and the enormous pistol. With Regus watching out of the corner of his eye, Music wrapped pistol, musette bag, and Regus's miner's cap in a rag and put them on the floorboard.

"They's a feller back yonder who's gonna be lookin fer us to come back with a couple of pigs. What tale you gonna tell him next time?"

"I don't know," Music said. He looked out the window as the last of Fivemile's wretched company housing fell behind. "I think we ought to find another way home."

Regus nodded. "I reckon we could go around by Harlan and there," he said.

"I think we better," Music said.

"I guess," Regus said. "Hit would save us comin through Mink Slide and Elkin with our tucker, though goddam Harlan ain't the place I'd pick to visit just now neither."

For a long time then they were silent, while the Model T made its fusty, clamorous way down the road and the climbing sun caused the frost, which lay everywhere, to creep toward the shaded lee of the hills. Slowly Music's spirits began to rise. Hell, he thought, if they were smart and had a little luck, they'd make it to Bristol and back all right; and it

236

was a grand thing just to be on the move for a change, just to be going somewhere again, no matter what the circumstances.

When they got to Pineville and Music saw a little café with its windows all but painted over with the list of fare, he almost laughed aloud. They'd had no supper to speak of and no breakfast at all, but unlike most times in his life, he had money, well over twenty dollars tucked in a tobacco sack in his breast pocket. He was hungry, and it was a wonderful thing to be hungry when you happened to be a man of means.

He pointed out the café to Regus, but Regus said he'd just as soon find a grocery store where he could get some crackers and sardines and maybe a little cheese.

"You goddamned hick," Music said and laughed. "We are going to have some hot food and coffee and a piece of pie. I'll stand you to it."

And although Regus argued that it didn't seem right to pay some stranger extra to cook and serve them victuals on a dish, Music said he wasn't going to be done out of proper food just because Regus was afraid to eat in a café. "Well, goddamn you then!" Regus said and pulled the truck over. He gave Music the little chrome-plated derringer to stick in his pocket, since it was obvious he meant to leave the Colt hidden on the floorboard.

Music wouldn't have admitted it, perhaps even to himself, but the simple matter of sitting at the counter of the little café made him feel better than he had in months. Ella's good cooking aside, it just wasn't the same. Nor was it simply that he could choose, among many possibilities, just the sort of thing he craved—a bowl of, by God, chili and a piece of apple pie, never mind that it was breakfast—no, the matter of eating in a café was on a whole different basis. It was out in the world, fraternal, cash-and-carry, and no strings attached. Somehow in a woman's kitchen a man felt forever obliged and bound in some odd way. Sure, from the first time they stuck a tit in a fellow's mouth until they buried him, they presided over the simple pleasure of eating. He hadn't felt so good since he was in Chicago, before his luck, and the luck of the whole world, seemed to turn bad. The chili was fine stuff with a special hot kick, and there was a big bowl of crackers between them to crumble into it. And pie. It was a wonderful café, rich with the smell of coffee and many kinds of food; even the underlying, pissy odor of old grease was just as it should have been.

He could have lingered far longer than they did, but the time came to check himself against the bill of fare and prices chalked on a blackboard behind the counter and count out what he owed: ten cents apiece for the bowls of chili, ten cents apiece for the generous slices of pie, the coffee being free, coming as it did with the food. He even left a nickel tip, and when the counterman called them gents and told them to hurry back, he didn't feel like just another stiff down on his luck, but, for a fleeting moment, a man of potential and promise.

They stopped again for gas, and when the Model T was pecking down the road once more, Regus said, "I never had no chili fed me until this day and I'll admit to it, but I'll hand it to ye, I could eat a bowl of that six times a week." He jerked his chin to one side and sucked his teeth in affirmation. "I wonder what they put in them old kidney beans to make em taste so grand."

"We'll stop somewhere on the way back and have some more," Music said.

"Well, now, I'll hold ye to that, Bill Music; I surely will," Regus said.

They made good time and had no more trouble until just before they crossed the Virginia line, where they were stopped once more by armed men and asked their business. Music told his story about the uncle in Tennessee with the pigs, and once again they were allowed to pass.

No one bothered them in Virginia, and they saw no more than two coal tipples in that whole corner of the state, although there were many small farms. As they were passing one, which looked particularly fertile and well kept, Music sat up suddenly in his seat. "Pull in here," he said. "By God, I've got a notion we can drive right past them gun thugs on the way back."

But when Music asked the farmer if he could buy some hay, the man shook his head sadly and explained that hay wasn't worth anybody's time to sell. Last year and the year before, those who had raised it for market could hardly give it away, so no one fooled with more than they needed for their own stock. At last, however, he gave Music the name of a man further down the road who just might have extra.

At the second place they had better luck, and for a dollar they bought a load of alfalfa that filled the truck. The farmer seemed very surprised with his good fortune and looked at the dollar bill Music gave him carefully before he tucked it away into the bib pocket of his overalls. When Music offered him another fifty cents for the sweat-stained, hard-worn straw hat on his head, the man was struck dumb. He looked at

Music. He took off his hat and looked at it, turning it this way and that in his hand as though to discover the source of its secret value. "Son," he said, "I reckon the hay's worth nearly four bits, but this hat never cost me more than twenty cent and it new."

"I'd like to buy it," Music said, for it seemed just the touch to make their disguise complete; he stretched the half-dollar toward the farmer. The man looked at the coin a moment, then took it, and thrust his hat toward Music. With a smile Music put it on and gave the crown a snappy pat. "Pretty good fit," he said.

"I hope the Lord don't strike me," the farmer said, tucking the fifty-cent piece away as well, "for I never lied to ye."

The spare tire thrown atop the load of hay to hold it down, they puttered and pecked through the streets of Bristol, stopping now and again to ask directions. They asked no policeman for fear he would know at once, somehow, what they were up to and send word back to every sheriff, mine guard, and gun thug in Kentucky to be on the lookout for their return. Still, at last they found the proper street, although they didn't believe it, if only because they hadn't expected to be among houses almost as large and fine as Kenton Hardcastle's. Certainly they were better kept, if not so big. They'd expected a defunct warehouse, or a big tent such as revivals were held in, or maybe a shed off some alley. "Well," Music said, "park it and let me go and see." He looked from the slip of paper Arturo Zigerelli had given him to the house number hanging from a lamp beside a long flagstone walkway. The house was a large stucco affair with a red tiled roof. "Hellkatoot," Music said, "this just ain't right. That little sucker gave us the wrong address."

But although the man who answered the door couldn't place the name of Arturo Zigerelli, it was not the wrong address. "We are expecting men from Consolidated Coal Company in Jenkins and from Hardcastle Coal Company—that terrible place where the young organizer was murdered," the man said.

"That's us," Music said.

"Wonderful," the man said and shook Music's hand and patted him on the back. "Marie," he shouted over his shoulder, "come! Come! Well," he said, "how goes the fight?"

"There wasn't any fighting when we left this morning," Music told him and realized at once he had mistaken the question. It made him feel foolish and stupid. "Well, I guess a good many miners have been evicted, and we've about run out of something to eat for sure," he added.

239

"Marie," the man shouted over his shoulder, "I want you to meet the brave miner who has come from Hardcastle Coal Company!"

Music wanted to explain that he was not a miner, but at that moment a young woman appeared, staring at him as though she wanted to fix his face forever in her memory, her eyes already a bit wet as though she might weep. "It's an honor," she said in a husky voice, and to his great surprise, stepped forward and hugged him fiercely for a good many seconds. He looked over her shoulder at the man, wondering if he was her husband or brother or what. He didn't seem to mind, whoever he was. He merely stood nodding his handsome head as though Music were a present or some sort of pet he had bought her. Dressed in hound's-tooth trousers and a soft sweater, his hair parted in the middle with a gentle wave over each temple, he reminded Music of an advertisement in a magazine.

"Uhhh," Music said, "you don't reckon you could tell me where the supplies we came to fetch are at?" He wondered what the hell Regus was thinking, watching all this from the truck. "Some folks are sorta anxious for us to get back," he said apologetically. Abruptly Marie stepped away, held him at arm's length, and looking at him with eyes as dark and dusky as wet plums, said, "Of course."

"Our garage is packed from floor to ceiling with food and supplies," the man said, "but your truck seems to be full already."

Music waved Regus into the driveway. "Yes," he admitted. "Goons stopped us twice this morning and asked us what we were up to. I thought if we went back looking like a couple of farmers with a big old load of hay, we might stay out of trouble."

"Very clever indeed," Marie said.

When Regus had driven around the house to the garage and stepped down from the truck, the man said, "Another brave miner from Hardcastle," and took Regus's arm as though to lead him into Marie's embrace, but she gave him only a firm, brisk handshake.

They could have put a couple of pitchforks to good use, but there was nothing like a pitchfork anywhere about, so they had to haul the hay off the truck by hand. There was, however, a wealth of goods in the garage: tents and blankets and cases of tinned meat and canned goods, perhaps a ton of flour in ten-pound bags, dried beans, potatoes, coffee. They got the feeling they could take as much of anything as they desired. It was like robbing a bank while the bankers held the doors open and inquired after the health of their families. They wished for a bigger truck. They regretted the necessity for taking tents, which, though they were folded

240

marvelously flat, took up considerable space. From time to time they glanced at each other and agreed with no more than a small shake of the head or a fish-eyed nod that tinned meat was more important than blankets or that dried beans had it over another sack of potatoes. And all the while, with what appeared to be something like joy, the man and woman asked endless questions about the conditions of the coal miner and life in a company-owned town. Music was happy to let Regus do the talking, since he himself wasn't exactly an expert; but then too, Regus seemed to be taking pleasure in painting as grim a picture of coal mining as possible. And he had a talent for it, being able in the fewest words to give them a world far colder, hungrier, and more dangerous than they seemed to expect. After a while, Music sensed they'd spied more misery than they could quite get their minds around, more than they had a taste for. It seemed no longer to flatter them, and they grew quiet and began to be a bit more help in loading the truck.

"Hellfire," Regus said at last, standing back as though to get a perspective on the tremendous load of goods, "I don't think the truck will haul it."

"Yes, it will," Music said.

Regus jerked his chin to one side. "I don't know," he said, "but if we go up any higher, and we hit the first bump, the whole damned load will fall over."

"We'll tie her down," Music said. "Think of the folks we can feed with just one or two more layers of them canned goods stacked on."

"Sure," Regus said, "but we can't feed nobody if we don't get there."

They compromised at a half dozen more cases of canned goods, but even that put the load a bit higher than the stake body and cab of the truck. Still they unfolded a tent and covered the load with it and tied it all down with tent rope, and then set about disguising the whole business with hay. They'd left a few inches of space between the sideboards and tailgate and the stacked supplies, and that space was easy enough to fill and pack tight with hay, but rounding off the top was more difficult, and they had to use a great deal of rope to secure it, tying the spare tire, at last, on the very top like a bottle cap on a pumpkin.

When they had finished, Regus stood gazing at the truck and shaking his head.

"That's just the way it ought to look!" Music told him. "It looks like too big a load to be anything in the world except just hay."

Regus scratched the back of his neck doubtfully. "Lord God help us if we have a flat," he said.

When the awkward moment for parting came, the man, dressed so fine in his hound's-tooth trousers and handsome sweater, began to blush. "A word of caution," he said. "If you should happen to get caught, it's very important that you do not mention us or this address." He laughed a panting sort of laughter. "It's possible we could get in serious trouble if you did."

"Don't bother yer head about that," Regus said. "Won't nobody get one word from us."

"It's just that we want the supplies to be here for others," the woman said.

"Absolutely," Music said.

There was a great deal of solemn, earnest handshaking all around, but no more hugging, and Music and Regus climbed into the truck and pulled out into the street.

"Sweet Jesus," Regus said, "feels like I'm drivin a mountain. I'd hate to try to outrun anybody loaded like this."

"Hell," Music said, "we couldn't outrun anybody in this truck if it was empty unless they were afoot. If you want to worry about something, worry about how far it will take you to stop it after you tell it whoa."

Regus got out his plug of tobacco and his pocketknife. "Hot damn!" he said. "What a haul! Ain't we got a load of tucker on here though?"

"Yeah," Music said. He shook his head soberly. "How come I still feel we went to the wrong address?"

"Ha," Regus said. "I don't know, but I don't reckon the joke's on us."

Music put on his straw hat and rolled himself a cigarette while Regus drove, spat out the window, and, every few minutes, chuckled to himself. But he turned serious when the truck had to climb the first long, steep grade, for the Model T was beginning to steam when it growled slowly over the crest in low gear. Going down the far pitch was sobering too, for the load wasn't merely heavy; it was top-heavy. Twenty or twenty-five miles an hour was all they dared on level road, and on a grade, far less.

At Big Stone Gap they stopped to get chili for Regus and water for the Model T. They had filled the radiator and bought some gas, and Regus had opened the cock to check the oil, when the service station man said,

242

"Yawl must be a-carrin a load of hay over to the stock barn in Francis."

"Sure," Music said.

"I reckon they'll learn, hereafter, about fillin their damned barns with wet hay," the man said and laughed.

"Fire?" Music asked.

"Well, hell, you know they wuz a fire or ye wouldn't be a-haulin hay to em," he said and made a funny face.

"No, well, I mean I didn't know it was wet hay that started it," Music said.

"That's what I hear," the man said.

"Oil's up to the top cock," Regus said. "I got my fanger in her. Where's the best place around here for a man to git a good bowl of chili?"

"They's an eatery down by the depot," the man said. "I don't know much about the fare, but it's the onliest place it is around here, for sure."

"Would you have a jug or somethin to carry water in we could buy off ye?" Regus asked.

"Sholy," the man said. He got them a jug and filled it with water for the radiator, but would take no money for it; and they went off to find the depot and the eatery, where Regus had two bowls of chili and declared them: "Wonderful tasty, nearly as good as I've ever et." Although later, when they were back on the road again, he confessed the chili that morning had been better because it had more kick and was a little runnier, so a man could crumble lots of crackers in it.

They talked for a long while then about the National Miners Union and whether or not the strike would work, and Regus grew very thoughtful and serious. The little Italian was right, Regus said; the operators had stolen out of the miner's pocket to underbid each other until there was nothing left to steal, except from themselves. Coal mining was eating itself up. Who could tell? he said; maybe the National Miners Union could stick it out and win. There was no figuring the fool operators and how hard they would fight when their backs were against the wall. Still, the time seemed right. The miner didn't have much of anything to lose by striking, and the National Miners Union was a new bunch, not one of the others that had already failed. Yet, Regus said, it didn't feel right someway; he didn't know just how. Maybe it was that

243

both sides seemed worn out with the struggle and desperate, which might cause them to fight crazy or just throw up their hands. Who could tell? And those folks in that fancy house with their garage heaped full of supplies for the goddamned ragged-assed coal miners—now that was like the sun coming up on the west side of the hill. He couldn't figure them into the situation at all, but it put a funny taste in his mouth someway.

About the time they crossed the Kentucky line, Regus said, "Why do you figure that fancy woman grabbed on to you like that? She scooped you up like a sugar daddy; I seen it from the truck!"

"I've been thinking about that myself," he said. "I don't know. Maybe she thought I was good-lookin."

"Ha," Regus said, "maybe so, maybe so. I've hear it said that rich folks are kindly queer. Maybe that's all it is to it."

But Music was thinking of the summer he was twelve and had been baptized at the Shulls Mills Lutheran Church. Two or three women he hardly knew had hugged him just as fiercely. Yes, and they had looked at him in just the same way, their eyes dark and moist. Somehow they had felt it necessary to welcome him into the fellowship of Christ with their bodies, rather than the way a man would, with words or a handshake. He was wondering whether or not it was too personal or foolish to talk about when he saw the long narrow bridge ahead of them and, at the other end, parked cars and men with badges and guns. "Hellfire," he said, "look yonder."

"I done already seen em," Regus said, pulling the throttle lever back and testing the brakes.

Music settled the farmer's hat more firmly on his head and threw up his hand to greet the sheriff, who, with four other men standing behind him, was blocking the center of the road. "Howdy," Music said.

"I see you boys got one hell of a load of hay," the sheriff said, coming up on Regus's side of the truck. "Where you headed with it?"

"Francis," Music said, leaning forward to talk across Regus, "over to the stockyard."

The sheriff pursed his lips. "Ain't that peculiar?" he said, "Francis bein behind you, like it is."

"Ha," Regus said, "my brother can't half hear. We *come* from Francis. Hay barn burned down over yonder, and we thought we had this load sold, but I reckon everbody else beat us to it. We live over in Leslie County, and we just goin home."

Jesus Christ, Music thought to himself; he could feel his face heating up, feel his ears warming the sides of his head.

"Is that right?" the sheriff said, looking from one of them to the other in a way that made Music suspect he saw right through them.

"Wouldn't have any need for a load of alfalfa, would ye, sheriff?" Music asked. "We'd let the whole truckload go fer three dollar and a half. Save us a-haulin it all the way back home."

Another man had come up by Music's side of the truck. "Alfalfa hell," he said, looking up at the load, "looks like broomstraw to me."

"Hit's alfalfa and as good a crop as we ever made," Music said.

The man pulled a great handful of it from between the sideboards of the truck bed, ragged it between his hands, and smelled it. "I'll give a dollar for it," he said.

"I guess we could let it go for three, just to save us a-makin a long haul fer nuthin," Music said.

"What do you say to a dollar and a half?" the man said.

"Why don't you shut up, Cal?" the sheriff said.

"Well, I didn't get all my hay in and I'm a little short," the man said in a peeved and querulous voice. "I'll give two dollars, and that's my final offer."

The sheriff looked to be losing his patience, and Music allowed himself to hope that they were going to get away with it after all.

"I'll eat the goddamned hay myself before I'll sell it fer two dollars," Regus blurted before Music could do any more bargaining.

"All right, two and a quarter," Cal said, "but I won't give more."

"I told you once to shut up!" the sheriff said. He looked from Regus to Music and back to Regus, turning the whole thing over in his head, Music could tell.

"What's all this about anyhow?" Regus said. "Hit ain't against the law to transport hay across the county line, is it, Sheriff?"

"Well, now, it ain't," the sheriff said, "but we've got us a bunch of red agitators stirrin up the miners here in Harlan County, and, ever little bit, them communist bastards try to truck in stuff to help em make more trouble. That keeps us on the lookout and a little suspicious, don'tcha see?"

"Well, I'll be damned," Regus said and hit such a false note that fear seemed to blow around Music's heart. He saw the sheriff's eyes narrow at once.

"Cal," the sheriff said, "why don't you slip in beside that old boy there.

245

Henry," the sheriff called to one of the other men, "bring yer shotgun and climb up on the running board here. Old man Cox's farm ain't but about a quarter mile down the road, and I reckon he'd loan you a couple of pitchforks." The sheriff stepped back and looked up at the load of hay. "You boys take this here *alfalfa* down by about half and poke around a little, and if it ain't nuthin but cow food, I reckon you can sling it on again. These gentlemen won't mind givin you a ride back. Otherwise, I expect to see em hog-tied when you get here."

"This ain't no way to treat folks," Music said, but his voice sounded thin in his ears, and his chest felt as hollow as if it were missing half its parts.

"Now, that's right," the sheriff said, "and if you boys ain't haulin nothin but hay, you'll find out I can make as pretty an apology as you're likely to hear. Take em on," he said to the man called Henry.

Cal crowded in beside Music, who tried to scrape the Walker Colt, musette bag, and Regus's miner's cap with him toward the center of the floorboard, but he couldn't manage it. Still, they remained covered with the rag, and perhaps the man couldn't feel through the soles of his shoes what was underfoot. Henry climbed up on the running board. "All right," he said.

When they had gone about fifty yards, Music said, "This just ain't no way to treat folks. I don't see how people around here could vote a man like that in."

"It's the coal interest that's mostly put him in," Cal said, "and that's what he looks after."

"We've done spent half a dollar driving this load around all day, and now we've got to unload it and load it back and scatter it about. It ain't right," Music said. "I'd just as soon go on and sell it to you fer two dollars as do that. Wouldn't you?" he asked Regus.

Regus scratched his chin and looked at him, trying to read in his eyes what he was up to. "I guess," he said at last.

"I don't know," Cal said. "Hit's three and a half or four miles to my place, and I don't want him on my ass."

"Well, if we're gonna have to unload the stuff anyway to prove it's what it is, we might as well unload it into yer barn. But I guess if you can't afford to cross the sheriff . . . " Music said.

Henry leaned down into the half-open window. "Turn right just past that sycamore up yonder," he said.

246

Regus began to slow down to make the turn.

"Well, hell," Cal said, "a few minutes one way or the other, twon't make no difference. Keep on."

When Regus speeded up, Henry ducked down again. "What in hell you doin? I said to turn this truck off!"

"We gonna put this hay in my barn," Cal told him.

"The hell, you say," Henry said. "I don't want that son of a bitch on my ass."

"I'll tell him whose ass to get on," Cal said. "It won't take but a little bit."

"I'll tell him I was agin it," Henry warned.

"I'll tell him myself," Cal said. "The son of a bitch."

Music got out his tobacco and papers and offered them to Cal, who shook his head. With a great deal of effort, Music rolled his cigarette and then pretended to search his pockets for a match, closing his hand, at last, around the derringer and cocking it before he drew it from his pocket and shoved it under Cal's jawbone. "If you say one word," he whispered, his mouth nearly too dry to speak, "I'll shoot the top of your head off right now!" Instantly Cal stretched toward the ceiling and his body turned rigid as a post.

"What in hell we gonna do now?" Regus whispered.

"Hellkatoot," Music whispered back, "I don't know, but we've got one of them. Drive and maybe we'll think of something."

But Music couldn't think of anything. He seemed to himself to be thinking furiously, but it was as if the machinery in his head, the wheels and gears, refused to mesh. Still, it didn't matter, for a moment later Henry leaned down to the half-open window and said, "We got to change places; I'm near froze to whatinhellyouletmegit!" and tried to bring the ungainly length of the shotgun to bear upon the three of them in the cab while Regus opened his door and jammed his shoulder against it, trying to knock Henry off the running board. The truck careened from one side of the road to the other, and for a moment Music thought Henry was gone, but he must have had a firm grip on the bed of the truck behind the cab, for in the next moment the butt of the shotgun came crashing through the window, breaking off the top part of it and slamming Regus in the side of the head. "I'll shoot," Music reminded Cal, who stiffened his legs against the floorboard as though he were trying to run his head through the roof. The truck almost turned over. Regus fought to control it and Henry, who—apparently having decided it would be easier to beat Regus to death with the butt of the shotgun than to get the long barrels through the window, or maybe realizing that to shoot Regus and Music was to shoot Cal as well, jammed together as they were—clung to the side of the truck like a spider and thrashed away. But somehow Regus caught and held the stock of the shotgun as Henry jabbed it in the window, and the truck slewed to a stop off in the shallow left-hand ditch, which loosened Henry's grip, at last, and sent him spinning off the front fender and into a patch of blackberry briars and old broomstraw. "You sucker!" Regus said, kicking the door of the truck open, getting out, and dragging the shotgun through the window all in the same motion.

"Get out," Music told Cal, and got out with him, holding the barrel of the derringer against the hinge of his jaw just under his ear. For a moment none of the four of them moved, and then Regus and Music looked at each other.

"Jesus," Regus said.

"Hellkatoot," Music said. He looked up and down the road curving away in the evening sun. No one was in sight in either direction. "Let's tie em the hell up and get gone," he said. He poked Cal under the ear with the derringer. "Go sit in them briars with your buddy."

Quickly, while Regus held the shotgun on the two men, Music cut any spare rope he could find from the load of hay. "Stand back to back," he told the two men when he'd gathered as much rope as he could. He bound their wrists together tightly and then their ankles and, having some rope left over, bound their arms again just above the elbows. "Christ," he said to Regus when he was finished and got a chance to look at him, "your left eye is closing up. Can you see out of it?"

"Some," Regus said. He walked around in front of Henry, who was facing away from the road, and began to go through his pockets.

"So," Henry said, "you ain't just communists, but robbers too."

Regus stood still and considered him a moment and then began to go through his pockets again. When he found, at last, a half dozen shotgun shells, he put his face up close to Henry's and said, "Since you ain't got the shotgun you tried to beat my head off with, you don't need no shells," and then stepping in front of Cal, he gave him a gentle push in the chest, which caused the two men to fall over as stiffly as a chopped tree.

"Oooof!" Henry cried from the bottom. "Goddamned briars! Get off!"

"Now just how the hell can I get off?" Cal said, looking straight up into the sky.

"Let me drive," Music said, "and you stay down outta sight. One man with a straw hat on, driving a load of hay, won't look as suspicious as two."

"You still think yer gonna fool somebody, do ye?"

"We might," Music said.

"Don't leave us here; we'll freeze to death!" Henry cried, his voice somewhat muffled and breathless.

"I expect the sheriff will be along in an hour or so," Regus said.

"But he'll turn off way back at Cox's place," Cal said.

"That's true," Regus said, "but then he'll come on along, I'll vow."

"But hit'll be dark by then," Henry cried in his muffled voice.

"Well, you'll need to yell out," Regus said.

"Dammit," Music said, "get in the truck and let's go." Regus got in. "See if you can get down in the floorboard," Music said. While Music backed the truck up, Regus tried to situate himself in the floorboard, but there wasn't room. "Okay," Music said, "but if we see anybody and when we come to towns, bend down low."

Regus unwrapped the Walker Colt from the rags, blew the dirt from it, and wiped it on his shirt sleeve. "All right," he said, "but you wear this damned hand cannon, cause we can't stand a close look anyway; and if we git one, I aim to shove this shotgun in their faces, and you might as well show that thing too, and maybe that will persuade them to let us pass on. I'm gettin kindly tired of this horseshit." Gently he felt his left cheek and eyebrow and shook his head. "What in hell made you say we were going to Francis when we'd done already got into Kentucky? You might have known Francis was in Virginia."

"I don't know," Music said. "I was going to make up a name where we were going, but I got excited, and it just came out."

"And I'll be damned if I didn't think you was gonna sell the hay to that feller. What would you have done, Bill Music, if you'd struck a bargain?"

"I wasn't gonna strike no bargain, and I about had that sheriff convinced hay was all we had till you opened up."

"Yeah, well . . . " Regus said, but he didn't finish; he merely got out his tobacco and pocketknife, cut himself a chew, and letting out a long whistling sigh, bit the chew off the blade of his knife.

"You know," Music said, "now that I think about it, once I had old Cal pinned to the roof, you could have drawn that thirty-eight and stuck it in Henry's belly and saved everybody a lot of trouble."

Regus sighed again. "You just took me a little by surprise," he said and grimaced. "Goddam," he said, "it hurts to chew."

They drove on, deciding to avoid Leslie County altogether since the sheriff might call ahead once he found out what had happened. And anyway, the long way home wasn't much longer. And much to their relief they discovered that one man in a straw hat driving a Model T truck full of hay did fool people—no doubt the broken window helped a little too—for twice more they passed armed men and were not waved down.

Still, when they crossed the Switch County line, Regus said he was, by God, home and through riding with his head down between his knees. Instead he sat straight up in the seat with the shotgun cradled across his chest, and Music didn't argue since, no doubt, the truck would have been recognized at first sight in any case. But they drove right through Valle Crucis and into the ragtag squatterville below Regus's house without being challenged, and days went by before they found out what a cold night Sheriff Farthing and half a dozen special deputies had spent just below Mink Slide, waiting for them to come back the way they had gone.

# 22
## THE PICKET LINE

BELOW REGUS BONE'S homestead the winter grass was trodden into the earth and the earth trodden into a substance hard as pavement as the citizens of squatterville began to settle in. Tents went up. Squares of canvas were cut away and patched with tin and sheet metal to accommodate stovepipes. Clotheslines were strung. Tubs, washboards, tables, and chairs were cached about outside. And here and there tents grew crude additions or roofed front porches, some made of cardboard, some made of lumber and corrugated iron painfully carried and dragged all the way through the woods from the Bear Paw coal camp, where scavenging reduced the tipple to a skeleton and one or two of the tumbledown, unoccupied shacks all but disappeared. One ambitious fellow collected empty food tins and cans and stamped them into the earth to make a colorful metal floor for his shelter, which caused the value of empty cans to rise so sharply he couldn't beg enough to pave his front stoop as he had planned. A wit put up a sign naming the uneven row of tents where he dwelt "Easy Street." The next morning those who lived a little way up the hill raised a sign of their own, calling their string of tents "Silk Stocking Row." And every morning, when the five o'clock whistle blew, a tough and plucky group marched down the road from squatterville to harangue the miners still working for Hardcastle and to plague and bait the mine guards as well.

As for Music, the new spirit of the evicted miners astonished him. He

251

wouldn't have thought one truckload of goods, which plainly wouldn't last forever, could put so much fight in them. He wondered if what he witnessed and felt in himself wasn't merely false courage. Still, it fooled everyone concerned, even Sheriff Hub Farthing. For certain, when the sheriff and his deputies arrived on the picket line that first day and ordered the striking miners off the main street of Elkin, neither he nor his men seemed prepared for the jeering that followed. All the white strikers were armed, and so were many of the blacks who had come up from the Bear Paw to join them. For the first time in months their bellies were full. And when the sheriff threatened to arrest and jail them, he was hooted down before he could even finish his say. He was told the law by men who had no idea what the law was. The main street of Elkin was the public way, they told him, and many among them cocked their pistols and rifles and leveled their shotguns at Hub Farthing, deputies, and mine guards alike. If it was a bluff, it was the best kind. Music himself wasn't sure and drew the ancient Walker Colt and rested the ball of his thumb anxiously on the hammer while his innards jittered and he waited for someone on either side to do something untoward. For a little while the sheriff considered the men on the picket line—whether to accustom himself to their new behavior or try to stare them down Music couldn't say—but, at last, Hub Farthing seemed to think it best to let the strikers keep the main street of Elkin. He had a quick conference with the mine guards, left his two deputies to stand with them, and climbed back into his car.

When he pulled away toward Valle Crucis, the ragged men on the picket line laughed and hooted and shook their fists. And when he did not return that day, or the next, or the one following, even Regus began to think they had won some sort of victory. "Boys," he said, "be damned if it don't look like ye faced that bastard down."

In the first few days the union men persuaded three miners to trade their company shacks for tents on Easy Street and Silk Stocking Row, although there was no doubt that one of the three, a man named Glen Dunbar, joined them because he could get no more credit at the commissary. Dunbar wasn't much of a miner, and he had five hungry children and a shiftless wife, and Music wondered, from time to time, how many victories like Dunbar squatterville could afford to win. But he needn't have worried, for after those first three converts, relations between the union men and the miners still working for Hardcastle began to harden and grow bitter. The men on the picket line lost patience with

252

arguing and pleading, and when the working miners sifted through them to trudge on toward the tipple and drift mouth, names were called after them they didn't care to answer to. And, finally, those who crossed the picket line had to risk rough handling.

Music thought such a tactic was no way to win men over, but no one in squatterville seemed to take his advice. Even Regus merely shrugged and said, "Hit's the way she always goes. The union will get only so many, and the others ain't gonna come out with ye. Ye can be satisfied of that. Hit always comes down to fightin and ill feeling. Ain't nothin to do now but hold what we got, make hit hard for the scabs to pull their shifts, and cost ole Kenton Hardcastle as much money as we can. And it's a-costin him, don't ye worry. Look at all them mine guards he's got workin around the clock. Ha, mine guards don't come cheap; it costs good money to hire sons a bitches, always has. Sure," Regus said, "we're a-doin way the hell better than I ever thought we would."

But Music had misgivings. It was plain that an unspoken set of rules had grown up from the first day on the picket line, but he didn't know how long they would last. From the beginning, main street belonged to the union men, and mine guards and the sheriff's deputies did not venture into it, nor did the union men set foot on Hardcastle property. Also, from the first day, the men on the picket line badgered and harassed the mine guards and deputies, but except for Cawood Burnside, they did not answer back, choosing to keep a grim silence and earn their money without doing anything that would provoke a shooting. Cawood, however, was sensitive over the beating Music had given him, and once or twice when he was goaded sufficiently about that, Grady had to restrain him. And though, for the most part, everyone's behavior seemed to have grown as predictable and formal as a dance, tensions were growing. Every day the miners still working for Hardcastle got rougher treatment, and although neither Music nor Regus ever laid a hand on anyone, or took part in badgering the guards, one day, Music suspected, some knucklehead was bound to go too far, and everyone would be drawn in to what followed.

But for the time being, at least, there was no great trouble. The weather held good, there was no sickness, spirits were high, and every soul in squatterville had something to eat. An older miner named Lewis Short had been put in charge of the stores. He had a partially crippled arm and not a tooth in his head, but the people liked and trusted him for his even temper and good humor, although they didn't like seeing him

253

send the evicted blacks off with their gunnysacks heavy. But when they came trudging around and down the ridge from the Bear Paw, he never turned them away empty-handed. "They went for the union just like us," he'd say. "They ain't scabbin agin us, and nuthin I ever heard about a nigger makes me think he don't get as hungry as a white man. I'm gonna see nobody don't get more than his proper share," he'd say, "fer if'n I don't, the time will come soon when an ole sproutin tater will look as good as a cured ham."

Indeed, for the time being, squatterville's luck was pretty good; and, on some level or other, Music was almost content. Nearly every afternoon Merlee came up from Elkin to see him, and they took walks up the mountain, or sat about in Ella's kitchen, or sought a private place to make love. So it was hard not to feel blessed. And when he wasn't on the picket line or with Merlee, he labored to make a serviceable plow out of the rusty plow point he'd discovered in the barn. He'd found two young hickories just the right size, and he cut, soaked, bent, and bound them to cure into handles. He'd made a singletree, and after a great deal of scouting, he had found a locust big enough to make the beam.

One day when Merlee didn't come, he cut it down and dragged a section to the barn and began to rough it out. It was good to work with an ax and drawknife and auger and to have the sweet-smelling chips and shavings collect around his feet. It was a little like writing a letter to his family, which he could not do. They would know nothing of unions and gun thugs. They wouldn't understand any struggle that set him against sheriffs and the law. But working on the plow in the barn—abandoned once more to the cow and him—setting his hand to something plain and useful, made him feel almost as if he had written and explained.

He worked very late and felt particularly good, and after supper when he was in the kitchen with Ella and Regus, it was a fine surprise to have Merlee knock on the door and appear, come to show him the dress she had made, at last, from the material he'd bought her. She looked like a young girl dressed up to go to a party, and compared to the drab and ragged women of squatterville, she was so pretty that none of the three of them could speak. Even Regus was stunned and unable to tease as it was his habit to do. Finally, an awed, faraway smile on her face, Ella said, "Why, Merlee, child, ye look like a picture stepped out of a book in this sorry place." And she did, Music thought, at least down to her shoes, which were so walked over, worn out, and altogether wrong beside the dress, they were funny, although he hadn't the slightest urge to laugh. "Sit ye down, child," Ella said, "and I'll fix ye a sup of broth."

As though the dress were even able to subdue her and make her shy, Merlee didn't protest as she usually would have done.

"Hit's a pity and a shame they's all this nonsense a-goin on. You youngins ort to be goin out to a dance," Ella said, setting the cup of broth on the table before Merlee and laying her hand for a moment on the crown of Merlee's head. "Hit ain't right," she said, "and it aggravates me to think about it."

"It's the purtiest dress I ever had on my back," Merlee said, looking straight into Music's eyes.

"Well, I should hope so," Ella said. Abruptly she poked Music on the arm. "Can't you say nothin a'tall, boy?" she asked him.

Music shook his head.

"I don't know, but I'll declare if it don't seem young men are even goofier than they was in my day," she said, with such exasperation that all of them were released from the spell of Merlee's dress and began to laugh. "Now, I forget myself," Ella said and laid the back of her hand fondly against Music's cheek. "I didn't mean to shame you by speakin out of turn."

Regus shook his head and guffawed. "You gettin in deeper all the time, Momma," he said. "Cain't nobody call back the shot when they've done already hit the target."

"You hush," Ella said.

"I'd just as lief you didn't call the rest of us goofy just because of Bill Music, though," he said.

"Hush up," Ella said. "I won't have this youngin picked on in my house."

Regus sputtered and laughed and wiped his eyes. "I'm a-gettin outta here," he said, "while I can still remember who said what," and he got up and went out upon the dogtrot, scratching the back of his neck and giggling to himself.

"Now, I got some mendin to do," Ella said, "if you two young folks will pardon me." And she went off into her room and left them too.

But Regus and Ella might have stayed for all that transpired between them. They did not even touch or, for the longest time, speak. Still, never before in his life had he accepted or returned a woman's gaze for so many long minutes. It was the most intimate time he had ever spent with her, and he would have wanted no one present.

"Hit was foolish, I guess, to sneak out against the curfew when I could have come on up tomorrow in the daylight," Merlee said.

"I'll see you home safe," Music said.

255

"I just this evenin finished hit, and I wanted you to see how elegant it made up," she said and smoothed the material under her hand as gently as though it might break, as though it didn't belong to her and never would. "I never sewed such tiny stitches in all my life."

He shook his head and smiled. "I can't even see them," he said.

He didn't know how many shots were fired; maybe fifteen, maybe twenty. He heard two or three *whick* into the wood of the house before he could get to Merlee and drag her down to the floor. The volley was very brief, with many reports overlapping, which meant there had to be two or three people pulling triggers. Unscathed, Ella appeared in the kitchen, and Music told them both to stay inside and bolted out upon the dogtrot just as a stick of dynamite went off somewhere along the first line of tents, and then a second stick went off perhaps thirty yards to the north in the ditch. "Don't move from this house," he told the women and dashed down the hill toward Silk Stocking Row and Easy Street, where shouts and cries and weeping had begun.

Miraculously, only one person had been killed, a young man who had had part of his skull blown away; although Glen Dunbar's wife had been shot through the calf of her leg, and a small boy through the elbow. Neither stick of dynamite had hurt anyone. The first had landed almost directly beneath a ragged, stuffed couch belonging to Lewis Short and sitting a few feet in front of his tent. The explosion sent part of the couch through the front flap, missing the first pole but hitting the rear one and collapsing the tent on those inside. The next-biggest piece came back to earth between Easy Street and Silk Stocking Row, but wood and hunks of cotton batting were everywhere. The second stick of dynamite had done no damage at all. Music suspected that some goon had lit it and then had to get rid of it even though the car or truck, or whatever he had been riding in, had passed squatterville by.

No one had gotten a good look at the vehicle, for the man on guard had been talking to a friend and neither of them heard it coming until just before it appeared from behind the line of scrub maple along the road. It's headlights had been off and the goons in it, or on it, had started shooting the moment it was clear of the slash, so he and his buddy only had time to dive to the ground and try to get behind anything they could find for cover.

Music helped Regus and Glen Dunbar get Glen's wife and the boy who had been shot into the truck so that they could be taken to the mine doctor in Valle Crucis, and since the mine doctor was also the county coroner, they wrapped the dead young man in a blanket and laid him in the truck bed as well, Glen Dunbar standing over him with Regus's shotgun in his hands and his eyes round and vague as the eyes of a child who had been wakened from a deep sleep.

When Music had posted an armed guard on the road fifty yards on either side of squatterville and seen to it that two other guards were armed and waiting among the tents, he went back to the house. "There's one dead and two hurt," he told the women. "Regus is taking them into Valle Crucis."

"Sweet Lord," Ella said. "You see this child safe home, and I'll go down and see if I can help."

"No," Music said, "you stay in this house till I get back," and he took Merlee's hand and they hurried away.

Just before they reached the hardscrabble path that ran beside her shack, they stopped a moment to hold each other. "If I didn't have little Anna Mae and Aunt Sylvie to look after, I'd make ye run off with me; I'd make ye run away from this awful place. I know I could," Merlee said. "I could make ye."

"Yes, you could," he said and held her while she trembled.

"So you'll know me, hit's not a day I don't plan to do it even so." Abruptly then, she drew his face down, kissed him, and ran away.

Long before he got to Regus's pasture on his way back, he could hear the mother of the young man who had been killed. It was a sound that raised the hairs on the back of his neck, for if he hadn't known otherwise, he wouldn't have thought such keening could come from a human throat. And on and on and on it went.

He had given orders to shoot the hell out of any vehicle that approached with its lights off, but because of the woman's screaming, and because he did not quite trust the road guard not to shoot Regus when he returned, he took the place of the man guarding the road from Valle Crucis.

# _23_
## BURYING

WHEN THE NEXT morning finally arrived, damp and cold and hiding the tops of mountains in clouds, the citizens of squatterville could not decide what should be done. One or two of the men wanted to go back down on the picket line to show the goons nothing had changed. The angry young miner with the consumptive wife said he, by God, had blasting powder and he knew some of the other men did too, and if he went into Hardcastle Coal Company, it wouldn't be to stand in a picket line; it would be to show some sons a bitches what last night's raid had fetched them. There was a great deal of argument and counterargument until someone suggested that folks had been shot and dynamited and one person killed, after all, and somebody ought to stand up in the sheriff's face and demand some justice. The angry young miner hooted. Some of the others jeered and laughed bitterly. The suggestion seemed to satisfy no one; and yet, at last, four men were chosen to drive to Valle Crucis and confront Sheriff Hub Farthing while the rest stayed behind to clean up the damage and protect the camp. Regus and Music were to go, together with Glen Dunbar and Charles Tucker, the father of the dead young man. Tucker had not spoken a word to anyone all morning, but he went into his tent, scraped off his whiskers, put on a collarless white shirt and his Sunday suit, and climbed into the truck bed. Music rode into town beside him, trying not to look at the man's haggard face, nicked from shaving, or his eyes, which seemed somehow burned out, as though his wife's terrible grief had eaten through them like acid.

Regus had left his pistols with other men back in squatterville, but he had the gall to carry his shotgun with him right into the courthouse and the sheriff's office. "When yer dealin with curs," he'd told them, "you need something they can see and appreciate." Still, out of some wisdom Music was not quite sure he understood, Hub Farthing chose not to see it.

"I'm sure hit ain't news, but we come to tell you that the folks livin on my property was shot up and dynamited last night," Regus said. "Two was hurt and one was killed."

"Yes," Farthing said with perfect calm, "the coroner called me up. He tells me you were not willing to give the body up to the mortician, which means you ain't got a permit to bury."

"We come to see what ye've done and who ye've arrested for murder," Regus said.

The sheriff leaned back in his chair and shook his head as though in disbelief, as though surprised by their stupidity. "Now what in God's name makes you think you can curse and beat honest miners, who ain't after a thing but to get to work in the mornin, without gettin some of yer own medicine back?" The sheriff let out a short bark of laughter. "Them nigger strikers down at the Bear Paw got shot at and dynamited last night too, but at least they had the good sense not to come draggin in here to me when they know damned well they brought it on themselves."

"What we do, we do in broad daylight," Regus said. "We ain't attacked no women and children. We ain't shot nobody and we ain't throwed no dynamite. Hit's murderin night riders we come to talk about, and how ye aim to deal with em."

"That's what I'm tellin you," the sheriff said. "I can't look after no red, Russia-loving troublemakers who go around beatin up honest workin men, and I wouldn't if I could. However," he said and knitted his fingers across his belly, "I reckon I done you one favor by tellin that foreign Zigerelli son of a bitch that, one way or another, messing with the good folk of Switch County would get him killed. That's right, I happened to come along and find him lying out beside his car in the ditch, and whipped good he was too; and I told that dumb foreigner just what I'm tellin you: the people of Switch County are honest, hardworking, God-fearing people who won't put up with a bunch of Reds stirrin up trouble and ill feelin." Hub Farthing leaned forward and tapped his desk with his forefinger. "Yes, and I told him if any decent member of this community or any officer of the law got killed as a result of his seditious troublemaking, I'd see to it that he was hung. The syndicalism law backs

259

me up on that, and I quoted him chapter and verse. So if you ain't seen that little son of a bitch for a while, I reckon you can thank me for that much help anyway."

Sheriff Hub Farthing leaned back again and knitted his fingers over his belly. "So there won't be no misunderstanding and you'll be clear on it, that same law applies to you," he said. He looked them up and down. "You people are outlaws as far as I'm concerned," he said. "And outlaws don't come to a sheriff and ask to be protected." He hocked and spat in the waste can beside his desk. "As far as I know," he said, "no decent human being has yet been seriously hurt by your—"

With a deliberate, stiff dignity, as though it had never occurred to him that someone might try to stop him, Charles Tucker brushed Dunbar aside and took hold of Regus's shotgun.

Music caught him in a bear hug from behind and pinned his arms. But even with such an advantage, he found himself being flung into walls and doorjambs as he tried to get him outside. Oddly, even Tucker's bursts of strength seemed to come only now and again and with a stubborn deliberateness. And through it all he did not utter a sound of any kind, although Music grunted and swore and talked without ceasing, trying to calm him down. But he was calm enough already; he was merely determined, which was another matter, Music knew.

When at last he got Tucker outside, he didn't know what to do with him. He was afraid to let him go. People passing by stopped to stare and point while Music asked over and over again, "Are you all right? Are you all right now?" and squeezed the man against his chest.

"Turn me aloose," Tucker finally said; and, finally, Music did so, fearing what would happen. But the man only stood where he was and gazed across the courthouse square and far away.

"Are you all right?" Music asked him again.

"Yes," he said, "yes, I'm all right," and he began to walk away.

Music watched him climb into the bed of the Model T and wondered if he could trust him to stay there, but it didn't matter, for Regus came down the courthouse steps in the next moment.

"Well?" Music said.

Regus looked at the solitary figure waiting in the bed of his truck, dark and still as a scorched fence post in a burned-over field. Then, distracted by the onlookers who seemed to find someone in a miner's cap armed with a shotgun as curious as they had found Music's earlier struggle, Regus eyed them until they dispersed nervously and went on about their business. "Less us git on home," Regus said, "or somebody will have to grab me in a minute."

But Regus told him later what had gone on in the sheriff's office after he'd fought Tucker through the door. The sheriff had threatened them all with charges of criminal syndicalism and made it sound as though they could be arrested and charged for provoking others to murder them. And that had provoked Regus to make some threats of his own. Regus had told the sheriff to warn all the scabs and goons he was in bed with that any car or truck coming by squatterville at night with its lights out would be shot off the goddamned road; and to warn Kenton Hardcastle that Regus Patoff Bone didn't fancy having his house shot up, and if it ever happened again, he was going to count the bullet holes and multiply by two before he returned the goddamned favor. Finally Regus had told the sheriff that any trespasser spied on Bone property was going to be treated like a murdering night rider and shot out of his boots.

They were sitting on the front edge of the dogtrot when Regus told him what had happened, Regus leaning forward resting his forearms on his knees, his hands folded before him. "So," he said, "I reckon it's done got mean." His shoulders were hung forward as though he were weary, and he pursed his lips and made a long, breathy, almost inaudible whistle. After a moment he got out his plug of tobacco and his knife and cut himself a chew.

"Well, we'll have to put on more guards, I guess," Music said. "But we can still break ole Kenton Hardcastle down. We can still get a union in here."

Regus looked down on squatterville, his forehead wrinkled thoughtfully, and he shook his head.

"Pretty soon we'll need to get some more supplies someway, so we can hold out. We done it once, and I expect we can figure a way again," Music said.

"I ain't sure it would matter," Regus said. "Ain't no tellin how much money a man like Hardcastle's got or can lay his hands on. For sure he won't never run out of poor, dumb stiffs to dig his coal. Ha," he said and shook his head sadly, "they's just too many; it's what Kentucky's got most of, and every other state too, I reckon. Nawh," Regus said. "We can strike him and we can fight him, but we can't make him hire us." Regus rubbed the palms of his hands together and looked at Music, his eyes wrinkling at the corners. "Since hit nearly always comes down to that, you'd think we'd learn after a while, wouldn't ye now?"

261

Music said nothing.

"But, hell, maybe that don't matter either," Regus said, rubbing his palms slowly together. "Once the fightin starts, hit's a little like two roosters facin off over a chicken yard; ye forget what ye wanted before long and just get down to the peckin and spurrin."

They sat on the dogtrot and looked down upon squatterville, the tents, the trodden earth, the brown winter grass, all shades of sepia under the grey sky; and Music felt an unbidden, unwilling love crowd into his chest, as well as a stubborn, deep resentment against Hardcastle and all the forces he could muster. There were people gathered around the tent where the young man had been killed, from which the Tucker woman's voice, ragged and soft now, yet rose from time to time to cry out or moan. And Charles Tucker stood by, still wearing his dark, baggy suit.

Men were digging a grave in the little cemetery at the top of Regus's pasture, from which, now and again, the clink of a pick or shovel striking a stone would reach the dogtrot. Music had learned the body of the young man had been washed, dressed in his finest, and sewn into a canvas shroud, but that Charles Tucker had been persuaded to take the shoes from his son's feet at the very last minute, since they were only a few months old and the boy's mother had all but walked out of her own. It would be a sin, the neighbors told him, to bury such good shoes in the ground in the middle of winter when his wife could put them to use. A man came into the world without shoes, they told him, and surely the Lord God, born in a manger, would understand a miner's son leaving without them.

Music hadn't seen the body, but he had a picture of the boy in his head: all dressed up, his hair tamed and combed just so, and his big feet ridiculously white and bare. He rolled himself a cigarette and lit it, and then almost immediately snapped it away. "I reckon I'll go up and help with the digging," he said.

Regus merely nodded.

When the preacher returned, he would read over the body, so there was no ceremony in the little graveyard. The boy's mother was not present; she had collapsed at the bottom edge of the pasture and had been carried back to her tent. The rest of them, standing awkwardly and stiffly about the cemetery, seemed to know the young man's death was indiscriminate—even if his mother did not—a random, deadly hit among all the shots fired and dynamite thrown, and therefore senseless and stupefying and outside the province of things to be mourned. Even Charles Tucker seemed to know that. But if the woman had been there, it would have been different. She knew something else, which Music had heard the night before in her screams. Fate had singled her out among all the others and willfully chosen to tear her son from her, and she would have taught them to grieve.

Lewis Short came up to Music after the grave was covered over to tell him that one of the families had decided to move out. And it was true. The father and mother and two daughters—everyone except the little boy who had been shot through the elbow—had tied up such belongings as they could carry and were about to leave that very moment and on foot. The man's brother owned a little ragtag farm better than forty miles away, and they intended to walk.

"The hell, you say," Regus told him. "If yer bent on leavin, help me load what ye own in the truck, and I'll carry ye."

"I'm obliged," the man said, "but it's not a goon in Switch County that don't know that truck, and I'm feared . . . " The man looked at his feet. ". . . I'm feared the missus couldn't take bein shot at no more."

"God damn you for runnin out," the angry young miner said, but the man paid him no attention, except to color around the neck and ears.

"Anyhow," the man said, "won't nobody bother us, we bein afoot. We'll git there tomorrow or the day after, and I reckon my brother won't be so likely to turn us away and us a-walkin." He shook hands with Regus and Music and some of the others, but the angry young miner would not shake his hand. "I reckon anybody that wants hit, can have what we've left. God knows," he said, looking toward his tent and the few possessions in and around it, "hit ain't nothin there that's fitten noway."

"Yer a coward to let Hardcastle run ye! Ye know that!" the angry young miner said, but the man only nodded to him and to the rest of them as though he'd been wished a safe journey, and he ushered his family into the road.

"Hell," another man said, as the family strung out along the highway toward Valle Crucis, "I reckon I'd leave myself if I had airey place to go."

"Well, God damn you too then!" the young miner said.

"Yer a-missin a good chance to keep yer mouth shut," Charles Tucker said calmly, not even turning to look at the young miner, but watching the family's slow progress north, all of them carrying bundles except the little boy, who carried only his ruined arm, thick with bandages, strapped to his chest.

263

# 24

## THE MINERS COME HOME
## FROM CHICAGO

IT RAINED STEADILY, a cold rain that kept Music's teeth chattering despite the piece of canvas he clutched about his head and shoulders like a shawl. Crouched in the slash beside the road, he didn't even have to ask himself what he would do if a car approached with its lights out. Exactly when his uncertainty about such things had left him, he didn't know, but it was gone. If night riders came, he would draw the Walker Colt and, providing his powder was still dry, show them, by God, its ancient thunder and lightning.

But no night riders appeared. The rain rattled against his leaking canvas shawl, the muscles in his legs cramped, and periodic waves of tremors shook him when they pleased. Perhaps because he'd had no sleep the night before, long stretches of time passed when there wasn't a single thought in his head. He was awake, his eyes were open, but it was as though the stations of his brain could only note the dark road and his chilled, unstable flesh.

After what seemed like hours, he tried to make himself a cigarette, but his fingers, all puckers and wrinkles, were numb, and he tore the cigarette paper and sprinkled his britches and damp hands with clinging flakes of tobacco. He warmed his hands in his armpits, dried them as well as he could on his shirt front, and tried again, producing, finally, a loose creation which he tucked into the corner of his mouth. His matches were damp too, and the heads of three or four of them crumbled against his

264

thumbnail before he found one that snapped and flared. He lit his cigarette and in the light of the match checked the time on Regus's pocket watch. Almost an hour and a half to go, but hellkatoot, he told himself, that was nearly nothing. It wasn't as if he couldn't do it. He took a drag on the cigarette and a terrific seizure of shaking rattled his bones.

It occurred to him that if there were gun thugs about, they might have seen the flare of his match, might, at that very moment, be taking a bead on the glowing coal of his cigarette beneath the hood of canvas, but it was a consideration that lacked the power to disturb him. Almost as if he were taking their side in the matter, he muttered, "You better hit me with the first shot," and smoked stubbornly until the cigarette grew so short it burned his lips and he had to spit it out. It was as though he were out of patience and had lost all ability to discriminate. Perhaps standing by the fresh grave had done it; perhaps wrestling Charles Tucker from the courthouse, which made twice, by his count, he'd kept some poor son of a bitch from shooting the sheriff or vice versa; perhaps it was watching the family set out to walk forty miles to kinfolk who likely wouldn't be able to support them any more than they could turn them away. He didn't know exactly what had put him in his present mood, but he felt as if all things had lost their power to signify, and doing one thing was no better or worse than doing another. It seemed to him that, in a proper world, all things ought to signify. But in this one, the one he knew, who could stand it? Not him.

His teeth rattled. His flesh seemed bound to shake loose from his bones. He stared down the road, and it was a long time later when he managed to strike another match and read by Regus's pocket watch that his three hours of guarding the road were more than over. To his surprise, his legs nearly refused to raise him up or carry him. They felt like posts, like brass pipes, and they jarred him when he walked. Even his feet were clumsy and had a great deal of trouble accommodating the uneven ground. Still, as unwilling as the cold machinery of his body was, it brought him into the huddled shelters of squatterville, where he stuck his head into Lewis Short's tent. He could make out nothing in the damp, fetid space inside, but it didn't matter, for somewhere among the shifting sounds of sleep, Lewis's voice said softly, "All right," and Music backed out into the far colder outside air to wait.

A little while later Lewis stepped through the tent flap, carrying his shotgun, and Music gave him Regus's watch. "You're welcome to this piece of canvas," Music told him and took it from around his shoulders, which turned them icy and caused his teeth to chatter. "It won't keep you dry, but it keeps the air from stirring around you so much."

"Sure," Lewis said. "The damned stuff leaks when ye touch hit. We been mostly all right, but Turl, the damned fool, tried soapin his tent to keep the rain out, and he's near swamped."

"Get him to move in where them folks left," Music said through the unstable quaking of his jaw.

"He already has," Lewis said. "Damnation if ye don't look all used up, son. I'll see you in the mornin," he said, and raising his hand in a gesture of parting, turned away to wake the others and change the guard.

When Music got to the house, he was almost unable to light the kerosene lamp in his room. He thanked heaven for the dry clothes hanging just inside his door on a nail, and he fully meant to put them on and sleep in them, but by the time he had dried the cap-and-ball pistol, put it aside where he could reach it, and shucked, at last, out of his wet clothes, he thought it best to wrap up in his quilt and sit down on his straw tick to rest a moment. He did not rise again. He thought of Merlee and her lovely dress and how beautiful and shy it had made her. He heard her telling him again how she could make him run off with her; he heard the pleasant, snug sound of the rain against the house, a soft xylophone upon the roof and windowpanes; and he had no memory at all of lying down or having his thoughts plucked away by sleep.

During the night the weather cleared, and the next morning, after Music had done the milking and he and Regus had eaten their breakfast, they stepped out upon the dogtrot to a mild-as-spring day. Clotheslines were strung everywhere in squatterville, and the whole tent city was steaming with the first touch of the sun when Arturo Zigerelli's Dodge drove up and the three men who had gone off to Chicago began to disentangle themselves from each other and the cramped confines of the car. They stood for a moment with the mud curling around their shoes and blinked at Easy Street and Silk Stocking Row before their families began to hail them and rush out to greet them. Zigerelli merely watched, one foot propped on the running board of his car, until he noticed Music and Regus on the dogtrot and started up through the mud and steaming tents. He came very slowly, as though he had walked many miles, and as he drew closer, they could see he truly had been beaten. A dark, crusted wound intersected one eyebrow and extended to the bridge of his nose. Both his eyes were discolored, and even his jaw was puffy and out of line.

266

When he reached the steps, Regus said, "Well, now, the sheriff promised we'd seen the last of ye."

"And did you believe him?" Zigerelli asked.

Regus scratched the back of his neck, looking thoughtfully at the Italian. "I reckon I did not," he said, "but it ain't like I never been fooled."

The Italian nodded solemnly. "And why are you not among the others to welcome the great travellers home?"

"We can let that wait a bit," Regus said. "The last time them three fellers seen us, me and Bill was mine guards. Wouldn't hurt to let them git use to a different notion before we butted in."

"They know whose side you are on," Arturo Zigerelli said. "I have told them." He looked from one of them to the other with something disturbing and peculiar in his eyes. "It is Arturo Guido Zigerelli they see as their enemy at this moment." The Italian shrugged his shoulders and turned his cupped palms toward them, then merely let his hands fall again to his sides. "I must tell you now a thing of great importance, and I wish you to believe I would have told you in the beginning if it had not been forbidden." Without turning away from them, he tipped his head toward the tent city. "It is what those three are saying even now, although they have so little understanding they mistrust those who have come to them as brothers and comrades. The preacher, the Bydee Flann, believes in his heart he has seen the gates of hell and touched them. Yes, and that I will grow horns from my head and a tail. He has this conviction because he has learned that the National Miners Union is not the simple, weak, foolish effort he thought it was, but a part of the great struggle of communism against all those who enslave the poor. Yes, yes, I tell you now with pride, Arturo Zigerelli is a Communist," he said and thumped himself upon the chest. "Are you now my enemies too? Do you see horns growing from my head?"

Regus raised his hand and made patting motions in the air with it. "Wait now, wait a little," he said. "You talk faster than a man can listen." He looked at Music, both surprise and disbelief in his expression, and then, oddly, he simply sat down on the dogtrot. After a moment he began to wag his head and laugh. "Every time my poor, dumb poppa joined a union, they called him a Communist, a goddamned Red. Jesus, but they beat him over the head with it, and I'd vow he never in his life knowed what a Communist was, but he denied it all his days like a man would deny he was a son of a bitch." Regus wagged his head again and wiped his face with one of his large, chapped hands as though he'd stepped into a spiderweb. "So," he said to the Italian, "you claim to be the genuine article, do ye?"

"Yes," Zigerelli said.

"Hell," Regus said and turned to Music, "I ain't a damned bit better off than my poppa. What do ye know about this communist business, Bill Music?"

"Why do you not ask one who can tell you?" Zigerelli said.

Regus patted the air with his hand. "We'll get around to you," he said. "I want to hear what Bill has to say."

From the first moment the Italian had begun to talk, Music had felt dread, as though he had somehow guessed what was coming, but, even so, he had trouble believing what he had heard. "I don't know anything about them," Music said. "I know they had a revolution over in Russia and killed a lot of people, and once or twice when I was in Chicago, there'd be a man standing up on an orange crate, or some such place, going on about communism like a circuit preacher. Sometimes I'd hang around to see what he had to say, but usually a fight would start, or the police would come around and run the fellow off. They don't think a fellow has a right to make his fortune and hold on to it. They think everything ought to belong to everybody, if I understood them. They don't believe in God, and I guess they figure this here country is just about wrong from top to bottom."

Regus sucked his teeth and looked at the Italian. "Do you own up to any of that?"

"If I understand what you are asking, I say yes to you; what Mr. Music says is much naked, but it is true."

"Ha," Regus said, "here I thought I was bein a fool for messin with a union." He shook his head in wonder. "I guess I just didn't know how many different kinds of fool I could be. There don't seem to be no end to it. Ha," he said, as though he couldn't get over it. He got out his plug of tobacco and his pocketknife and cut himself a chew. He stared at the space of hardscrabble earth directly in front of the Italian and worked the quid of tobacco into his jaw. "Maybe I ain't yet got it straight, but hit sounds like ye've set me and these other dumb suckers up for a fight, not just agin Hardcastle, but agin religion and the whole damned country. Is that the way you see it?"

"I believe the worker gets only crumbs, although his labor produces the whole loaf," Arturo Zigerelli said, "and I believe he will get only crumbs

268

until he makes a revolution against the capitalists who enslave him; yes, and rejects the god of suffering he has been taught to worship."

"Ye won't sell that line in Kentucky, bud," Regus said. "Hell, not even to a coal miner."

"To some of the young we have done so. Yes, and to a few of the others as well," Arturo Zigerelli said. "For Bydee Flann and those like him, perhaps there is no hope. The Kentucky miner has valor, but no one is more innocent. Ah, Mr. Bone and Mr. Music, I know everyone will not throw off the yoke or give up the sad god of the cross at once," Zigerelli said, "but we can teach them. I was not born a Communist." Zigerelli smiled faintly, which made his lopsided jaw and the bruised, discolored flesh around his eyes look ridiculous. "I was as innocent of knowledge as any here. My good mother spent part of each day upon her knees, thinking to send messages up to heaven. And I too . . . "

"Did you know a young man was killed here night before last, and a woman and a little boy shot?" Music asked, his surprise and disbelief having boiled down, at last, to anger.

"I learned of it," Zigerelli said, "as I learned of the attack upon your Negro comrades at the Bear Paw as well."

"And, goddammit, not one of them had a hint of what your union was up to!" Music said. "How many do you think would have joined if they'd known?" Music started down the steps toward the Italian, but found himself facing Regus.

"Whoa now, Bill," Regus said.

"If I'd had the choice, I would not have deceived you," Arturo Zigerelli said.

Music started to step around Regus, but Regus caught him by the shoulders. "Bill, Bill, Bill!" he said, until Music was looking at him instead of over his shoulder at the Italian. "Hell, I don't think it's goin to matter," Regus said with a faint, tired squint of a smile around his eyes. "I expect it wouldn't make no difference if he was a Communist, a Baptist, a Democrat, or a goddamned airplane pilot. I reckon that's the pity of it."

"It matters to me!" Music said.

"No," Regus said, "likely it won't matter to any of us. What you gonna do? You gonna bend yer pistol barrel around the little guinea's head? Looks like somebody else already done that once or twice. You gonna shoot him?"

Music didn't know what he intended to do; he hadn't thought about it.

He took a deep breath. "Nawh, hell," he said, "I ain't gonna shoot him."

"I understand your anger, Mr. Music," Arturo Zigerelli said, "and I am sorry for it."

"No, you don't," Music said. "I argued against taking you to the sheriff that first night down at the Bear Paw."

"I see," Zigerelli said. "But even now, if I were gone, another would come to take my place. And I think the sheriff would not have held me. Many times he could have put me in the jail, Mr. Music, but I think he wants to send me away with so much fear that no other will come here again. I think now perhaps he will kill me because I do not run away."

"I think we need to set down and talk to this feller a little bit," Regus said.

"You talk to him," Music said, and he stalked back up the steps and out to the barn, where Ella's laying hens clucked and blinked their idiot eyes at him while he fumed. The more he thought of the betrayed people of squatterville, the more helpless he felt; until, at last, he found himself, head in hands, sitting on the milking stool among the shavings of the plow, having lost all track of time. He had no notion whether one hour or three had passed, and what brought him around, even so, were the people plodding by the house and up through the pasture toward the small graveyard. The preacher, he realized, was going to hold the Tucker boy's funeral, and he left the barn and followed like a man obliged to share their grief.

From the height of the land he could see—even though Zigerelli's car was gone and the funeral had begun—men still remaining in squatterville, Regus among them, and they appeared to be arguing. But those who were gathered about the grave drew his attention. They had put on their best clothes. The men were shaved. The women were tidy and had fixed their hair. And even the children looked almost clean, their woolly heads wetted and combed. He himself was not clean, and his face was rough with stubble, so he kept his distance, although he would have done so in any case. He could hear only a word or two of what Bydee Flann was saying, and when the preacher bowed his head to pray, he could distinguish nothing, as though the rite were not meant for the likes of him, and he found that just and proper, after all.

The Tucker woman was there, looking so pale and worn out Music doubted she would have been able to stand upright if her husband hadn't

270

held her. Ella was there in a dark dress he had never seen. She looked strange without her constant apron and with her hair twisted into a bun and held with combs. But he would have known her anywhere, for her shoulders were as broad and square as any man's, and her head, even bowed, was bent to one side as though the very earth spoke to her and she listened. Lewis Short was there, dressed in a black suit nearly as green and shiny in its worn places as the wings of a dragonfly. Worth Enloe. The consumptive woman. And there were others whose faces were perfectly familiar but whose names he had never learned. And he was there, William Music, who should have been merely passing through, who should have had no influence on their lives.

At last the little preacher lifted his head and raised up his Bible and began to read in a ringing voice.

Lord, thou hast been our dwelling place in all generations.

Before the mountains were brought forth, or ever thou hadst formed the earth and the world, even from everlasting to everlasting, thou art God.

Thou turnest man to destruction; and sayest, Return, ye children of men.

For a thousand years in thy sight are but as yesterday when it is past, and as a watch in the night.

Thou carriest them away as with a flood; they are as a sleep: in the morning they are like grass which groweth up.

In the morning it flourisheth, and groweth up; in the evening it is cut down, and withereth.

For we are consumed by thine anger, and by thy wrath are we troubled.

Thou hast set our iniquities before thee, our secret sins in the light of thy countenance.

For all our days are passed away in thy wrath: we spend our years as a tale that is told.

The days of our years are three-score years and ten; and if by reason of strength they be fourscore years, yet is their strength labour and sorrow; for it is soon cut off, and we fly away.

Who knoweth the power of thine anger? even according to thy fear, so is thy wrath.

So teach us to number our days, that we may apply our hearts unto wisdom.

Return, O Lord, how long? and let it repent thee concerning thy servants.

O satisfy us early with thy mercy; that we may rejoice and be glad all our days.

Make us glad according to the days wherein thou hast afflicted us, and the years wherein we have seen evil.

Let thy work appear unto thy servants, and thy glory unto their children.

And let the beauty of the Lord our God be upon us: and establish thou the work of our hands upon us; yes, the work of our hands establish thou it.

The preacher stood for a moment longer at the foot of the grave, his chin raised, his eyes on the mountain rising above the pasture as though he were looking after the sound of his own voice. "Amen and Amen," he said at last, and as he went over to speak to the Tucker woman, Music took himself back to the barn. He was there, sitting on the milking stool among the shavings, the drawing knife idle in his hands, when Regus entered and squatted by the stanchion.

Music pondered the unfinished beam of the plow, not bothering to acknowledge him. "One of these days I'll need to get into town," Music said after a while. "I've got to have some big bolts and a clevis or two."

Regus looked around at the bound hickory handles, the singletree, the beam. He nodded. "Hit'll be as fine as any I could order from a catalogue, I'd vow, when ye get her done."

"No," Music said, "but I guess it will serve. It's gonna cut a little shallow, I think, but if you can't get a good team, that might be better."

Regus let out a long sigh and shook his head. "Hell, you may be right after all," he said.

"About what?" Music said.

"About me farmin this place," Regus said.

"Ah," Music said, as though he had forgotten that was a possibility, as though he had forgotten that was the purpose behind building the plow. "We'd have been a leg up on it, anyway, if we hadn't got mixed up in a goddamned union. We'd have had the hogpen built, and a plow, and maybe a loft in this barn," he said, musing up at the rafters.

"I've heard people say a hundred times that one miner by hisself might have a little sense; but if you put two together, they'd have half as much sense as one; and three would have less sense than two; and any more than three wouldn't have any sense at all."

"I've heard you say it," Music said.

Regus tipped his head toward the highway. "Down yonder in squatterville you can see the proof if ye doubt me. They's three or four of them suckers wanting to load up their guns and take over Hardcastle

272

Coal Company. I mean right now!" Regus said. "Then they's Bydee Flann, and I'll be goddamned if he don't want to go straight to Kenton Hardcastle, the sheriff, the county judge, the preachers, the schoolteachers, and every other soul in Switch County and tell em the Communists have come to overthrow the government and carry us all to hell." Regus wagged his head from side to side. "I believe we could do without goons for makin trouble in squatterville. I believe we could just about make enough of our own from here on in."

"What are you going to do?" Music said.

Squatting jug-butted and weary by the stanchion, Regus sighed and rubbed the copper stubble on his face. "That's sholy the question, ain't it? What Zigerelli thinks is that the coal operators have got to be hurt. Have got to be put in danger of losing what little contracts they've won. And he thinks it's got to happen right now and all across the state. He's trying to make his bosses understand if the National Miners Union doesn't make a strong move soon, they won't have any membership left."

"It sounds to me," Music said, "as though he's talked you around."

"Ha," Regus said, "miners ain't never been able to win out against just the operators. What chance we got with this communist stuff puttin us crosswise of damned near everybody? No, what I think is that we have shit and fell back in it." Regus rubbed his hands together and seemed to muse upon them. "But at least the little son of a bitch never took up a collection on us."

"Somebody took up a collection somewhere," Music said.

"And he ain't run out and left us flat, and that puts him ahead of anybody my poppa ever dealt with. No, he ain't talked me around, Bill Music, but it's hard not to listen just a little bit."

"You listened to me once too," Music said.

"Ha," Regus said, his eyebrows assuming for a moment their old humorous posture, "you ain't gonna hold that against me, are ye?"

"Yes," Music said. "Absolutely."

"Ha," Regus said, "you are the peculiariest man I ever run up against." He braced his hands on his knees and rose. "I expect I'll let ye get back to yer plow makin, if that's what ye've a mind to do. But I come to tell you that we're gonna have a meetin in squatterville this evenin, and I'd be obliged if ye'd help us talk this mess over. Hit'll be right hard, I'd vow."

"You can ask me to do anything but that," Music said.

"I'd be obliged all the same," Regus said. "Squatterville needs to make

273

peace amongst itself, if it can, before Zigerelli comes back. Hellfire, don't go soft on me now. It wouldn't be a'tall right if you weren't in it with us."

In his eyes Music saw the spark of humor, or maybe it was simply a strange sort of tolerance which he had always mistaken for humor. Still, it was there, appearing to take a longer view of things than seemed quite humanly possible. And under its influence, Music nodded, and Regus nodded too and winked.

# 25

## THE FINAL ATTACK

SOMETHING WAS WRONG in the very fabric of the night. Music could feel it in the pit of his stomach and along his spine, although he thought it came from the men standing about the fire, who were so full of their futility and their anger. Later, when Regus had been shot down and killed, he thought otherwise. But he never mentioned it to anyone, for if such instincts existed, he suspected a man ought not to have them, any more than he ought to have dewclaws or bristles down his back.

"They said they wasn't no hell ner any heaven. They said the closest thing to hell was here in this country and the closest to heaven was Russia. They'd hired out this big, grand auditorium for a meetin and ever soul in it had a red flag to wave. They give me one too, but I throwed hit down, and I tore up my union card before the meetin was over. They said they could make Jesus and sell him for a dime and get richer than airey capitalist has yet got," Bydee Flann said. "I'll not cast my lot with such as them, and they ain't any kind of hard times, ner any man here, that can make me."

"I don't want to make ye," said the angry young miner. He spat into the fire they were all gathered around. "I want ye to shut yer Bible-thumpin mouth!"

"Tom Loflin!" Charles Tucker said and aimed his finger, "you speak to the preacher with a better tongue and some manners or I will undertake to keep you quiet."

275

"You think you can do that, do ye?" Loflin demanded. "Step right up then!"

"If he can't, I reckon I can," Worth Enloe said.

"Or me, or the three of us together anyhow," Lewis Short said.

"He ain't even a preacher," Loflin said. "He just decided to call hisself one. I got youngins a-wearing rags patched together; their stomachs ain't been proper full in years; my wife sick and not a nickel to fetch a doctor ner any medicine; and he's tellin me about folks wavin red flags and sellin Jesus. I don't want to hear it! He ain't even a preacher."

"He got the call just like Moses and John the Baptist done," Charles Tucker said. "I reckon he's preacher enough for me."

"No," Bydee Flann said, shaking his head slowly, "I ain't no Moses. I ain't a thing but a lay preacher and a coal miner like the rest here, but I don't aim to sell my soul for a few victuals or a coat for my back. Hit's a trade no child of God ought to make."

"All that means to me is that you are whipped like a dog and happy with it. Don't talk to me about no god that made the hell me and mine been livin in! I'd sell anything I got to get out of it," Loflin said, "my soul first off!"

"God made the world and suffered folks to make the hell," Bydee Flann said. "If you understood that, ye might be more content, son."

Music stood on the dark outside fringe of men gathered around the fire. He had nothing to say, and even Regus had not yet spoken a word. But it was easy to see how the lines were drawn. Three of the men were anxious to do whatever Zigerelli wanted: Turl, whom Music remembered struggling up the road with his arms around his radio, who had soaped his tent hoping to keep the rain out; Clifford Smith, the only one of the three who had been to Chicago; and Tom Loflin, who seemed to have only anger to brace himself against his troubles, his children, his wife, pale and listless with consumption. The others were moved by the preacher, and if they were not ready to confess to Kenton Hardcastle that they'd been tricked into joining a bunch of godless Reds and beg him to put them back to work again, as Bydee Flann was, they were in deep despair.

Afflicted with his strange sensibilities, Music had listened to the miners returned from Chicago, seldom even looking at whoever might be talking, yet hearing things they didn't quite say. In the timbre of their voices he heard the distances they had traveled, the cities beyond imagination they had seen; the distances alone able to both belittle and make more precious the narrow Kentucky valley they had come from; the cities, no less than the Communists, able to confound them and make them skeptical. Even in Clifford Smith's voice Music had heard an edge of doubt, as though he wondered if the currency he'd brought back from Chicago hadn't somehow lost its value along the way. Worth Enloe sounded weary, almost too weary to be angry, as though he'd made a long journey only to witness a circus, a freak show. But in Bydee Flann's voice Music heard outrage and alarm. What he had seen was no plan to help the miner, nor merely a joke or a sideshow, but an offense to God which could spread itself like a disease through the land. Music heard all that and more, or at least he imagined he did.

When each of those who had been to Chicago had spoken and ceased, Lewis Short wagged his grizzled head and scratched the back of his neck. "I reckon I know Kenton Hardcastle as well as any man here, save maybe Worth. Before his health went bad on him, he used to spend as many hours down at the mine as the foreman did. He was a stubborn man even when times were good and he had it all his own way, but he's worse now. He's growed old and sour, and I have to tell ye, Preacher, I don't think he'd take airey one of us back on, no matter how ye crawled."

"He won't," Worth Enloe said, "not when it ain't to his advantage. He's got more than enough men left to fetch his coal without the help of any here; the best way he can use us now is for a lesson to them others."

"Yer a-talkin whipped too, then," Turl said. "Sayin we're beat where we stand."

Perhaps because he didn't want to hear himself admit it, Worth Enloe did not speak at all; he merely looked at the fire and, after a moment, spat a stream of tobacco juice into it.

"If you'll hear me," Regus said, "I ain't had my say about this National Miners Union business."

"Ye've as much right to speak as airey man in this crew," Lewis Short said.

"All right then," Regus said, "it ain't nuthin new for a coal miner, but I reckon we been flimflammed. We joined an outfit that didn't tell us what they were up to. And even if we could make peace with that and were all of one mind, I reckon we'd still get skinned." There was a solemn nodding of heads except for Turl, Clifford Smith, and Tom Loflin, who cursed and muttered and seemed about to break in with opinions of their own. "I don't look for Hardcastle Coal Company to be unionized by this bunch here, nor the rest of the Kentucky coalfields either," Regus said. "So I'm willin to own up that we are beat. I just ain't willin to say that we're whipped." Regus ran his finger back and forth under his nose. "How much tucker we got left, Lewis?" he asked.

"Not much," Lewis said; "grub is gonna run thin in less than a week, I'm thinkin." He rubbed the back of his head and looked around at the circle of men apologetically. "Hit's gonna come down to beans and bulldog gravy, except without the beans," he said.

"Well, boys," Regus said, "if it was summer, we might last a good while on nearly nuthin, but not this time of year. The weather's been good to us, but hit could clamp down cold tomorrow. Folks can put up with cold, or they can put up with nearly nuthin to eat, but it's damned few who can stand both for very long. So," Regus said, "that's where we stand. Now that little guinea tells me they's supplies aplenty down in Knoxville, Tennessee, if we got the grit to collect em and try to run em back into Switch County. Me and Bill Music made one haul from Bristol, and I reckon we could try another from Knoxville. If we took off west, where they ain't so much coal minin, and then dropped down to Knoxville and come back the same way, we might not run into bad trouble this time. And we ought to make a good haul, since we don't need no tents. Anyhow," he said, tipping his head toward Music and grinning wryly, "if we took a couple of men with shotguns and left off all that hay."

"I'll ride with ye," Turl said.

"Yes," Charles Tucker said, "I'll travel along."

Bydee Flann shook his head. "We should have nothing more to do with this outfit boys, for they ain't no proper union."

"Preacher," Regus said, "these here folks have got to eat, but they don't have to believe nothin they don't want to. Them Communists ain't got the power for that. Did they make you buy what they were sellin?"

"No," Bydee Flann said, "they did not."

"Sure," Regus said, "they got no power when all a man has to do is say *no*."

"You were not in Chicago to see them," Bydee Flann said.

"I can't deny it," Regus said, "but they ain't down here in Switch County to see me either, and I'd say that puts us even."

For a while no one spoke. They stood around the low, guttering fire, shoulders hunched against the approaching cold of the night. "I reckon it's hard to fault what ye say," Worth Enloe said at last. His ruined eye twitched as though in memory of the powder charge that had gone off in his face and blown in coal dust where vision used to be. "But it galls me to throw in with them that's played us fer fools. It galls me, that's all," he said and sucked his teeth.

"Fools is what we are," Regus said. "The operators have played us for fools from the first day we walked into the mines to make their money for them."

"You were a mine guard, not no miner," Tom Loflin said.

Regus considered Loflin for a long moment. "I was a miner until I came here, and my poppa was a miner before me. Maybe I wasn't no fool when I went to work for Hardcastle, but I'll thank ye not to remind me of it further, if you think to call me friend."

"You know as good as any what he's done fer us," Lewis Short said, frowning at Loflin from under his eyebrows. "He taken us in and stood by us. They ain't no reason to bring up such as that."

"Maybe," Clifford Smith said, "but I'd like to know, Mr. Regus Bone, if you intend to stick with the union or if you don't."

"Hell, son," Regus said, "they just ain't gonna be no union to stick to, not this time around. Even that little guinea knows that. He won't say it straight out, but he knows it. There won't be anything to stick to before long but this here tent city."

"Then what do you mean we ain't whipped?" Loflin said. "You said we wasn't whipped."

"I mean we'll truck that grub up from Knoxville, and we'll take our picket line down to visit the scabs and goons in Elkin every single goddamned day," Regus said. "Ha, we can't make Hardcastle hire us, and we can't make him pay us good money, but we can sure as hell make him spend it."

Bydee Flann was looking at the ground, shaking his head slowly and steadily and much more in sadness, it seemed to Music, than disagreement. "I'd like to stand with ye," he said. "I'd wager my life fer you boys, I reckon ye all know that; but a man's faith ain't for wager. I'll pull my watch tonight same as the next man, and me and mine will leave out tomorrow."

"Where do you expect to go?" Charles Tucker asked. "There's shelter and grub here. We'll ask ye to do nothin agin yer conscience."

"I reckon, Lord help me, hit's agin my conscience to be beholden to

279

that National Mines outfit for my victuals and a roof," Bydee said. "But I will pray for all of ye here."

"We'd have you stay, Preacher," Regus said.

Bydee shook his head. "They'll be a shack down at the Bear Paw until the Lord shows me where to go and what to do."

"Ha," Turl said, "they's nigger Communists down at the Bear Paw, and they done took everything with more than two walls and a roof a-standin."

"No," Bydee said, "that Italian told us when he brought us home that those poor colored all moved into the main drift of the old mine after the night riders attacked them. There will be some sort of shelter."

"So," Turl said, "they done gone back to livin in a cave like they done in Africa. Ha, what do ye know?"

"Ha, yerself," Clifford Smith said. "If the drift ain't full of water, it might beat this place here. They'd have high ground on any night riders. It'ud be easy to guard and hard to attack; and, hell, they've got the whole mountain over em to keep the rain and snow out."

"I'd have you stay, Preacher," Regus said again, as though he didn't even hear Turl or Clifford Smith.

"Hit ain't in me," Bydee Flann said, "but may God bless you for your charity."

Regus rubbed his face with one of his big, knob-knuckly hands and seemed about to say something else to Bydee, but, if so, he must have thought better of it, for he merely shook his head. "All right then," he said finally, "I'm ready to be down on the picket line in the mornin. I hate to think of them mine guards loafin around, smilin and pickin their teeth, or them scabs feelin so smart and righteous." He ran his forefinger back and forth under his nose, and his eyebrows assumed their old humorous posture. "Ha," he said, "the next time a union comes to town, old Kenton Hardcastle might just decide it's way yonder cheaper to live with it. Sure, he might just ast to join up, hisself."

A few of the men snorted with laughter, and for a moment Music thought a little of squatterville's spirit might return, but there wasn't much joking and boasting. As for himself, his edginess would not leave him and had begun to afflict his stomach like a great hunger or sadness.

Regus decided to put the three who had come back from Chicago on the first guard shift, for they were weary from their travels and would soon be done and allowed to rest. Bydee was given Regus's little nickel-plated derringer since, although he apologized for it, he said he could not shoot a man in any case. Still, Regus merely told him to stay in squatterville and shoot the derringer in the air if he got wind of trouble. Clifford Smith and Worth Enloe, who had no such compassion for night riders, were posted as road guards. Turl, Lewis, and Tucker would take the second shift, and Regus, Music, and Loflin would take the last one. Although, as it turned out, they were hit before the road guards even quite got out of camp.

Long afterwards they would agree it had been an awful failing to expect trouble to come from the highway and nowhere else. Still, it wasn't merely because that's where the first attack had come from. It was always the miner who had to sneak about being careful not to be seen, who had to avoid the public way. Men with badges traveled the highroad and came right up in your face, not from a lack of imagination, but because they had everything on their side: the legal rights, the power, the gall. And long afterwards, too, Music wondered about his awful presentiment, if that's what it had been. For Ella, who was gifted in such matters if anyone was, had none until the first pistol shot made her heart grow cold.

He and Regus were climbing the washed-out wagon road, and he was no more than a step behind, when Fetlock barked from beneath the dogtrot. Having been confused and all but cowed by the comings and goings of those in squatterville, Fetlock seldom made a sound and would allow anyone to approach the house without a challenge, but bark he did. And even if it was only one clipped remark, like a hammer blow, it caused Music to drop back another step. The hair at the nape of his neck beginning to rise, his eyes coming around toward the elderberry bushes across the springhouse branch, he was not completely taken unaware when the volley came from just that spot. Nor was there any doubt that Regus had been hit; Music saw how his head was tossed and how he fell without any effort to right himself. Just as, in the next instant, he knew with absolute certain knowledge that the jerking of Regus's broad, bony shoulder and the trembling of his arm were aimless reflex winning out over an effort to draw a weapon. He saw all that with utter clarity, despite the darkness, despite his own death, which missed him by no more than an inch, tearing the air beside his cheek, and missed him a second time, plucking, as though with regret, at the coattail fanned out behind him as he dived into a tire rut in the washed-out road.

He was aware of the commotion and the shouting in squatterville and

281

of Ella Bone appearing on the dogtrot with the kerosene lamp from the kitchen, but only as a kind of inconsequential background, an irrelevant climate surrounding what had happened to Regus, and surrounding him as he thumbed back the hammer of the ancient Walker Colt. He did not need the notch in the hammer nor the blade at the end of the barrel, didn't even see them; nor did the deafening reports, the successive recoil, or the nimbus of fire fanning out from the cylinder distract him in the least. As much by instinct as by sight he located the dark shadows where the muzzle flashes had been, and his first shot struck one of them down. The second dark shadow scuttled to the side and fired on him twice, but he tracked it with the long barrel of the Colt, thumbing back the hammer and firing again and again until he saw the indistinct contortions of its fall and heard the branches crack and break under it as it went down. And through it all he had been as innocent of fear as he was of bravery or mercy or remorse.

When he scrambled up to where Regus was lying, Ella was already there. But Regus stayed only a moment. "So, Momma," he said, but all at once his back began to dance against the ground, and his breath rattled out.

There was no time for any promises, even if Music had been the sort to make them and had had them ready. And although he saw it come, the news of Regus's death didn't seem to reach all the areas of his understanding for months or even years afterward, so that it took a very long time to come to the end of his grief.

# SWITCH COUNTY, KENTUCKY, SUMMER 1979

IN THE SUMMER heat he walks down the road into Elkin, her small, soft fist gripping the forefinger he has stuck down for her to hold. She is four, the youngest of his grandchildren up from Knoxville for a visit, and when they get into town, she will have a soft drink, or a Popsicle, whichever strikes her fancy more. He would have bought her a treat in any case, but now it will be, in some part, a reward for forgetting so easily what her older brothers were so curious and worked up about.

"Pappaw," she says, "will you carry me?"

He looks down at her and sees that she is flushed, that under her eyes and across her upper lip there is a fine mist of sweat, and he swings her up and sets her astride his shoulders and walks on. She is a small, light life to carry, and in that alone she seems to offer a gentle, if not quite perfect, absolution for an old man's crimes. For long periods of time he is able to forget them, to put them away so completely that now they seem not quite retrievable. And why should they be? For who would want to remember them as though they were something to be celebrated? He decides he will try to explain that to his grandsons, and maybe to their father as well, when he and his wife come back from their vacation to collect their children once more. He will call him aside, yes, and tell him plainly that there are some things a fellow doesn't strut and crow about.

Beside the road a fence is lush with a burden of honeysuckle, and he steps down into the ditch and plucks a piece of the vine covered in blossoms. "Do what Pappaw does, Darlin," he tells the little girl, "and ye'll get somethin sweet," and he bites off the stem end of one of the flowers and sucks the nectar out before he passes the thick tulle of blossoms up to amuse her. But as he walks along the road with the child astride his neck and flowers of honeysuckle sifting down around him, a bit of his old anger comes back to gnaw at his stomach. The anger is no longer quite so pure, but it remains. And he remembers well enough his time in the Switch County jail waiting for his trial, and he remembers the trial too. Perhaps he would have lost if the National Miners Union hadn't sent a lawyer over from Pikeville to defend him, but there is no gratitude in him. He knew, even then, whose interest the lawyer had come to defend. A few months later, when it was clear the union was broken, the organizers and lawyers and all the rest of the National Miners Union people vanished like smoke. Nor did Arturo Guido Zigerelli ever once show up in Switch County again. Still, that was smart too. For if the people around there were used to men killing each other for one reason or another and found the business between William Music and the Burnsides too close to call, they might have hanged Zigerelli.

Even Turl and Tom Loflin had gotten five years in the penitentiary for blowing up the power plant at Elkin in the wee hours after Regus was killed. But, of course, they couldn't plead self-defense.

"Why are you laughing, Pappaw?" she asks him, bending around to stare at him owlishly from above and a little to one side.

"I don't know," he answers her. "I didn't know I was."

"Would you like a honeysuckle?" she asks him.

"Absolutely," he tells her, and while she reaches down the small trumpets of honeysuckle to his lips and he takes them by touch, he thinks of the mockery of his trial: the prosecutor trying him more for being a member of the National Miners Union than for killing the Burnsides, and his own lawyer trying harder to defend the union than the shooting. They were both the same, those lawyers, he thinks; strutting and posing like senators giving speeches, and the truth nowhere in them. He nibbles her small, silky fingers and she giggles.

"Don't bite me, Pappaw," she says.

"I can't help it," he says. "Ye've made me so hungry, I've got to snappin." But oh, he thinks, when Bydee Flann and Charles Tucker and Ella Bone gave testimony, they turned that trial around. He remembers absolutely the way Ella Bone looked, coming forward to testify on Merlee's arm, her worn hands folded into her dress front, her head held humbly to one side. She and Bydee and Charles Tucker, at least, were an embarrassment to both attorneys; and for a little while what had been a stage for wild invention became merely a crowded, slightly too warm, country courtroom where one could smell the rank tobacco in the spittoons, the odor of unwashed bodies, and the mustiness of clothing ordinarily packed away for special occasions. A place where, momentarily, the humble truth appeared and grieved.

When they get into Elkin, he reaches up and takes her hands and swings her around and down to the ground. "Now," he says, "what do ye crave, Missy? Will ye have a cold drink or a Popsicle or what?"

"I want a Popsicle, an orange one," she tells him, and together they climb the steps to the gallery. It is Green's Supermarket now, not the Hardcastle commissary, but it is the same building; and inside, the wooden floor pops and groans as it did, and it even entices the nostrils with the same smells, never mind that it is air-conditioned. He buys the five pounds of sugar Merlee has sent him for and two orange Popsicles, which he and his granddaughter eat sitting in split-bottomed chairs on the gallery. Now and then people pass by and speak to him, inquire after his grandchild and tell him she is pretty. They call him Mr. Music, for none of them date back to his time or are so familiar as to call him Bill, although there are a few left alive who do so.

But he isn't paying much attention to them. Because of the mood he is in, he looks out on what used to be Hardcastle company housing and tries to resurrect it in his mind. It is hard, for there are some dowdy shops and stores where the first row of houses used to be; yet behind them, a few of the shacks remain. They are painted now, and one or two of them have additions built on, and there are some trees and grass. When he and the little girl walk back, he knows he will look toward the place where the tipple and power plant once stood, and he will try to resurrect them as well, and that will be even more difficult, for no trace of them remains, and even the mountain, which rose above them, is being unwound from strip-mining. Peeled like an apple.

His legs are crossed at the knees, and at the end of his raised, skinny shank, one scuffed work shoe keeps time with his heartbeat while he eats his Popsicle and considers his life. It is not the one he had in mind when he started out, or the one he would have chosen, but merely the one that claimed him. And, all things considered, it has been good enough. Still, years ago he confessed to Bydee Flann that a feeling of homesickness bothered him now and again. But Bydee, while he lived, never lacked an answer for anything. He had been born and raised in Switch County and, except for the trip to Chicago, had never been as much as fifty miles away, and he was homesick too, he told Music. "All men are homesick," he'd said, "ever since God Almighty scourged them from the garden."

Maybe so, Music thinks, but he suspects otherwise. He suspects home is simply not a place after all, but a time, and when it's gone, it's gone forever. He twiddles his foot and agrees with himself.

"What did you say, Pappaw?" she asks him.

He has no idea. "I said less us get on back and see what them mean little brothers of yours are a-doin."

The sun is dropping behind the ridge above Mink Slide, and it is cooler. He looks, as he knew he would, at the mountain across the river, at its raw and naked terraces, and he clucks to himself. Hellkatoot, he thinks, if Regus were alive, he wouldn't even know where he was, nor would Ella. And all at once, out of nowhere, he understands something. He understands why his two small grandsons, clearly too young for such matters, were told he had once shot down a pair of deputy sheriffs. It is suddenly as plain as a pikestaff to him that he has become some sort of oddity, some sort of curiosity, to his youngest son. No doubt Switch County has too. And why wouldn't it be all right to tell any kind of story about an oddity, after all? Sure, going off to school, living so long away from home in a city with a good job and a fine house, has given the boy notions. Music realizes he has sensed it before and couldn't quite put a name to it. He can even understand it a little, but he decides it cuts no mustard with him, is no proper excuse, and he intends to collar his son and take him aside.

In a little while he and his granddaughter come in sight of the huge chicken house he raised in the forties, the field around it covered with hundreds of white pullets; and a little beyond, the new house he built in the fifties, where the kitchen garden used to be; and a little beyond and below that, the old one, still standing, which he could never persuade Ella to leave. And somehow he relents a little. The boys have been sent off to fish the river with their brand-new and untried rods and reels. They will catch very little, for he could see at once they had no experience to help them. Perhaps he should teach them real fishing, depression fishing, where you wade the river and, when the fish spook under the bank or under rocks, you reach in after them and grab them. It was one of the ways he got grub for Ella and Aunt Sylvie and Merlee and Anna Mae during the hard times, and he feels up to showing his grandsons how.

As he and the little girl mount the dirt road up to the house, he remembers with perfect clarity a particular March evening in 1932, and how he had climbed up out of the river, his bare feet purple with the cold and his clothes soaked, but carrying enough fish in the sack over his shoulder to feed the five of them, for he had worked hard and culled nothing. He remembers sitting in the withered bracken to lace his brogans about his sockless shanks, realizing at last that the worst of the season was over. Already a few red-winged blackbirds had shown up to ride the slender tips of the elderberry bushes along the river and fluff their feathers and creak to each other like rusty hinges. In no more than a week or so, he knew, he would be able to gather pokeweed and dock and other wild greens for them to eat. He remembers climbing the riverbank to the highway and coming in view of what had once been Easy Street and Silk Stocking Row, and how nothing remained of them but the heavily trodden earth and a little debris, as though what had once been squatterville might have been only the abandoned site of a carnival. And he remembers vividly how, in the aspect of that particular evening, he could look upon the place without so much bitterness and shame.

Yes, he thinks, he will teach his grandsons a different manner of fishing. And perhaps he will tell them stories, and if not quite the story they wish to hear, then maybe stories about Chicago and riding the freights, or getting caught sleeping in Regus Bone's haystack. Perhaps, indeed, he will tell them Regus's story about shooting the bear and getting trapped in the hollow tree with its mother. He wonders, after all, if it won't be all the same to them.